DULVERTON

3|22

SOUTH PETHERTON

91 24

DUL

Please return/renew this item by the last date shown on this label, or on your self-service receipt.

To renew this item, visit **www.librarieswest.org.uk**, use the LibrariesWest app, or contact your library.

Your borrower number and PIN are required.

MORE OR LESS ANNIE

TRACEY GEMMELL

First Printing, 2019

ISBN 978-0-9976137-2-8
ISBN 978-0-9976137-3-5 (eBook)

Tracey Gemmell Publishing
W5317 Highland Drive
New Glarus, Wisconsin 53574

Cover design: Anita B. Carroll, Race-Point
Cover photo: Message in a Bottle © Shaiith/Dreamstime

Author photo: Steve Howes

email: tracey@traceygemmell.com
Website: www.traceygemmell.com
Twitter: https://twitter.com/TraceyGemmell17
Instagram: https://www.instagram.com/traceygemmellauthor/
Facebook: https://www.facebook.com/author.traceygemmell/

To Scott

*for the journey behind us –
and the journey to come*

PROLOGUE – RAINDROPS ON FOREHEADS

St Albans, England· 1969

Annie's father twitched the curtain aside. The raindrops on the windowpane shattered the light from a streetlamp into tiny sparkles. Annie smiled at their glittery downward wriggles.

'Why's Dad playing with the curtains, Mum?' Lizzie frowned, her new Etch A Sketch dangling in her hands.

Lizzie missed nothing, Mum always said. Both a blessing and a curse, Mum always said.

Annie sometimes wondered which she was. She didn't know which one she was supposed to be. Now didn't seem like a good time to ask, so she sucked patiently on her thumb, which was too old to be sucked, according to Lizzie. Dad paced to the other window in the living room, squeezing between the wall and the couch. He grabbed a fistful of curtain fabric in each hand, allowing the wriggles back into the room before touching his nose to the pane. He pulled back quickly like the glass had cut him. Playing with the curtains got you yanked backwards off the couch, in Annie's experience. About now, Mum would start yelling about the house rules.

Instead, Mum stood with her arms folded, leaning against the kitchen door jamb. 'Wondering why he's doing that myself, poppet.' Her lips disappeared, sucked inwards, her mouth a tight, straight line.

Straight-line mouth usually meant straight to bed.

Dad's eyes raked the room, settling on the newspaper he'd been reading until the curtains drew his attention. He grabbed the front page, allowing the other sheets to drop to the floor. He pulled faces. The paper in his hands trembled. Tugging at his shirt collar, he opened his mouth to say … what?

Mum strode across the room and snatched the paper from Dad's hands. She read out loud: 'Police Say More Arrests Likely.'

Dad stole the paper back, throwing it on the sofa. He prowled back to the window and scanned the road, as Annie did when the ice cream van tinkled its siren call. How had two shiny raindrops landed on Dad's crinkly forehead? They couldn't have jumped in the window. It was closed.

Mum's face wriggled and twitched into unhappy shapes. 'What, Joe? Why are you getting all daft over that newspaper story? It was years ago. What's it got to do with you?'

'Nothing. Nothing, Pat. Now, let me think.'

Annie watched her mother let her father think. After a few seconds, Mum's eyes opened wide. 'Do you know those blokes?'

'Of course not!' Dad's lips pulled back over clenched teeth. It wasn't a smile.

Mum eyed the paper on the couch. 'Stealing like that. It's not right and lots of the money still missing. Hang them crooks, I say.'

'Be quiet, woman!' Raindrops from Dad's forehead now drizzled down his cheeks and neck, darkening his shirt collar. He turned wide eyes on Lizzie for several seconds before resting them on his 'littlest treasure'. Annie held her father's gaze, slowly removing her thumb from her mouth.

The movement was so swift, Annie flinched. Her father rushed into the bedroom of the small flat, knocking into the doorframe hard enough to almost lose his balance before reappearing with his coat, his hat and a briefcase.

Mum's mouth wasn't straight anymore. It made a big, wide circle – wide enough that her eyebrows had to shoot up to make room for it. 'Where're you going?' No answer. Louder. 'What's wrong, Joe?'

Annie ran behind her sister and wrapped her arms around Lizzie's tiny waist, shielding herself from Mum's shout.

The man in the suit didn't look like Dad anymore. He gripped Mum in a bear hug. 'Nothing. Nothing's wrong,' he said. 'I just need to go out for a bit.' He let Mum go.

Rushing across the room, he scooped his girls into his arms, kissed them hard on the cheek, then again on the top of their heads. Annie pulled away. His grip made it hard to breathe.

The man ripped open the door and called over his shoulder, 'You take care of each other for me, and I'll … I'll be back in no time.'

He was back at no time.

1 – LOSER'S LUCK

Verston, England· Present day

Tolerating criticism from inanimate objects began as a hobby. It was now a lifestyle. The burn marks on the bottom of the iron, the worn carpet and the pile of bills all passed regular judgement on Annie Hardcastle. This didn't strike Annie as strange. Which was strange, though attributable to years of practice – and the fact there were few animate opinions she respected.

Today's featured judge and jury were seated under her eyes. The dark, mottled circles dulled the metallic surface of the iron. Her distorted likeness trailed up and down the shirt fast enough to soften the facial wrinkles to 'not too critical', the shy grey hairs tiptoeing through the brunette to 'not too vocal'. But those eclipsed half-moons still taunted her: 'You've given up on yourself, girl.' She thunked the iron down, picked up the spray starch and squirted her reflection until it blurred.

Annie felt a hundred years old – without the respect, or the congratulatory letter from the Queen. She sagged forward and rested her hands on the ironing board, then stood upright and pinched her waist with her fingers. A little softening around the middle. Could be worse. Four flights of stairs carrying groceries had a silver lining.

Flipping the shirt over to get the other sleeve, Annie waited for Lester's programme to end in the living room – a rather misnamed room, she always thought, as not much living went on in there. The dreary clarinet of *Coronation Street*'s theme music signalled Lester to either fall asleep or head to the Fox and Rabbit. She didn't care which. The iron thumped and hissed its agreement.

'How'd you get this Mickey Mouse machine to work?'

Annie cringed at the banality of Lester still finding it funny to call computers 'Mickey Mouse machines'. Twenty years was enough, surely?

Another 'tut' from the living room. Annie sensed her husband's irritation oozing on to the keyboard, heaping guilt on the old laptop, as he did everything else.

'Turn it on.' Annie's clipped tone from behind her ironing board shield echoed Lester's peeved attitude.

'Why's that circle thingy going round and round? Stupid machine.'

'It's thinking.' *You should try it.*

'Where's the internet?'

'The blue "E" picture.' Icon was too complex a concept to explain. Every time Lester tried to use the laptop, she wanted to rechristen it 'slaptop'. The iron pounded the shirt again.

'Dear God, this thing runs slow.'

'You could always wait for the paper in the morning.'

'I don't appreciate your tone, Annie.'

And it doesn't appreciate you.

Annie's hand slowed, suspending in air the steamy-breathed iron dragon as it spat at its prey. When had she become this … bitchy? She used to be nicer, didn't she? Looking down at the name patch on the pocket of the shirt, she wondered, not for the first time, why she had to iron Lester's polyester, oil-stained work shirts. She smooshed the iron down on the name tag and leaned her weight into it.

'Finally, I'm in.' The pride in Lester's voice left Annie the impression he'd discovered water on the moon rather than simply navigated the search bar. 'Now to check those lottery tickets.'

Annie raised an eyebrow. 'Why are you doing that?' Usually Lester threw the tickets at her to check the numbers.

'We never win when you do it.' Lester laughed at his own wit. Someone had to. 'Not a single number on that one. Not a single number on that one …'

The brittle crackle of lottery tickets as they were shredded into strips tore desperate hope from Annie's soul. Lester's voice faded into the sizzle of the iron. 'Not a sssssingle …'

Single. A lovely word. Annie relished the silence emanating from the other room; the minutia, the disregard, the years of settling momentarily stilled. She hung the stiff blue shirt on a wire hanger, then moved to the kitchen window. Her gaze followed the vapour trail of a jet heading out of Luton Airport. As always, she imagined a sunny destination, the amped up lives of the people on board.

The sun deflated behind the roofs of the flats across the road. At least it had bothered to show up today. She flicked the curtain back to follow the steps of a neighbour as he crossed the street. The fabric's motion stirred something in a dusty corner of her memory: loss, disgrace, unknown history.

Hiding.

'Annie.'

'What?' She turned from the window and spread another polyester sacrifice across the ironing board.

'Annie!'

'What?' Annie gripped the iron harder over the proxy shirt.

Lester's shadow filled the kitchen doorway. 'Er … can you come here a minute?'

He'd never asked nicely before.

The computer screen stared, unblinking, devoid of all sense. The couple stared back.

Lester swallowed, ran his hand through his thinning hair, then across a couple of his chins, finally dropping it down to rest on years' worth of beer. 'Am I right?'

He'd never questioned himself before.

'It would seem so.'

'Huh.' Lester's breath shallowed, each exhalation panted slightly. 'We're rich then.'

'We are.' Annie's knees buckled, sliding her limp body down to meet the sagging sofa cushion. Plopping down on the faded fabric this time felt novel; not because her knees lacked the will to stand, but because something noteworthy had happened. It was a Noteworthy Plop. A Plop to Remember.

'Fifty-two million quid. Fifty-two million ...' Lester's widening eyes signalled the dawning of incomprehension.

Fifty-two million life jackets. Fifty-two million ...

Annie struggled to tune out the ringing phone. It hadn't stopped all day. 'I thought we were keeping this quiet until we'd had time to think?' She glared at Lester and rubbed her chest, tasting the bitter burn of a stressed lunch: sardines on toast followed by the Cadbury's Mini Eggs she kept hidden among the tea towels – like much of her life. Lester wasn't supportive of luxuries. His beer didn't count, apparently. The fact he never dried a single dish meant the tea towels kept her contraband safe. As an additional insurance policy, she hid little individually packed bags of Quality Street chocolates in the back of the freezer. Pull in case of fire. She pulled. Frequently.

Lester rubbed his hands together, glee all over his face. 'It was just the lads at the pub last night. Can't hold out on them, can we now?' The phone stopped ringing.

'Then, how come everyone at the factory knows?' Annie shifted her weight from one hip to the other. Lester had left for work that morning as normal; returning only a couple of hours later. His presence, apparently, distracted the other workers. Annie had left a message on the bakery voicemail last night saying she was sick. Lester's indiscretion made a liar of her. Again.

'Like I said, I only told the lads at the pub.'

'And you swore them all to secrecy, I suppose?' Annie twisted the thin, worn, golden noose around her finger, faster and faster, as though wringing a neck. She hadn't shared the news with anyone since she and Lester had checked the tickets. Not even her mother. Especially not her mother.

The irony of her current situation wasn't lost on Annie. She'd spent countless hours – years – imagining a more exciting life; the world of travel, of celebrity, of Twitter followers. She'd wanted to taste all that, hadn't she? Yet, at a moment when that world was only a lottery cheque away, when others were, for the first time, interested in her, she sought solace in the silent phone. Her stomach roiled at Lester's stupidity.

The phone rang again. Mum. She'd have to talk to her sooner or later.

Mum was out for blood. 'I've called a million times. No one's answered. Why the hell am I the last to know?'

Because you can't keep your mouth shut? Because for once in my life, I'd like something good to keep to myself instead of all the crap? 'Hello, Mum.' Annie leaned her head against the yellowing wallpaper.

'Imagine! The hairdresser had to tell me!' Pat poured indignation down the phone line and more acid into Annie's stomach. 'Of course, I pretended I knew, after the shock nearly stopped my heart. My own daughter doesn't want to share her good news with her poor mother.'

If it were only the good news you wanted, I wouldn't have minded telling you. 'I'm sorry, Mum. It's all a bit of a shock to us right now. We're trying to regroup.'

'By all accounts, Lester did a great job "regrouping" at the Fox and Rabbit. Drinks all round, apparently. Shameful. I was that upset, I had to take a pill last night.'

Annie had refused to go for a drink, confident in the knowledge her husband would never keep the news quiet until they could sort things out – mainly because she'd suggested it.

A knock at the door. Lester jumped up from his chair to open it. Annie flinched; not at the knock, but at Lester's rapid movement. It had never been his job to answer the door before. Her world was changing extraordinarily fast.

A flash of light turned Annie's head away from the phone in the hallway. Another flash winked and her singed retinas made out the shape of a microphone and a large lens. 'Mr and Mrs Hardcastle! Our hometown multi-millionaires! How does it feel? Come on now, share with the *Tri-Counties Gazette.*'

'Champion. Feels champion, doesn't it, luv?' Lester called over his shoulder, beckoning Annie to the door.

'I'll have to call you back, Mum. Paper's at the door.'

'How can you read when your mum's upset?'

'No, Mum. The reporter from the paper is at the door.' Annie's vision of her own celebrity hadn't included being photographed or written about – or seen at all. Hiding had been part of her DNA for as long as she could remember – if only she could remember why. She sighed, welcoming the reporter on her doorstep with enthusiasm typically reserved for a delivery of anthrax.

'Talk to complete strangers before your old mum, would you? Don't worry about—'

Annie hung up the phone. She'd pay for that later. Her trembling hands patted her lifeless hair, then pulled the pilled sleeves on her sweater down from their potato peeling spot above her elbows. She sidled up behind her husband, knowing if she ignored his beckoning, it would turn into a different sort of front page story.

Lester pulled her up beside him and threw his arm over her shoulder, the hand hanging loosely. Possession without connection. Another flash of light caught her grimace.

The reporter, who couldn't have been older than sixteen, tutted. 'You must be happier than that, Mrs Hardcastle. Come on now. A big smile for the front page.' He modelled the smile he wanted, as though he knew exactly what a lottery winner should feel like. Annie considered the fact she should know what a lottery winner felt like. She didn't. Unless numb was appropriate.

Annie's insides knotted at the prospect of sharing herself with strangers. She clenched her teeth and lifted the corners of her lips. Wallace, from the animated films, came to mind. All that would be missing on the front page the next morning was Gromit rolling his eyes.

Obviously satisfied with the photo, the reporter prattled on. 'What are your plans? Big house? Spain? Bentley in the driveway?'

Secrecy until we've had time to think.

'Oh, big plans. Lots of big plans.' Lester hooked his arm closer into Annie's neck. His big plans pressed on her carotid artery. 'But we'll not be sharing them yet. Got to get things sorted a bit. Will be talking to the bank manager, though. Give him back some of that cheek he's been giving us all these years, right, luv?'

Annie grimaced at the exaggerated wink thrown her way. 'Bank manager's been rather accommodating through the years, actually.' The sound of typically internalised dialogue surprised Annie. Did Lester notice the dig? Oh, so proud Lester? She'd never worked out what he was proud of.

No second car rather limited career options in a small village. Annie settled for working part-time at the bakery in the high street. Endless batches of stodgy, murky fruitcake batter for wedding cakes provided the perfect analogy for the triumph of hope over marital reality; darkness plastered over with sticky sweetness. There'd be no wedding cakes when she was the owner of the bakery she'd dreamed of since childhood. Instead, there'd be commitment-free, light, melt-in-the-mouth petit fours, floral cupcakes and whimsical confections. Pop in the mouth luxuries. Well-earned treats, no strings attached.

But sweet indulgences lay trampled underfoot during her puddle-strewn walks to work before dawn. She occasionally wondered if her ungodly early hours were the reason children had refused to join the Hardcastle clan. She could only assume they knew they'd never get decent childcare early in the morning. The prospect of Daddy Lester providing breakfast probably scared them into pretending to sleep through the fertilisation process. Annie often did the same. The first ten years had been the worst. The second decade served as little more than confirmation her eggs knew what was best for them.

Lester's arm jiggled around her neck, jolting her back to the reporter. 'Yeah, well,' Lester said. 'He's accommodated out of a job now, isn't he, that bank manager.' He dared Annie to contribute more.

Was her husband afraid she'd share details of their overdraft protection plan? As though she'd ever share that – or anything. Standing in the fading light, it struck her: at least she had something worthy of sharing now. For a split second, a lightening in her chest; a dawning sense that maybe things were about to change. It was a dream she'd dared to dream before, just never dared to dwell on.

Lester whooped before slapping the boy reporter's shoulder and shouting, 'Fewer bank managers, more bartenders!'

The reporter beamed. 'That's the headline on tomorrow's front page!'

Fewer husbands, more …? A brave internal headline; incomplete.

The reporter shoved his camera into his backpack and took off in pursuit of his deadline.

Annie closed the door with a weary click. 'Why'd you tell everyone?'

Lester smirked. 'Didn't tell your mum, did I?' He struggled with Pat at the best of times.

Annie blew out her cheeks and held her breath, before letting the air out between her lips in little puffs. 'And I'll pay for that for the rest of my life.'

Lester returned to the living room to wait for his dinner. Annie leaned her forehead on the front door and closed her eyes. As her breathing slowed, a recessed lightbulb flickered in her head: subtraction was the lottery luxury here, not addition. *Is this a normal reaction?*

How long she stood at the door, she wasn't sure. The opening blast of music from the six o'clock television news reminded her the potatoes wouldn't peel themselves. Rousing her tired body, she turned towards the kitchen at the exact moment the front door flew open. It flung her across the hallway as though she'd been shot in the back. She spun to face the intruder and discovered her reverie had lasted long enough for her mother to scurry across the village green.

Pat's hulking outline blocked the light. Enter stage centre. Panting and clutching her side with one hand, she dared any rich relatives to deny her existence.

'Passed a little blighter running down your stairs. Bet he nicked something.' Pat stared around the hallway, eyes wide. 'Where's that reporter, then?'

Annie stared at the woman in front of her, then covered her own mouth with her hand. 'Oh, dear God!' Her mother wore a gaudy smear of red lipstick, most of it on her teeth. She never wore lipstick.

Those blood-like slashes seared themselves into Annie's timid soul, screaming 'spotlight!' to an unknown audience. She fought for control of her anonymity, hammering down the switch on the electric kettle, throwing tea bags in the pot and grabbing a mug for her mother – who was now ensconced on a kitchen stool. She peeled potatoes at double speed and wrestled pork chops under the grill. In her heart she knew it was too late.

Breaking news! Pandora's Box Contains Lottery Ticket!

2 – ROOM WITH A SHRINKING VIEW

Chicago, USA· Present day

The bus belched fumes directly into Taylor's face, blowing her pristine power cut around like a nest in a storm as she wrestled her heel out of the grate. The shredded Chanel leather glared at her: imperfection! Her cost/benefit analysis of beating the morning sidewalk rush hour by running across the grate proved faulty.

Poor planning.

Strategic error.

The peeled heel negated the precisely coloured hair, the perfect middle-age-erasing make-up, the Burberry armour suit. The additional fifteen seconds she'd spent yanking the heel out would have to be made up somewhere. Maybe Friday … evening?

'Great.' Taylor's teeth clenched. Down to one income now, she'd have to repair the heel rather than replace the shoes.

'Can I help, madam?' A hand hooked under Taylor's elbow as she struggled upright.

What is it about a British accent that irritates me? Oh, yes. I remember. 'I don't know what backward Shakespearian village you hail from, but grabbing someone in this city will get you shot.' Taylor jerked her elbow free of the hand, about to direct a curse at the audacious act of civility. She looked up in time to check herself in the reflection of a toddler's wide eyes. The toddler stared unblinkingly back at her. Taylor congratulated herself, again, for remaining childless – a decision made decades ago, long before it was cool to relegate a womb to the Goodwill pile.

'Well, enjoy your day.' The chirpy toddler wrangler wouldn't quit.

'I'll do anything I want with my day, Mary Poppins.' Taylor's only nod to civility was muttering the words under her breath.

You can be anything you want, Taylor. Anything. But it would mean a lot to me if you would be kind. Her grandfather's words always came to her too late. Who had time for all that anyway?

The elevator stopped on the fifteenth floor, and Taylor exited. Her heel preceded her, incurring the stare of the receptionist and the snicker of the interns. Imperfection was unacceptable at Ashcroft Realty.

'Do you have a moment?' Ed Ashcroft's door seemed to open by itself as Taylor passed.

'Of course.' Taylor flicked on her warm, bright smile. She entered the office, which oozed eighteenth hole ambiance, or as close as one could get in a glass high-rise building. The golf clubs in the corner were probably still warm to the touch from the weekend. Her boss closed the door behind her.

'Exciting news for you.' Ed's smile matched Taylor's. 'Expansion op-portunities have arisen.'

Who says 'arisen' outside a pulpit? The hairs on the back of Taylor's neck arose under her silk scarf.

'You're held in high regard, as you know.' Ed looked up, and to the left.

The sweat prickled on Taylor's upper lip. Her brain skipped: London, Paris, Tokyo? Something in the golf clubs said no.

'We need boots on the ground in Central America. Costa Rica to be exact. Expanding into this new … exciting arena.'

Uh-oh. Since when had Costa Rica been the centre of the luxury housing market? Taylor had been there many times. Gorgeous? Yes. Paris? No.

'The team we have in place in North America is strong enough to spare you, and your twenty years here make you a perfect candidate to spread Ashcroft Realty into new territory. Of course, you'll need time to consider your options.' Ed finally made eye contact.

'Of course.' Taylor struggled to contain the snake-like hiss of her final 's'. She didn't doubt the potential in Costa Rica. The problem was, to her mind, it was entry-level potential. It was twenty-years-ago potential. This opportunity had nothing to do with potential. It had everything to do with punishment: punishment for the sins of her husband. Or rather, the sins of his company. It didn't matter Charles hadn't personally sinned. He was more shocked than anyone to discover his investment company had poured huge sums into a Ponzi scheme. Those decisions had been made in places other than the boardroom, Charles tainted by association. And, it appeared, so was she. She hated the fact she would have done the same thing in Ed's position. Business was business. She couldn't sell properties to those whose fortunes had been damaged in a scandal she was married to.

'Should you conclude this isn't for you, we could find another arrangement to your liking, I'm sure.'

Sure. 'Other arrangements' are always to everyone's liking.

Ed tucked his thumbs in the lapels of his jacket. 'Give me your decision by the end of the day.'

Taylor nodded. For once, words completely failed her. Luckily, a career spent perfecting the poker face, never tipping her hand, meant autopilot flicked the warmth button up a notch. Mouth puckered into a tight smile, she backed out of the room.

The slamming of her office door dared her assistant to make eye contact. She threw herself down in her leather-backed chair and spun to face the towering steel and glass jury lined up in city blocks across Chicago. The jury stared back, the decision already defined in the penthouses she'd sold and the second home deals she'd negotiated on the shoreline of Lake Michigan.

Heel. My word of the day.

Taylor flipped her hair at the jury and turned to the phone. 'Screw you, Ashcroft. I'm the best there is at what I do, and I'm innocent of all charges.'

But innocence wasn't the issue. Perception was the issue.

Perception greeted her in each of the phone calls she made over the next few hours. Phone calls to CEOs, CFOs, sales directors, construction companies she'd made millions of dollars for, colleagues she'd worked with, side-by-side, for decades. She'd become tainted goods because her husband had devoted his life to a company hijacked by corporate bandits.

With her last phone call, the jury came back.

Guilty: in the banter skipping around the suggestion of a job offer. Guilty: in the calls not transferred farther than the assistants' desks. Guilty: in the 'let's do lunch sometime' platitudes.

Panic had never been part of Taylor's corporate or personal vernacular. Until now.

'Great job, Charles!' Taylor stared at an empty picture frame where, in anyone else's office, a husband's photo would have smiled back. She'd meant to get to that.

With heart pounding, Taylor dialled her boss's extension. She put him on speaker and leaned back in her chair, rubbing her temples. Ed hated being put on speaker.

'Why Costa Rica?'

'Good fit for you, I think.'

'It's shooting fish in a barrel, Ed, and you know it. My secretary could sell condos there and she can't even get a tall, half-caff, soy latte at 120 degrees order right. Why are you expanding down there anyway? I don't have a single client asking for a second home in Central America.'

'Well, that's your job, isn't it? To convince them that's the place to be.'

'No. I convince them to buy the penthouse rather than the almost top floor. I convince them to buy an entire building in Paris.' Her volume increased. 'I don't convince them to sit by a pool while the nanny plays with the kids.' She took a breath. 'This is about Charles, isn't it?'

Silence, followed by a sigh. 'We're in a tough position on this one, Taylor. Not of our making, I hasten to add.'

'Not of my making. Not even of Charles's making. You know that.'

'But we've had … complaints. I can't give you clients who've lost money on Charles, or who even associate with people who've lost money on Charles. You must understand. There needs to be distance between you and Chicago clients.'

'You mean between you and me?' The hush said it all. Taylor grabbed the phone and slammed it to her ear. She wanted her next comment to smack Ed right between his.

'I've given you twenty years. I deserve better than this crap, so here's my decision: sand is for mixing into concrete for skyscrapers, not for getting in between toes on a beach. I quit.'

She broke a nail as the phone hit the desk, but, despite the injury, power gushed through her pumping veins. Even if she hadn't had a choice in the matter, she'd been un-brother-like.

Brother. She wasn't surprised he'd came to mind during a time of failure. At his funeral, the pastor's phrase 'Richard chose to be with God' suggested he'd had purpose, contrary to all evidence over the last decade of his life. Taylor pictured her father that day – hunched, shorter – as he'd sealed his golden boy under golden granite.

Men weren't allowed to fail; not in her family, anyway. In that same warped clan, women weren't expected to succeed, which was ridiculous because if allowed into the family business, she'd have shown them all. *Screw you, Dad.*

She spun her chair to face the glass power towers of the dearly beloved gathered to mourn the career of Taylor Newman. A wave of grief washed over her for the sweet brother she still missed; the brother ploughed under by her father's ambition. The irony wasn't lost on her that the same paternal expectation that stole her brother was still her motivation for trying to prove herself. Why did her father's opinion still matter? Whatever. She'd shown him. She'd been everything her deceased-by-choice brother wasn't. She'd been successful. Until now.

Taylor grabbed a file box and tipped out all the sales leads she'd accumulated over the past few months. Panic? No time for it. Fear? Overrated. Taylor? Unconvinced.

The former assistant, former receptionist and former interns to Ms Newman scrutinised the cardboard box she carried out of her office. The sales awards and empty photo frames she'd planned to fill one day scrutinised Taylor all the way home in the taxi.

The box containing Taylor's non-personal effects sat on the dining room table. Like an urn. She hadn't said a word as she plonked the ashes of her career down in front of her husband. His own box had been placed on the marble table in the hallway a few months earlier, containing more shock, more grief, but otherwise similar contents. Except his photo frames had smiling faces in them.

'Jesus, Taylor.' Charles folded the *Wall Street Journal* along its original crease lines and placed it at right angles to the edge of the glass tabletop. He stood and walked over to the floor-to-ceiling windows, staring out into the drizzle with his hands in his pockets. Taylor poured a glass of Pinot Noir, then kicked off her heels as she brought Charles up to speed on the few details the box didn't already convey.

'Bastards.' Charles didn't turn around from the window. He rested his forehead on the glass as a ring of condensation, huffed from his nose, briefly clouded the view.

'No warning.' Even as Taylor spat the words out, she knew they weren't true. There were always warnings. The new hotshot associate towing multi-millionaire clients. The meeting she wasn't invited to. The write-up in the *Chicago Tribune* on her husband's now defunct company. No, her goose was cooked before her Congratulations-on-Twenty-Years-With-Ashcroft cake was baked. The goose honked its last honk when the Feds swooped in on the board of directors meeting at Charles's corporate headquarters.

Former headquarters.

'What now?' Not a question Charles normally asked. He always had a plan, was always heading into the wind, full sails, nose sniffing for opportunities. Two months becalmed in a jobless sea with sharks circling the boat had changed him. Taylor's heart broke as her husband stared over the jagged rooftop fins towards Michigan Avenue.

'Not this. Obviously.' Taylor waved her hand at the apartment, sleek clean lines, sharp edges. Was that a pulled thread in the Alexander McQueen rug under the table? Her pulse quickened.

Fear. Not a word many associated with Ms Taylor Newman of Ashcroft Realty. Control was the word everyone associated with Ms Taylor Newman.

Charles turned and headed back to the table, squeezing Taylor's shoulder as he steered her into a chair and sat beside her. 'In many ways, this makes things easier.'

Taylor snorted.

'No, hear me out. We aren't tied to Chicago anymore. Let's face it, my career's over here.' Charles didn't need to add Taylor's was too.

Taylor buried another snort in her wineglass. 'Like Chicago's our only problem. New York's not going to be any better … at our ages.' They both knew age wasn't the problem. 'LA? Miami? Minneapolis? Des Moines?'

Charles brightened. 'We could start out on our own. Work virtually from the porch in Door County.'

Their weekend home in Egg Harbor, Wisconsin, had been a place to celebrate mega-deals, providing a fleeting escape from the city's pressure cooker mentality. Taylor placed herself on the porch, wine glass in hand, the waters of beautiful Green Bay emanating peace. Her mental Polaroid image further developed to reveal her mobile phone on her lap, a pile of new Chicago listings at her elbow, a to do list on a legal pad. That's how she spent her days there. Without that, what did the view even mean? Taylor cringed at the thought of lasting more than a long weekend wrapped in tranquillity.

A grin spread across her husband's face. She upended her wineglass onto tight lips then smacked the glass down onto the table. 'Would love to hear what you find humorous.'

'The thought of you in your nightdress at eleven in the morning, chatting with the neighbours.' Charles's smile petered out.

Taylor poured a refill from the bottle standing between her and Charles. 'Not funny.' She calculated the combined worth of the golden kick-in-the-butts they both stood to receive. Plenty, some would say; though not if Chanel and Alexander McQueen were to remain ghostly houseguests. 'I veto Egg Harbor. Big picture. What's next and where are we going to do it?'

Charles leaned back in his chair, stretching his long legs under the table. He folded his arms. 'What we already do. Anywhere it's not already being done.'

Taylor's fingers stopped in mid-drum. The wineglass didn't make it to her mouth. Her lips twitched the first hint of a smile. 'How do you feel about Costa Rica?'

'Costa Rica? Thought we were trying to avoid Costa Rica?'

'We were. Because that's where they were sending me to die in the Ashcroft elephant graveyard. Now, hear me out. What if I go there, not as their employee, but as the president of my own real estate company? If that's where they're thinking about setting up shop, that's where I go to screw them. I steal their clients right off the beach.'

Twilight reflected in the glass Taylor held, then in her eyes. Twilight changing to dawn. 'Ashcroft's right about something. Central America's waking up and America's going to sleep, if that's what you do during baby-boomer retirement.' She shuddered before leaning forward and holding Charles's attention with a piercing gaze. 'Combine the two: retirement communities, condos, spas, strip malls for all the crap they miss from home. Pool facilities for the grandkids. Health clinics. Marinas. Fast food—'

'Sounds awful.' Charles grimaced and blinked hard. 'We love the ambiance of Costa Rica the way it is. Why take all this with us?' He waved his arm at the windows; at America.

'We've only been down there for long weekends. Five days at the most. If we planned to stay longer, we'd need at least a little of this.' Taylor cast her gaze out the window at America before returning her focus to Charles. 'Besides, Costa Rica's aesthetic is expendable if it means getting back at Ashcroft.'

Charles swirled the wine in his glass and studied the residual ruby hue as it clung to the crystal. 'Huh. What do you know of their plans?'

'Nothing. Must have forgotten to send me the memo.'

'Huh,' Charles said again. First time in two months Taylor had seen that twinkle in his eyes.

3 – HIT SEND

Lester tore his eyes from the football results. 'Costa Rica? Why on earth would we want to go there? Why would we want to go anywhere? Quite happy here, thank you very much.'

Annie threw ten more begging letters on the table and pointed to the blinking light on the answering machine. 'Have you been paying attention at all? It's constant. One phone call after another. The postman even complained today about all the extra letters he's got to carry up the stairs. Then there's Mum.'

Lester rolled his eyes and grimaced. 'Yeah. Your mum …'

'If you'd kept quiet,' Annie continued, 'we wouldn't have the whole world trying to butter us up for money, now would we? The solicitor advised us to leave Verston until things calm down.'

Nigel Yates had offered plenty of advice, even suggesting he accompany the couple anywhere they chose to go to ensure the transition went smoothly. Annie wasn't sure he'd been joking. But he appeared serious when he mentioned he'd recently returned from a property search in Costa Rica. Great investment opportunities, he'd said. Great place to hide, he'd said. He'd keep it quiet, he'd said, tapping the side of his nose. Annie knew no one else to trust and nowhere else to go.

Lester sighed. 'Might not be a bad idea to get away for a bit. The lads at work are being a bit pushy. Did you know Mike's Betty has diabetes?'

Bet Mike's Betty didn't know it, either.

Lester pouted as he spoke. 'But why Costa Rica? What about Benidorm? We love it there.'

'Yeah, well, everyone in Europe's familiar with our name, thanks to you alerting the papers.' Annie folded her arms and stared at Lester. 'Besides, I've had a good look at Costa Rica online. It's nice. Same as Benidorm. Without the fish and chips.'

Lester's mouth dropped open, fear in his eyes. Annie instantly regretted her words. She cleared her throat and rephrased her argument. 'Mum's never heard of Costa Rica and once I mentioned they didn't have pork pies and sherry trifle there, she stopped pushing to come with us.'

And the winner is …

Lester blew out his cheeks and exhaled. 'Okay, luv. Show me the place on that Mickey Mouse machine. I'm not promising anything, but I'll take a gander.'

The irony of having to lug Lester along as she ran away from home wasn't lost on Annie. For years she'd dreamed of breaking out, of casting off the lines and setting sail solo. Yet here she was, about to drag her boat anchor with her. A tiny twitch in one corner of her mouth reminded her of her rationale. Her subtraction epiphany, the day after the win, led to time mulling over the exact meaning of subtraction – or more specifically, what stood between her and subtraction. Lester bought the ticket. Could he prevent her getting the money if she left him straight away? She'd lasted twenty years. She wasn't going to blow it now by leaving too soon.

No. Get all my ducks in a row. Then shoot them.

Lester studied the laptop screen over Annie's shoulder, rubbing his three-day stubble with his large hand. 'There's a travel agent in St Albans to do all this stuff, you know. Bet she could get us a place on Tamarindo Beach.' Annie hadn't shown Lester where they were really going to stay: Hermosa. She planned to confuse his workmates if Lester spilled the beans.

'Oh, yeah, there's a travel agent,' Annie said as she typed in the dates. She recalled Lucy's interrogation a couple of years ago during their last visit to her office. 'Let's trust our plan to Lucy, shall we? Safe as houses with her we'd be. They'd have to torture her to get it out.'

Lester shrugged acquiescence. His movement signified once again how much her life had changed. This man was now following her lead. He'd always been such a windbag of unearned confidence on all topics, in all contexts. Yet, over the last week, she'd seen doubt in his eyes. His bravado hadn't lasted longer than three or four rounds at the pub and one press interview. It hadn't survived the assumption he'd pay for the upgrade from beer to Scotch, the strangers stopping him on the street or the calls from his Yorkshire cousins. Lester pontificated proudly at every opportunity about his Yorkshire heritage, despite barely remembering the cousins' names when they'd called.

All those years of pretending they had enough, only to find the reality of enough unnerving. Lester unnerved. Annie couldn't believe she'd lived to see the day.

She skipped competently around the Travelocity website. Lester didn't ask where she'd gained her skills, so she didn't have to explain she spent hours on the site while he was at work. She'd pick a country, peruse the beaches, the mountain hikes, the river cruises and the hotels. Plug in dates, pick flights, choose a room. Then sit back as it all timed out; the plane and the room ticked away, the screen faded to black. Back to dreamless sleep. Then she'd make tea, giving the website time to forget her silly games. It always shocked her when she opened another window later to find the screen reminding her of her previous search. 'Do you still want to go to Sydney? Tenerife? Rome? San Francisco?'

Why, yes. Yes, I do. Just not today.

Her finger paused over the 'return date' button. *Leave it blank?*

'Are you sure we should go for two whole weeks?' Lester folded his arms. 'They'll fall apart on the shop floor without me cracking the whip.'

Annie's funny bone twitched. She kept quiet. He didn't ask how Shirley at the bakery would get by without her for two weeks. Lester was unaware she'd quit her job the day after the win. He never noticed whether she was in the house or not anyway. Her finger hovered interminably over 'number of adults'. Every fibre of her finger resisted, her hesitation ending with a resigned stab at the '2' option in the drop down box.

Annie swallowed hard and entered unknown Travelocity territory. She entered her credit card number. Clicked 'book now', held her breath – *tick tock* – waiting for the Travelocity Wizard to recognise her and shift her reservation to the 'just kidding' pile. Fade to endless, flightless black. The confirmation number popped up on screen. Annie gasped and fell back in her chair as though she'd been stung.

Lester patted her shoulder. 'What's for tea? Better eat up in case those islanders don't have English sausages.'

Costa Rica's not an island, you pillock. Annie promised herself she'd call her husband a pillock to his face. Soon. Maybe on a beach somewhere.

Lester sprung for a couple of miniature Scotches on each leg of the journey from Heathrow to Liberia, Costa Rica. He then slept, bolt up-right with his arms folded, as only a man can. Annie dutifully placed a napkin over his tee shirt to catch the drool when his head finally sunk onto his shoulder.

She declined the offer of alcohol – the trip itself enough of a buzz. She stared out of the plane window, disbelieving; not convinced the dream wouldn't end. Her heart thumped in anticipation of the plane's interior peeling back and the pilots flying out the cockpit door, to be re-placed by the Verston launderette. She rested her forehead on the oval window, letting the coldness convince her of the flight's authenticity, before huffing on the pane and writing in the condensation, 'My turn to live'. Lester snorted in his sleep beside her.

Seconds later – or a lifetime, Annie wasn't sure which – she staggered out of the airport into the Costa Rican heat. Gazing up at palm trees sil-houetted against a shade of blue she'd only ever seen through a screen, she stopped dead. Something slammed into the back of her. She turned to apologise, but before the words took shape, a female American voice shouted at her.

'Wake up and move out the way!'

'Sorry,' Annie mumbled, untangling her suitcase from her legs and sidestepping to let the woman pass. Their eyes locked for an instant. Annie inhaled sharply. Fear – and something else she couldn't name. The sensation passed so quickly, Annie lacked the certainty she'd felt it at all.

Lester grabbed her arm, breaking the tension building in her chest. 'Hurry up or we'll miss the shuttle bus.'

Annie silently cursed the wonky, broken wheel on her suitcase and followed Lester.

Twenty minutes later, she tipped out of the crowded bus into the ClubSol lobby. On TripAdvisor, more than a few reviews mentioned the hotel had seen 'better days'. Annie gawked at the outdoor bar, the pool glinting in the sunlight and the maids pushing their carts full of cleaning materials she'd never have to use. The reviews were right: it all looked like better days.

Lester 'ho ho hoed' beside her. He ignored the shuttle driver's subtle hand itching for a tip and swaggered through the open-walled lobby. 'This is champion, girl. Told you this would be great, didn't I?'

No. You said we should go to Benidorm. Annie wrestled to keep her suitcase moving forward instead of in circles. 'Where are the walls?' The palm frond roof floated overhead on lofty intermittent wooden posts. Not a solid wall in sight. 'What happens when it rains?'

'Shop!' Lester banged his hand on the reception desk before leaning on a proprietary elbow, the other hand placed on his hip. He leered at the ladies on the wicker couch in the lobby.

'Stop it,' Annie hissed at Lester, as he moved to bang the counter again. Unsure of fancy hotel etiquette, she was still almost positive shouting 'Shop' wasn't appropriate.

'Welcome to ClubSol.' A floral shirt and khaki shorts appeared from the back-office doorway, only to disappear again to answer a ringing phone.

Was that a Manchester accent?

Lester whispered, 'She wouldn't be answering the phone if she knew who we were.'

'That's the whole point.' Annie glared at her husband. 'Our solicitor said they don't get the *Daily Mail* out here. No one knows who we are.'

Lester mouthed, 'Oh, right', with a wink and a tap of his nose. He craned his neck towards the bar. Annie sighed, convinced the bartender would be the first initiated into the Hardcastle circle of confidants.

Manchester came out from the back room, flicking her red curls from her sweaty forehead. 'Sorry for the wait. Bit short-handed today. Welcome to ClubSol. Your name, please.'

'Lester.' Lester stared intently at Manchester.

Annie palm-slapped her forehead. Did he really think he could go by one name now, like Adele or Sting?

'I'm sorry I don't seem to have a reserve—'

'Hardcastle. It's under Annie Hardcastle.' Annie lowered her gaze, avoiding Lester's irritated scowl. *I suggested it, found it, booked it, named it.*

'Ah, yes. Here we are. The Garden Room. Nice tropical views.' Manchester tapped away at the scuffed keyboard. 'Two weeks, I see. Must be a big celebration.' She swung her eyes away from the screen to Lester's face for confirmation.

Lester inhaled to speak. Annie silenced him by patting his hand with a warm smile and a 'Yes. Big celebration.' Lester's mouth dropped open. A friendly pat hadn't happened in years.

'Right. I'm Maggie by the way, and I'm here to make you comfortable in any way I can. That's legal, anyway.' She shot Lester a sideways glance. He smirked back. 'José will take you to your room. Here's the keycard and a brochure of activities. We'll be happy to help you book fishing trips, spa treatments, jet-skiing, or horse riding. Enjoy your stay.'

José reached for a suitcase. Lester grabbed it back saying, 'Point us in the right direction and we'll do the rest.'

Annie whispered over Lester's shoulder, 'Why not let him do his job?'

'Because he'll want a tip,' Lester whispered back. 'Like the shuttle driver did.'

Annie glanced over her shoulder at José. 'We can afford it, you know.'

Lester snorted through his nose and, barely moving his lips, said, 'You insist we keep that to ourselves.'

Annie softened a little. She, too, was struggling to process this new reality. Flipping a lifetime of spending habits on its head wasn't going to happen overnight. Where to start? Exhaustion seeped into Annie's arms and legs. *Ugh. Seriously?* Rich, newly arrived in a fantasy location, and all she dreamed of was a nap? Who'd have thought being a millionaire would be more tiring than not being one?

Annie bobbed José an apologetic nod and followed Lester. Passing the hotel business centre on the way to her room, she had an idea: an internet search. She knew how to do those. 'Beginners Guide to Being a Millionaire Dot Com.' *Righty ho. I'll start there.*

4 – FOLLOW THAT TAXI!

The airport in Liberia, Costa Rica, wasn't even recognisable. On Taylor's last visit, only eighteen months prior, it had been an open-air hangar with a huge central fan churning hot air over the incoming visitors. A couple of immigration officers had sat at desks with laptops. No cameras, no glass partitions. The cab drivers had stood right next to the luggage carousel.

'Maybe Ashcroft's right,' Charles said, as they walked through the shiny new terminal. 'Things are a-moving and a-shaking down here.' The only indications it wasn't a small airport in the United States were the brightly-coloured sarongs and scarves in the gift shops.

Taylor busily counted heads, assessed the cost of suitcases and jewellery, listened for where passengers were asking the taxis to take them: Papagayo, Flamingo, Tamarindo. She picked her targets with laser-like precision.

The wall of Costa Rican heat used to hit her the instant the flight attendants opened the plane door. Now, the blast was deferred until the door leading to the taxi stand opened. Taylor asked no one in particular, 'Wonder if air conditioning is standard or an upgrade in new construction?'

Charles harrumphed good-naturedly. 'Jumping the gun, aren't we? Shouldn't we focus first on tracts of land for sale, investment companies, architects?'

'No. Look at that couple over there.' Taylor inclined her head towards a man in a 'Yorkshire Men do it Moor' tee shirt. The woman next to him radiated confusion. 'And that family, and that guy in the suit or the cowboy in the hat. What do they all have in common? Sweat. We need AC in the initial plans and breezy locations. The why leads the how.'

Charles shot an appreciative grin at his wife. 'And that, my love, is why you take the lead on this deal. You hunt down dream homes like a bricks-and-mortar bloodhound.'

'I can't do it without the money, honey.' Taylor's favourite phrase. 'And you're the financial guru.' *Former financial guru.* She avoided eye contact.

Taylor threw out an arm, New York style, to hail a taxi. As she charged towards the kerb, a woman stopped dead in front of her. She crashed into the back of her, which spun the woman's body round. Confused Woman. Eye to eye with dark circles and a pale, worn complexion, Taylor tutted. 'Wake up and move out the way!'

'Sorry,' the woman mumbled, untangling her suitcase from her legs and sidestepping to let Taylor pass. Their eyes locked for an instant. Confused Woman inhaled sharply. Taylor was almost certain she saw fear cross the woman's features. *Geez. She'd never last in Chicago if such an innocuous comment scared her.*

The man in the Yorkshire tee shirt grabbed the woman's arm before Taylor could say anything else. 'Hurry up or we'll miss the shuttle bus,' he said.

Taylor dismissed them both, intent on securing a ride. Louis Vuitton shoved Wonky Wheels out of the way before being stuffed in the trunk of a taxi. Charles climbed in beside his wife. The driver knew their destination before Taylor even waved her hand: Paradise Resort, Papagayo. It was only a five-star resort because there weren't any more stars to be had. Charles timed the trip from the airport, while directing his attention to the copious 'For Sale' signs along the road. Taylor worked her phone, searching property sites on the Gold Coast of Guanacaste Province. No shortage of single family mansions, condos and old beach shacks waiting to be torn down; their ghosts buried in marble bathtubs and wrap-around teak porches. She turned her phone to show Charles a hilltop retreat, infinity pool merging into the deep blue of the Gulf of Papagayo.

Charles whistled. 'Why aren't we living here already?'

'More to the point, have we missed the boat already?' Taylor's mind raced. How much coastal land was left? What resources were supplying all these foreign homeowners? Taylor knitted her eyebrows and rubbed one side of her flight-kinked neck. As the taxi sped along the tree-lined roads towards the coast, she caught sight of a couple of howler monkeys swinging in the branches. Which reminded her …

Taylor tapped Charles's arm to get his attention away from his phone. 'Where's second-rate, half-assed Ashcroft International going to locate their new office?'

'No idea. No mention of their Costa Rican intentions anywhere on-line. But that would make sense if they intended you to be the lead scout. They need time to find someone else.'

'Probably send my ex-secretary,' Taylor replied.

'Bastards,' Charles and Taylor said in unison before high-fiving each other.

Charles placed both hands back on his phone: swipe, tap, enter, save. 'We sure won't be the first in, but judging by all the land for sale, there's still plenty of room for growth.' He transferred billboard phone numbers into his mobile as fast as his thumbs would work. His razor-sharp memory meant he only had to inspect the billboards for a second to capture the details.

Taylor envied him. Her once impressive memory was nothing more than a distant memory now. She didn't admit weakness often, even to herself. Meticulous planning and visual supports helped disguise this particular facet of her menopausal disability. Shame it couldn't disguise the hot flushes. She clenched her jaw. Those young hotshots in Chicago weren't going to usurp her – even if 'hotshot' had taken on new meaning in her sweaty new world.

Her father had never believed she could be a hotshot.

There'll be no 'told you so', Dad. Something big was going to happen here in this tropical new-business-potential paradise. She sensed it in her beautifully chiselled, calcium-supplemented bones.

Taylor led the way into the hotel room. She scanned the acre of bed-linen, the granite wet bar and the bottle of wine in an ice bucket on the table; a welcome gift from the manager. The top floor terrace offered the shade of potted trees and the sun of the private lap pool in equal measure. One-hundred-and-eighty-degree views of the Gulf of Papagayo, framed by the tree-lined coast and dotted with rocky islands, astounded the senses. Even Taylor's somewhat jaded traveller's eye widened with pleasure.

Charles tipped the bellhop in the nonchalant manner of an American abroad, peeling off dollar bills – because everyone, everywhere, liked dollars – and placing them in the hands of the recipient without ever losing eye contact. The nonchalance didn't last beyond the closing door. Charles appraised the suite before addressing his wife over his glasses. 'A little extravagant, isn't it, given our circumstances?'

'First rule of attracting high-end clients: act like you don't need them. Act as though they need you.' Taylor gave Charles a sly grin. 'Besides, this all becomes a tax write-off when "Newman Gold Coast Realty" starts up.'

'True that, Ms Genius.' Charles strode over to the terrace, pulling Taylor with him. He wrapped his arms around her waist. They rocked for a moment, leaning into the jasmine-scented breeze, eyeing the sail-boats and checking out potential customers at the main pool bar below them.

Taylor released herself from Charles's arms and headed back into the room. She kicked off her wedge-heeled sandals. 'Shut the doors and crank up the AC. We've got work to do.'

On the phone, she said all the right things to realtors to garner their interest: she was a wealthy city slicker looking for a second home and financial opportunity. All true. Though she'd prudently left out the bit about her wealth ticking down like a Chicago parking meter and revenge playing as big a role as opportunity. No need to show all one's cards. The realtors salivated down the phone line at the opportunity to sell an ocean-view home, seven figures, all cash. Taylor found people believed anything if one threw numbers about like discarded champagne bottles.

'Why aren't you telling them you're a realtor?' Charles frowned as Taylor ended the last call. 'I'm sure there's room for more people selling real estate down here.'

Taylor sighed. Despite her husband's former profession, Charles was as ethical as they came. She loved him for it, even as she sometimes wished he'd stamp on the 'Do Not Walk on the Grass' sign.

'Simple. Ashcroft. I don't need him knowing where I am before I know where he is. I need to feel this place out before tipping my hand.'

'Are you sure he even chose this part of Costa Rica?' Charles asked.

Taylor checked off points on her fingers. 'Only a two-and-a-half-hour flight from Houston. Doesn't have the malaria concerns of other regions. Basic infrastructure in place. Plenty of room for growth and improvement, meaning it's easy to convince clients they're getting in ahead of the curve. If they wait until all the asphalt goes down, it'll be too late to grab the rocket by the tail. All Ashcroft strategy.'

Charles rubbed his chin, then tapped his lips with his pointer finger; his 'unsure' tell signs. 'Understood. I just ask that you don't get so absorbed in beating Ashcroft you lose sight of this beautiful place and the reason people want to be here. Don't set yourself up as an untrustworthy outsider on a mission.'

Taylor acknowledged the comment with a slightly irritated, 'not-like-I-didn't-know-that-already' bow of her head. Irritating or not, Charles's honesty and kindness deserved respect. He demonstrated an affinity with others she'd never quite mastered and people warmed to him instantly. He was one of the good guys. That he'd been tarnished by the deceit of others galled her.

She smiled at the top of his salt and peppered head, at his tapping toe beneath the desk, an unconscious work habit that made him seem jolly even during complex tasks. Had her father ever tapped his toes? Taylor made a mental note to add a toe tap to her work routine.

Removing a bottle of water from the minibar, she asked, 'Found any good properties yet?'

Charles jumped. His fingers skittered across the key board, leading Taylor to conclude he'd hurriedly closed a couple of windows. The toe tapping stopped.

'Er ... lots of spectacular homes you'd be quite happy to buy.' Charles turned the screen towards his wife; an image of a modern villa under construction. Taylor wasn't into quaint or traditional.

'Hmm. Nice. What else have you got?'

Charles flicked through listings of a million dollars and up while Taylor studied his face: determined chin, kind eyes, laughter lines, the corners of his mouth always turned up, ready to smile at a moment's notice. Her smiles required scheduling in advance. His easy charm balanced her thrust and parry, but his kindness wasn't a weakness. People made that mistake at their peril. Charles was a savvy businessman.

What was he trying to hide? Should she ask? No, she trusted him. But she trusted her own gut feeling well enough to be certain he was up to something.

5 – CAKE, ANYONE?

Annie slept for a few hours, exhausted from the sleepless, though dream-filled, journey. The unfamiliar hum of the air conditioning had at first distracted her, then lulled her to sleep. She awoke, resisting the urge to open her eyes. Was this the moment the dream dissipated? Would the crack in her bedroom ceiling appear? The lorries on the A5 heading towards St Albans rattle the windows?

The hum. It was the hum that reminded her the dream lived on.

She sat up, spun her feet onto the cool tile floor and blinked at the bright sunlight. The translucent sheer curtains framing the patio door rippled in the breeze. Verston curtains didn't ripple. They flapped. These curtains appeared almost haughty in their rhythmic undulation. If curtains could look down their noses …

Oh, for crying out loud! Now you're allowing bits of cloth stuck on poles to judge you?

Annie scanned the room. Lester wasn't there. An internet search for instructions on how to be a millionaire would have to wait. Lester may already be drinking like one with no professional guidance.

Annie splashed water on her face, her lips sealed together, refusing to trust the water. Something else to add to the long list of untrustables.

Habit made her reach for her cardigan and handbag. Awarding herself no points for knowing where to head, she found Lester at the bar, nestled amidst the cleavages of two barflies. How many drinks had he bought them?

Lester waved her over and had the brains to pull up another bar stool for her. She tried an air of wifely possession. Failed. She didn't even want to succeed.

'Meet Gloria and Beth. They're from Dublin.'

Aren't we a bit old to giggle, ladies?

'Nice to meet you.' Annie smiled, trying hard to let her hair down an inch. Beth and Gloria seemed to be having no difficulty in that area. Loud laughter, full faces of makeup, draped confidently over their barstool, the women sapped any self-confidence Annie possessed. Her spine sagged into the shape of a question mark, forming an apology on the bar stool.

'What'll it be, luv? Our maestro bartender, John, stands ready to serve.' Lester saluted John, who saluted back. 'They've got Samuel Smith, would you believe?'

Annie did believe. The four English beer bottles in front of Lester were credible character witnesses.

John waited for her order; his wrinkled sleeveless shirt and three-day stubble adding to the impression he may have partaken in a tipple or two. She focused on a blender behind the bar and recalled an image she'd seen on the telly once. 'I'll have a Piña Colada.' Her hair slid down a fraction of an inch. The effort left her clutching her handbag more tightly into her lap.

'Ohhh, get you, Annie!' Lester egged her on. 'Didn't take you long to drink like a local. Soon be wearing one of them …' Lester's eyes found the ample, exposed mounds on Gloria's chest, barely contained by the sarong that appeared to be loosening with each passing beer. 'One of them sheet thingies.'

Closer to three sheets, if you ask me. 'I saw a piña colada on that Death in Paradise television programme. Might as well try it,' Annie said. The glass plonked down in front of her in a manner that suggested Lester hadn't spilled any secrets to John. Yet.

The creamy froth oozed over the rim and down the sides of the sweating glass. The pineapple chunk skewered next to the cherry split in two and Annie caught the falling half in her palm.

The first straw-full tasted heavenly. The cool glass felt heavenly. The heavenly gates opened farther, welcoming the splash of a cannonball into the pool behind her, the crackle of palm fronds above her head. The scent of coconut, pineapple and rum mixed with salty ocean and citrusy sunblock caused a light-headed swoon. Annie closed her eyes to reduce the stimuli entering her brain; too much one second, not enough the next. Slowly opening her eyes, she caught the sunlight glinting through the palm-leaf roof. It lay speckled on the bar, like rippling glitter. She trapped it under her glass after each sip. Bottles and concoctions – like trips on the Travelocity website – lined up along the wall behind the bar, waiting for her to click 'buy now'.

A sense of control shocked her to her core. She could afford any damned drink she pleased. Unfortunately, so could Lester. He had more experience with control.

'Annie!' Lester scattered the glitter. 'Did you hear me? The girls are going to dinner in Coco Beach later and want to show us the town. It would be ungentlemanly of me to let them go alone. You're in, right? Of course, she's in.' Lester chuckled towards Gloria and Beth. As if Annie wouldn't go where he said she was to go.

'Well, it's our first night. Shouldn't we eat here? The two of us?' Annie peeked up at Gloria to Beth. She got no support from either.

Lester winked. Had he always winked this much? 'We can eat together anytime. Been doing it for twenty years. Come on. Time to shake things up a bit.' The bravado he'd lost at the Fox and Rabbit returned to the stool under the palm-fronds.

'All right, then. Kind of you to offer.' Annie tried to raise her glass to the two Irish lasses, failing to emulate the action of the sophisticated women she'd watched on screen at the cinema. The other half of the pineapple chunk fell into her lap.

Annie and Lester elbowed for space in front of the bathroom mirror. Lester wore the effects of refusing sunblock; his inflamed cheeks and V-shaped neck line stood in stark contrast to the insipid skin flanking them.

'This is not to turn into a multi-millionaire's coming out party,' Annie said. 'Keep it subtle, Lester. Until we've got everything settled financially, keep it subtle.' Annie wasn't sure Lester knew what subtle meant. 'Keep your mouth shut.' *That'll do.* 'Please.'

'I'm not stupid, y'know.' Lester splashed Old Spice on his cheeks. He winced at the burn. Certainly, his odour wasn't going to give away the fact he was rich. 'But surely we can have a few drinks and a bite to eat without going into the witness protection programme?' He picked something out of a tooth and hitched his shorts up over his beer barrel abs. The shorts promptly settled back in the cellar region.

Lester headed out the door first, leaving Annie to lock up. She followed him to the lobby where their dinner dates were waiting. Annie swivelled her head side to side to keep her eyes off the bobbing foursome. Lester didn't even try.

Must have paid excess baggage for all that bosom. Where did you even buy those sorts of dresses in Dublin? Wasn't it cold there like it was in England? Annie's black and white striped midi dress seemed appropriate for the climate, and the occasion. But as she trailed the Guinness twins to the hotel shuttle bus, her acres of fabric may as well have been a burqa.

Annie perched on the edge of the seat next to Lester, their backs to the driver. Gloria and Beth sat opposite. The bumpy road didn't help the situation. The driver kept manoeuvring the rear-view mirror, Annie assumed to get more than a rear view.

'We've been here a week. Four days left.' Gloria's voice proved unable to peel Lester's eyes upwards. 'We've been to every bar in town and eaten everywhere, so tell us what you fancy and we'll tell you where to go.'

'Fish 'n' chips, goes without saying.' Lester said it anyway. 'But nowhere makes them better than old Britannia. No point trying to find good ones here. What about roast beef? Don't expect Yorkshire pudding, of course, but it's the gravy makes all the difference anyway, right, Annie?'

Annie knew it was Marks and Spencer's made all the difference – when you could afford it. She raised her tourist map to block most of the coastal mountain ranges bouncing in front of her.

'You won't be finding the gravy here, Les.' Beth's Irish brogue oozed condescension.

Les? He hates being called Les!

'But fish they've got. No batter though.'

That got Lester's attention. 'Who eats fish without batter?'

Beth battled on. 'What about paella? Will you be liking paella, now?'

'Oh, yeah, love that stuff …' Lester's voice trailed off and Annie stifled a giggle. Les had no idea what paella was, and she had no idea if Les's new friends knew about the meal ticket they could be sitting on. If they did, they hid it well.

The bus dropped them off in the bustling resort town of Coco Beach. Annie followed the boobs … *girls* … into the street, the dust from the dirt road catching in her sandals.

The shops remained open, despite the evening hour. Baskets of beachwear, flip-flops, shell jewellery and pottery painted jade and orange intentionally spilled their wares onto the sidewalks, slowing the progress of tourists and locals alike. Sundresses billowed on hangers from doorways. Sunhats of tropically-coloured straw waited patiently, ready for the pouty-lipped selfie sure to follow the squeal of 'This one's cute!' Sea air mingled with spices and fish. Annie, still waiting to wake up in Verston, took in the sounds, sights and scents like a sailor on shore leave.

Lester droned on about the Indian food back home. The Dubliners prattled on about the dresses they'd love to buy if they weren't out of money. Annie mentally patted her handbag; more specifically, the credit card inside it.

I could buy that entire shop full of dresses.

45

She studied the bright fabrics carefully before concluding they didn't cover enough flesh. Her travels through the Harrods and Paris couture websites had taught her real money tended to cover up more at her age. But the knowledge she could afford it all gave her an unfamiliar sense of belonging to a world once only reflected through a computer screen.

Lester marched forward, followed by his dinner guests, followed by Annie. Her companions faded from her consciousness as she drew her fingers through flowering vines tumbling over fences. The street ended at the beach. Red-flowered Malinche trees swayed rhythmically, matching the rolling waves. Annie swayed, too. The breeze lifted her hair. Maybe, just maybe, it had grown another inch since the bus ride. She raised her face to the setting sun and closed her eyes. The image was the same, open or shut. Never before had the dream and the reality matched.

'Annie! What are you doing?' Lester's voice rained down from somewhere above her.

Annie snapped her eyes open. Lester waved a beer bottle from a restaurant balcony. She had no idea how long she'd been standing on the beach or when she'd separated from the others.

'You're missing all the fun, standing there dreaming.'

You're kidding? Standing there dreaming was the most fun she'd had in a decade.

She found the staircase up to the restaurant and a waiter showed her to the table on the balcony. Gloria and Beth had arranged themselves one on each side. Les sat next to Gloria. Annie sidled into the chair next to Beth.

Gloria giggled. 'Cosy.'

Seeing as everyone already had drinks, the waiter addressed Annie. 'What can I get you?'

Until the Piña Colada, she'd only rotated through three drinks: beer, Babycham at Christmas – her mother's cheap champagne substitute – and the house red. Her eyes raked the surrounding tables.

'I'll have one of those.' Annie pointed to a tall, cool glass filled with liquid sunset, held by a young woman feeding her toddler with her free hand.

The waiter smiled at her. 'Sex on the Beach?'

'I beg your pardon?' Annie clutched her handbag and turned to Lester for backup.

Gloria and Beth broke into howls of laughter.

'That orange drink,' Gloria said, stifling her honking laugh with her hand, 'it's called Sex on the Beach. Have you never heard of it, now?' Her lilt did nothing to mask the harshness of the jab.

Lester chimed in, reaching across the table to take Annie's hand. 'She's not a lady of the beach world.'

Annie snatched her hand back. *You've never allowed me to be a lady of any world, you pillock.*

'Go on. Try it, luv.' Lester directed another infuriating wink at Beth.

'No, thank you.' Annie glared at the waiter. 'I'll have a red wine.'

'Which—'

'Anything that's open.' Annie snapped her mouth shut and watched the waiter back away from the table. She defied her table mates to make further comment.

It was Annie's turn to gloat when an enormous dish of paella landed in the centre of the table. Lester took one look at the mussels, shrimp, scallops and chunks of white fish on a mountain of pinky-orange rice and turned pale.

'Is this Costa Rican food?' Lester reached across the table and poked the head of a shrimp with his fork.

'Spanish, I think,' replied Gloria.

'Nah.' Lester jutted his chin, defiantly. 'Never saw this in Benidorm.'

Annie rolled her eyes so hard she worried she'd pulled an extraocular muscle. She flapped her napkin onto her lap and proceeded to serve her husband a pile, heavy on the shrimp. *Wonder if he's allergic …?*

She served herself, then tossed the serving spoon at Gloria. The clatter of the spoon dared Lester to complain. His attempts to feign paella pleasure between frequent swigs of beer fooled no one, but Annie enjoyed the spectacle.

Conversation round the table waxed and waned in rhythm with the water lapping the shore below the balcony. Annie asked the Dubliners what they did for a living – clothing shop managers. They asked Lester what he did – foreman at a corrugated cardboard manufacturer. 'For now,' he said, looking at Annie. She'd have to kill him if he winked again.

No one asked Annie what she did. Was it so obvious? 'I'm a bakery shop manager.' She threw it out there – 'manager' a given, like five-star reviews, smash hits and jaw-dropping dresses. 'Wedding cake specialist.' Annie pointedly directed her gaze at two empty ring fingers.

Beth giggled at Gloria. 'We've both had wedding cakes. Picked the wrong ones. Too many nuts in mine.'

'Not enough icing on mine.' Gloria snorted a little wine out of her nose, which made Beth hoot.

Annie hadn't even had a cake at her wedding. It all made sense now.

Of course, they'd paid for dinner. Les said it was the gallant thing to do for two poor divorced ladies trying to get back on their feet. *Back on their backs, more like.* Annie spent the shuttle ride home torn between blocking the coastal ranges with her map and trying to keep an eye on her husband's efforts to map those ranges – visually and manually. Luckily, the local beer and the local time zone put a damper on his mountaineering, and Annie easily convinced him to end the evening. He fell asleep in his underwear, sprawled face-down across the bed.

Annie slid open the door to the patio and sat down on a plastic wicker chair. She pulled its twin into position, slipped of her sandals and put her feet up. The humiliation of finding herself an exotic drinks virgin and all-round stranger in exposed-breasted paradise ebbed with the tide. The stars peeking through the palm trees twinkled close enough to touch. Sounds of the jungle startled and soothed in equal measure; though Annie questioned whether this was, in fact, a jungle or a rainforest. What was the difference?

Though her special package deal room didn't face the ocean, Annie delighted in the roll and retreat of waves as they whispered in her ear. Entranced, she stood up; beckoned by a watery snake-charmer that led her from her patio and through the deserted pool area. Once across the lawn – her bare feet registering the unique sensation of the spongy, succulent groundcover – she stepped over the rocky border onto the cool sand. No sandals. No cardigan. No handbag. She swept the abundant fabric of her dress up and draped it over one arm, freeing her legs to take longer strides. An unencumbered stranger in paradise. Or anywhere.

Despite the lateness of the hour, the waters of the bay lapped warm and inviting against her legs. Annie's toes elongated as they reached deeper into the sand, unafraid of the little crabs scuttling about, their shells glistening in the moonlight. They had never met before, these creatures of paradise and Annie from Verston. It surprised her that she instantly trusted them to do her no harm. She bent down to pick up a scurrying, pinkish native. It ran across her fingers, then settled motionless in the bowl of her palm. *Oh. It's you.*

'My first friend,' Annie whispered, before placing the crab gently on the sand. It darted away, carrying its home with it.

Home: a void, acknowledged but never addressed. In the moonlit reflection of a new world, a reckoning: continue to blame, delay, dream? Or acknowledge, plan, execute?

The breeze lifted her hair from her forehead, sweeping her eyes clear. Her toes dug deeper into the sand, gripping, rooting. A whisper – a promise – to the moon. 'A home. A real home. For me and only me.' She lifted the fingertips of her right hand to her lips: a kiss to seal the deal.

The splash of a waterfall interrupted her vows. Annie spun to face the inky water cascading into the pool. Another night, another torrent of dark water onto concrete. Flashing blue lights, the smell of smoke.

'Don't go down there, Annie!' Neighbours standing helplessly on the pavement. Running to save her sister, a policeman catching her roughly, swinging her off her feet and pushing her against a squad car. Water from the hoses gushing off the roof, washing her past, present and future into the gutter. Screams dispersing into thin air, like the spray from the hoses.

Lizzie couldn't hear her. Not then. Not now.

6 - HOW BIG WAS THAT FISH?

Taylor dressed carefully: linen, silk, silver and Chanel No. 5. Effortless took effort. The empty – and expensive – bottle of Châteauneuf-du-Pape from last night's room service sat on the table. She'd forgotten limitations, all be it briefly. Tucking the room keycard into her handbag, she left the room.

Charles, in crisp cotton shirt, designer jeans, no socks, Italian loafers, matched his wife stride for stride through the lobby. A large SUV swept them down the tree-lined driveway and onwards to Playa Flamingo.

The properties were exquisite, the vistas stunning, the sellers motivated and the information gleaned from the realtors … disappointing. Ashcroft Realty remained an unknown entity. Taylor and Charles returned to the car and headed, empty-handed, back towards the Paradise Resort.

The glint of gulf water through trees reflected in the window of the car. The flashes of light peeking, bobbing, hiding, goaded Taylor. Why couldn't she find Ashcroft? Why was it important she did? Why not leave him in the dust billowing out behind the car? It would be the mature thing to do, the professional thing to do. Just not the Taylor thing to do. She took no prisoners, turned no other cheek.

'This makes no sense.' Taylor poked at the phone in her lap. 'Ashcroft's such a pretentious jerk, he'd announce his arrival with a parade, not hide in the shadows.'

'Maybe he's not here yet,' Charles said. 'Maybe he's still trying to find someone to take on the position after you turned it down. You have big shoes to fill, and he must have been shocked you quit.'

'Shocked I didn't jump at the chance to maroon myself on a beach, you mean?'

'Or, maybe he's not in Costa Rica, period? I've pulled in quiet favours from my international contacts; those still speaking to me, that is. No one's aware of Ashcroft anywhere in Costa Rica.'

Taylor bit her lip. 'I know him. If he says he's going to do something, he's going to do it immediately. He's here somewhere. Giving up isn't an option.' Taylor glared at her husband, aware he was smarter than to suggest it.

Charles didn't suggest it. 'Relax, it's a small country. We'll find him. Meanwhile, you need to get your Costa Rican real estate license before he pulls his Caesar impersonation.'

Her husband also knew better than to suggest she relax but she let it pass. 'I've almost finished the paperwork. It's not as complicated as in the States, luckily. Bet I could finish it over something bubbly.' Taylor batted her eyelashes at Charles.

The car dropped them at the lobby of the Paradise Resort. The couple strode into the beachfront restaurant with the confident gait of gunslingers: gunslingers that fired cell phones and threw glossy real estate brochures down on the saloon bar.

Deep-cushioned wicker chairs welcomed the guests. Silent ceiling fans wafted luxury across the tile floors, past the huge planters of exotic blooms, across the pool with its centre island of palm trees and out into the bay. Servers appeared; silent apparitions anticipating needs, suggesting wants.

Taylor opened her laptop. 'Prosecco and a Perrier.' She ordered without paying any regard to the waitress.

'Can you recommend a local beer?' Charles smiled at the server, who responded to Charles's interest in her country's home-produced beer the way everyone responded to Charles: warmly, openly. The server named several Costa Rican brews and Charles chose Imperial – not the drink of kings; the drink of global ambassadors.

'She likes you,' Taylor said as the server left.

'What's not to like?'

Taylor had to agree. How many times had she watched her husband in action and vowed to emulate him the next time the opportunity arose? Unfortunately, she always got busy, focused, immersed, and the moment passed. Whispers reached her in bars and boardrooms, across negotiating tables: 'She's a cold fish.' At best.

An old promise to her grandfather found Taylor placing her laptop on the table. 'I'm … hard, sometimes, aren't I?'

'Sometimes?' Charles winked at his wife. 'But what brought that up?'

'Insecurity, I guess.' The words shocked even Taylor.

'Whoa! Wait a minute, Ms Newman. Insecurity?' Charles leaned towards Taylor and gently took her hand. 'You're feeling insecure just because your husband's a crook with no job prospects and you've been ousted from your corner office onto the unemployment line?'

'You're not a crook.' Taylor had never questioned this about her husband.

Charles sighed and let go of his wife's hand. 'Said Nixon, with the same effect as when I say it to the guy poking me in the chest at Starbucks.'

Taylor knew how much hurt Charles tried to hide. She forced a weak smile. 'You're the most honest crook I've ever met.' She patted his leg. An image of her father entered the room, uninvited. Taylor tutted out loud, causing Charles to raise an eyebrow in question. Taylor pushed her laptop further onto the table, making room for her elbows as she talked. 'You know, if anyone in my family could be a crook, it would be my father, not you.'

'You never mentioned this before. You let me marry into the Godfather family? You really are hard.'

'According to the press, you're a perfect fit.' Taylor winced at her words.

'I was in the wrong goddamned place at the wrong goddamned time when the shit hit the fan.' Charles rarely swore; his words now the only outlet for the anger bubbling beneath the veneer of good sportsmanship he showed to the world. Only someone who knew him inside and out recognised the cracks. Taylor's heart shuddered at the injustice.

Charles regained his outward composure. 'But I have to ask, what makes you believe Alan could have been a crook?'

'Oh, I don't know.' Taylor pictured her father's eyes; shifty, veiled. 'Always wheeling and dealing in public, stuffing his success down people's throats at parties, like a tuxedoed ticker tape feed. However, at home he never answered Mom's questions. By my teenage years, she was a full-blown alcoholic. I guess she gave up asking then.'

Charles smiled at the server when the drinks arrived. 'Maybe some things are best left unknown.'

The young woman moved on before Taylor remembered to smile. She gazed into the pale glittery liquid of her Prosecco. A friendly, bubbly, crisp beverage. Celebratory. Light-hearted.

Not today.

Taylor blinked the mistiness from her eyes, her father's harshness still able to reduce her to the mental age of six. She imagined him dissipating into the air like carbonated bubbles. It worked enough to allow her to focus back on her husband. 'You don't deserve the stigma of the scandal. You know that.'

Charles tipped his glass in thanks. 'It doesn't matter what *I* know. I have no control over other people's perceptions. The question is, what do I do now?'

Taylor sniffed and shook off any remaining pity – for herself or Charles. 'You drink yourself stupid while I become a realtor in Costa Rica.' She tipped her fluted glass back at her husband and set to work completing the online forms that would allow her to beat Ashcroft at his own game. Toe to toe with alpha dogs; a comfortable spot for her, despite her father's antiquated views of women. Or maybe because of them.

Stop it, Dad! Go back to sleep. She raised a silent prayer that her brother slept soundly too.

After the low-calorie, high-priced lunch, it was back in the waiting car for the afternoon appointment at the bank.

The banker, specialising in international clients, provided Charles and Taylor a comprehensive education in the many ways to bring money into the country. A growing economy, eco-tourism skyrocketing in popularity, and infrastructure upgrades a priority for government and local administrations alike: all good signs. There were builders a-plenty, architects a-hungry and buyers a-salivating. Taylor scribbled notes. Everything the banker shared convinced her success here was a given – except in one area. After careful and discreet probing, still no news of Ashcroft. It was a somewhat subdued walk back to the car. Taylor nodded distractedly at the driver who opened the door for her.

'Is he using a cover? Another agency?' Charles continued to work his phone contacts from the back seat. Not all his former business associates had abandoned him, but they weren't prepared to acknowledge him publicly; tainted goods, no matter how good.

The coastline raced alongside the car as Taylor sifted through her notes. 'It doesn't make sense. What's Ashcroft playing at? The job was an immediate transfer. I had to decide within hours. He must have had wheels in motion. Coldwell, Remax, Saville, Fine and Country, they're all here already. Someone should be aware of a big fish trying to muscle in by now.'

'I heard of big fish.' The driver's comment snapped two heads away from electronics. 'Sure, sir, madam. I heard big fish staying Hermosa.'

7 – PEPTO-BISMOL DREAMS

Lester groaned from the bathroom floor. 'They'd better have Pepto-Bismol in this place.'

Annie swept the sand she'd brought home from the beach out of the bed. 'You wouldn't need it if you hadn't drunk too much.' It was late-morning. Lester had only just managed to roll his fuzzy head off the pillow and into the recovery position, his cheek pressed against the cool tile. She smoothed the creases from the sheets and pulled the floral comforter up, aware there was maid service, though not quite sure what that entailed. She refused to appear slovenly to strangers.

'It was a bad shrimp,' Lester moaned from the bathroom. 'I didn't have but a drink or two.'

Per minute.

'Then how come I'm not sick?' Annie picked Lester's clothes off the floor and wiped down the bedside tables. 'We ate the same thing.'

'I had no idea pie … pie-allo had crawling sea bugs in it. You should have known it would give me a funny tummy. This'd never happen at the Fox and Rabbit.'

Annie stopped folding clothes and gazed out of the sliding patio door. The Fox and Rabbit. Though it had only been a few days, she couldn't quite place it.

'Hurry up, Annie. Go get me something to fix this.'

She could still place her husband, unfortunately. 'All right, though a lie-down and a drink of water would fix it soon enough.' She grabbed her handbag and headed out the door, nodding to the maids in the hallway and hoping she'd done enough tidying. She passed the pool where mothers draped towels over loungers and sloshed lotion on the kids. Only a hint of maternal regret remained after twenty years; she'd never blamed a baby for not wanting to become a Hardcastle.

Maggie tapped away on her keyboard behind the reception desk. Annie waited in true British style to gain attention but Maggie remained glued to her computer screen.

'Er, sorry.' Annie slapped her thigh. *Why am I sorry?*

Maggie jumped. She scrambled to close a window on her screen like a teenage boy when his mother burst in with the laundry.

'Good morning.' Annie clutched her handbag, hoping she hadn't offended anyone. 'There's no one in the gift shop and I need help.'

Maggie patted her chest and smoothed on a smile. Her cheeks flamed to match her hair. 'You startled me, Mrs Hardcastle. Gift shop? Right away.' With a leading hand and a slight bow, à la Basil Fawlty, she scuttled around the counter.

Arriving at the gift shop, Annie paused at the pottery stand, the bangles, the postcards. She felt no urgency to alleviate her husband's selfish stupidity, if that was even an option.

'Can I help you find anything? Sunblock? Snacks? Haven't seen Les … Mr Hardcastle yet this morning. Sleeping in, is he?'

'Pepto-Bismol.'

The women exchanged a glance.

'Oh. I see.' Maggie tightened her lips. She reached down behind the counter and got out the smallest bottle of the pink liquid Annie had ever seen. It was barely big enough to hold all the numbers on the price tag.

'Not giving it away, are they and surely even a travel-sized version should hold at least one full dose?' Annie squinted at the price tag again. She considered telling Lester they didn't have any. The idea faded quickly. Exorbitant price or not, it was worth the expense to keep Lester off her back.

Maggie printed out a weekly grocery bill-sized receipt. Annie signed it, now understanding why guests needed to win the lottery to come here. She figured she'd probably still have to sell the car if she wanted a swimsuit.

'Can I send lunch to your room?'

'Um … no.'

'Can I bring it to you by the pool?'

'Um. Oh. Lovely.'

'I'll make arrangements straight away. For one or two people?'

'One.' Single. Alone. Heaven.

Leaving Lester to dine on Pepto-Bismol at his toilet-side table ('You can't leave me here!' 'Yes. Yes, I can.'), Annie headed back to the pool. Her flip-flops conversed in a foreign language. Her sarong, found at a consignment shop in Benidorm half a decade ago, smelled of the back of her Verston wardrobe. Her handbag insisted on accompanying her and completed the picture of a foreigner to these shores, or to this life.

A table waited for her in the shade. Maggie poured the water – which Annie eyed suspiciously. 'What would you like?'

'What I'm really craving is breakfast,' Annie replied. She'd waited hours for Lester to wake up and missed the allotted breakfast hours.

'No problem, madam. I'll get you a menu.' Maggie walked away, to be confronted by an Australian guest who also wanted breakfast. Maggie refused his request which resulted in him glaring at Annie. She moved her chair, turning her back towards him.

Maggie handed over the breakfast menu. Annie spent a few joyous moments translating it into the vernacular of her favourite grocery chain, Tesco's: Eggs Benedict (ham and eggs on a crumpet with sauce), strawberry compote (fruity yogurt), huervos rancheros. *Who the heck eats beans, rice and spicy tomatoes for breakfast?*

'Eggs Benedict sounds lovely.' She handed the menu to Maggie, confused as to why the receptionist was now her attentive waitress.

As she waited, sipping the coffee that arrived unheralded, Annie caught the eye of bartender John as he arrived for his shift. He held a brief conversation in the lobby with Maggie before heading to his palm-covered work cubicle. He continued to catch Annie's eye each time she looked up from the ham and eggs.

Summat's up. Annie huffed in irritation at using one of Lester's Yorkshire turns of phrase; the one he used every time 'something was up' in a crime show. It annoyed her every time.

'Summat' was left on the backburner. After breakfast, Annie spent the rest of the day getting the hang of tilting her head upwards at the drinks server to signal a refill. She practiced nonchalantly tipping each server the way she'd seen in the American films; though on one occasion, she ended up scattering notes around her chair. The server retrieved them from the breeze and handed them back, looking down his nose like Annie needed them more than he did.

If he only knew.

Old habits die hard. Mid-afternoon, Annie ordered a pot of tea. She had to repeat her request twice. The server peered up at the sun and wiped sweat from his brow, shrugging his shoulders. When the tray arrived, a snigger emanated from a couple sitting next to her. She poured. The steaming liquid fogged up her sunglasses, making her realise how infrequently she'd drunk tea in England wearing sunglasses. After a couple of sips, sweat prickled her upper lip before plopping into her mug. The melting sunblock on her hands caused the handle to slip between her fingers. She ended up taking the mug and placing it on the side of the pool, climbing in and standing chest deep in the cooling waters, only then able to consume the liquid without fearing heat stroke. The couple sniggered again, which meant Annie had to finish the whole pot. British resolve and all that.

With each passing hour, Annie sunk deeper into her lounge chair. A Mai Tai, followed by a mango Margarita, encouraged her spine to lose the shape of an apology and take on the curves of a woman at play. She practised living; in and out of the pool, in and out of her book, in and out of incredulousness.

And, she noticed, in but never out of Maggie's peripheral vision.

8 – SHE WORKS HARD FOR THE MONEY

The Newmans set off from the Paradise Resort to hunt Big Fish – Ashcroft Fish. Fish for filleting on the Newman Gold Coast Realty table. Apparently, that big fish, speaking with a British accent and travelling with his wife, was at ClubSol in Hermosa. Or so said the Newman's driver.

The car purred to a halt under the hotel awning. José aided Taylor out of her climate-controlled chariot. He smelled big tip at the first American syllable.

Feeling naked without her linen, jewellery and Chanel, Taylor studied the lobby. It was exactly as the photos online had promised. Which was why she'd dressed down – if four-hundred-dollar jeans constituted dressing down. Charles blended in a little better, having left his watch in the hotel safe and rolled his sleeves, leaving his shirt untucked. Though exposed shirt tails had become accepted practice all over the world, Taylor struggled with its implications of excess weight and inattention to detail. Regardless of her efforts to blend, she wasn't fooling the restaurant guests or the staff. Multiple eyes tracked the Newmans across the lobby and into the restaurant.

As they were led to a table, Charles scanned the scene. 'This is going to be difficult. We don't have a name or a description. I doubt it's going to be any of the key players from your office.'

'Whomever it is should stand out here like a Yaley at a Harvard banquet.' Taylor spoke with her head down, eyes squirting out to each side.

Charles chuckled. 'Having been to both banquets, I can honestly say I can't tell the difference.'

'Blasphemy!' Taylor smirked, before catching the eye of a sunburned tourist entering the restaurant. A small bulge in his shorts pocket caught Taylor's attention. *Is that the lid of a Pepto-Bismol bottle?*

She sensed it first. A ripple of interest in the room. A straightening of staff backs, a quicker step to a table. She glanced at Charles. He nodded acknowledgement; he'd caught the vibe too. Using the cover of crossing his legs and sipping water, his eyes strafed the room for the source.

A waiter arrived. Charles spent a long two seconds scanning the wine list before ordering a bottle. Taking the opportunity to visually rake the entire restaurant, Taylor's heart sank. The sacrifice she was making to eat here was going to be completely wasted. Damn that driver.

'Keep track of the sommelier. Check out what he's bringing to various tables.' Taylor mentally palm slapped her forehead as she registered the dime-store detective in her voice.

Charles spluttered water down his chin and shirt. 'Sommelier, my ass. You won't even find "sommelier" in the dictionary at this place.'

Taylor gasped, momentarily taken aback – her husband never acted the snob – though she had to concede the point. She tipped her head towards the bartender, cigarette under the bar, damp cloth over his bare shoulder. Her grimace became a thoughtful pout. She added one-bedroom condos to her mental colonisation plan. Inland a bit, of course.

Pepto-Bismol Guy had been ushered to a prime table, then moved to one closer to the toilets.

Taylor's nose wrinkled. 'Dear God. What a mess.'

Charles contorted his face into a 'yikes' then nodded casually towards another couple. 'A bit more bling. Not sure it's Ashcroft bling though.'

Taylor observed the party seated a few tables away. She agreed they didn't match the Ashcroft brand. In fact, nothing about this place matched the Ashcroft brand. 'Maybe they won't be out in the open. If the Ashcroft guys are trying to hide, they're ordering room service to fly under the radar?' The words rung false, even to her ears. Ashcroft never flew under the radar.

Her pulse quickened. Heat burned her cheeks. *He knows I'm here already!* Of course! Now he'd fight dirty to ensure she knew her place. Which meant she'd fight dirty to make sure he knew her place, teaching him the same lessons her father had learned years ago. She'd rubbed her success in Dad's face with every newspaper article written about her, at every awkward family dinner, at each sales awards ceremony.

On each anniversary of her brother's death.

Her success forced her father to acknowledge what Richard could have been, if only he'd stood strong like his sister. With renewed verve, she determined to fight on. Squaring her shoulders, she stared round the restaurant; the view rather anticlimactic compared to the battlefield in her head.

Luckily for her, Charles demonstrated a more pragmatic approach to warfare. He caught the attention of a redheaded employee and beckoned her over to the table. 'Hi. This is a sweet spot you've got here.' The redhead smiled back. 'We're thinking about changing hotels. Can you give us a rundown of your services?'

Red Head swivelled her upper body left and right as though searching for inspiration. 'Um … complimentary beach towels. Gift shop.'

Taylor forbid her eyes to roll. She folded her arms and leaned back – then unfolded her arms and leaned forward, feigning interest. *Why all these infuriating British accents?*

The hostess continued her sales pitch. 'Pool's cleaned every day.'

Taylor gaped at the pool through the window in horror. *Some pools aren't?*

Charles grinned at his germophobic wife. 'Sounds lovely, doesn't it, honey? What about room service? Twenty-four hours?'

'No, sir. Stops at ten.'

'Of course.' Charles nodded. 'Bet room service is busy now then.'

'No orders tonight, sir. Everyone's eating in the restaurant except the family reunion. They went into town for dinner tonight.'

The waiter arrived and began to uncork the wine. Red Head said, 'Ask for Maggie if you want to make a room reservation.' She dipped her head at the wine. 'That's a grand bottle you've ordered.' With that, she left the table.

Taylor wouldn't have used this particular bottle of white wine to flush a red wine spill out of a cocktail dress back home. She managed a sickly-sweet smile as the waiter left.

'We could die here. You know that, right?' Taylor tutted at herself. She took ownership of her snobbishness – usually – but tonight something about it didn't sit right. Maybe it was Richard's ghostly presence at the table. She swivelled her head, taking in all the diners who appeared perfectly content with their surroundings. Why was nothing good enough for her these days? When had she changed? She recalled the childhood aroma of baking, replacing the smell of leather car seats and cigars, as she gleefully transitioned from her father's Cadillac into her grandfather's rural Illinois home. Her dad never came in; his absence commonplace in any environment. Back then, she'd preferred cosiness to the spacious precision of her parents' Chicago penthouse box, preferred clutter to order. She and Richard would skip happily into the arms of Grandpa, free of the ridiculously premature pressures of fulfilling parental expectations. She'd slip under the old quilt on the squeaky mattress in the shabby bedroom and eat cookies by torchlight while Richard talked of running away to sea or becoming an astronaut. He never spoke of taking over the family business during conversations with Grandpa. Grandpa would pull off his glasses and give them a good clean on his sweater before a conversation with his grandchildren. Taylor loved the way he cleaned off the world to see and hear her better.

'Can girls be as smart as boys?' The echo of a question asked of a grandfather a lifetime ago. Taylor needed reassurance then, unlikely to get it from her father.

'Oh, yes.' Grandpa peered over his glasses at his granddaughter. 'Boys are stupid things.'

Taylor giggled. 'But you're a boy.'

'So I know what I'm talking about.' He sipped on his lemonade and listened to the bees.

She'd been kind then. And smart. And a girl. Yet here she was, a grown-up snob, constantly fighting for success, but forgetting to fight for kind. She'd sided with one over the other a long time ago.

The right shoes delineated life from death in her world now, more so than the promises she made her grandfather to be kind, and to her brother they'd always be best friends; maybe set up a business together far away from their father. She'd played in puddles then. Now swimming pools needed sterilising daily to keep her happy. It saddened her she couldn't channel the child she'd been. Pathetic relief that her grandfather hadn't lived to see her now saddened her further. When had she become her father? She'd wanted desperately to be her grandfather.

The waiter arrived with his notepad. She took a deep breath and ordered the burger.

To blend in.

When she removed the bun, the onions and the burger, nibbling only at the lettuce and tomato, she recognised she'd failed to filter back into Grandpa's world. She did thank the waiter, however, as he cleared the dishes. 'Kindness is a muscle that needs exercise,' Grandpa always said.

The bartender did his best to clean up after his trip and fall. 'I'll never get the stain out of this shirt,' Taylor muttered in the car as they left ClubSol. Despite the offer of the roll-on travel stain remover from the lady at the next table, the white shirt had lost the fabric-versus-barbeque sauce fight. 'I doubt I'll even bother taking it home.'

Charles stifled a laugh. 'Think of the money, honey.'

'I am. About how much this shirt cost.'

'I mean the money you're going to make when you beat Ashcroft at his own game.'

'Oh. That money.' Taylor sniffed at the barbeque scented air. Was it worth the effort?

As she got out of the car at the Paradise Resort, Taylor vowed to hunt down the driver who had given them the big fish information. He owed her a shirt. Back in the room, she hurled the stained fabric into the trash, showered, then plonked herself down on the bed, wrapped in a thick spa robe. The scent of barbeque sauce followed her.

Charles checked the bottom of his shoes. 'Are you sure we didn't tread in it?' He placed his shoes in a bag to be collected for cleaning – just in case – before continuing. 'So much sacrifice and we're no further ahead than we were before dinner.'

'This all makes no sense.' Taylor drummed her fingers on taut sheets. 'Why would Ashcroft ship someone from England to stay at a hotel like that?

'Same reason we're staying here,' Charles replied. 'To settle on a plan before tipping their hand.'

Taylor perused her luxurious surroundings. 'And why on earth would any hotel tout cleaning the pool as an upgrade? I much prefer the way we're travelling incognito to the way they're doing it.'

'Make the most of it.' Charles frowned. 'We're living off our golden handshakes, remember. They won't last forever.' He headed for the de-contamination shower.

Taylor settled onto her back on the bed. The drapes waved in the air conditioning. No, the money wouldn't last forever.

Think, Taylor.

'I may have left my purse at your restaurant last night.' Taylor wore more bling this morning. Maggie's eyes roved over Taylor's bedecked arm and throat.

'We were chatting with your "important guests".' Taylor dipped her head conspiratorially, the dollar notes folded in her hand with a corner sticking out. Maggie noticed that, too.

'All our guests are important, madam, though I bet I know who you mean. Please wait here.' She trotted over to the bartender, and they conversed for a moment. She trotted back.

Casting her eyes everywhere but at Taylor, Maggie said, 'John wishes to apologise again for the barbeque sauce incident.' She cleared her throat before continuing. 'He also says no purse was handed in and you didn't talk with the Hardcastles in the restaurant last night.'

'Who's taking my name in vain, then?' A voice, containing equal measures of arrogance and condescension, startled the two ladies. Pepto-Bismol Man sauntered up and leaned on the counter. His eyes perused Taylor, up and down.

Taylor vowed to take another shower.

The man winked, one eye at each lady. Taylor pictured an owl – without the aura of wisdom. 'I'm sure I'd have remembered talking to you, Ms …?'

'And I'm sure I would have remembered you, too.' Taylor attempted to substitute warmth for irritation in her smile. She doubted she was successful. 'We seem to have crossed wires here, Mr Hardcastle.'

Lester grinned. 'Any time you want help uncrossing your wires, give me a call. Ask for Lester.'

Taylor nodded curtly before turning back to face Maggie. 'Sorry for any confusion. My thanks for checking for my purse. I'll search again back at my hotel.'

Taylor left a five-dollar note on the counter and strode across the lobby. *How on earth could the stupid woman think that jerk's the important guest?*

She scuttled back to her side of the bay in the waiting limo.

Charles stopped typing on his laptop as Taylor cruised towards his poolside table at the Paradise Resort. She didn't acknowledge the waiter as she ordered a Bloody Mary.

Charles waited. When Taylor said nothing, he prompted. 'How'd it go?'

Taylor remained silent. When her drink arrived, she took a huge gulp before turning her phone screen towards Charles.

His mouth dropped open. 'That's a photo of Sit-by-the-Toilet-Man from last night.'

'Shh. Listen to this.' Taylor directed the screen back to face herself and read from the *Tri-Counties Gazette* website, checking first no one else could eavesdrop: '"Lester and Annie Hardcastle are the winners of fifty-two million pounds." That's pounds. Sterling!' Taylor widened her eyes at Charles. 'Quick. Check the exchange rate.'

Charles clicked a few keys on his laptop then let out a low whistle. 'Jesus H. Christ! That's a lot of money.'

'Yeah.' Taylor struggled to keep her voice hushed. 'Tens of millions of dollars sitting on a bar stool at ClubSol, drinking Pepto-Bismol. I still don't believe it.'

Charles scanned headlines, his eyebrows lifting higher and higher. 'They're all over Twitter in the United Kingdom. We need to meet these people.'

'I already did. Lester, anyway.'

Charles raised his glass at his wife. 'Your first luxury villa sale can't be far behind.'

'Oh, think bigger, honey. We need a plan. Fast, before Ashcroft gets them.'

Charles slammed his laptop screen closed. Grabbing drinks, Taylor led the way back to their room.

Inside Command Central, they worked the angles. Based on her interaction with Lester, Taylor doubted the Hardcastles even knew they had an angle. All she knew for certain was she needed to stick right by their side until they worked it out.

9 – IMPROVING IN LEAPS AND BOUNDS

Lester nursed his head in tremulous hands while Annie flicked through the activities brochure at the breakfast table. Her finger stopped at the photo of jet skis. Great idea: choppy water and loud engines to remind Lester not to drink to excess again.

An hour later, Lester eyed the apparatus; mechanical dolphins beached on the sand. Then he examined the wide expanse of Papagayo Bay. Annie ducked her head to smirk at his discomfort. The half-mile swimming certificate he'd earned at secondary school had long expired.

Lester rubbed his chin. 'They'll give us life jackets, won't they?'

'Of course, they will.' *Unfortunately.*

'You brought the Pepto-Bismol, right?'

'No. That stuff's more expensive than the jet skis.' Through the side of her mouth, Annie whispered, 'First pay-out's not in our account yet. Pace yourself.'

Lester swallowed. He'd hardly left the bar since their arrival in Costa Rica. Sitting and drinking wasn't unusual behaviour for him. Back home – Annie struggled again to picture it – Lester visited the Fox and Rabbit several times a week, but he had his limit for work days and even at weekends remained mindful of budget. Annie was grateful for it, aware some women viewed this the epitome of gallant behaviour. However, the lottery win appeared to have expanded her husband's alcoholic horizons. Annie was struck by the idea Lester's flippant 'more bartenders' statement to the reporter may in fact be his new business plan.

As Lester wrestled his arms through the wrong straps on his life jacket, Annie studied the man before her. Did an unlimited bar tab signify the pinnacle of his millionaire imagination? Could first-name terms with the bartender be akin to social climbing? She pictured her favourite romantic film, *Sabrina*: working-class woman wins high society – and gorgeous – man, social consequences be damned. Annie knitted her eyebrows. What did social class even mean anymore? Did she want ball gowns and titles? *Nope. Though if Harrison Ford were available ...*

'Are you coming?' Lester 'So-Not-Harrison-Ford' sat astride a jet ski bobbing in the water, life jacket buckled, white-zinced nose pointing nautical north. He revved the engine a few times. 'Bit sticky, this throttle. Nothing I can't deal with though.'

'Pick another jet ski.' Annie selected one with pink lightning bolts on each side.

'Nah. This one'll be grand. Let's go.'

The jet ski operator went over the rules before pushing each jet ski deeper into the water. With a wobble, Lester and Annie set off.

Once she'd worked out it was best to head straight into the waves rather than let them hit her sideways, Annie savoured the wind tousling her hair, the tingling coolness of the spray, the exhilaration of cornering without the constraints of tarmac and centre line boundaries. On one occasion, suspended airborne over a larger wave, a sense of daring, of flying, overpowered her.

Even Lester laughed. 'Uff! The landing gets your bum, doesn't it?'

Annie couldn't remember the last time she'd laughed with her husband. Moments later, he accidently steered into the plume of water arcing out of the back of her jet ski. He had to turn back to scoop his hat out of the deep blue. Annie laughed again.

She went on ahead, passing a couple of tiny islands covered in birds, heading for the peninsula that denoted the end of the curved bay across from which nestled the town of Hermosa. Annie slowed down to enjoy the view of the coastline.

White beaches basked in the sun, the sand speckled with trees bedecked in vivid red blooms. Luxury villas peeked out from rocky ledges; the manmade intrusions artfully screened by native vegetation. Heat shimmered off the roofs yet the whole scene was cooled by cobalt waters and winds moving playfully through branches. Annie lifted her face to the sun, tasting the salt on her lips, calling birds laying the sound track. Warmth permeated to the depths of her soul. This place, this was where she should be.

I can afford one of those houses.

She cut the jet ski engine. Waves calmed. Birds silenced.

'I can totally afford one of those.' The enormity of the statement left Annie breathless. Shaking, she closed her eyes and contemplated all the ways the rug could be pulled out from under her feet.

The rug spoke. 'Don't you mean *we* can totally afford one of those?'

Annie motioned Lester to cut the engine on his jet ski, and they bobbed along next to each other. 'While we're out here, away from listening ears, we should talk about … things.'

Lester pulled his tee shirt over his head and placed it in the seat compartment. 'Well, I've been thinking.'

Annie bit her lip. 'When, exactly?'

'It's not all fun and games at the bar, you know.' Lester's stern scowl sent twitches through Annie's shoulders in an effort to stifle the snigger.

'I've been thinking,' Lester said again. 'It's all well and good, sitting around doing nothing all day, but we need to get on with our regular lives at some point.'

Oh, no, we don't!

'There's our jobs to worry about. Are we going to quit or not? Are we going to buy a new house or fix up the flat we've got? Are we going to get a car each?'

Annie inhaled, forgetting to exhale until forced to by dizziness. Such minuscule deliberations! Surely, the answers were a given? Surely, they weren't either/or choices? 'You do understand we won fifty-two million pounds. Not fifty-two thousand? Don't you?' Annie wrestled to contain her incredulous expression. She'd hated it when the Dubliners directed a similar one towards her on discovering she'd never had a pedicure.

'Of course I understand.' Lester tutted. 'That doesn't mean we're turning into plonkers, all cigars and la di dah.' He folded his arms. The jet ski handles spun round, requiring him to throw out his hands to catch them.

'Plonker' is exactly what you became at the Fox and Rabbit the night of the lottery win.

Lester continued, as though he had in fact given much thought to everything they shouldn't do with their lives. 'No going all bleached blonde and ignoring our mates. I won't have it.'

Annie cringed. She knew exactly what he meant, having attempted the bleached blonde look in the early years of their marriage. Results were disastrous. Lester had called her a scarecrow with boobs. In front of everyone.

'I'm not saying we should do that.' Annie shifted her attention from Lester to the houses on the peninsula, trying to equate them with a mere cigar. 'But surely you're not thinking about going back to work?'

'Haven't ruled it out.' Lester puffed up defensively. 'Routine's important.'

'But isn't there a lot of space between us returning to our old lives and turning into plonkers? Isn't there a third option?'

Lester scratched his head. 'Well, what's your plan?' His chin jutted defiantly, like he knew she'd never come up with anything more exciting than their old life with better biscuits.

Annie stared at her husband. Lester dished out forethought like he was being charged for it by the ounce, but, surely, he was smarter than this? Horror filled her at how quickly he'd given up picturing something better. Had he no dreams? He must have had a bucket list or why would he have bought five lottery tickets every week for the last ten years?

Annie collected herself. 'I thought … places I'd never been before. I thought my own cake shop, with a website and hunter green delivery vans.' Annie paused, waiting for Lester to notice he hadn't been mentioned yet. 'Then I thought … here.' She swept her arm across the gulf. The wind carried her voice over the waves to settle on the roof of a stunning villa by the beach, an infinity pool inviting the viewer to spend infinity in its waters.

'Well, that's a lorry load of dreaming, my girl.' Annie's skin crawled at Lester's pompous tone. 'I suppose you'll be throwing out your good clothes and driving a convertible next.'

Now you mention it …

Annie said nothing. There was nothing to say. The jet skis bumped together, scraped along each other's sides, floating at awkward angles to each other. Bobbing out of sync.

She hadn't shared all her dreams for the future. She'd wanted to give it one more chance, to work out if she and Lester had anything even remotely in common now they didn't have to be themselves. She sighed. She knew better.

As she wallowed in old territory, a new thought struck her: she knew less about her husband of twenty years than she knew about paradise. She lived her married life clueless as to whether Lester yearned or dreamed, imagined or regretted; whether he aspired. An intense stab of jealousy shook her; jealousy towards the tipsy, balding, beer-bellied owner of a 'Yorkshire Men do it Moor' tee shirt. If he did none of these things, he was the genius of the two, she the time waster. Something else shook her: a hint of understanding. If she knew nothing of him, how could she expect him to know anything of her?

Annie blinked back tears – tears for wasted time and unexploited potential. *Enough!* She didn't want to contemplate her failings anymore. She wasn't ready to shift the blame entirely to herself yet, either.

She pasted on a smile. 'We'll have to give it all more thought, then. Let's head over to the cove we saw in the poster hanging at the hotel.'

While talking, they had drifted closer to a beach they hadn't seen before. The coloured umbrellas and the waiters carrying drinks to pampered guests sparked new dreams in Annie.

'NQOCD,' she muttered towards the tanned bodies sipping on expensive cocktails. The acronym her mother used for 'Not Quite Our Class Dear' had always been applied to those lower down the food chain when Annie was growing up. Annie tended to use it about those higher up the food chain. Nodding her goodbyes to the exclusive beach club, she fired up her jet ski.

Lester did the same. Nothing happened. Lots more pressing start buttons. Lots more nothing happened. Annie shut her engine off and waited.

'Let's 'ave a look then.' Lester took charge, standing up and lifting the seat that covered the engine. 'Got fuel. No leaks. What's this? A bit rusty, whatever it is. Oh, probably the throttle cable.' He fiddled with a wire, then pressed the start button. The engine roared. Lester grabbed the throttle handle and twisted it back. The engine roared louder.

What happened next, Annie wasn't sure. The seat cover crashed down and Lester took off across the water; an ocean-going kangaroo, gripping the handlebars, belly down on the seat, legs flapping out behind like kite tails. The jet ski bounced across the shallow water and pogoed up the sandy beach, coming to a halt inside an upturned beach umbrella. Sunbathers scattered, and sand sprayed into the eyes and drinks of every patron of the Paradise Resort within fifty feet.

Annie covered her eyes, then her ears. Surely, the screaming was excessive? No need to attract attention like that.

10 - SPECIAL DELIVERY

Taylor shook out a sandal while acknowledging the disconcerting reality that if she planned to sell shoreline properties she'd have to get used to sand between her toes. Picking up the glasses from the bar, she made her way across the private beach, concentrating on not spilling a drop of the exorbitantly expensive drinks she carried. She should have let a server carry them for her, but she'd decided to experiment with, 'No, that's okay. I'll do it.' Charles always got a smile from waiters when he said that. Her server had just looked suspicious, like he knew the other Newman shoe was about to drop.

Charles pulled two lounge chairs into the shade of an umbrella. Taylor handed him her cocktail to hold, scanning beach patrons as she removed her sarong. No laptops, no leather briefcases; just beautiful people doing what beautiful people did. They made relaxing look effortless – even enjoyable – forcing her to question where her drive to perfect the art of relaxation had gone. She recognised the skill as necessary for long-term health, but she just couldn't build up any stamina for it. Maybe it would help if she added 'relax' to her appointment notifications. She vowed to do exactly that. Tomorrow.

'I've checked everyone here,' Charles said. 'No one's sporting the Ashcroft logo. Wiley as a bunch of spooks, they are.' He sipped his Chiliguaro.

Taylor never understood how he tolerated the spicy cocktail on their trips to Costa Rica, given the possibility of being confused with a dragon afterwards. It lingered on the breath for days. Taylor sat down and sipped her Flor de Cana and Diet Coke.

One sip. Two sips. Relaxation time over. 'How are we going to corner those Brits before Ashcroft does?'

Charles raised an eyebrow. 'Are you sure you want to? After meeting this Lester guy, is his business even worth the money, honey?'

'Ha ha.' Taylor had to admit the prospect wasn't pleasant. Neither was losing the Hardcastles to Ashcroft. 'What do you think people like that do for fun?' She cringed, recognising her father in her comment. 'I mean, we'll bond with them—'

A shadow fell across her drink, followed by a split second to register the screaming. Then, she was airborne, briefly, before rolling in sand, a bikini bottom wedged in places it shouldn't be. Darkness. The smell of salt and dragons. Burning exfoliation of the skin on her cheeks – all of them. Pain across her stomach.

Face down, wearing her lounger like a turtle shell, sand stuck in infinitely more places than between her toes, Taylor slowly lifted her head. She peered through crusty eyeballs at Charles who was plonked on his backside, legs spread-eagled, arms tangled up in the ribs of his beach umbrella. He appeared to be finishing his drink via his nasal passages, gasping as though he'd been pepper-sprayed. A jet ski lay next to him.

Security arrived quickly. As did the bartender and a lawyer – or six. All Taylor could hear through sand-filled ears was, 'So and so, Attorney at Law.' The so-and-sos extricated her limbs from the mangled lounger, their narrowed eyes assessing her level of emotional distress. Taylor guessed they'd multiply it by a thousand and come up with a number before Charles even finished choking. One of the lawyers proffered Taylor his card as she spat sand out of her mouth. She gaped from his Speedo to the card. Not sure where he'd pulled it from, her fingers refused to take it. A bartender offered Charles a towel to wipe her rum and coke from his chest and the Chiliguaro from his eyes.

75

The Speedoed lawyer gave the jet ski driver the once-over. 'Probably couldn't get much out of him,' he said before ambling off back to his drinks. His departing body clearing the way for Taylor to notice two jet skis: one filling a large divot where her beach chair used to be, and the other in the shallow water. A woman on the second jet ski appeared to be fighting to steer it to shore, her face frozen in horror.

A couple of teenagers put down their phones – Taylor guessed photos of the event already on Instagram – and made their way towards the woman, splashing through the water and dragging her and her jet ski up onto the beach. The woman looked like she'd rather be pushed out to sea. She staggered off her jet ski and wobbled slightly, head down, no eye contact. She walked slowly towards a man, rolling off his beached jet ski onto the sand.

Everything smelled of fuel, rum and dragon's breath.

'I … I'm so sorry,' the woman stammered in Taylor's direction. 'Obviously, a major mechanical malfunction. Are you all right?'

Shouldn't the man be the one asking? The beached whale next to her made silent fish lip movements. One of the teenagers attempted to close-range video the welt forming across her stomach. Taylor swatted him across his head, then grabbed her towel to cover up. Through her irritation, she found herself face-to-face with the photo from the *Tri-Counties Gazette:* Annie and Lester Hardcastle.

Act cool, Taylor. Act cool.

Charles stood upright, about as angry as Taylor had ever seen him. He opened his mouth to speak.

'Now, now, Charles. No real harm done.' Taylor hustled over to him and brushed sand off his shoulders. She peeked over her own at the stunned-looking couple behind her.

Charles glared at Taylor through alcohol-induced pink eye. 'Since when have you been the one to turn the other cheek?'

Taylor winked several times at Charles, who clearly didn't get the hint. She tried another tactic. 'Drinks are in order.'

Charles appeared in no mood for civility. 'We're owed an—'

Taylor cupped Charles's chin, mouthing into his astonished face, 'Annie and Lester Hardcastle.'

'—owed an explanation of the drinks specials.' Charles pasted on a tight-lipped smile before tipping his head to one side, seeming to clear the Chiliguaro from his ears and sinuses.

Taylor led the bedraggled group over to a table, as unobtrusively as possible removing wayward sand and straightening her swimwear.

Charles waved a server over.

'Oh, we couldn't possibly,' Annie squeaked. Her fingers wandered to the waterproof money canister around her neck. 'We have to get back.'

'Nonsense.' Taylor took charge. 'We couldn't possibly allow you to get back on those machines and head out into deep water until we're sure you aren't suffering from delayed shock.'

Lester's oral movements calmed somewhat, but he was still the picture of a man struggling to comprehend his situation. That suited Taylor fine.

'Charles, please retrieve any possessions these poor people have left in the jet skis. Then we'll introduce ourselves properly.'

Taylor shuffled a few steps away from the Hardcastles and grasped Charles's arm. From the side of her mouth, she issued orders into his ear: 'Give those teenagers an exorbitant amount of money to ride the skis across the bay and abandon them on ClubSol's beach. Without saying a word to anyone. Surely, even kids staying here need cold, hard cash.'

Charles nodded. 'No need to question your motives, I suppose?'

Taylor turned away before he could pull anymore of his holier-than-thou crap. She bounced back to the table, disguising the pain in her hip with a slight hop. 'Right, I need a drink.'

Annie held her hand over her heart. 'Maybe a drink would help steady the pounding in my chest. I'm Annie, by the way.'

'Taylor Newman, and you are …?' Taylor's hand reached for Lester's. He didn't appear to recognise her. At least he didn't offer to help her uncross her wires again.

'Lester Har— ouch!' Lester glared at Annie. 'Lester. That's me.'

Taylor registered the kick under the table. She pulled out a chair for Charles as he returned from his errand. 'Nice to meet you both. This is Charles, my husband. His eyes aren't normally red, by the way.' Taylor attempted a chuckle. Charles obviously didn't find the comment amusing. He plonked himself down with a grimace as the ripening bruise on his thigh hit the arm of the chair.

'What will it be, then?' Taylor waited for Annie's order.

Annie checked out the other tables and homed in on a beer a man in a Speedo was sipping. 'I'll have one of those, please. Beer's always a safe bet.'

Taylor pondered what she meant. Lester ordered a Samuel Smith.

'Excellent choice,' Charles said. He handed the couple the tee shirt and the sarong he'd found in the seat compartments of the jet skis.

The drinks arrived while Annie was still struggling to tie her sarong around her neck with shaky fingers. Taylor's mouth set in a straight line. The wrinkled, wet and obviously cheap fabric didn't help Annie blend in with the silk kaftans, Dior swimwear and gold belly chains at other tables. It did help hide the one-piece, black swimsuit. Taylor homed in on the baggy elastic in the legs; a fashion faux pas sniffer dog. Lester struggled into his 'Yorkshire Men do it Moor' shirt. Taylor stifled a shudder. At least the other beach goers knew she hadn't invited these guests.

'So,' Charles began. 'How'd you find this place? I mean Papagayo, not this beach. I'm intimately familiar with how you found this beach.' Weak chuckles. It was too soon.

'Recommended by our solicitor, actually.' Annie surveyed the scene. 'We typically stay in Europe this time of year. Wanted a change so thought we'd try it.'

The medicinal qualities of the beer seemed to be working wonders on Lester. 'Stay in Europe?' In an accent Taylor recognised from Downton Abbey – upstairs Downton Abbey, not downstairs – he continued. 'Oh, yes. We're usually on the Flamstead Riviera about now. Unless we get bored, then we take the Bentley up to Harpenden Common.'

Taylor had no idea what Flamstead or Harpenden were, but surmised they weren't holiday destinations.

Lester chortled at his joke until Annie's scowl silenced him. Lester smoothed down his tee shirt with his free hand and finished his drink. He wasn't a sipper. Taylor waved over another round and made small talk about Hertfordshire villages for what seemed like hours.

'What about you two?' Lester directed his thumb around the beach. 'I'd guess successful bank robbers. Costs a packet to stay here, I bet.'

Taylor couldn't take her eyes off Annie. Was the woman trying to smack her forehead or swat a fly? Her hand missed whatever she was aiming for, catching only the tip of her ear. The peculiar woman threw her hand an accusatory scowl. She carefully picked up the second glass, gaping at it like it was an apparition. Something was wrong.

'No, we're not crooks. I'm in real estate.' Taylor answered Lester's question while flicking her eyes at Annie and back, signalling Lester to pay attention to his wife. He didn't get the hint. Maybe Annie's behaviour was normal in jet ski circles. Taylor reassessed her plan for one-bedroom condos. They may be more trouble than they were worth.

'What do you do, Charles?' Lester carried on, oblivious to his wife's struggles with her sarong. She muttered something as she wrestled with the knot behind her head.

'Also not a crook. Banking. Retired,' Charles replied.

'Cake decorator. Active du … duty.' Annie finished with the knot and appeared rather surprised at her words She cast long, slow blinks in Taylor's direction before scrutinising her beer as though about to ask it a question.

Taylor threw Charles a silent, wide-eyed 'OMG' stare before continuing. 'We're mixing business with pleasure. Searching for real estate investments. After all, who wouldn't want to live here?'

Annie nodded, rather too vigorously.

Lester frowned. 'There'd have to be a chippy close by before I'd move here.'

Taylor took mental notes: *Build a chippy. After finding out what a chippy is.*

'Oh, I bet the chef here could rustle up something to your exacting tastes.' Charles turned to his wife. 'Fish and chips is the chef's speciality, isn't it?'

Taylor nodded Charles a grateful affirmative. 'Oh, please, be our guests for dinner. We insist; to show we're all friends here. No matter how we met.'

Lester appeared chuffed. Annie gesticulated, hands spasming awkwardly; words attempted and aborted.

'Are you all right, luv?' Lester peered at his wife. 'Oh, my good gawd. She's drunk! I haven't seen her drunk in fifteen years.' He laughed and patted Annie's back.

'I thought she was brave to order the Tumba Calzones,' Charles said. 'Kick harder than a fifth of vodka, those things.'

'Whaza Tunbra Cahone?' Annie spoke as though through Novocaine.

'A Costa Rican beer,' Charles explained. 'But the name tells you all you need to know. The translation means "panty remover".'

Annie slid off her chair, knocking her beer glass to the ground. Taylor leapt up as the cold liquid splashed her lap. Wafting up from the floor, slurred and sleepy-sounding: 'I'll have a Babycham.'

11 – PARADISE UPGRADED

Annie peeled her eyelids open. Blinding whiteness and the nauseating motion of a slowly spinning fan slammed them shut again. Opening one eye a tiny chink, Annie registered she was lying in a bed the size of a cricket pitch. Her fingers sunk into a fluffy robe, exotic scents tickled her nostrils. An apparent gap in the time-space continuum led to a disquieting sense of panic. It started in Annie's toes before spreading towards her rational brain centres – what was left of them.

'You're awake.' A voice floated in on the breeze from an open door.

Am I?

A lady in white got bigger and bigger, as though rolling in on silent wheels. Her head eclipsed the fan.

'What happened?' Annie struggled to sit upright. 'And please stop shouting.' *Oops. My voice. Sorry.*

'You had a little run-in with the locals – or rather the local beer.' A man appeared from behind the white lady and smiled down at Annie.

Wavy visions of floating beer glasses and trying to speak through molasses. A vague recollection of walking, aided on both sides, up a beautiful pathway. The flowers had spoken to her. Had it rained? Annie fingered her damp hair. She recalled someone singing. Panties. Something about panties …

'Stop right there!' Annie gripped the sheet to her chest. She held up her palm, making it quite clear these shenanigans were to go no farther.

'About time you woke up, luv.' A familiar voice. It should have provided reassurance but didn't. 'You missed a nice sunset from Chuck's terrace.'

'Who the heck's Chuck?' Annie continued to clutch the sheet, but at least she was now aware it was Lester speaking.

Lester pointed to the smiling man beside him, whose eyebrows suggested he was somewhat surprised to find out he was Chuck. 'Charles and Taylor. They sell houses. Don't you remember anything? Honestly, I can't take her anywhere.' Lester grinned at his audience.

'I remember a flying jet ski,' Annie snapped back.

Lester's grin disappeared. 'Accidents happen, you know. Luckily, we're all still friends.' He thumped Chuck's arm.

Charles directed a somewhat pained smile at Annie. 'Lester and I will leave you ladies to get ready for dinner. You slept through lunch and the whole afternoon so maybe a little bite to eat will taste good?' Charles led Lester to the door of the suite.

Annie's instinct was to refuse food. It had been a long time since she'd suffered overindulgence, but she remembered not wanting to eat for days the last time it happened. Surprisingly, her stomach disagreed. Maybe beer had changed over the last fifteen years. Maybe she'd changed – toughened up a bit with all the exotic alcoholic experiences of the last few days. She felt rather proud of herself.

She had barely enough time to wonder what Lester was wearing before he disappeared out the door with Charles.

Taylor followed Annie's questioning glance. 'We took the liberty of a trip to the resort boutique to tide you and Lester over until you get your things.'

'Why do we have to get our things? Have we been thrown out of ClubSol? What did Lester do while I was asleep?'

'Nothing,' Taylor said. 'But we have a room for you here, as our guests until you recover.'

Annie couldn't imagine sleeping in a bed this size. 'Oh, no. We couldn't possibly. We have to get back.' Her brain worked frantically. There was a catch. There had to be a catch. If only she could catch it …

Focus. Focus. Both eyes needed to agree to work together before that could happen. Annie concentrated hard on Taylor's noses until they sluggishly became one. 'Wait a minute. We've clonked you with a jet ski, messed up your bedsheets, cost you a trip to the gift sho—'

'Boutique.' Taylor bit down on her lip.

'Boutique, then. But what's going on?' Annie's panties were now fully restored to their rightful place, regardless of the beer's reputation.

'I'm trying to help,' Taylor said. 'You've been through a terrible trauma and—'

Annie threw the sheets back and swung her legs over the side of the bed. 'The only trauma I've been through is finding myself dressed in someone else's nightclothes in a strange bed.'

'Lester did all that. No need to be alarmed.'

'Lester? Helped me shower and put me to bed?' This was the biggest trauma of all. Certainly, the biggest surprise. He'd slept at the neighbour's house when she'd had the flu last year.

Annie's eyes narrowed. She studied the other woman. 'Have we met before today?'

'I don't think so,' Taylor replied. 'Have you ever been to Chicago?'

'Ha! Hardly.' Annie fixed Taylor with a stare. 'Have you been to Benidorm?'

'No. Should I go?'

'No. Unless cheap is your thing.'

'Cheap may well be my thing. Unlike you—' Taylor sucked air through her teeth.

Annie folded her arms – on her second attempt. *And there's the catch.* 'So that's what this is all about. You know who we are.'

Taylor glanced down, then up again from under 'you got me' eyelashes. 'Yes, Annie, I did a little research. There are worse secrets to have, you know.'

'You haven't been on the receiving end of my mother's begging and the postman's complaints.' Annie shook her head, aware her words came across as a tad ungrateful. She exhaled. 'Sorry, not big on secrets or fortunes. It's all been a bit stressful.'

'I'm sure.' Taylor nodded. 'Lots of secrets in my world. Never tipping your hand is a mainstay of business, and it's exhausting. I can also imagine I'd be overwhelmed if I suddenly had access to mega amounts money. Changes in fortune – up or down – aren't all they're cracked up to be, are they?'

Annie appreciated the commiseration for her plight. It felt warranted. Didn't she deserve a shoulder on which to weep out her unimaginably good fortune? She almost let her hair down a full two inches; until she remembered she'd been fooled before.

'Right. Thank you.' Shields – and hair – up. 'You'll also understand why we can't accept your charity. We certainly aren't going to buy a house from you, if that's your game. We need to get back to our hotel.'

'I understand,' Taylor said. 'But just stay for dinner. The men are already in the restaurant.'

Annie's stomach growled its empty complaint. Breakfast had been a long time ago. She stood up gingerly. 'All right then, though only for dinner.' She patted at her bathrobe. 'Er, is this one of those spa places where you wander around in your nightclothes while pan pipes waft through the potted palms?' She'd visited the websites frequently.

Taylor laughed. 'No, but I may never view my spa treatments the same way again. Don't worry. I have something for you to wear.' She collected a garment bag from an enormous closet and hung it on the back of the bathroom door.

Annie eyed it suspiciously. 'As soon as we've eaten, we're going back to our hotel.'

'Ah. Here's the thing about your hotel.' Taylor placed her hands together in apology. 'Apparently, the staff have known about you for a couple of days. A certain Maggie contacted the press. Our driver tells us you have a surprise party being thrown in your honour tonight, probably financed by the reporter from *The Daily Scoop*. He flew in from London today. There will, of course, be strings attached to your celebration.'

Annie sunk back down onto the bed, completely sober. She pictured thirty or forty Gloria-and-Beth-types in a Conga line around the pool, all pushing email addresses into her pockets and promising to send

Christmas cards. She pictured Lester in the middle of it all, handing out cigars and passing drinks over strangers' heads, delighted not to be discreet anymore. She pictured her mother showing the ladies at the hairdresser's the front page of *The Daily Scoop*.

Despite the fogginess in her brain, a question swirled in and out of focus. She may be struggling to define 'normal' in her new world but wasn't there something strange about this scenario?

'I don't get it.' Annie's brow crinkled. 'I mean, I understand Maggie wanting a bit of attention for ClubSol and herself. What I don't understand is the British press flying all this way to hunt us down?'

As desperate to break out of her tedious life as she'd been, *The Daily Scoop* wasn't what she signed up for. Why was it interested, anyway? She couldn't remember seeing photos of lottery winners on beaches.

Sitting down next to Annie, Taylor took her hand. 'I've been asking myself the same question.' The pondering continued behind faultlessly mascaraed eyelashes. 'I have no answer but you have no reason to talk to the press.'

Annie pulled her hand from Taylor's. 'I have no reason to talk to anyone.'

'True,' Taylor said. 'Certainly not to me. You're aware I sell property, so you'd be right to be suspicious of my motives. I wouldn't have much respect for you if you weren't.' There was sincerity in Taylor's voice. 'But let's take this one step at a time. The first step is to get you away from the spotlight until you're more comfortable. Charles and I can help with that. We'll pick up your things, book you in here under our name, keep you behind the security gates. No obligation. All right?'

Annie took a moment to assess this Thelma to her Louise. 'All right, but we're paying for the room, and the clothes.' She wasn't naïve enough to bestow BFF status yet.

'Deal,' Taylor said.

Annie got the impression Taylor knew all about deals.

Her skin had never felt this coddled. Annie gently stroked the fabric, its coral shade accentuating her sun-kissed cheeks, then twirled in front of the mirror. As the skirt floated back down to caress her legs, she wondered what it was made of. If she had to guess, silk. Hard to get a feel for texture through a computer screen so she couldn't swear to it. The creamy, whisper-soft cashmere wrap draped across her shoulders, providing her with a modicum of security. A low boat neck and a fitted bodice left her feeling exposed, yet she had to admit the look suited her. The strappy sandals wouldn't do well in British puddles, but the buttery leather felt soft against her toes. Shock − or maybe gratitude − at a positive assessment of herself in the mirror found her hand resting on her chest and patting gently.

Taylor waved off Annie's thanks for help with the outfit as they stepped into the patio restaurant. 'You look rich,' Taylor said.

'I don't want to look rich,' Annie replied. 'I want to look happy. That's what I need to practise.'

Taylor stopped in her tracks before speaking. 'You're a surprising woman, Annie Hardcastle.'

'I'm a shocked woman right now.' Annie surveyed the scene − right out of *Lifestyles of the Rich and Famous*. She should know. She'd watched enough old reruns of the show, tutting the host, Robin Leach, when he wished her a life of champagne and caviar. Now, in front of her very eyes, Tiki torches, moonlight on water, crystal on linen tablecloths, floral arrangements taller than herself. She held her breath to stop her mouth hanging open, Robin Leach echoing in her head, telling her she deserved the best.

Taylor and Annie criss-crossed between tables in the restaurant. 'You know,' Taylor said, 'my brother used to say, "I'd rather be happy than rich". Unlike my father, who thought the pursuit of money was worth any price.'

'Don't remember much about my dad, but money didn't mean much to him.' Annie brushed an orchid with her finger as she passed a stunning arrangement. 'He certainly didn't think his wife and kids needed any.'

'Is he still alive?'

'No idea.' Annie's eyes reflected prisms of light from the raindrops of water falling in the restaurant fountain. 'He's not big on keeping in touch. What about your brother? Is he rich, or did he go with the happiness bit and become a monk?'

'Something like that.' Taylor's face set rigid. Annie figured it was none of her business.

Charles stood up – Lester did not – as the ladies arrived at the table. He met the eyes of first one woman, then the other, appearing confused. Annie guessed he hadn't thought she'd clean up so well. 'You look lovely in coral, Annie.' He smiled down at her.

'Er, thank you?' Annie had no idea how to take a compliment.

Lester pointed with both hands to his outfit. 'Yorkshire Men do it Moor' showed through his new white shirt, untucked from the linen trousers. Annie had to smile. Charles had obviously tried.

A guitarist played in a corner. He walked up to a table to play a refined tribute for a special occasion. The gentle waters of the Gulf of Papagayo almost lapped the legs of their table. Lights twinkled on the opposite coastline and Annie wondered if they belonged to ClubSol. She almost expected a searchlight to sweep the bay, to hear the frustrated bellows of a reporter trying to get his expenses paid. How many guests in a place as fancy this read *The Daily Scoop*? Not many, she supposed. She began to relax. She even smiled. She was a step ahead. For the first time in a long time – or ever. Wanting to stay that way, she ordered an orange juice.

The drinks arrived on a silver tray with a gracious bow.

So not the Fox and Rabbit.

Charles held his glass aloft. 'What are we drinking to?'

Lester raised his beer bottle, having refused the glass. 'How about privacy?'

Annie's heart thumped. 'So, you know?' She expected a tirade about how *The Daily Scoop* would never have followed them to Benidorm.

'Oh, I know all right,' Lester said. 'Chuck told me all about that Maggie woman.'

Charles nodded in Lester's direction. 'The news produced some colourful language from Lester, which I won't repeat here.'

'To privacy,' Annie said quickly, hoping to keep more colourful language out of this elegant restaurant.

'To privacy' echoed around the table. Annie sipped her juice. Startled taste buds zapped to attention. Was even the orange juice spiked? She realised this must be how fresh-squeezed juice tasted. The little bits got caught in her teeth, but the flavour was pure liquid flowers and joy.

Lester was presented with a custom-cooked plate of fish and chips, which, according to Lester, tasted 'almost as good as home'. This was thanks to a sous chef from Bristol, who brought the dish to the table himself. Annie chose Arroz con pollo. Rice and chicken agreed with the remnants of the beer in her system.

Annie sighed over the last mouthful. 'I'll never settle for boiled potatoes and carrots again.'

Lester inspected her plate suspiciously. 'Nothing wrong with meat and two veg.'

'Can't boil potatoes or carrots myself, so you sound a rather inventive cook to me,' Taylor said. Lester hooted at the joke.

'She's serious,' Charles stage-whispered.

Lester's face was a picture. 'Who cooks your tea then?'

'How … quaint,' Taylor said.

Annie cheeks burned at the humiliation of Taylor's attempt to be kind.

Kindness ruled the next couple of hours. Annie absorbed it like sunshine: Charles and Taylor paying kind attention to subjects of which they could have no knowledge – Manchester City football; Annie kindly not rolling her eyes at everything Lester said about Manchester City football. Lester praising the sous chef from Bristol; Charles praising Taylor's choice of dress for Annie. Kind. Not a bad way to spend an evening. However, with each passing minute, the enormous gap between her life and the one sitting across the table widened. The ease at which

Taylor directed waiters, handled her cutlery and spun a yarn triggered flashbacks to her own awkward upbringing. Did she and Taylor intersect as a species at all? Was there any common ground or experience that could relate them? Unlikely. It would take more than an outer layer of silk. Annie determined to enjoy her visit to this alien world, sure she wouldn't be back any time soon – money or no money.

After dinner, Charles and Taylor walked Annie and Lester to their villa, away from the main resort areas. Annie tried to quash the feeling the isolated location could have been intentional on Taylor's part.

Taylor smiled at Annie's feet. 'How about a pedicure tomorrow?'

Annie studied her fingernails. 'No, they're okay, thanks. Maybe we could meet for ice cream?'

'I haven't eaten ice cream in thirty years,' Taylor replied.

Charles dug his wife gently in the ribs, a gesture Annie couldn't interpret. Taylor inhaled, as though about to correct herself. Nothing came out. Annie took in Taylor's toned, slim body and kicked herself. She may as well have suggested they find a local heroin dealer – ice cream a gateway drug to an extra five pounds and forbidden love handles. Annie sucked in her stomach and attempted nonchalance.

Charles led Taylor away, smiling apologetically over his shoulder. 'We'll call your room tomorrow and make plans. Sleep well.'

Lester entered the room first, found the remote and threw himself down on the couch. The sounds of a car chase soon filled the previously tranquil space. Annie closed the door behind her and walked slowly through the suite. Exotic flowers decorated the many tables; towels became sculptures, folded and shaped into elephant heads on the bed, a single blossom held in each trunk. Sheets were turned down with the precision of origami artwork. Chocolate mints wrapped in jewel tones glinted on plump pillows. Fancy toiletries filled the bathroom with scents of bergamot and jasmine; Annie learned this from the labels on the bottles. Once again, the internet had not prepared her for how luxury felt in the flesh; how it wrapped the senses in gold and aligned the stars to shine down on a single person.

When Lester made his moves that night, at least she had something interesting to watch. A large palm-leaf-shaped fan rotated serenely above the bed. She pictured one on her bedroom ceiling at home, before tutting out loud at her lack of ambition. The tut didn't distract Lester.

Hours later, still awake, Annie contemplated the man she'd said, not exactly 'yes', but a resounding, 'I suppose so' to all those years ago. Could she walk out on him? Would that make her a carbon copy of her father – the man who left his family for a neighbour woman, so her mother said? No. She wasn't her father, because Lester wasn't a child or a cheated-on mother. She wondered how it felt to be cheated on instead of simply cheated. At least there was a modicum of excitement in being cheated on.

'Choose carefully, my girl,' her mother would say. 'Make sure you find yourself a good man. Then you won't have to kick your husband out like I did.' That was the only reference Pat made to a father.

Not much chance of finding a good man when your mum was your roommate, a role she'd taken on after Annie lost everything in the fire. The water from the hoses swept Annie downstream, back into the muddy waters of dependency. Dependency on a roommate who cracked too many jokes at the pub, hooted at the sitcoms on televisions and talked too loudly. A mum determined to act dumb. Annie had always hated the way her mother expected nothing of herself; how she hid in the shallow waters of life. Why? Why was she content to accept that role?

Like mother like daughter. The words blazed through Annie; lightning tearing through a black sky. Her body jolted upright. Raging eyes aimed at Lester's sleeping form, searching for anything that spoke of home or comfort or family. Anything that suggested she'd made a strong, life-affirming decision in marrying him. Instead, the sleeping man became akin to a glass of stale water on a bedside table. When you'd poured it the night before, you figured it would provide life-sustaining refreshment if needed during the night. In reality, it tasted dull, flavourless, lukewarm, with a slightly hairy quality. You drank it with a grimace and only if nothing else was available.

Was nothing else available to Annie from Verston? She hugged her knees, raising her eyes to the slowly rotating ceiling fan.

Lester, twenty years ago, sitting with a couple of his mates across a bar. Herself, alone on a bar stool, only there because if she had to suffer through one more episode of *Coronation Street* with her mother she was going to die. Lester's glance in her direction coincided with a wave of paralysing dread about returning to her mother's flat – her tedious life. She met Lester's eyes with the empty realisation that culinary school would never be within her financial grasp. That her existence as it was then was existence as it would always be; a poor imitation of a real life. Lester's wink spoke of breaking out, of a new start, of a refreshing glass of water. He moved fast. She did too. Boxes packed, address on her bills changed before they'd even signed the marriage certificate. On her wedding day, the only indication it was a special occasion was being offered a starter with the meal. She'd splashed cocktail sauce on the fake silk flower bouquet that had clashed with her borrowed yellow dress.

What would Lizzie have made of Lester? Would her sister have stopped her exchanging one boat anchor for another? Would she have persuaded Annie she was worth more, deserved better? Maybe she didn't deserve better. In fact, she was sure she didn't, or she wouldn't have let the last twenty years happen. No one had gifted her the words she was worth more. Was she capable of gifting them to herself now? With all her new riches, could she gift herself all she really needed?

She wheeled away from Lester, gripping the starched sheets between her fingers.

Never again would she sip from that stale glass of water.

Five the next morning found Charles dressed in shorts, dark glasses and one of the boutique's more flamboyant tee shirts. He borrowed a car from the Paradise Resort – thus avoiding any indiscretion with a hired driver – and headed to ClubSol.

Charles tapped the steering wheel with his fingers, his own internal wheels spinning. 'Why is the press following the Hardcastles?' He'd spent an hour after dinner the night before searching the internet for news coverage of previous Euro Lottery winners. There wasn't much to see: an initial burst of smiling photos announcing the life changing event, then silence until the shocking bankruptcies were announced. 'Sixty Million Pounds Blown on Rare Stamps and Exotic Fish!' one headline screamed. Apart from that, he found little mention of life between the arrival and departure of the windfalls.

Sneaking into the Hardcastles' room with the key card he'd taken from one of the jet skis, Charles searched for anything that may provide useful insight into these newly minted millionaires.

Who the hell displays Pepto-Bismol? Charles stared at the empty medicine bottles arranged on the windowsill the way most people displayed exotic liquor bottles after a stag night.

Trying to keep his mind off all the stomach aid, Charles emptied every drawer and grabbed Annie's dress from the closet. He found nothing to suggest the Hardcastles were hiding anything that would make them targets for the media.

He pulled the small, wonky-wheeled suitcases to the lobby and woke the night reception clerk.

'There's been an emergency,' Charles said. 'I need to check the Hardcastles out. Yes, paying with cash today.'

The clerk asked no questions. Charles was away long before he believed *The Daily Scoop* reporter woke up.

He drove back along the pot-holed dirt roads that skirted Papagayo Bay and called Taylor's number. 'I ask you again, why are reporters chasing the Hardcastles?'

'No idea and Annie doesn't seem to have a clue either,' Taylor replied. 'She doesn't strike me as one with lots of secrets.'

'Me neither but we'd better watch our backs.'

'Agreed. We need to dig deeper. I need to make sure our first Costa Rican clients are reputable.'

Charles swiped his wife's name off his screen, throwing the phone on the passenger seat before pulling into the driveway of the Paradise Resort. Something wasn't right here. Not right at all.

12 – TWO PLUS TWO MAKES HOW MANY?

Annie stirred from sleep to the sound of waves: waves breaking on the beach beyond the patio door, waves of gentle air from the ceiling fan, waves of tingling new life coursing through her body – and waves of snoring from the lumpy mass beside her.

Three out of four wasn't bad.

She pulled on her swimsuit, tied her sarong and promised herself she'd visit the boutique for an upgraded version of both later. Sliding open the patio door, she slipped away from the lumpy mass and headed off for five-star better days.

A pathway wound down the slope to the beach. Annie followed it to join a couple of early risers strolling the sands; one hunting for shells which she placed in a string bag, the other sipping on a cup of coffee as his eyes scanned the horizon. Annie scanned it too. Across the bay, she picked out the beach at ClubSol; its existence as dreamlike now as hometown Verston.

Verston. Her street, her bedroom, her life, left only in shadowy thoughts; someone else's faded photo album. Was it possible to spend a lifetime somewhere, yet instantly disconnect from it at the first opportunity? Maybe not surprising, given her nomadic childhood. Endless boxes, endless run-down flats, new schools, judgemental eyes, whisperings.

She'd worn the scent of something she didn't understand. Despite the numerous relocations, her life had encompassed only a miniscule amount of 'world'. Until now.

Today was a new day; a day to plan. Did the past always shape the future? Annie hoped not. But then, she'd hoped a lot of things throughout her life, until fading hope itself became her life. Now, hope stared back at her, smiling. She breathed in the ocean.

Options. Opportunities.

'Hi.'

Annie spun round to find she stood several feet in front of a man who was either not quite right in the head or practising yoga. Not sure which, she backed away.

Airborne feet waggled at her. 'It's okay. It's yoga.'

Do yogis read minds? 'Do you always do yoga upside down?'

'Not always but it wakes you right up.'

Annie struggled to readjust her line of vision to the man's face at sand level. Anything higher wasn't at all appropriate in this instance.

'This isn't a spectator sport, you know.'

'From my viewpoint, I'd guess that's all it is.' Annie balked at her bold statement. The twitching grin on the head stymied her instinct to apologise. The smile said she didn't need to. How refreshing.

'Not true. I'm working hard here,' Yoga Man said. 'Keeping all thoughts at bay is exhausting and takes extreme concentration. Bet you couldn't do it for one minute without collapsing. I'd have to resuscitate you.' The American accent sounded soft and gentle, not harsh as she tended to find the ones in the films.

'Well, that's a line no one's used on me before.' As the words tumbled out, Annie realised she hadn't had any lines used on her before. Lester hadn't used lines; more squiggles trailing off into assumptions, leading to resignation and silence.

'Zen masters don't use lines. They lull you into acceptance.' The mouth was serious now. The eyes were not.

'Sounds peaceful. In a creepy sort of way. I sense I shouldn't immediately run for it but should prep my inner being for flight.' *I'm bantering!*
With a stranger! Since when have I bantered with strangers?

'Ah. The gut check.' Yoga Man tried to nod. The elbows each side
of his head wrestled to maintain balance. 'And what's your gut saying
right now?'

What was her inner self saying? She didn't usually listen to it. In fact,
she'd spent years perfecting the art of tuning it out. 'Well, it says I'm
hungry and breakfast is waiting.'

'Then listen. I find the breakfast gut compelling.' Yoga Man dropped
his feet to the beach and stood up slowly, brushing the sand out of his
hair. A little shorter than Annie expected now he was the right way up,
crepey flesh above his elbows and salt and pepper hair gave a shout-out
to the passing of decades rather than years. He whistled and picked up
his towel.

'My canine Buddha is also quite astute when it comes to noting breakfast time.' A Labrador trotted over and licked Annie's hand. 'That's
doggie Zen for "Wash your hands before you eat".'

'Will do.' Annie gave the dog a little hug. She left Yoga Man with a
nod and headed towards the resort.

Don't look back. Oh, like he's looking back at you, you daft muppet.

'Beginner's Guide to Being a Millionaire Dot Com' had assumed
more urgency since last night's dinner. Annie worried to distraction
she'd spill something on her new dress. Inanimate objects taunted her,
the cutlery on the table disoriented her. Afraid to touch anything, she
glanced surreptitiously at others for clues as to which fork they used
before picking up her own. She added a multitude of extra words to
sentences when speaking to Charles: '*The Daily Scoop* is something to
which I have never subscribed.' Even as the words tumbled out, Annie's
insides churned with humiliation. What to do? Being herself seemed

excruciatingly inappropriate in this setting; a setting she'd dreamed of frequenting for so long.

Frequenting? Who says 'frequenting'? Even her thoughts rebelled, refusing to represent Annie Hardcastle authentically. She stamped her way to the business centre, dragging her insecurities with her like naughty children.

In front of the computer screen, dining etiquette dropped to second place behind checking email. It took three attempts to remember the password to her new account. The solicitor recommended closing her old account at their first meeting. The suggestion implied paranoia, Annie thought. After receiving over two hundred emails in the first three post-lottery days, she'd complied. Had anyone coined the term 'lottery chasers' yet?

She hadn't even imported her old contacts to her new account. Scrolling down the list of names, she registered no loss at deleting most of them. They'd call her ungrateful, or a cold fish, or a snob, or … what? For the first time in her life, why should she care what anyone called her?

The door to the business centre opened and a grandmotherly-type entered, nodded at Annie and sat down at the terminal dedicated to printing out boarding passes. Maybe grandmotherly was pushing it. She fit the age criteria, but Annie couldn't imagine her pushing a small child on a swing or playing with glitter and wiping a chocolatey face. The perfect make up, the layers of jewellery, the immaculate nails, the coordination of outfit, sandals, attitude. No room for fingerprints.

Annie straightened her posture, then remembered her crinkled sarong. She smoothed the front over her sucked-in belly.

Trying to compete with septuagenarians now, are we? She rolled her eyes at her computer and opened her inbox. A message from Nigel, the solicitor. Was she having fun? … blah blah blah … wished he were there … blah blah blah … a bunch of zeros …

A whole bunch of zeros. 'Whoa!'

Grandma Couture peered at Annie over her diamanté glasses. Or were they real diamonds? Annie mouthed an apology.

She moved her lips, silently reading, 'The first payment from your lottery win has been paid into your account. Should cover any little expenses.'

Or a small country's national debt. She recognised zeros; gaping holes on bank statements, open mouths waiting to be fed. However, numbers in front of the zeros were a new phenomenon. She mouthed the numeric combinations over and over, unable to herd the thousands, tens of thousands – was that hundreds of thousands? – into meaningful columns. Still unsure, she wrote out all the numbers on a notepad displaying the resort logo at the top. She separated zeros with commas, rearranging combinations over and over. It still made no sense. Delightfully unbelievable. *I'm going to buy a racehorse and call it Delightfully Unbelievable.* Joke? Maybe not.

Annie drew a smiley face after the last zero. The smile spread to her own face, seeped into her pores, emanated from the racing heart beneath the crinkled sarong. A euphoric grin reflected in the screen as she closed her inbox and shut down the computer.

Forget about learning how to be a millionaire from websites. She'd experience it, make up her own rules. First rule: wear only new swimsuits.

Rising gracefully from her chair, she met the disapproving eyes of Grandma. Annie nodded coolly. *We must do lunch, Grandma. My treat.*

Almost to the door, Annie stopped dead, spun around and returned to tear the page off the notepad. Didn't want Grandma sharing her business around the bingo tables, if they had such a thing at the Paradise Resort. With a jaunty wiggle of her shoulders, Annie strutted to the door –without her sarong, which had snagged on the corner of the desk.

Annie fumbled to untangle the torn fabric, accompanied by a 'tut' from Grandma Couture.

Charles entered his hotel room dragging two wonky-wheeled suitcases behind him as Taylor got out of the shower. Charles grabbed his laptop and sat on the upholstered stool next to the marble bathtub.

'Were you followed?' Taylor's concern was as much about his choice of shirt as his covert mission.

'A bit cloak and dagger, don't you think?'

'Not when we have no idea what we're dealing with.'

'Good point. I didn't check the rear-view mirror, but no one turned into the resort after me.'

'Maybe from now on we should check.'

'From now on, Daniel Craig will wish he'd shadowed me to learn a thing or two about stealth operations.' Charles assumed a seated karate position, or the best imitation a former captain of the Yale rowing team could produce.

Taylor drew her chin back and raised her eyebrows. *Casino Royale* was her husband's favourite guilty pleasure. She doubted it would help him in a fist fight. 'No, seriously, be careful.'

'Is it such a stretch to picture me as James Bond?'

Taylor contemplated her husband as she stroked her chin. 'Newman. Charles Newman. Sorry. It's a stretch.' She began applying copious amounts of moisturiser to her legs. 'We need to keep the Hardcastles to ourselves for a little longer so it's important we're discreet.'

'Discreet. That's me,' Charles said, and Taylor believed him.

'I have a two-pronged plan of attack.' Taylor screwed the top back on the moisturiser. 'The Hardcastles aren't solely potential clients; they're also Ashcroft bait. When we're ready, we dangle them over a luxury villa infinity pool and wait for Ashcroft Realty to leap out of the water. If they do, we've exposed them. If they don't, we sell Lester and Annie the villa anyway. Win-win.'

'And what do the Hardcastles have to say about sitting in this luxury chum bucket?' Charles waited. Taylor inwardly cursed him for his incessant need to play the good guy.

She applied blush to her cheeks with military precision. 'They'll want a villa. We'll get them a villa. It will make little difference to them who they buy it from which means I'm not taking advantage. Besides, though she seems a rather dull person, I quite like Annie. Lester, on the other hand, I could do without. How on earth does he get away with being so … I can't even find the word.'

'Victorian?'

'I doubt Queen Victoria would have put up with Lester.'

'Edwardian, then.'

'Maybe that.' Taylor finished her make-up and left the bathroom. Charles followed her, cradling his laptop. 'Still, makes no sense to me, how Annie tolerates him. She's obviously a deeper thinker than he is. Wonder what she saw in him?'

'People say that about me and you, you know.' Charles dodged the flying pillow and sat down at the desk. 'Yes, I like Annie too, but I'd guess she's led a rather staid life. That said, there's more to her than meets the eye. Watch out if all this money gives her the confidence to explore her potential.'

Charles's laptop pinged an automated alert he'd programmed in to search for key words.

'I don't believe it!' He bolted up from his chair, holding his laptop out in front of him as though it contained a Boa Constrictor. 'What the hell?'

Taylor scooted around to read over Charles's shoulder. 'KIDNAPPED!' The headline on *The Daily Scoop* website seared itself into her eyeballs. The subtitle was no better. 'Kidnapper sneaks into hotel room and makes off with lottery winners. Police expect ransom demand shortly.'

Taylor glowered at her husband. 'Still think you were discreet, Mr Bond?'

13 – JUST TRYING TO HELP

Kidnapped?' Pat shrieked into the phone, clasping her ancient woolly jumper across her pyjama top. She steadied herself on the wall. 'What do you mean, kidnapped?'

Within seconds the neighbour's door slammed. A shadow fell across the window of Pat's ground floor flat. 'Bloody thin walls,' Pat muttered. They ensured Becky Dagny missed nothing. Pat switched her attention back to the voice still speaking on the crackly phoneline.

'No, you idiot, I know what the word "kidnapped" means.' Pat pursed her lips at the phone. 'I mean what do you mean my daughter's been kidnapped?' Silence. 'Where's Lester? Oh, he's missing too? Now, this is a fine how'd you do.' Pat leaned on the wall, needing time to think, but the voice kept talking.

'A stranger you say? Paid their bill, snuck out and they haven't been seen since?' Pat's brow furrowed. She'd watched *Broadchurch* – twice – and every version of Sherlock Holmes filmed since the 1940s. She knew criminals. They didn't pay the victim's bills first. Though, this was Costa Rica. Things were strange in Africa.

'What? No! I haven't received a ransom note. As if I've got any money. What? No! I'm not calling you if I hear anything.' Pat slammed the phone down, the shadow in the window rooted to the spot. Pat ignored it.

Could Annie truly be missing? Pat's hands shook and her head spun, dredging up another phone call, another notification of a daughter lost forever. That wasn't going to happen again. She could save this one. She must save this one.

Think, Pat. First question: if the reporter on the phone was in Costa Rica, had he contacted the fuzz in England yet? She should have checked before hanging up. No matter. She'd visit the police herself.

'This tea's bloody awful.' Pat sniffed and puffed out her chest. She glared at the Police Superintendent across the interview table.

'Sorry, Mrs Rickman. We do our best.' Superintendent Jane Williams let out a sigh and glanced at the young officer standing behind her. 'Now, let's start from the beginning. Why did you take the bus in to St Albans rather than calling 999? Is this a matter of the utmost urgency, as you told the officer at the front desk, or not?'

'I always do the shopping on a Wednesday, so thought it'd be quicker to stop in at the station on my way to the market. But, rest assured, my daughter being kidnapped is serious business.'

Jane snorted. Yes, she often heard the weekly vegetable run was on an even plane with the kidnapping of a family member. 'Why do you think your daughter's been kidnapped.'

'This man from *The Daily Scoop* called and—'

'Did you get his name?'

'Bob or Frank or ... no.'

'Phone number?'

'No.'

'Where he was calling from?'

'Costa Rica. That's in Africa.'

Jane realised Pat wasn't pulling her leg by the deep furrows in her brow. 'That's not in Africa, Mrs Rickman.' She glanced over at her colleague. PC Jarvis's shoulders were shaking. He'd learn to cry about things he currently found funny as his police career progressed; unless he had no soul. Sometimes Jane worried about her own.

'So, you get a phone call from this man, who presumably followed your daughter to Costa Rica, and he tells you Mr and Mrs Hardcastle have been kidnapped.'

'Yes.'

'How'd he know they'd been kidnapped?'

'Said he was staying in the same hotel as Annie and he spoke to people who witnessed the crime.'

'And what hotel was that?'

'Don't know.' Pat thrust out her chin.

Surely a daughter would share these details with a mother? Jane moved on. 'You think the reporter was telling the truth?'

Pat's chin became several chins as they concertinaed backwards; her expression somewhat crestfallen. Would it be a huge disappointment if Annie was, in fact, safe and sound? Or, was it more that Pat would be upset if she was lied to? Nothing was ever as it seemed in police work. Jane noted the stiffening in Pat's spine. *Here comes the defence.*

'Oh, I'm used to the police not believing me,' Pat said. 'Like when I told you people my dad was Richard Burton or that I knew nothing about those crooks.' Pat's eyes shot to Jane's face, then anywhere but Jane's face.

'I'm confused. When did you mention this?' Jane flicked back and forth through her notes.

'Never mind.' Pat studied her hands in her lap. 'Long time ago. Doesn't matter now. Anyway, why would the reporter lie?'

'Oh, I don't know. To get a story, perhaps?'

Shadows chased across Pat's features as the woman appraised this alternative. 'If he wasn't a real reporter, how would he know they were in Costa Rica? Even I didn't know until they were practically headed to the airport.'

'Why would Annie keep the trip a secret?'

'They'd recently won the lottery, like I said, so they had … security issues.' Pat leaned forward and tapped her nose. 'Didn't want the riff-raff knowing where they were.'

'So, they told you they were going to Costa Rica but not specifically where in Costa Rica?'

'Not specifically.' Pat wrinkled her nose and squeezed her eyes shut. About to cry? Jane bided her time. 'You're just making me out to be daft. I'm not daft. Of course, if they'd taken me with them we wouldn't be in this mess, would we? I'd have protected them. I could have cooked for them too. Then they wouldn't have to eat foreign muck.'

PC Jarvis stepped forward and whispered in Jane's ear, 'I have an idea why they didn't inform Mum of their whereabouts, ma'am.'

Jane swatted him away.

Pat pulled herself up straight in her chair and slammed her cup down in the saucer. 'Stop wasting valuable time. I need you to send in the flying squad.'

The explosive laughter-turned-cough got Jarvis a nasty glare from his commanding officer.

'All right.' Jane tore a blank page off her notepad. 'This is our special flying squad form. Fill in names and addresses of all those who may have a motive for kidnapping your family. Then fill in the section about how long they've been missing and what you've done yourself to try to find them.'

Pat frowned. 'Reporter didn't say how long they'd been missing.'

'Did you arrange a time for them to check in with you each day? If you did, you calculate how many check-ins you missed—'

Pat slammed the pen down. 'Listen to me, young lady. We didn't arrange to contact each other, I don't know their hotel information, I don't know who would kidnap them, I only know what the reporter told me. Now, get the flying squad in the air and go find them!'

Jane, almost twenty years on the force, multiple decorations for bravery to her name, stood up slowly and leaned over the desk towards Pat, making her sink down in her chair. 'Mrs Rickman. It's impossible to conclude a crime has been committed based on this crackpot call. We certainly can't call in the flying squad. Which, incidentally, doesn't fly. So, buy your vegetables, go home and contact us if you hear something worth our time.'

Pat rose slowly from her chair, threw one last disgusted glare at her teacup, and stamped out of the room.

After the door slammed behind another dissatisfied customer, Jane flopped back down on her chair. She rubbed her temples. *I'm not paid enough for this.*

'Word from the flying squad, ma'am. Over Africa now. Arriving Costa Rica 1300 hours.'

'Shut up, Jarvis, or I'm transferring you to parking enforcement.'

'Shutting up, ma'am.'

Jane took angry sips of tea. The brew soothed her enough to allow rational thought; not the first time tea had proved miraculous. The more she calmed down, the more disappointed at herself she became. She'd dismissed a mother who had all the hallmarks of a life of struggle. Whatever else Pat Rickman was, Jane worked for her. Maybe she should at least dig a little deeper.

'You heard of these lottery winners, Jarvis?'

'Of course. All over the papers.'

Jane rarely read the papers. 'The notion someone may be trying to get money out of new millionaires isn't exactly out of the realm of possibility, is it?'

'No, ma'am.'

'That Mrs Rickman would be susceptible to a scam is obvious.'

'Yes, ma'am.'

'Then let's check her phone records for verification of a call from Costa Rica.'

'Righty ho. One question first, ma'am. Why would *The Daily Scoop* be in Costa Rica before the lottery winners were kidnapped?'

Jane pushed her colleague aside and headed towards her office.

'Smartest question you've asked in a week.'

14 – YOU'RE NOT HELPING

How does this even happen?' Annie sat in the Newmans' hotel room and stared at the headline. Taylor, a face like thunder, had pulled her from her room a few minutes earlier and marched her into the Newmans' suite. Charles had plucked Lester from the breakfast buffet, though Lester had refused to leave his plate behind. The plate sat forgotten on the bed now.

Lester paced the room and wiped his hand across the nape of his neck. 'What the heck do we do now?'

'We'll have to call Mum,' Annie whispered. 'She'll be making a right meal of this.'

Charles spoke, garnering Annie's attention like a flotation device at a shipwreck. Did he have a plan to save her from her mother? 'Something's not right here,' he said. 'A reporter follows you to Costa Rica and cares enough about you to assume a kidnapping when you check out of your hotel. I'm missing the plot. Lottery winners aren't usually that interesting. No offence.'

'None taken.' Annie sighed.

Lester disagreed. 'Offence taken. I'm missing breakfast.'

Taylor pushed Charles's point. 'Are you hiding something? Something the press would go to all this trouble to expose?'

'No!' Annie jumped up. 'And I resent the implication.'

'Sorry. Sorry, Annie.' Taylor shrugged her shoulders at Charles.

Charles walked over to Annie and encouraged her to sit down again. 'We have no right to get into your business but we seem part of it now. We're kidnappers, according to the press. Someone's going to come hunting for us soon. Can you explain what's going on here?'

Lester pulled himself up to his full height. 'I've got nothing to hide.'

'I have no idea why a reporter would be interested in us,' Annie said. 'I've never been even remotely interesting to anyone. My life's been much too boring to have secrets.' Her words hung in the air, heavy and accusatory.

Is that true? Annie sat on her hands on the bed. She'd always held the vague notion her mother had tried to hide her children from something. They'd bounced around from temporary home to temporary home for as long as Annie could remember. Never an explanation of why they had to change schools, or leave the flat that had a nice tree outside the window. It was 'Pack your stuff, girls', and off they went. Why would this train of thought bubble to the surface now? A half-buried, ancient question: would she ever be more than just a temporary lodger in a temporary building? Rubbing her arms, Annie desperately wanted chocolate. The Quality Street stash in her freezer seemed a million miles – and aeons – away.

Lester broke the silence. 'I'm going down to the bar, because I doubt you've got Samuel Smith in your fancy fridge.' Lester glared towards the wet bar.

'Not a good idea,' Taylor said.

'Definitely not,' Annie added. 'It's ten o'clock in the morning.'

'I'm more worried about the press finding him or the police being called,' Taylor said.

'Oh. That too.' Annie sunk her head into her hands.

Lester scowled at Taylor. 'What? We're your prisoners now?'

'Of course you're not prisoners,' Taylor said. 'But it's a good idea to lie low for a while until we can sort out this mess.'

'Lie low? I never wanted all this cloak and dagger stuff in the first place. Running off to Costa Rica indeed when we could have gone to Benidorm. Where everyone speaks English, by the way!' Lester directed his anger at Annie. 'I could be sitting in a proper English pub there, drinking a pint. Instead, I'm spending my holiday in a …' Lester searched the tile floor for the right word, 'in a marble mausoleum.'

Annie blinked. She wasn't used to hearing big words from her husband.

Taylor's peeved expression morphed to a conceding shrug as she perused the room.

Annie moaned. 'I'm sorry. I thought getting away was for the best. We were being hounded at home and this seemed a safe place to wait out the storm. Turns out it wasn't. I'm sorry, Lester. I really am.'

'I'm sorry, too.' Charles patted Annie's shoulder. 'I had no idea two lottery winners were in such high demand. They don't usually get this much attention until the bankruptcy is announced.'

Lester swivelled stunned eyes in Charles's direction. 'You mean we're going to go through all this, only to end up penniless at the end of it? That's bull—'

'Surely, we won't go bankrupt?' Annie's hands moved to her throat. She pictured ironing Lester's shirts in her old kitchen. She pictured the sun deflate once more behind the block of flats with all the excitement of a damp candle. Here, in Costa Rica, the sun exited stage centre in a burst of citrusy glory, spreading across the waters of the bay like a billowing, magical, technicoloured dreamcoat.

'We won't end up penniless,' she stated, with resolve of such depth it surprised even her.

'Atta girl,' Charles said. 'I didn't mean to insinuate *all* lottery winners went bankrupt. Only those who didn't seek professional advice. You sought professional advice, didn't you?'

'Oh, yeah. We got advice, all right.' Lester folded his arms and narrowed his eyes at Annie. 'A wally in a suit suggested we come to Costa Rica. How much did we pay for that little gem, Annie?'

Annie's shiny, new resolve dulled a little. 'We've only been here a week or so. Only been rich a bit longer than that. We've got to allow ourselves time to adjust. This kidnapping nonsense has thrown a bit of a spanner in the works, I'll admit. Let's sort it out and go back to thinking about what we're going to do with our lives.'

'How much time?' Lester's face took on the qualities of a child who'd flushed his pacifier down the toilet. 'I miss me sofa. I miss me mates. I miss me shows on the telly. I miss real food and I miss going outside my room without asking permission.' His voice grew louder. 'In fact, I've had enough of all this island stuff. I want to go home. Now!'

Charles shrugged his shoulders at Taylor and mouthed, 'Island stuff?'

Lester prowled the room. Annie knew how important routine and familiarity were to him. Curiously, despite these weird circumstances, unrecognisable drink names and strange people, Annie couldn't equate home with sanctuary at all. A cold chill rattled her spine when she pictured Verston, contrasting with the warm glow emanating from somewhere around her heart muscle as she took in the view of the beach. Her toes bunched up, gripping at the floor.

Shouldn't it be the other way around? Shouldn't she be craving the reassurance of familiar faces and places to ground her, to provide a comforting pillow on which to rest her weary head during these turbulent times? But she couldn't muster a sense of belonging at all – to anything or anyone. Her family were a convoluted tangle of missing links, hearsay and denial and her home was a prison cell. It struck her she'd stopped caring about her family and prior homes a long time ago.

Taylor's voice dragged Annie back into the room. 'Now, friends, please let's not act rashly. We'll order brunch from room service and put our heads together. Yes, the whole kidnapping angle is a bit of a surprise. We'll need your help to fix it.' At this, Taylor focused her piercing eyes on Annie. 'Are you sure you can't tell us why the press is interested in you both?'

Lester gaped at Annie. 'Well? Is there something we aren't telling them? Because I'd love to hear it.'

Annie's shoulders sagged. She clasped her hands, trying to identify a nagging sense of déjà vu. Was there a reason the press may be hounding her?

Charles sat down next to Annie and put his arm around her. A knock at the door startled the group.

'Room service.'

Lester marched over and grabbed the door handle.

'No!' Taylor bolted towards Lester as he flung the door wide and a barrage of clicks assaulted the ears of those in the room.

'Will you be demanding a ransom?' The camera panned over to Annie and Charles on the bed. 'Is this a case of Stockholm syndrome?'

Taylor lunged forward. She pushed Lester out of the way and, grabbing the door to try to close it, trapped the photographer's arm against the doorjamb. The camera swung for a tantalising second within Taylor's reach. An ugly oath emanated from the reporter. Charles leapt to his feet and hurtled over to assist his wife. He grabbed the camera strap, attempting to wrestle it into his possession. Despite Charles's best efforts, the photographer proved stronger and quicker. He wrenched the camera away, taking off down the hallway like his expense account depended on it.

Lester remained stock-still. Taylor slammed the door and leaned against it. She struggled to catch her breath, her eyes flicked from one shocked face to another. Slowly, she pivoted towards Lester. 'Why on earth did you open the door?'

'He said "room service". We were going to get food, you said.'

Taylor rubbed her wrist. 'We. Hadn't. Ordered. Yet.'

The ceiling fan spun slowly above Lester's head.

Annie finally managed to react. 'That was brave of you both, to fight off the photographer. Thank you.'

Charles appeared pleased. 'I'm typically more adept at negotiations than physical stuff, but the time creates the man, as they say.'

Lester's shoulders twitched, then straightened. 'Yeah, and you – the man – created this problem by kidnapping our suitcases.'

'Point taken.' Charles trapped the air in his cheeks before expelling it. 'So, our cover is blown. What now?'

'We stay hidden,' Taylor said.

Lester pouted. 'I'm not used to being a prisoner and I'm not used to hiding out, either.'

Not used to hiding out from a man serving food, that's for certain. Annie rubbed her eyes.

Taylor moved from her place by the door, nodding her head as she paced. 'From now on, we must assume we're being watched. This is what we should do—'

'What *we* should do?' Lester's fists were clenched.

Annie knew what was coming next.

'What *we* should do? Since when have you been we? Since when have you and your fancy boy been in charge of the Hardcastles?'

I've certainly never been in charge of the Hardcastles. The truth hit Annie hard.

Lester inhaled several deep breaths through his nose, for all intents and purposes looking like a bull right before it charged. 'Seems to me, things have gone from bad to worse since we met you. What if you called the press, eh? How do we know you aren't being paid by those geezers? What are you getting out of us, dressing us in fancy clothes and the "oh, we'll help hide you" act?'

A good point. The whole world must be going mad. Lester never made good points. But if there was one thing Annie knew by now, it was money didn't buy you friends or loyalty. From the Fox and Rabbit to the ClubSol reception desk, the Hardcastles were nothing more than dangled meat. Her view was confirmed by the somewhat sheepish expression crossing Taylor's face. She steeled herself for confrontation, not a position she relished; neither was owing Lester anything. But she'd dragged him here and insisted he keep quiet, neither strategy proving successful for flying under the radar.

Annie covered her cheeks with her hands, the heat of indignation flaming in them. 'Lester has a point. What are you getting out of this? And don't say "nothing". We may be country bumpkins compared to you high-flying folk, but we're not stupid.' Annie surprised herself. Hadn't she been accusing herself of exactly that for living the life she'd been given rather than the life she wanted? But it was one thing to call yourself stupid; quite another to have someone else call you stupid. She joined Lester's team. 'Come on. Out with it. What's your game? Is this all about selling us a house?'

'You've got it all wrong,' Taylor said. 'You needed help and we thought we could offer it, that's all. We don't need your money.'

Taylor's cheeks flushed rose. Annie noticed and decided it wasn't too much of a stretch to assume guilt was the cause. She pushed back. 'Obviously you need something from us. You put up a rather strong resistance back there. Really went to bat for strangers. Strangers with millions.'

'All right, all right.' Charles put his hands up, mea culpa. 'Come on, Taylor. We owe them the truth.'

Annie's last hope she'd found allies faded with Lester's aspirations for room service.

When Taylor remained silent, Charles took over. 'We want the best for you, by the way, but there's more to it.' He sat on the bed and placed his hands on his knees. 'We came down here to find someone, or rather an organisation. This organisation did us wrong and we wanted to get back at them.'

'The Mafia?' Lester screeched, leaping from one foot to the other, then clasping his hands behind his head. 'You've got us involved with the Mafia! For certain this would've never happened in Benidorm!'

'The Mafia?' Charles's eyebrows almost hit the back of his head. 'No, no. There's no mafia here. Calm down and let me explain.'

Taylor perched on the edge of the dresser and rubbed her temples. 'Screw it, I'm ordering room service. I need a drink and at this point, Piers Morgan could deliver it and I wouldn't care.'

She dialled and ordered mimosas and beer, a fruit plate for herself and sandwiches for everyone else without consultation. Annie silently fumed at the snub.

Charles recounted the Newman story while they waited for room service to arrive. He talked of Chicago, of losing their jobs, of Ashcroft

Realty and of wanting to use the Hardcastles as bait, though he worded it differently.

'We were going to offer to help you find investment properties here. Then put the word out and wait for Ashcroft to crawl out of the wood-work, or the cocktail glasses ...' His chuckle died in his throat. 'We didn't want your money. We needed your reputation.'

Annie huffed. 'Oh, well, that's all right, then.'

'I mean, we needed your status as wealthy potential homeowners in the area. That's all.'

'Oh, that's all, is it?' Annie stood up. 'You offered a nice friendship carrot and *forgot* to mention the stick? Well, get this. We don't need your carrots. We buy our own carrots from now on.'

Annie grabbed Lester's hand and pulled him out of the room, col-liding with the room service cart in the hallway. A beer bottle fell to the floor. Lester tried to reach for it, but Annie dragged him away.

Tears welled up in her eyes as she marched towards her room to pack. Lester was right. This place was nothing but trouble. But what hap-pened to all her options and opportunities? She couldn't come up with a plan fast enough, slapping her thigh and cursing her own stupidity as she scurried down the pathway.

No Plan B? Who's the pillock now?

Lester breathed down her neck as she opened the door to the beau-tiful hotel room they were about to evacuate. Annie blinked back tears, determined Lester wouldn't see her cry. She clamped her jaw and pre-pared to run away again; a subconscious default instinct apparently, years in the making. But run where? Verston? For now, Verston would have to do. Distressing as it was, she'd have to go home.

Even more distressing, the question screaming in her head: when had running away ever solved a problem?

Annie shoved open the door of the flat with her shoulder, having hauled her suitcase up four flights of stairs. The doormat hid under piles of envelopes and newspapers. A jacket had fallen off the coatrack and lay on the hallway floor like a dead soldier. Annie closed her eyes and held her breath. If the flat didn't notice she was back, maybe she wouldn't be.

Lester arrived behind her, panting. He pushed her through the door into their home.

'Cuppa tea. That's what we need, luv.' Lester stood with his hands on his hips in the living room, surveying his domain. 'Great to be home, isn't it.' It wasn't a question.

Annie let out the breath she'd been holding. Her eyes swept the dusty surfaces and her mind struggled to picture the kitchen and the tea kettle, to recall where the teabags were stored. Heavy feet carried her through the hallway in the direction of Lester's needs. Heavy hands found their tea-making rhythm, the clatter of spoons on mugs both distantly famil- iar and strangely disquieting.

'Cheers.' Lester reached for his tea with a contented smile. Already enthroned on his recliner, his lap full of post, he searched for the paper with the racing results.

Annie sank onto the couch, the physical exhaustion of international travel eclipsed by a deeper weariness. She took a scalding sip of tea. The sombrero caught her eye. That damned, dusty, faded sombrero from Benidorm hanging in judgement from its rusty nail pulpit. Not in a living room, but in a dying room.

Her pulse quickened in her ears. 'What was I thinking? I can't do this. Even temporarily.'

Lester pulled his nose from the paper. 'Do what, luv?' He followed the track of Annie's eyes as they jumped from almost dead plant to sombrero to dust-covered table. 'Oh, you mean the cleaning.' Lester acknowledged the dust with a sweep of his finger across the side table by his chair. It was the only sweeping he'd ever done.

'Shoulda told your mum we were coming back early. She could have come round to clean up a bit.'

His straight face compounded her panic. Life with Lester would nev- er change, no matter how much she needed it to or how much money they had. Her eyes flitted round the room – this 'home' of twenty years. *What the hell, Annie?* What kind of idiot would still be waiting for Lester? But she froze; terrified this would prove to be the moment she'd wake up and find the lottery win nothing but a dream. She'd die if she woke up now.

Lester's voice cut through her fear. 'You all right? You look peaky.'

'I can't do this. Can't … do this.'

'For goodness sake.' Concern morphed into irritation in Lester's voice. 'It's a bit of dust, Annie, not tornado damage.'

Annie leapt from the couch, spilling tea and dread on the carpet. 'This life. I can't do this life.'

Lester rolled his eyes. 'That's a bit dramatic, isn't it? Dusting makes you suicidal? Better think twice before we go on holiday again.'

Still gripping her mug in one hand, her free fist clenching and un-clenching, Annie tracked a fly crawling along the windowsill. She was inside the *Mary Celeste*; her old home a ghostly shell, the crew's where-abouts unknown. Maybe the crew had never existed at all, the flat mere-ly an empty hull filled with assumptions about how the inhabitants had once lived and what made them abandon ship.

Annie knew why she had to abandon this ship. A somewhat maniacal chuckle escaped her lips. First payments had been transferred to their joint account. It was safe to leave Lester now, wasn't it? She crossed the fingers of her free hand.

Lester scraped the post off his lap and stood up, pushing out his chest. 'Sit down, Annie!'

'No need. I won't be here long.' Annie unkinked the apology from her spine, vertebrae straightening from question mark to exclamation mark. She met her husband's eyes dead on. 'Just long enough to tie up a few loose ends and say goodbye.'

Lester's eyes widened, then narrowed. He opened his mouth to speak, but the doorbell rang. Annie jumped at the sound of the alarm. Hot tea slopped against her leg. With shaking hands, she placed her mug on the table.

Lester bolted to open the door. 'Better be someone with a bloody duster,' he called over his shoulder, before announcing, 'It's your mum.'

Pat walked past him into the living room where Annie stood, rigid and still shaking. 'Annie! Welcome home.' Pat clutched Annie to her chest and kissed her cheek. 'And what a relief you escaped from your kidnappers. Was it the flying squad got you out? They didn't share the details—'

'How'd you know we were back? It's only been an hour,' Lester said. 'Paparazzi?'

'Becky. Walking past as your taxi pulled up,' Pat replied. 'Sometimes a know-it-all neighbour has her uses. She was the first to tell me you'd been freed, though it would've been nice to hear it from you.'

Lester flopped into his recliner again. 'Phone calls from Costa Rica aren't cheap, and we figured we'd see you soon enough. Besides, we weren't kidnapped. Don't care what you read in the papers.'

Guilt flooded Annie's conscience. She hadn't considered her mother at all, what with packing and changing flights and trying to suppress her grief at leaving paradise.

Lester continued. 'Anyway, we're back now. I'll let you take Annie's breakdown from here. She's bothered about the dusting.'

Pat peered at Annie. 'Is that why you look out of sorts? The dust?'

'Oh, for crying out loud!' Annie didn't often yell. It was Lester's turn to jump. 'This has nothing to do with dust!'

'What's going on?' Pat steered Annie back down onto the couch and sat beside her. Annie bobbed back up like a bottled SOS message tossed into the ocean.

'I can't live this life anymore, Mum. I tried to believe I was coming home, but I'm not. I'm not home. I never was home. This will never be home.'

Silence.

'Sunstroke.' Lester had the nerve to look satisfied at his diagnosis.

More silence.

'I said, it's sunstroke.'

Pat hushed Lester with a finger to her lips. 'Annie, you're scaring me. Don't you recognise where you are?'

'Oh, I know exactly where I am and I'm not home.' A smile twitched at the corner of her lips.

'Oh, I get it. Becky told you already.' Pat clapped her hands, then reached into her plastic ostrich-skin handbag. 'She gave you the news.'

Annie's smile faded. She couldn't even muster the question.

Lester heaved himself out of his chair and headed towards Pat. 'We haven't even seen Becky yet. What news?' He took the brochure Pat pulled from her handbag. Flipping through the photos, comprehension spread across his features. Annie brushed away thoughts of a knob of butter on warm toast. 'Ho, ho, ho. I see where this is going.'

Annie grabbed the brochure and turned the pages, slowly, methodically. The inner workings of her mother's – and now Lester's – mind lay spread before her in glossy colour.

'You've always liked this one, luv, haven't you?' Lester's comment astonished Annie. She had no idea he knew what she liked.

She surveyed the three-bedroom, two-bath detached house with two-car garage, small back garden and separate in-law accommodation, close to shops with views of the village green. She calculated how far it was from her current location – one-and-a-half-minutes. Then she calculated how much effort it was going to take not to scream.

Flinging the local estate agent's brochure across the room, Annie screamed.

Pat's hands flew to her face. Lester gawked at his wife.

The screaming subsided, replaced by laughter, which appeared to scare her audience more than the screaming. Laughter hadn't been part of this flat in a long time. Pat alternated between rubbing her cheeks and patting her chest as Lester hopped from foot to foot, blinking rapidly.

Lester reached for Annie's arm. 'Now, now, luv. It's all a bit of a shock, I know. Got to get used to our new life, haven't we? And this house is a great idea. I'd already thought about buying one.'

His condescending expression sealed his fate; tangible proof of the depths of his inability to imagine or empathise or … know her at all. She spun away from him.

'I thought you'd love it,' Pat said. 'It's such a pretty house and close to the high street for the bus. When I saw it for sale … eureka! Nice granny annex in the back.'

Lester grabbed the brochure off the floor, scanning it with renewed concentration while Annie fought for control of her senses. 'Love it? Love it?'

Pat's face crumpled like a punctured balloon. 'What? You don't love it?'

Annie snatched the brochure from Lester and threw it in the air. It zigzagged to the ground.

Lipstick on a pig! 'This is your plan? Moving a few yards down the road and all living together is the culmination of a lifetime of dreaming about breaking free of … this?' She flailed her arms at her surroundings. Words pushed through her teeth like ground beef through a meat grinder. 'A lawnmower and room for a bigger television is paradise to you?'

'Well, yes. Actually.' Pat's eyes followed the arc of the flailing arms.

Lester smiled. 'Be nice, won't it? You not having to carry the groceries up the stairs. Nice little garden to sit in? I can't believe I'm having to explain the idea of moving up to you.'

'I can't believe it either,' Pat said in a moment of solidarity between in-laws.

Lester rocked backwards and forwards from heel to toe, hands on hips. 'Don't worry about a thing. I'll take care of it all. I'll find a better solicitor than the idiot who sent us to Costa Rica and he'll do all the clever stuff. We'll have a new house in no time.' Lester radiated smugness; a man who'd pulled something over on someone.

He had. Himself.

Annie's jaw muscles ached from the pressure they exerted on her teeth. She woke up, not from the dream of winning the lottery but from the nightmare of life unlived.

'I'm sure you and Mum will be very happy in your new house. But if you think we'll ever live together again, anywhere, don't care if it's Windsor Castle or the moon, you're seriously mistaken.' Annie steadied herself with a gulp of air. 'What was I thinking when I came back here to hide? I've done it all my life. I don't even know why. It stops now.'

Pat bent down to pick up the brochure.

Lester rubbed his chin sagely. 'We could get a cleaning lady to help you.'

'Shut up!' Annie slapped her hands to her ears. Her shriek tipped Pat onto the carpet.

Lester hauled Pat to her feet, then came up with a new plan – or rather an old plan that had worked for years. 'Put the kettle on, Pat. A nice cup of tea and we'll have a good laugh about this. It's excitement, that's all.'

'You're right, Lester. It's excitement. I'm leaving you.'

'Don't be daft.' Lester turned towards Pat with a nervous laugh. 'She's being daft, isn't she?'

Pat's mouth hung open. Annie's head swivelling from one dumbfounded face to another. Neither her mother nor Lester understood a single thing.

'Did you expect nothing to change, Lester? Did nothing about being rich trigger the need for a drastic re-evaluation of our lives?'

Lester brandished the brochure in front of Annie's face. 'This isn't a drastic change? A garden and no stairs aren't drastic changes?'

Pat nodded mechanically.

'So our new clothes are a drastic change too?' Annie threw her hands up and let them fall with a smack to her thighs. 'That shirt Charles chose for you was all you needed to become a new man?'

'Stupid shirt wasn't even comfortable,' Lester said. The shirt Charles had helped Lester pick out at the Paradise Resort lay crumpled in a tangled mess in the still unpacked suitcases. Never worn again, shed with no more thought than a surface layer of sunburnt skin.

Annie's own skin peeled to the depth of her soul. Her eyes flicked to the doorway; a tiger noticing the cage had been left open. 'Now I understand why I came back. I came to unshackle the chains, not move them to a new house. I came to say goodbye, Lester, not to make your tea and carry on as though nothing more has happened than a rather nice banking error in our favour. We have twenty-six million pounds each. You, apparently, want to use yours to stay here. I want to use mine to not stay here.'

Her words sliced through the stagnant years, the detachment, the futility; flashing knives at a hibachi restaurant slashing her old world to pieces before she threw the dismembered bits in Lester's face. 'We'll need a solicitor, all right. Oh, yes. A divorce solicitor.' There would be no ambiguity.

'So …' Lester scratched his head and stared at the brochure again. 'Is the garden too big? We could change our minds, buy a different house—'

How was I ambiguous? 'Our minds, Lester? I'm not changing our minds! Our minds are separate entities now.' Annie bowed her head in the belated knowledge they always had been.

The ticking clock on the mantle marked the length of the following silence. That same clock had been marking her life for decades, recording her compliance in this sham.

She pulled herself up to her full height. 'It's pointless arguing or explaining. All that's left to say is I'm off in search of a new life. I'll leave you to your old one.'

'You can't leave your husband, Annie,' Pat said, voice strained and somehow pitiful. 'Husbands are supposed to be for life.'

'Exactly, Mum. For life. Not for a long, slow death.'

'I resent that,' Lester said. 'I gave you a nice flat, a drink on Saturday nights. A good life.'

Annie stood stock still in front of this stranger-of-twenty-years – defeated. It wasn't all his fault. 'You're right. You gave me all I expected. I just should have expected more. I'm sorry.'

Lester beamed. 'Apology accepted. Now, about that tea …'

If ever there was a reason to kill another human being, Lester's request for tea was it. Annie contemplated the repercussions. She'd already done twenty years to life. *Not doing any more.*

She turned on her heels, went to her bedroom and searched for a reason to take anything in it with her. She picked up a photo of her sister from the dresser. The facial features were faded, but it was the only surviving photo of Lizzie. The others had gone up in the fire, along with the little cash Annie had saved for culinary school. The cash Lizzie had shot into a vein before torching the sofa in Annie's first – only – independent flat. Annie stroked the picture frame and recalled asking her mother all those years ago if she blamed herself for what happened to Lizzie.

'She made her own bed,' Mum had said, looking left.

No more talk of family.

Annie marched back to the hallway, thrust the photo into her suitcase and scanned her old life one more time. Scanned Lester one more time. He'd always taken up all the room in the flat. Now she sensed herself expanding, pushing back, filling her fair share of atomic space.

The front door hit the wall as Annie threw it open and lifted her case over the threshold. As an afterthought, she strode back into the living room, threw her arms around her mother, and hugged her with such strength her mother gasped.

'I'll leave you and Lester to it. I'm happy for you. Really. I'll be in touch.' She returned to the door, grabbed the suitcase handle and lifted it down the first of the steps.

'Where're you going?' Pat wailed as she leaned over the banister railing. 'Shall I put the kettle on? I bought your favourite biscuits.'

Annie threw her head back as the explosive 'Ha!' burst forth. 'All the Hobnobs in the world couldn't lure me back into that cage.' With her gaze directed up the stairwell, she locked eyes with her mother, real fear captured in the brown pools surrounded by a widening rim of white. Pat placed her palms together and pressed her index fingers to her lips. Another parting hung in the air between mother and daughter, the same question asked of a man with a briefcase as he headed for a door. Annie had never found the answer to that man's question. It was time to give up trying. All she could do now was find answers to her own quandaries.

Lester leaned over the banister and shouted at the top of Annie's disappearing head, 'Are you leaving me for that rich geezer, Charles?'

Annie shouted back, 'You're a rich geezer! But no, I'm not leaving you for a man. I'm leaving you for a life. Oh, and by the way, you're a pillock!' *One more thing off the bucket list.*

Lester receded; smaller, less relevant with each turn in the staircase. Fragmented dialogue floated above her head.

'Where's she going, Lester?'

'I thought she'd enjoy that house, Pat. I really did.'

His footsteps echoed down the stairwell as Lester stamped back into the flat. Her mother's followed him slowly.

Annie – formally of Verston – listened no more.

She hadn't mapped out what she'd do once the portal at the foot of the four flights of stairs opened. All she knew was she could go anywhere. Do anything. She stood perfectly still, rooted to the spot. The bus pulled up across the road, disgorging an old lady tugging her wheeled shopping cart behind her. The bus offering at least a meagre option; a place to sit and think. Annie bolted for it. She trundled her suitcase down the aisle, apologising as the handle caught the jacket of a man on his phone. She sidled into an empty seat, pulling her suitcase up beside her.

There. All settled. We're off. Annie smiled to herself as the bus pulled away. The windows of first the laundromat, then the convenience shop, then the Fox and Rabbit attracted her attention. Her head rocked left to right, left to right, like the carriage on an old typewriter as the windows receded into the past. She checked the buildings off her list of things to leave behind. Her smile waned. She swallowed hard as her eyes swept the few passengers in the seats in front of her.

Why the hell am I on the bloody bus to St Albans?

She sat in incredulity as the fields along the A5 flitted past the window. The cathedral on the hill came into view, presiding over the human ants whose lives had been scurrying around its foundation for millennia. The bus wound along streets threaded with history: from Iron

Age settlement to Roman Verulamium, 1700 years of pilgrimages to the shrine of St Albans, home of the only English pope. This was her heritage, yet she felt herself a nomadic stranger.

Getting off the bus in St Peter's Street, she dragged her suitcase past the shops and the Wednesday open-air market, a fixture of the town since the ninth century. She walked past the electronics shop housed in a Tudor building, its windows lined with screens flashing images of other worlds. 'Flat screen' made sense to her now. The images bore no relation to the real thing: no smells, no tactile sensations. To stand in the middle of a 360-degree view and meld with it could never be confused with 'viewing it'. The virtual reality glasses for sale next to the screens promised to 'take you there'. They wouldn't. She knew that now.

Trudging past the medieval clock tower and under the archway, she steered her wonky-wheeled suitcase along the confined alley. It opened up to reveal the enormity of St Albans Cathedral. Engulfed by the sheer scale of the building, disorientation overwhelmed her. This was home. This was her history. Yet, it all felt incredibly foreign. Her breaths came in short, panicked bursts.

She halted under the ancient Yew tree in the courtyard; the one she'd run around as a child in a frenzied attempt to conjure up the ghosts said to inhabit it. Where was her intensity of purpose now? A clear idea of what she didn't want had swept her onto the bus. Now, that decision took on the infantile characteristics of a tantrum – hardly a plan in and of itself. There were many steps between 'Don't want this anymore' and 'This is what I want'. Complete freedom paralyzed her completely.

Her stomach assumed control. She headed for the rectory café, serving teas and cakes, sandwiches and light lunches. Fatigue no longer an issue – surprisingly, considering how many hours she'd been awake – sausage and mash sounded good. For fun, she ordered a slice of Victoria sandwich with a lemon curd filling. Arriving with her tray at the check-out counter, she realised she hadn't read the prices on the large menu board before ordering.

First. Time. Ever.

Annie beamed at the lady taking the money. *At least not knowing what I'm doing doesn't include not knowing where the next penny's coming from.*

She ate slowly, numbly, unaware of how long she'd been there when a lady asked her if she could take her plates. Annie rose and left the rectory, heading into the heart of the cathedral itself. The staff in the gift shop eyed her suspiciously, but her suitcase screamed 'Sanctuary!' They let her pass.

Entering the vast nave, Annie bumped the shoulder of an elderly man. Her mouth formed an apology, sound momentarily trapped in the gaze of a stone saint on the wall.

'Sorry,' she mumbled, eyes still on the stone effigy; the word that ubiquitous British 'sorry', practiced since birth for use when treading on the floor or accidentally breathing the air. Oh, how Annie felt she'd practiced; a devout disciple of guilt. Her simple word covered crimes unknown, people unknown, reasons unknown. An exhausting, all-encompassing apology – both for and to herself.

Flopping down on one of the nearest wooden chairs, Annie drew her suitcase close. She wrapped her arms around it and rested her head on the handle. It smelled old, just as the sunken couch cushions in a childhood flat had smelled old. Everything in that flat had smelled of someone else's life, including her satchel and her school uniform. An image: her mother bolting across a room, a vague recollection of an earlier rapid movement of a half-remembered man. Her mother reappeared with a couple of cardboard boxes, throwing one at each daughter.

'Pack your stuff,' her mother had said, before packing her own case.

'It's all right, Mum.' Lizzie's chin wobbled. 'We don't need to move again. It scares Annie.'

'I'm not scared of anything,' Annie shot back, scared of everything.

'Don't just stand there! Go and pack!'

Her childhood self turned tail and ran to her bedroom. Throwing the box on her bed, the emptiness of it taunted her. Emptiness tracked her still, like a fifty-year-old homing pigeon.

Running. Why?

Annie blinked up at the altar. She'd never understood religious customs. She couldn't separate her culture's rituals from those shown on National Geographic programmes about tribes in the jungle. What was the difference – prettier windows? Missionary attempts to convert from one set of rules to another seemed to her a complete waste of time. Until now.

In that moment, Annie envied the woman kneeling at the altar in prayer. How lovely to believe a deity controlled the universe, and all you had to do was hand yourself over for all to be well. The praying woman didn't give off the vibe all was well. Rather, sadness shaped her features.

Organ music blasted from somewhere above her head. Visitors turned to listen. Waves of sound crashed down on her, bounced off lofty arches and pillars that had seen much and cared little for the struggles of human life. Candles flickered. Dust particles swirled, dressed in vibrant hues from the stained-glass windows. A man hanging on a high cross winked at her. She closed her eyes, willing the takeover by a higher power. Seconds later, her eyes snapped open. 'Oh, no. Not again. Not in this lifetime.'

A tap on her shoulder. Annie leapt out of her chair.

'Are you all right, madam?' The man in a black robe spoke kindly, then cautiously regarded her suitcase. Annie realised it must look like a distress flare. Which it was. 'Can I help you? Help you find something? Pray with you, perhaps?'

For a respectful moment, Annie pondered the clergyman's request. 'No thanks, vicar.' She grabbed her suitcase: disorientation now realisation. Faith, from now on, would be in herself.

Annie left the building. She hauled her life past the lake in the park at Verulamium, past the descendants of the ducks she'd fed as a child, and up Fishpool Street to the swanky hotel she'd only ever seen from the outside. Annie met the slightly condescending look of the receptionist head on. His expression changed when she booked the most expensive suite.

Once in her room, she made two calls from the phone beside the four-poster bed: one an ending, one a beginning.

15 – PARADISE MISLAID

Taylor lay on the bed, her laptop lodged on her knees. Focus should have been on her new business but something nudged her to peruse the luxury apartments currently listed in Chicago. Pages and pages of them, each photo a reminder no one missed her at all. Two weeks in Costa Rica and her old life appeared obsolete.

The Chicago skyline in the photos shocked her, never before viewed as a tangled, chaotic, confused mass of humanity. It had been exciting and tameable if you knew its secrets. She'd mastered it all, responsible for selling most of the luxury suites in the towering monuments in the images. The penthouse suite sale; the golden ticket. Important. Celebrated. Blah, blah, blah.

What? Lose a job and a wealthy customer and suddenly success is overrated? Speaking of losing something, Taylor wondered what the Hardcastles were doing now. No mention of Annie and Lester in the news websites; strange given the intense interest of a week ago. She hated secrets. Knowing Annie and Lester had one – a big one – gnawed at her and compounded her sense of failure at losing them as clients. She dragged her eyes back to her screen, then groaned loudly enough to draw Charles's attention from his own laptop.

His brow furrowed. 'Is there a ghost in there?'

'I don't belong.' Anxiety about her own life replaced her interest in the Hardcastles. 'I don't belong in Chicago anymore. Seriously, I'd forgotten that. How could I possibly have forgotten that?'

Charles took his glasses off and pinched his nose. 'What are you talking about? Of course you belong there. You grew up there. Did really well there.' Charles sighed. 'Until recently.'

'Sure. A high-flyer who'd never fall off the wire.' Taylor threw her laptop aside on the bed. 'I fell off the wire when I assumed I was too good to fail.'

'We're all too good to fail, until we fail.' Charles's voice couldn't contain his resentment, ever present since the authorities swarmed his company headquarters, escorting management and secretaries and maintenance workers and lawyers to the door or prison cells or unemployment lines.

'True that.' Taylor matched her husband's sigh with one of her own. Failure brought her father to mind; her high-flying father had failed too. Before heading out to the church for her brother's funeral, a family friend suggested Richard's name for a rehab centre.

'Hell, no!' Her father smashed the Waterford wine goblet he'd been holding into the wall. 'I'll not plaster any of my money on a building for him.'

Through her grief and anger, Taylor had smiled up at her father in that moment of defeat, her disdain never forgotten by either of them. She let that grief – as stale and as fresh as ever – wash over her now. Her father's failure, her brother's failure, accentuating her own.

'Are we doing the right thing, staying here?' Taylor laid her head back and acknowledged this new world of vulnerability. No one was immune. The anger of being fired dissipated. The bravado of trying to pull one over on Ashcroft dimmed. 'I ask again, what are we doing here and what do we really want for ourselves?'

'I want to stroll down Michigan Avenue without an angry retiree who lost his nest egg to my company shouting abuse at me.' Charles flipped his legs round off the bed and stood up. 'I'd settle for credibility again. I used to believe I was one of the good guys, you know? Now I'm only what the world thinks I am. The good, the bad and the innocent all carry the ugly brand now.'

'The world hasn't been fair to you.' Taylor scowled. 'It just spun your story to direct outrage at anyone and everyone, regardless of the facts or the consequences. Speaking of spinning stories, I'd love to find out what happened to Annie and Lester. Someone at *The Daily Scoop* saw enough smoke to chase them around.'

Charles closed his eyes. 'A tiny puff of smoke turns into a giant wild-fire and if there isn't any smoke, someone will bring a bottle of it to get the party started.'

Taylor checked her watch. Old habits die hard. Typically, by this time of the morning, she'd be three deals into the day. Now, she sat with no-where to go, with no one waiting for her call, with no agenda beyond getting back at Ashcroft and contemplating starting a business in a place she wasn't sure she wanted to be. It was the most terrifying ordeal of her life.

'Maybe I did see a ghost in that screen just now,' Taylor said quietly. 'A ghost of me, disappearing when the lights came on.'

Charles patted Taylor's hand. 'This isn't you at all. We need to buck ourselves up. We're better than this. We have options and assets we have to believe in again.'

'Bravo.' A little fight returned to her voice. She tapped a key on her laptop with gusto. 'I just hit send on my Costa Rican real estate licence application. What have you done today?'

Charles shrugged, sheepishly. 'I've come up with a plan. Not ready to divulge it yet, but I'm optimistic about its potential.'

'Can you at least give me a clue?' Taylor tried to snatch Charles's laptop from where he'd left it on the bed.

Charles snatched it back and closed several windows. 'All in good time. All in good time. First, we need to ask ourselves where we're going to live if we've decided to stay down here. All this paradise is getting way too expensive.'

Taylor pulled a face. 'You're such a buzzkill at times.'

16 - ANNIE, MEET ANNIE

Annie binge-watched all the Jason Bourne films while hiding out at the hotel. She ordered room service, sneaking out for walks at night, just in case *The Daily Scoop* still had any interest in her. The why of that whole scenario completely escaped her. Occasional glances at their website suggested all was forgotten, the Hardcastles replaced by a royal pregnancy complete with extra-terrestrial father. Still, laying low remained a safe bet. Jason Bourne had nothing on her and after five days spent setting her new life in motion and staying off the grid – more to hide from Lester and her mother than anyone else – she headed for Heathrow airport.

Twenty hours later, the taxi pulled to a stop outside the reception area of the Paradise Resort. The driver cleared his throat as he held the door open. Annie filled her lungs with scented air and swung herself into motion. She tipped the driver from her bundle of cash, then pictured waiting for a Verston bus in the rain. *Never again.*

She figured no one would assume she'd come back to the same place. Jason Bourne hid right under the noses of those searching for him. She tugged her straw sunhat lower over her eyes and congratulated herself on her plan, which didn't involve checking into the Paradise Resort.

Who knew if *The Daily Scoop* reporter had followed her back to St Albans or followed her on her return to Costa Rica. All she knew was staying away from newspapers and online news sources took priority. As was staying out of Taylor's way, if she was still here. But she would use Taylor one more time, imagining a silk dress, Italian sandals, a handbag with room for a company cell phone and an appointments book. Attitude. She would channel Taylor's attitude.

Keeping her head down, she headed for the first of the boutiques. This Taylor-Annie asked thrilled employees working on commission to dress her: swimsuits and exercise gear, dresses and linen trousers, cloud-soft sweaters and elegant sandals. Annie never wore accessories. They got in the way of peeling potatoes. This Taylor-Annie, however, wore silver bangles, turquoise necklaces, a classic watch, silk scarves. She carried handbags that matched her outfits, but never contained a bus timetable. A pair of café readers – magnifying sunglasses allowing her to read on the beach without being blinded by white pages – completed the transformation. Though a little disconcerted the sales lady had pegged her as one needing such technology, Annie bought two pairs.

Taylor-Annie's last duty was to pay in cash. Dropping the hyphenation and refusing an offer to have the packages delivered to her room, Annie strode out of the last boutique, pulling her bulging, newly-purchased suitcase behind her. The condemned wonky-wheeled one followed sullenly behind.

As she passed the lobby bar, Annie smiled at all the exotic liquors on the shelves waiting to be concocted into beverages with ridiculous names. She vowed to taste every one of them, and even say their stupid names out loud.

She dragged the vestiges of Old Annie into the toilets by the bar, where she changed into a pair of shorts and a nondescript tee shirt. She stamped the clothes she'd been wearing to travel into a waste basket, then tucked her old suitcase into a stall and closed the door. She'd needed her former shell only long enough to escape. About to leave, she ran back to the suitcase and grabbed Lizzie's photo.

Zigzagging her way through the resort, avoiding the pool areas, hiding behind palm trees until she was sure she wasn't being followed,

Annie arrived at the back of the resort. She slipped through a gap in the fence she'd noticed during her prior stay, and disappeared.

Eat your heart out, Jason Bourne.

'May not have thought this through,' Annie whispered to herself nearly an hour later, as she brushed the branches away from her face and swatted a fly. 'But must be nearly there now.'

She studied the paper in her hand showing a hand-drawn map. The track widened as it wound through the rainforest and ran parallel to a narrow road. Having seen or heard no one for the entire journey, she knew she'd picked the right spot.

A mile and a half down the coast from the Paradise Resort sat a remote, well-screened villa with access to a secluded beach. Said villa was now secured for a long-term lease by one 'Dale Dante' from New York; an author escaping to finish her latest crime novel. An author who needed absolute privacy. 'Dale' refused the management company's offer of a welcome tour of the property, no handshake or visual contact of any kind required. Payment had been delivered via a bank courier and the key was waiting in a drop box outside the villa.

Annie admired the way Jason Bourne anticipated the bad guys' moves; the way he always had the skills and languages and money and passports available to reinvent himself at a moment's notice. His escapes thrilled her, no matter how many times she'd watched them. She hadn't appreciated why she'd enjoyed those films so much, but smiled now in the knowledge they'd been how-to videos. She planned to skip the scenes where she killed with her bare hands and drove a car backwards at 80mph, however.

She tripped over a fallen log. As she dusted herself off, she pictured the more sophisticated and dignified Purdey in the *New Avengers* television show from decades before. Glamorous, upper-class Purdey ran in high heels, took out the bad guys without ruffling her perfect bob cut, with not a drop of sweat showing in the armpits of her creaseless blouse. *Exactly how Taylor would've done this, no doubt.* Inferiority Woman – capeless and dishevelled – made a brief appearance in the film credits. There was nothing 'Purdey' about her. Ah, well. Purdey needed two men to help her. Annie was never going to need one of *those* again. Her euphoria at the sentiment manifested itself in a whoop. A gecko on a tree branch responded by licking its eyeball.

Annie left Inferiority Woman on the cutting room floor and strode onwards. She began to laugh, at first gently, then with gusto. What wouldn't the paparazzi give to snap a photo of her now?

A truck trundled by on the nearby road. She clamped her hand over her mouth and ducked down behind a tree and her suitcase. Once the coast was clear, she muttered something in Russian about stupid spy operatives – or it sounded Russian to her.

Another thirty minutes found her outside gates she recognised from the Casa Luna website. In the mailbox, a remote control for the gate and a key waited. Casting a furtive glance over her shoulder, she hit the remote button. The gates slide back, reminiscent of curtains at the cinema.

Identical to curtains at the cinema, Annie thought, transfixed. The opening portal revealed a winding, beckoning driveway of cobblestones bordered by swaying palm trees and shiny-leaved shrubs sporting colourful blooms. Succulent ground covers edged the driveway, drawing her eyes along the stones and into the distance. The villa hadn't come into view yet but she caught a glimpse of the ocean through the vegetation.

The sound of another car forced her mind back to her mission and she scooted her suitcase through the gates, hitting the remote before she even crossed the threshold. She imagined herself doing one of those rolling dives under a closing door at a top-secret facility, somewhere in the old Soviet bloc, but decided against trying it. The car passed by the hidden driveway as the gate clicked shut. A safe click, not a prying, front page click.

Leaves in her hair, dusty smudges across her cheeks, Annie Hardcastle from Verston took a deep breath, clutched her companion by the handle and set off towards Oz. Starting strong, her steps slowed, then faltered, as the villa came into view. Curved contours of the tiled roof followed the rounded outline of the vista beyond. The sparkling waters of the bay beckoned her gaze towards the small islands in the distance. Unfamiliar birdcalls emanated from the trees. A fountain in the courtyard tinkled its welcome as Annie crept onwards. With shaky hands, she placed the key in the lock of the wooden door, its surface decorated with carvings of flowers and birds. *Open Sesame.*

Leaving the suitcase in the cool, tiled entryway, Annie floated past the granite-countered kitchen with glass-doored wine cooler, past the open-plan living area with the cream couches, past tropical-coloured throw pillows, sea creature sculptures, the dining table for twelve and the exotic plants in huge ceramic containers. At the threshold between house and garden, she paused to adjust to the light – or was it the life? Gliding farther into the dreamscape, past the rocking chairs on the veranda, she came to a halt at the edge of the infinity pool. A waterfall cascaded from natural rock formations into the clear water.

She sank to her knees and cried. For joy, for rebirth, for life.

17 - WHAT'S IN A NAME?

They found her clothes in a toilet?' Pat perched on the edge of her sofa, hand over her heart. Becky Dagny patted her knee. Superintendent Jane Williams sat on the recliner opposite, with a crumpled copy of *The Daily Scoop* on her lap: 'Nothing Left But Her Clothes! Lottery Winner Disappears into Thin Air!' said the headline.

Pat glared at the policewoman. 'What have they done with her? They can't do this to one of Her Majesty's royal subjects!'

Becky nodded fervently, leaving Pat the distinct impression her neighbour belonged on a dashboard.

'Mrs Rickman. We don't know what happened yet, only what *The Daily Scoop* printed, which is probably worthless. I'm more interested in what you have to say.'

'I've told you,' Pat said. 'Annie stormed out of here over a week ago, and I haven't heard from her since.'

The policewoman checked her notes. 'Is it possible her motivation is simply to get away to think?'

'Why would she take her clothes off to think?' Pat knew her daughter. She wasn't the exhibitionist type.

'Becoming a multi-millionaire is a lot to process, Mrs Rickman.'

Becky stopped patting Pat's knee and astutely observed, 'Doesn't make your clothes fall off, though, does it?'

Pat pushed visions of her naked daughter out of her head. 'Lester was going to take care of the details. All Annie had to do was pack up her flat. Not much to process, if you ask me.' Pat dabbed her eyes.

Williams switched her focus from Pat to her notes. 'Did she want to move?'

'You've seen her flat, right?' Becky covered her mouth. Pat didn't bother responding.

Williams flicked through her notes again. 'None of this explains why Annie's possessions were abandoned in a public toilet in Costa Rica.'

'Throw the media hounds off the scent?' Pat nodded slowly as the thought took shape. 'Trying to outrun the paparazzi? Don't you remember poor Princess Diana?'

'Why would she leave her boarding pass with her name on it behind if she was trying to hide?' The furrows in Williams's forehead got deeper. 'Any fool would've checked their pockets first if they were trying to disappear.'

'And my daughter's no fool. That's why I'm positive she's been kidnapped.' Pat gave a final curt nod of her head and waited for Superintendent Williams to catch up.

Superintendent Williams let out a sigh. 'You concluded she'd been kidnapped before. It turned out not to be tr—'

'The reporter said he had proof.'

'I'm not here to discuss the reporting habits of *The Daily Scoop*,' Superintendent Williams said. 'I'm trying to find out why Annie has drawn this excessive attention from the media and why she may have gone into hiding. If that's what she's done. I've spoken to a couple of contacts of mine, can't share who exactly, and they say *The Daily Scoop* is planning to reveal a bigger story than fake kidnappings. Something about you and Annie having a secret past that may be of interest to the authorities; a past that may have been pushed to the forefront by the lottery win. Is there any possibility the media has something here?'

Becky turned her whole body towards Pat, her jaw slack. 'So, it's true. You *are* Richard Burton's love child!'

Pat stroked her hair. 'There's no proof, just lots of comments about my uncanny resemblance to him.'

Superintendent Williams cleared her throat. 'Richard Burton? Seriously?'

Pat resented the police woman's tone. 'That's what Mum said.' She waggled her head at Becky.

Williams continued. 'Parentage aside, let's get back to the possibility there's more to Annie's story than meets the eye.'

Pat fiddled with her necklace, then her bracelet. She flicked dust off her sleeve. 'You'd better leave, Becky.' Pat pushed out her chin. There would be no negotiating.

Becky packed her disdain into one raised shoulder and a head turn with pursed lips. 'Well, I never. Through thick and thin we've been—'

'That will be all, Mrs Dagny.' Williams rose from her chair, placed a firm hand on Becky's shoulder, and directed her out. The door slammed behind her.

'Right.' Williams opened her notebook. 'Where were we? Ah, yes. You were about to spill why the press may be hounding your daughter if it's not about being a lottery winner.'

Pat rubbed the back of her neck and fought with her mouth. It gyrated around the facts it was about to share – or invent. She wasn't sure which anymore. After all, it was long ago and she'd never known the full story herself; left to fill in the gaps during many a long, lonely night of hoping for better. If there was one thing she'd passed onto her daughters, it was a reason to hope for better.

'It may be her dad,' Pat said. 'He may be Number Three.'

Williams's reaction was somewhat disappointing. 'Number three … of what, exactly?' Her pen remained poised.

Pat didn't even try to hide her astonishment. 'How can any self-respecting police officer not have heard of Number Three?' She shook her head in disgust at the state of the world. 'Number Three from that train robbery.'

Williams looked pained but remained silent. Pat rolled her eyes. 'Rumour has it, Annie's father was the unidentified suspect known only as Number Three in the Great Train Robbery of 1963. Now you know.'

Not a single sound emanated from the recliner.

Pat tutted before standing up. 'I'll make more tea.'

'That's why he moved to Hertfordshire? To hide from the authorities in Buckinghamshire?' Jane had been stirring her tea non-stop for about five minutes. She hadn't taken a single sip. The police got fed whoppers all the time. Everybody lied to them. But Buckinghamshire was right next door to Hertfordshire. What kind of nutter stole £2.6 million, then hid out next door?

Jane put her cup down and glanced at her phone which showed the records she'd pulled up while Pat made tea. 'The Great Train Robbery of 1963 was called the Crime of the Century at the time, Mrs Rickman. In today's money, the £2.6 million stolen would be worth north of £40 million. This is a big deal.'

'Tell me about it.' Pat warmed to her subject. 'Fifteen blokes used a fake red light to make the Royal Mail train stop. They got away with sacks full of bank notes. Most of the money was never recovered.'

'May I remind you most of the perpetrators were.' Jane continued to scan her phone. 'A few of them quickly, others after a year or so, and the ringleader, Bruce Reynolds, about five years later. That said, there'd always been rumours of the three that got away, never identified.' *Someone wasn't a nutter.* 'What made you think your Joe was involved?'

'Oh, I wasn't sure of anything, but I had a long time to ponder it after …' Pat swallowed. Jane recognised a woman steeling herself for what was to come. 'Joe arrived out of nowhere in our little village of Markyate. Strangers didn't just arrive in Markyate. We all wondered where he was from. Smart shoes, briefcase, money for Babycham at the pub. All the girls were smitten, but I was the one he chose. Said I had Hollywood glamour, he did. Could be true, of course. I never met my dad.' Pat's eyes drifted for a moment.

Jane steered her back onto the train tracks. 'Please continue.'

'I didn't know anything about Joe and the Great Train Robbery. All I knew was he had a suntan when we first met. It was January 1964. Stood out like spaghetti on a Sunday roast lunch plate, he did.' Pat huffed down her nose. 'Between the tan and the suit, I knew he had money, but why would I jump to the conclusion he'd nicked it? Said he was a businessman dealing in currency. I only understood one thing about currency: I didn't have any.' Pat cackled into her teacup.

Jane cracked a weak smile, a show of support.

'Anyway, him and me took up together, got married a year later at the registry office with a kid in premature attendance, if you get my drift. That – plus Annie – was that for a few years.' Pat's pleasant reminisces shone on her face, briefly. The clouds closed in fast.

'I still don't understand why you thought Joe was Number Three. Lots of people had money they didn't get from robbing trains.'

'Oh, the shifty eyes in the pub, the phone calls on a Sunday evening, having to go out with no warning. Never having an office Christmas party. Everyone had an office Christmas party back then. "S'pose you'll be going up to London for a fancy do," my friends would say. Not true. I never met his workmates, though he'd leave for work in the mornings. It all made me a bit nervous, to be honest though I assumed only petty crime. Never dreamed it was big stuff. We weren't living large or anything.' Pat rubbed her thumb across the palm of her hand before continuing. 'One night – it was a Tuesday – there was a story in the newspaper about new suspects in the robbery. Joe kissed Lizzie and Annie, went out the door and we never saw him again. That was 1969.'

Jane considered her question carefully, sensing the answer may be difficult. 'And Lizzie is?'

Pat's expression turned to stone. 'Oldest daughter. Dead.'

Jane decided not to push for details about Lizzie yet. Her priority remained Annie. 'Must have been hard, raising kids alone. I have to ask, why didn't you say anything about Joe?' If Pat had been treated this badly by her husband, why would she protect him?

'Because I couldn't be certain. The police arrived the day after Joe left. Asked where the money was.' Pat sat up straighter. 'I showed the coppers around the flat in St Albans. Hardly a millionaire's hideout. I didn't even have a bank account. Joe gave me cash each week for the shopping. Police told me there was no bank account they could find in the name of Joe Rickman. No record at all of a Joe Rickman.' The sting of the ruse crinkled Pat's brow, then her chin. 'It was nice to have a man in the house who provided. Richard Burton wasn't the best of fathers when it came time to provide for his family.'

Jane softened. She witnessed the worst of human nature daily, but she never failed to feel for the lives destroyed by the lies of trusted loved ones. Pat had been betrayed by many, including her own mother.

'Did the police ever prove Joe was involved?' Jane asked.

'Nah. The anonymous tip-off couldn't be traced and no one could find Joe … because Joe Rickman never existed. Bit of a shock, that. Whatever name he gave me at the registry office was fake. Annie's grown up with a fake name. Oh, don't tell her! She doesn't need to learn all this. That's why we moved so often when she was a kid. Trying to keep ahead of the gossip.'

Jane was fully aware of how much damage neighbours could do with partial information, innuendo and rumour. She imagined Pat, abandoned and humiliated, trying to protect her children – Lizzie and Annie Fake-Last-Name.

'I never had the marriage annulled. It was something to hold onto. A pretend someone had pretended to make a pretend life with me. It was better than nothing.'

Jane hadn't liked the woman before her, thinking her nothing more than an attention-seeker hanging onto her daughter's lottery-win shirt tails. Now she acknowledged Pat's only crime had been allowing herself to dream of better days. She worried the past was about to trample those better days.

When the women's eyes met, Jane saw acceptance. Pat understood she was the pretend daughter of a legend and the pretend wife of a criminal. Her weary shoulders sagged. The motion kicked the toughened police officer hard in the chest, unshielded by her business suit.

Pat's reserve crumbled; broken chunks of ancient glacier. Tears compounded the icy flow. 'As far as Annie's concerned, I threw out a cheating husband. If she finds out the truth …'

Jane stood up. 'At least we understand the media interest now. Maybe we'll find Annie before the reporter does. I'll get working on it. In the meantime, I suggest you don't read the papers.'

A shadow scuttled past the open window as Jane reached the door.

Pat put her hand out to brush Jane's sleeve. 'Please help me. I lost one daughter to her dad. I'll not lose another.'

Jane vowed to tackle Lizzie's story later. She needed to find Annie first. She squeezed Pat's hand and left.

Becky was studying the wall outside the flat, fascinating structure that it was. Jane wondered how much this neighbour had heard.

Enough. Becky had heard enough, and friendship was an easy thing to sell. The headline in *The Daily Scoop* the next morning shrieked: 'Lottery Winner: Offspring of Richard Burton and Great Train Robber!'

Pat strode into Lester's living room, having barged her way past a dishevelled son-in-law. She threw her paper down on the coffee table, only to discover she needn't have marched across the village green carrying her own. Torn pages of Lester's copy littered the floor in the living room, the unwitting victim of someone's fury. Maybe she should have shared the policewoman's advice to not read the papers. Pat wished she'd listened herself.

She plonked down on the sofa and flapped her shirt collar in and out, attempting to cool herself down after the stair climb. 'We have to do something! We can't leave my baby to the vultures. Not in Africa, of all places! We'll never find her again.'

'Costa Rica's not in Africa.' Lester's teeth clenched. 'It's in the Caribbean, if you must know, and your baby left me, remember? Besides, I've got me own problems.' Lester flicked the curtain aside. 'That bloke with the telephoto lens is still parked outside.'

'Pushed a reporter off my doorstep, too.' She suffered a rare twinge of guilt. This wasn't Lester's fault.

'Let's focus on Annie,' Pat said. 'We've always taken care of each other, me and my little girl.' A second twinge of guilt. Pat vowed there wouldn't be a third. 'I won't abandon her now.'

'Wish those reporters would abandon me.' Lester belched. Pat tightened her lips at the sight of the beer can. 'A man can't even drink in peace. I get to the Fox and Rabbit last night and a bunch of geezers with cameras start asking where the money is. "It's in the bank" I say and everyone goes nuts. Ask if I'm confessing to the crime. "What crime?" I say. "Winning the lottery's not a crime," I say. That's when I find out I already had two million quid before I even bought a lottery ticket!'

Pat believed any accusation could always be allayed using a good dose of deflection. 'Oh, of course. Me and Annie lived high on the hog for years before she met you. Foreign holidays, mansions, a couple of Jags in the driveway. Decided to hide it all when you arrived on the scene, we did. We're hiding all the left-over cash in the cake tin for after you drop dead.'

'Funny,' Lester muttered.

Pat scanned the room. 'Annie wouldn't be living in this flat if we had money.'

'What's wrong with it?' Lester peered left and right. 'Nice view, central heating, new bathroom a few years back. Many as would be happy in this little nest. Mind you, making your own tea's tiring with the kitchen so far from the telly.'

Pat tutted. 'A real workout for you, I'm sure.' She couldn't deny Lester appeared tired, though not from work, as his bosses had asked him to stay away. Must be the all-night television. The line of beer cans on the sideboard snitched on him.

With no offer to make tea forthcoming, Lester ploughed on. 'Anyway, what's all this got to do with the fact I had no idea Annie and you were fugitives from the law?'

Pat stood up and walked to the window. Lester had a right to know. 'It's all idle gossip. Annie's father never said anything to me about robbing trains. When the coppers came round asking about him, I couldn't tell them anything. Not even Joe's real name. Don't you think for one minute I'm proud of that, either.' Pat's chin wobbled. 'Not only didn't she have a father, she didn't even have a real name. S'pose I should've told Annie all this long before now. How could I risk it after what happened to Lizzie?' She scanned the carpet, even into the corners as though still searching for her lost daughter. 'Can't do anything about Lizzie but now my poor Annie's going to find out from the paparazzi.'

'Are you saying Annie has no idea her dad was a train robber?'

'*Alleged* train robber.' Pat dug deep for any last vestige of loyalty to the man she thought she'd married.

Lester swept the car park with suspicious eyes one more time before returning to his recliner. He absentmindedly pulled the handle to lift the foot rest. 'And the name she grew up with wasn't real? Blimey. She's going to have a heart attack when she finds out.'

'What are we going to do?' Pat waited for the man of the house to take charge. She didn't have to wait long for the disappointment.

'How should I know?' Lester said with a yawn. 'Haven't a clue where she is. Though if I had to guess I'd bet my winnings on her being back in Costa Rica with that slimy Charles bloke.'

'What Charles bloke?'

'Never mind,' Lester said. 'If it's not him she's after, it's more of those piña coladas and beautiful sunsets. Every night she'd say, "What a beautiful sunset". I say, you've seen one, you've seen 'em all.' He yawned again.

Pat stamped her foot, worried Lester's minimal grasp on the issue was frittering away at rapid speed. 'So, there's a good chance she's back in Costa Rica? That's a good start. Now what should we do?'

Lester rubbed his chin slowly and came up with a plan. 'I'll ask me mates tomorrow.' His satisfied head nod suggested case closed.

Pat's eyes widened, though not in total surprise. 'That's it then? "I'll ask me mates" and we're all sorted?' She didn't have a good answer, but she was certain asking Becky Dagny wasn't going to help. 'Will your mates cushion the blow when Annie falls apart? God, you're thick.'

'I don't have to sit in my own home and take that, you know. Unless you can come up with something better, go away and let me have a nap. I'm still jet-lagged.' Lester sank down in his chair, eyelids at half-mast already.

Pat had no idea how long jet lag could be used as an excuse. She stood up wearily, put her hands on her hips and leaned back to stretch her stiff spine. 'I'm too old for this.' About to give up, her eyes caught sight of Lester's wallet on the sideboard. It practically screamed 'I have a plan!'

Pat began cautiously. 'You could send me to Costa Rica. You stay here and check with your mates for answers to our problems and I'll fly out to break the news to Annie before the press get to her. If I don't get there in time, I'll pick up the pieces the best I can. What do you think?' Pat waited.

'Righto.' Lester's eyes were almost closed.

Pat lowered her voice to barely a whisper. 'I don't have any money, Lester. You'll have to help.'

'Righto.'

Pat watched beer relieve Lester's brain of its leadership role. Not the first time she'd witnessed it. It just hadn't been useful before.

Pat picked up Lester's wallet and rifled through it. 'I'll just borrow your credit card for the ticket,' she whispered, 'and pick up a bit of cash for the journey, all right?'

'Righto.' Lester's final word. A purr, a murmur, a grunt.

Pat smiled as the snoring started. She'd save Annie. The least Lester could do was help her.

She tiptoed out of the flat, closing the door behind her with a gentle click. A bus ride later, the travel agent in St Albans helped her book a ticket to Liberia, Costa Rica. It had been years since her trip to Calais on the ferry for Christmas shopping. She clutched her tickets and wondered if the Caribbean was similar to Calais.

18 – LOOK WHO'S BACK

Annie's surfaced in the press again, and her story gets more bizarre by the minute.' Taylor scanned *The Daily Scoop*'s website; a familiar face stared out at her, next to an unfamiliar one. 'How could anyone relate this Pat woman to Richard Burton? Tim Burton, maybe?' Taylor squinted at her computer screen, sucking on her thumbnail.

Charles combed the internet for more information. 'Apparently, Tim Burton crossed with an unidentified train robber. You can't make this stuff up.' He grinned back at the screen. 'Oh, wait. Yes, you can.'

Her husband had never acted this way before; obviously enjoying his dip into the muddy soup of the tabloid press. A sensitive, intellectual man, he always considered other people's feelings – hardly the type to follow scandal without making a comment about the sorry decline of humanity. Taylor couldn't believe the change in him – but she had more to worry about.

She threw the laptop down on the bed. 'I hate to interrupt but we're supposed to be on a mission here. We're spending money like crooked bankers—' She cringed at her thoughtless comment. 'Anyway, to date, we have nothing to show for it but a less than helpful connection with a possible outlaw. If I were Ashcroft Realty, I'd go nowhere near the Hardcastles. I can't believe she came back to this area, anyway. Are you listening to me?' Taylor stopped. No, he wasn't listening to her.

Charles's eyes flittered around the screen on his laptop faster than a teenager's thumbs on Twitter. 'Look, look, look!' Charles stood up. 'Breaking news: the British authorities want to open an investigation. They say if there's any chance Annie is the daughter of one of the Great Train Robbers, they want to interview her. It appears £2 million – now worth about £40 million – of the Royal Mail money was never found. If Annie or her parents ever had it, NCIS wants—'

'You mean the TV show?'

'No, not Naval Criminal Investigative Service. That's American. This is the National Criminal Intelligence Service in the United Kingdom. Same as our FBI, I'm guessing. Anyway, they say it's worth going after Annie now she has the means to pay it back. The British public are demanding she be returned to face charges.'

Charles swept his hand through his hair, shaking his head in disbelief. 'We sure misread that little lady. How could someone with all this baggage come across as such a story-less nobody? And Lester? Hardly strikes you as someone juggling multiple secrets in the air.'

Taylor tutted. 'Big shock to me too but if you want a real shock, check out our hotel bill.' Charles didn't even blink. Taylor stuck her neck out and dug her fingernails into her hips. 'Hello? *Our* financial situation? Forget forty million anything. We have a future of our own to worry about and Annie Hardcastle is as much use to us as a pig in a tuxedo.'

Charles raised his eyebrows. 'A pig in a tuxedo?'

'You see! This is what happens when you start reading tabloid press.' Taylor yanked the laptop off the bed and turned the screen towards Charles. Below the photo of Annie and Pat, a pig wearing a tuxedo shoved his snout towards the camera from the back seat of a limousine.

'Pig Makes Millions on Stock Market', the headline read. Taylor stamped off to take a shower. Charles laughed the other side of the door for a long time.

In the shower, Taylor scrubbed at the concept of integrity. It was a slippery one. She wasn't above casting disdain on the reporters of the tabloid press or writing off Annie as disreputable. The problem was, she couldn't absolutely draw the conclusion staying away from Annie was better for her business. Top of the list under 'bad for business' was not taking advantage of the exposure Annie could bring her new real estate venture. 'Awful for business' was Ashcroft getting the glory. The world was watching. Integrity spiralled down the drain with the bubbles.

Wrapped in a towel, Taylor called the front desk and asked to be put through to Annie's room.

'There's no one registered here by that name, madam,' was not acceptable to Taylor.

'She's using a fake name,' Taylor said to Charles. 'Sly, I'll give her that. I doubt she'll be by the pool, entertaining questions about her parentage and whether she's going to pay back millions to the Queen of England. Think. She must be hiding close by or why would her clothes be here?'

Charles glanced up from his computer screen, where he spent all his time these days. 'James Bond would've done it because it would be the last place you'd look for him.'

'Would he take off all his clothes in the bathroom and leave them to be found?'

'If they paid Daniel Craig more, he might.'

Taylor cocked her head to one side, a distant gleam in her eyes. It was a lovely thought.

'Anyway, back to the Queen's money,' she said. 'No surprise the Brits are putting all these resources into catching the crooks. Annie just comes across as completely … clueless. I can't believe she's in on this.'

'Hard to picture, isn't it?' Charles steepled his fingers, creases of concentration lining his forehead.

Taylor tapped her fingers on her thigh. 'She must be holed up in a room somewhere. I'm going to find her. I'm not her favourite person right now, but she may need my help.'

'And a secluded villa, with security cameras and a gatehouse for seven figures?' Charles's eyes glinted over his glasses.

'Yes, well … a sale's a sale. We're not rolling in options here.' Taylor dared Charles to pull more of his nice guy crap on her.

Charles turned serious. 'Be gentle. Annie could do with a real friend about now.'

'I am capable of being nice, you know.'

'That's our little secret though, right?'

Another ping on Charles's laptop. He clicked a few buttons and his eyes widened.

Taylor didn't ask, just scurried round to read over his shoulder. A video played on *The Daily Scoop* website: Charles and Taylor, covered in sand and the remains of their drinks, being dragged out from underneath lounge chairs and beach umbrellas. Lester sprawled out on a dead jet ski, Annie in the background. Scrolling across the bottom of the screen: 'Great Train Robber's Daughter Knew Her Kidnappers!'

Taylor yelped as the camera panned in on the welt across her stomach. 'Where the hell do they get this stuff?'

Charles blocked the screen. 'Those kids with cell phones on the beach? Bet those lawyers wish they'd tried harder to get us to press charges now.'

Taylor clamped one hand to her stomach, the other to her mouth.

'So,' Charles said, a little too brightly. 'We can officially add "Accessory to Grand Theft Steam Train" to my growing list of crimes against humanity.'

Taylor flung her arms out then threw them over her face and groaned into the crook of her elbows.

19 – THE BEACH IS ALIVE

Annie sat on the edge of the pool, dangling her feet in the crystal-clear water. She'd washed them in the outdoor shower to remove any dust, scared to drop debris on the mosaic tiles lining the base of the pool. The paranoid compulsion to wipe down countertops, fold towels immediately after use and puff up pillows the moment she made an indentation on them hadn't lessened yet. It found her sneaking around the villa, waiting to be thrown out. But during the occasional moments she dared to believe she belonged, the sensation was … blissful.

A mosaic tiled King Neptune with his trident smiled up at her through the shimmering, cool blue.

How's your first taste of freedom, dear?

Nice. Very nice, thank you.

Last night, the sheets had remained cool and unruffled, the stillness unbroken, the sense of space around her skin – and mind – liberating. The act of living single was perhaps the most sensual experience of her life, heightened by the awakening knowledge of self, of … Annie-ness. Pure, unadulterated Annie-ness.

With each new experience, she stripped layers, rock strata, from the foundation blocks of Potential Annie: a layer of Mum, of hiding, of dead sister. A layer of Lester, of lost control. A layer of unrequited culinary school dreams. A layer of settling, of giving up. Independence and sunshine found the sculptor's careful chisel chipping away another flake, leaving a pile of old baggage around the base of the Annie plinth.

She smiled at her reflection in the pool and said simply, 'Hello.'

Dense vegetation also reflected in the crystal-clear water. Swaths of green, purple and yellow hues, both smooth and prickly textures, umbrella sized leaves and petite flowers provided canopy-to-forest-floor sanctuary. This living wall provided a protective embrace in a way the thick stone walls of St Albans Cathedral had never done. Neither had the yellow wallpapered barricade of her Verston flat. That barrier had threatened to suffocate her.

Home. Was this home? The one she'd dreamed of on the beach her first night in Costa Rica? She turned this way and that, gazed up at the sky, across the bay and down into the depths of the pool. Something felt different here. *She* felt different here.

It certainly fit the anonymity bill, tucking her safely away from prying eyes and cameras. Fortune without fame. Could there be any lifestyle more perfect than that? She'd only experienced media interest for a few days but had found it quite enough to cure her of any desire for more. Kidnapped indeed! Chased around, hiding in hotel rooms, indeed! Those shenanigans defeated the object of having money at all, trapping her every bit as much as the bank manager had in her old life. Losing control of her own narrative had been terrifying. She wondered how celebrities stood it; before conceding she'd lost control of her own narrative long before the lottery win.

Scanning the waters of the bay beyond the lawn, she noted a sailboat bobbed at anchor, no sign of life on board. It added to the postcard scene.

Hungry. Was it time for lunch? With a snort of glee, Annie relished the notion there was no 'lunch time' anymore. She could eat whenever she wanted. She'd learned quickly on this new planet a prepaid phone from the airport combined with cash rocked her intergalactic world. No one cared who you were when you left payments in the mailbox. Delivery drivers happily left food in a cooler outside the gate. Authors were such strange people, after all. Dale, using Google Translate, convinced a couple of local shop owners that disturbing Ms Dante would destroy a year's worth of written words. She laughed at the idea of Annie intimidating anyone, but Dale Dante wasn't to be messed with.

Unfortunately, the gourmet kitchen still intimidated the heck out of the Verston girl. Her goal for the day was to pluck up the nerve to leave a dish in the sink. She slipped her feet out of the pool and padded across the warm stone patio to the kitchen. After picking out a couple of cheeses and opening a packet of crackers from the well-stocked pantry, she placed lunch on a plate, adding a handful of grapes.

An envelope lay on the counter, addressed to her mother. It contained an explanation: she wasn't coming home, and she was divorcing Lester. It would be hard on her mother. Having a daughter with a husband meant a lot to her – a sure sign Annie had succeeded in life, apparently.

Annie tipped the letter into the rubbish bin. 'Why bother?' She carried her plate to the hammock slung between two trees on the lawn and climbed in. It was her favourite spot, dappled shade in which to rock gently in the breeze.

Balancing the plate on her stomach, she placed the sparkling water bottle between her thighs, noticing her light tan colour as she unscrewed the lid. In the bathroom mirror that morning, shiny eyes smiled back at her. Gone were the dark circles that once deflected light from her life; replaced with rosy absorbers of a new world. Her tiny crow's feet took on new meaning, reminding her she now laughed out loud – often – even though alone.

Should I be worried about that?

Her wedding ring caught a sunbeam, momentarily dazzled her. It was the only familiar aspect of her whole body; the scratched, thin, metal noose escapable now. It would slide off easily over her unclenched fingers. She'd kept it on to remind herself of unfinished business, but slipped it off now, dropping it onto her plate.

A rapid movement in the trees above her head coincided with a cacophony of screeches and howls. Cheese, crackers and fruit flew into the air, the grapes rolling into the pool with a plop. Shockingly cold sparkling water soaked her bikini bottom, resulting in a rapid, ungraceful exit from the hammock onto all fours. Annie pulled herself up in time to catch swinging tails disappear into the canopy of leaves.

'Damn monkeys!' Annie couldn't contain her laugh as she pulled the freezing fabric from her crotch. She still had a bit to learn about living in paradise.

A jump in the pool warmed up the bikini, and her bottom. Surprisingly, she felt no rush to clean up the mess. *Progress*, she thought, then laughed at the grapes on the pool floor. Floating on her back, she studied the howler monkeys. They appeared to find her uninteresting. Hanging out with monkeys was the epitome of interesting to Annie, only possible in her old world if she'd fallen into the monkey exhibit at Whipsnade Zoo.

Turning onto her stomach, she swam towards the edge of the infinity pool – head held out of the water, unaccustomed to swimming as she was – to take a closer look at the sailboat in the bay. She smiled serenely at the scene. Then froze.

'Reporters!' Annie slammed her hand over her mouth before she could yell again. The word bounced off her skull and popped out of her eyeballs. She dropped low in the water and clung to the side of the pool, facing away from the ocean.

'You stupid pillock!' she spat at herself. 'Of course, it's the paparazzi! How could you have thought you'd outsmart them when Jennifer Aniston can't?'

She ducked lower in the water, nothing more than her hairline showing above the edge of the pool. Bobbing up infinitesimally, she scanned the boat and the beach. No one. No ten-foot lenses, no ladders in trees.

'It's impossible they know I'm here,' Annie whispered. 'I'm safe. Breathe. Just breathe.'

As her heart rate slowed, her irritation grew, shifting to anger. The rental agent had told her no one ever used this beach, which meant someone now trespassed on *her* beach. She'd never had a beach before. She was amazed at her possessive attitude, but, by god, it was *her* beach!

Hauling her righteous self out of the water, then pulling on her robe and flip-flops of righteousness, she strode down the path to reclaim her beach.

Scratching and scurrying in the vegetation beside the path caused a little shrinkage of the cloak of righteousness; the cloak that should also make her invisible to snakes and other vermin. Annie hesitated, then jumped as a small lizard darted out of the undergrowth. Monkeys and lizards. Strange new neighbours.

From the protective cover of the treeline at the edge of the sand, Annie threw a furtive gander around before sneaking forward. There'd have been all kinds of clicking by now if a reporter was here, wouldn't there? A chuckle escaped her lips. *You're paranoid, Annie.*

Marching out of the shade and into the sun, she took a deep breath, filling herself with confidence. She let her hair down all the way, free and unencumbered. Gazing out across her new domain, her spine held no hint of a question mark now. Her beach robe dropped to the sand, followed by her flip-flops. She strode, barefoot and free, along her beach with the air of a trust fund baby. Oh, yes! She belonged in this world of beauty and tranquillity and security and home-delivered fruit baskets.

Annie began to skip, then run. Visions of Julie Andrews: arms outstretched and yelling something about hills being alive. Annie sang, pranced and twirled, then grabbed a palm tree as her dance partner. She went for the grand finale: a spin around the tree, a run into the water ...

'What the he—?' A booming voice drowned out Julie Andrews.

Annie's cheek hit two feet sticking straight up in the air behind the palm tree. She didn't have time to note what they were attached to, but they came with her as she fell. She landed with her head between someone's legs. That person was now shouting but it was somewhat incoherent as Annie's knee appeared wedged in the sound source. With sand flying and body parts tangling, a dog leapt into the fray, barking, then tugging at Annie's bikini bottom.

Between the dog and the superior strength of whatever Annie had landed on, Annie soon found herself on her back, pinned to the sand with a man straddling her chest. The dog continued to pull at her bikini bottom. The man turned to stop the dog but spun back, throwing a hand over his eyes. 'Sorry! Sorry! Stop it, Jackson! Leave it!'

Annie lifted her head a few inches and gawked up at a familiar face. The face stared down at her with dawning recognition.

'Breakfast Lady,' the man panted.

'Yoga Man,' Annie panted back. Her head dropped back onto the sand. She closed her eyes.

Well, this is awkward.

20 – THREE WEEKS TO BREAK A HABIT

How much scrutiny could we stand up to?' Taylor chewed a piece of grapefruit at the poolside breakfast table. 'I mean, when people start to dig in to anyone's past, they're going to find something, aren't they?'

'Lots to dig up about us, well, me.' Charles put his paper down and appraised his wife's face. 'You know, you look rested – and not just perfect make-up job rested. Maybe this place agrees with you.'

'Surprisingly, I have to agree.' Taylor cast smiling eyes at the ever-changing colours of the water in the bay. 'And yes, I am less uptight than usual. Didn't recognise the feeling. I figured it was indigestion.'

'You're even funny in Costa Rica.' Charles grinned. 'I like it.'

'More coffee, Ms Newman?' The waiter stood at her shoulder.

'Yes, but a fresh pot this time and hotter than the last cup you served me.'

The 'tut' from Charles made Taylor grimace, disgusted at herself. Her caustic comment struck her – too late – as ridiculously out of context. Why? The friendly Costa Rican vibe? Her own deflated sense of self-worth? Whatever the reason, her fresh link to her grandfather found her counting the number of insults she'd produced that day already. Too many – and it was only breakfast time. *Three weeks to break a habit. Three weeks to break a habit. Three weeks …*

'I'll take more from that pot you already have,' Charles said, smiling up at the waiter. 'Delicious stuff.'

The waiter poured and walked away.

'You made me look bad.' Taylor pouted.

'Oh, did you look bad?' Charles raised an eyebrow before scanning the paper, flicking the sheets and folding back the page to read an interesting article. 'Apparently there've been sightings of Annie in the Kremlin, a jazz bar in New Orleans, the Sydney Opera House, and the CIA's headquarters. Oh, and Blackpool – wherever that is.'

'Who's responsible for such competent journalistic insight?' Taylor glanced at the paper in Charles's hands. 'Of course. *The Daily Scoop*. Did you actually buy that?'

'It's not the official publication of the BBC, that's for sure.' Charles nodded slowly. 'But since the Annie story broke with its connection to this place, they're carrying it in the lobby. Someone here must be reading it.'

'You're enjoying it more than an Ivy Leaguer should.'

'Now who's making whom look bad?' Charles folded the newspaper with a flourish. 'Let's take a cruise around the bay. Time to check this place out properly.'

It struck Taylor she and Charles may have switched financial horses. 'Excuse me, Mr Money Bags, have you seen the credit card bill?'

'I realise we can't do this forever,' Charles said. 'But one last hurrah before you get your license and I become a house-showing widower again.'

'Except you were never home then, either.'

'True.' Charles sighed. 'Now I'm home all the time.'

'What *are* you going to do with yourself? Do you have any contacts in the financial world down here?' Taylor pictured Charles going to work with his briefcase bumping against linen short-clad legs instead of a suit.

Charles waggled his eyebrows. 'I have a plan. I'll fill you in when I'm up and running. Let's say, it's something I never expected to be doing.'

'Dog trainer? Spy? Hypnotist?'

'Cute.' Charles leaned across the table and kissed his wife. 'Now, let's scout out beachfront properties and find a boat.'

'Good idea.' Taylor perked up. 'And maybe we could find a realtor to pay for the boat.'

'That's my girl. Always thinking.' Charles stood to leave, placing a large tip on the table and smiling at the waiter.

Three weeks to change a habit. Be kind. She would make it her New Career's Resolution.

She threw her best smile at the waiter. His lips remained set in neutral.

The little sailboat ambled along, in no hurry to unfold the treasures of the shoreline to the passengers on board. The captain provided a running commentary concerning the little coves and the native plants, listing animals that favoured each one.

Donna Burk, from Remax, was all business, probing to assess exactly what the Newmans were in the market for. She read from the notes she'd taken over the phone. 'Something with privacy, yet open views to the water. Accessible to amenities but not in earshot or sight of the resorts. One point five to two million ... that's US dollars, correct?'

'Correct,' Taylor said, while framing a question to elicit the actual results she sought. 'That's a New York accent, right? How long have you been down here?'

'Coming up to fifteen years, now. Came on vacation with my ex. Lasted about a month after returning to the States. Couldn't work out why I'd give up all this to spend more time trying to rectify a mistake I made years before.'

Charles chuckled. 'Doubt I should leave you two alone.'

Taylor feigned more interest in Donna. 'So, were you a realtor in New York, too?'

'No. Investment banker. The quintessential rat race.'

Taylor flicked a glance at Charles, who turned away.

'I always say I've extended my life twenty years by moving here. Of course, the weather may help too, along with dropping the spousal boat anchor.' Donna smiled at Charles.

'Definitely not leaving you two alone,' Taylor said. Should she worry? Why did Charles close all those windows on his laptop when she walked by? *Enough. Focus.*

Though she was committed to leaving Ashcroft behind her and focusing on her own business, Taylor hadn't mellowed enough to miss taking a swing at Ashcroft if it presented itself. 'Must be a lot of foreign estate agents down here, hungry for this lifestyle.'

'Quite a few, but we all get along and there's plenty of buying and selling to go around. Was a bit shaky during the US recession, but things have been on the upswing ever since.'

'Anyone new on the scene?' Taylor thought the comment innocuous.

'Not that I'm aware of,' Donna replied. 'Oh, wait. There is one guy. Came down a little while ago. Rumours are conflicting. Some say he's a buyer, some say he's a seller. Not sure which as I haven't met him. However, I have access to more properties than anyone else here so let's dig into these brochures.'

Donna reached for the beach bag she'd placed on the deck. 'Here's a selection of homes new to the market.' She studied the coastline. 'We're coming up on one of them now, around that rocky outcrop there.'

The captain manoeuvred the boat expertly. Once around the outcrop, the view opened onto a small, crescent-shaped beach. A lone sailboat bobbed at anchor off shore.

'And there you have it, Casa Luna: four bedrooms, four baths, professional grade kitchen, satellite TV and Wi-Fi, on about an acre with manicured lawns, infinity pool, private beach, outdoor entertaining area. What do you think?'

No response. Donna looked up to find her clients focused on a tangle of arms, legs and dog on the sand next to a palm tree. Donna dropped the brochure. 'Oh, my …'

Taylor grabbed the binoculars that hung from the captain's chair. She needed only a moment to study the scene. Turning to Charles she whispered, 'Don't say anything, but that's Annie and I do believe she's having sex with a man … and a dog.'

Charles inhaled a long, slow breath before whispering back, awe in every syllable, 'I completely underestimated that woman.'

21 – THE HAND THAT ROCKS THE COFFEE POT ...

Yoga Man crawled off Annie on all fours. Annie struggled into a seated position and wrapped her arms protectively around her knees. A sailboat cruised by the beach.

A woman's voice drifted on the breeze from the deck towards the two sand-covered wrestlers. 'Er … not exactly a private beach, is it?'

A man's voice replied, 'Or maybe it's *too* private.'

Annie ducked her face down until the boat had passed on its way. 'I'm not moving until you fetch my beach robe.' She registered the mild hysteria in her voice.

Yoga Man took off at an impressive clip. Annie was left – eyeball to muzzle – with a chocolate Labrador. He panted, his ears flat against his head, a slight greying of the hairs around his mouth. She felt judged, coming up short of doggie expectations. This was no way a lady human should act. She broke eye contact and attempted to tie the remaining shreds of her bikini bottom together. She gave up and cast the tatters aside in disgust.

Yoga Man returned, threw the robe at Annie from a distance and averted his eyes. 'Please hurry. Jackson's injured.' Only then did Annie notice the Lab holding a front paw in the air.

'Oh, no! Did I hurt him?' Though impossible to know whose arm or leg or hip or head had caused the injury, taking the blame came naturally. Annie threw on her robe. 'There's blood.' She crawled closer to Jackson.

Before she could blink, Yoga Man was at her side, accessing the raised paw. 'It's okay, Jackson. Hold still.'

Annie tentatively wrapped her arms around Jackson's neck and was rewarded as he leaned into her. Yoga Man took his towel and wiped blood off Jackson's paw. He tutted and pointed to a jagged shard of shell protruding from a pad. 'Hold still. Good boy.' As he picked the shell from the pad, Annie noticed the man's fingernails, bitten to the quick; a strange juxtaposition to her no-worries image of a Yoga devotee. She stroked Jackson's neck and whispered in his ear all would be well.

'You're a dog lover then?'

It took a second for Annie to realise the man was talking to her, not Jackson. 'Oh, yes, though I've never owned a dog. Unsympathetic mother. Allergic husband.' Annie managed a weak smile. 'Sorry about falling on you. Didn't see you behind the tree.'

'Oh, that was you? I thought I'd been mugged by Julie Andrews.'

'Ugh.' Mortification. Time to channel her mother: deflect the blame. 'Is standing on your head your default setting? And is it safe for all us unsuspecting beach goers?'

'Beach goers, yes. Beach twirlers, no.'

Annie had to laugh. 'I'm An ... Dale, by the way.'

'I'm Rob. Nice to meet you, though those voyeurs on the sailboat probably assume we're on at least our third date.'

Annie groaned. 'With a bit of luck, they couldn't pick us out of a line-up.'

'We didn't commit a crime that would make it necessary. Did we?' Rob gave Annie a sideways glance. 'Anyway, I hadn't realised how much time I spent in salamba sirsasana until you and Julie came along. It used to be easier to find a safe spot to do it.' The corners of his mouth twitched.

Annie noted again his soft American lilt and had to catch herself, afraid she may reach out and pinch the face to check if it was real. When she dared to raise her eyes, she registered a few days' stubble and heavily salted hair that instead of washing him out, accentuated his tan. The most prominent features were his laughter lines. They formed arrows directing attention to his brown eyes, framing his mouth; his smile Harrison Ford-like lop-sided.

Annie wrenched her attention back to Jackson. 'I'm staying in the villa up that path. I haven't needed medical supplies yet, but if the medicine cabinet is as well stocked as the liquor cabinet, we'll find something to bandage his paw. It's my fault Jackson's hurt after all.'

'Very true,' Rob replied. 'Viciously attacked, he was. Though based on the state of your bikini, he fought back hard.'

Annie grabbed the shredded remains of her swimsuit and tried to hide it in her armpit.

Rob wrapped his towel around Jackson's paw, then effortlessly picked up his dog, cradling him in his arms. He followed Annie, first to her discarded flip-flops, then up the path to the villa.

The walk was silent, though – surprisingly – not completely awkward. Arriving on the lawn, Rob nodded at the mess under the hammock. 'What happened to your lunch?'

Annie scowled at the fallen plate, cheese and fruit sprayed across the grass. 'If you must know, the monkeys startled me, and I threw the plate. There was an icy water spill, a jump in the pool to warm up, followed by a bolt for the beach.'

'Had to attack a defenceless man and his dog in a hurry, did you?' It was Rob's turn to grimace. 'Too soon?'

Annie snorted. 'A bit. But I never miss an opportunity to pick a fight.' *What the heck?* She'd missed every opportunity to fight, making her comment tragic in her mind. She stooped to pick up the remains of lunch, slipping the discarded wedding ring under a cracker, before leading Rob into the house.

All business now, Annie located sterile pads, antiseptic lotions, Band-Aids and gauze wrap in one of the bathroom cabinets. She dumped the supplies onto the kitchen counter. Rob laid Jackson on his towel on the kitchen floor.

'That should cover it,' he said, smiling at Annie. 'So, new here?'

'How'd you guess?'

'Took you a while to find these supplies.'

'Or maybe I've been here ages, just never attacked anyone before.' Annie snapped her mouth shut. When had she become a stand-up comedienne?

Rob reached for another sterile pad. 'I see. Jackson, we've been singled out by this marauder for rough treatment. Get ready to run as soon as I give the signal.'

'But I have tuna fish as bait so Jackson will never leave. I also have wine, so you won't be able to either after a bottle or two.' *Oh, for God's sake, Annie!* 'I'm sorry. I …'

Rob laughed as he dabbed antiseptic lotion on the paw. 'Common mistake in rookie pirates. They apologise for everything, which is one more reason I don't think you've been attacking people here long.'

'You got me. Only a few days in this gorgeous spot.'

Rob nodded. Everything about this man radiated relaxation. Except the fingernails. The chewed, ragged stubs seemed completely at odds with his calm demeanour. His fingers struggled to peel the tape off the gauze wrap. Annie resisted the urge to offer assistance. The tape finally came free when Rob switched to his teeth.

He caught her peering at his nails and screwed his hands into fists around the tape dispenser. 'Throwback to a previous life. Had to change direction before I lost my hands completely. Hoping this place saves them.'

Annie lifted her eyes over Rob's head to the ocean view. 'Hoping it does the same for me, though my sanity may have been more at risk than my hands. Anyway, you don't need long for Guanacaste to grow on you, do you?'

Rob slowly and carefully wrapped Jackson's paw in the bandage. 'No, you don't, as I'm finding out to my cost. Was supposed to only be here a week myself. That was weeks ago. The sailboat absolutely refused to sail on by and my First Mate here was useless at quelling the mutiny.'

Jackson lolled over on one side with dewy eyes and a floppy tongue to take the belly rub Annie offered. This dog was going to milk his injury for all it was worth, and then some.

'Yep,' Annie said, 'He'd be pretty pathetic if subjected to torturous belly rubs. You're on your own, Captain.' Annie found herself quite interested in whether Captain Rob was on his own. She tried to fill the void of unasked questions. 'Must be nice to have complete control over your life, simply deciding to stay somewhere as long as the fancy takes you.' She'd forgotten this was now her life too.

'It's even nicer when the realisation hits you you've got no control over life at all.'

'Obviously, you've never been completely out of control.' *Great! Show him you're a bitter old witch, why don't you?*

'I've been controlled by others, all right,' Rob continued. 'But even worse was when I believed I controlled my own universe. Huge mistake.'

Annie folded her arms. 'That doesn't make any sense. Who wouldn't want to control their own universe? I've dreamed about doing that for years.'

Rob continued to wrap Jackson's paw, casting frequent short glances at Annie as he did so. 'Then I wish you more success with it than I had. I thought I controlled everything for a while, only to discover control is an illusion. You don't control anything. When you finally realise that, you jump ship for a life that doesn't pretend to offer you control.'

Annie buried her face in Jackson's neck. 'And here's me, believing I'd call the shots from now on.'

Rob finished the bandage and tied the ends. 'I'm sorry. I shouldn't have said anything. I'm not privy to your story.'

Annie pulled a few doggy hairs out of her mouth. 'It's a long story. Or rather a short one, lived over a long period of time.'

'And you must live it your way. All I can share is my story. I get up because the sun tells me it's time. I sail because the tides tell me it's time. I eat when my body tells me it's time and I sleep when I need to. There's no control in all that, simply the relief of accepting I'm nothing more

163

than a jellyfish or a piece of driftwood, swept along by the current. All my life I thought control would set me free. Took me way too long to work out giving up control would set me freer.'

Annie saw the truth of his words on Rob's face. For the first time in her life she identified true contentment in an expression – turned out it wasn't Lester's with a fresh pint in front of him.

Rob stroked Jackson's head. 'Alex Lowe said something about it being wonderful to be back among the oceans that reminded him of his vulnerability; his lack of control over the world.' He flashed Annie a sheepish grin. 'Actually, Lowe used those words about the mountains. I changed it to oceans because that's what speaks to me.'

'Who's Alex Lowe?'

'An American mountaineer.'

'Friend of yours?'

'No. Killed in an avalanche on a mountain in Tibet years ago.'

'That proved him right, then. He didn't control those mountains, did he?'

'No, he didn't. Let him be a reminder to you that you control nothing – and neither do the people who think they control you.'

What. The. Heck?

Rob ducked his chin and narrowed his eyes at Annie, a gentle reprimand before softening his features into a grin.

'Thank you.' Annie held Rob's gaze, not turning away; embarrassment and awkwardness forgotten. 'Thank you for that.'

'You're welcome.' Rob patted Jackson and stood up. 'But I lied about one thing. You absolutely control the coffee pot. It's the only thing in the world you do control.'

'Okay, okay. I get the hint.' Annie moved to stand up.

Rob rested his hand on her shoulder. 'I meant "you" figuratively. You, Dale, don't have to make anyone's coffee. They control their own coffee pots. I'll make it.'

Who the hell's Dale? Uh-oh ...

Annie battled the urge to share her life story, down to the minute details, such as her real name. She watched him open and close cupboard doors until he found what he needed. He worked the coffee maker expertly. She tried to picture Lester doing that. Then she tried to not picture Lester at all.

'So, big place for one person.' Rob looked around his surrounding as the coffee maker bubbled and hissed. 'And that's way too much wine, even for a whole crew of pirates. Expecting company?'

'Er … no, actually. If anything, I'm trying to get away from company.' *Jesus, Annie. Throw him out, why don't you?* 'I don't mean kidnapped company, just People-I-Know company.' Annie waved haphazardly at the remains of her lunch sitting on the kitchen counter. 'Broken crackers, anyone? Dirty fruit?'

'A gourmet chef, I see. Tempting but I'll stick with coffee.' He poured two mugs and sat back down on the kitchen floor with Jackson.

Annie pointed to the patio furniture. 'I do have nice chairs.'

'When you live on a sailboat, just stretching out your legs is a luxury. Chair or no chair.'

Jackson lay between the two coffee sippers. Annie luxuriated in the softness of Jackson's silky ears between her fingers, smiling at the thump of his tail, which continued wagging even though he was almost asleep. She relaxed and listened to the waves lap at the beach; she wasn't sure how long for.

Rob's voice made her jump. 'Well, I'd better get Jackson back to the boat while the tide's still low. Don't want to swim too far with him on my shoulders.'

'Right. Of course.' Annie smiled. 'And you don't want pirates to steal your boat while you lollygag up here.'

'Saving a dog's life is lollygagging, is it? You secretly detest animals, don't you?' Rob winked at Annie, then picked Jackson up and headed for the patio.

'But I *always* wanted a dog.' Impending loss overwhelmed her. The fact she'd never had a dog screamed of wasted time, missed opportunity. She blamed her mother, the 'no pets allowed' landlords. Lester. Life. Even Rob, as he carried her dog away.

Old Annie trailed behind the pair – control over her destiny question-able. Thanks to Rob's statement, she wasn't even sure if she was sup-posed to be trying to control anything. But she wanted to control this.

'I'm here for a while if you find yourself back in the cove. I'll even wash the fruit off next time.' Annie smiled, nonchalantly - going for not desperate, just inviting; indicative of good company with no expecta-tions. Who was she kidding?

'I may find myself back here. It's a great spot for salamba sirsasana. Or used to be. Thanks for the first aid supplies and the coffee.' Rob flicked his eyebrows upwards a couple of times – a swift action that re-mained in Annie's awareness long after he'd gone. He headed out across the lawn.

Did he look back at her? Annie thought so, then shook her head. She of all people knew you saw what you wanted to see.

Back in the kitchen, Annie tripped over something. Rob's towel lay in the middle of the floor.

22 – SOMEONE TO SEE YOU, MA'AM

Jane Williams's phone buzzed at six thirty on Sunday morning. National Criminal Intelligence Service wanted to talk to her. She wasn't surprised the Hardcastle case had been kicked upstairs to NCIS in London. She just wished they could have waited one more day. In her childhood police games, a call to action by Scotland Yard was the dream outcome. With the modern equivalent requesting her real-life attention, she felt cheated at not experiencing the excitement she'd expected. Maybe it was the early morning hour on her day off.

Rolling out of bed, she opened the wardrobe and lifted down the work suit hanging on the back of the door; always on duty. Agatha threw her a feline look of disgust that Jane recognised well. The lazy lap day her cat had been promised of watching reruns of *The Great British Bake Off* wasn't going to happen. Luckily, fourteen years of life with a police officer had trained Agatha to hope for a lap, prepare for a windowsill.

An hour later, Jane sat at her office computer, compiling everything she'd found on the mysterious Number Three into one file. It wasn't much, which was why, fifty-odd years later, he was still just 'Number Three'. She printed the original report of an anonymous tip called in from a phone box in Buckinghamshire. It led the police to a flat in St Albans in 1969. Jane recognised Pat's initial cocky belligerence in the transcript, followed by disbelief, followed by the painful realisation she'd been conned. Once more, Jane's heart softened for the probably-not-legally-married woman left behind to pick up the pieces and reinvent her life the best she could. Who had the right to judge Pat Rickman, or whatever her name was?

Jane printed out the last of the files just in time for the knock at her door.

'Commander Thorn to see you, ma'am.' WPC West moved aside to let a tall, imposing suit glide past her into the office. She offered tea, which the man refused, before closing the door.

The silver military-style buzz cut and toned physique suggested this was no regular paper pusher. Jane's hand lifted of its own accord to smooth down her blond bun. She hated women who acted that way in the office.

'Nice to meet you.' Jane thrust out a hand. 'Not sure which side of the desk I should sit when NCIS comes to call.'

'Happens often, does it?' Commander Thorn asked, flatly. 'Get a lot of visits from us around here, do you?'

'No, sir.' Jane's smile faded. *If that's how it's going to be.* 'Here's all I have on Number Three. Same as you have, I'm sure. Here are the interviews I've held with Pat Rickman. Bear in mind the initial interviews were conducted during the investigation of a possible kidnapping of Mrs Rickman's daughter, before we knew anything of the possible tie to Number Three. Nothing of interest in those interviews for you.'

Commander Thorn took the file with a glance over his glasses that said he'd be the judge of what was of interest to him. He read the transcript of the first interview with Pat Rickman. The corners of his mouth twitched.

'So, did you corroborate the story?' Thorn's eyes could have pierced armour.

'What story?'

'That Mrs Rickman always does her shopping on a Wednesday? Interview all the market stallholders, did you?'

'Well, I ... I ... didn't think it import—'

'Kidding, Williams, kidding.' Thorn threw the file back on the desk. 'If we're going to spend our Sunday together, we'd better at least have a laugh or two.'

Oh, wait until you meet Pat. She'll show you a laugh or two.

Jane picked up the file, walked around her desk and opened the door. 'Let's laugh our way to Verston then, shall we?'

The car wound through St Albans, heading for the A5, the drive punctuated with questions and answers about St Albans and the surrounding villages.

'Pretty countryside, nice pubs, lots of expensive cars and houses. Not a bad beat, for you, Williams.'

Not bad at all if you don't mind running street battles on a Saturday night with the local teenagers and enough theft to fell a forest in paperwork. Much like any other city. 'Yes, nice houses, sir.'

Commander Thorn looked out of the car window at the imposing silhouette of St Albans Cathedral. 'Worth a visit, is it? That church?'

'That *church* marks the oldest continuous site of Christian worship in Britain. It has the longest nave in England, medieval wall paintings …' Jane glanced sideways and gave up. 'They filmed part of *Johnny English* there. You know, the Rowan Atkinson spy spoof. Pretended St Albans Cathedral was Westminster Abbey. That's one of *your* churches, I believe.'

Thorn smiled. 'Touché, Williams, touché.'

Fifteen minutes later, they passed the Verston village green and its tiny church. Thorn opened the file again. 'Says here Pat Rickman lived, briefly, in several other Hertfordshire villages and towns since running all the way from St Albans in the early 1970s. Wonder why she settled here, though it seems a nice place.'

'Nice village, yes.' Jane indicated to turn left onto a side street. 'It straddles the old Roman Watling Street. The original road marched Romans legions from Dover to London to Wroxeter.' She rolled her eyes at herself. *A history lesson? Seriously?*

'History buff, are we?'

'Dad was.'

'Then I would have liked him.'

Jane fought to contain the spread of a rather goofy smile. How ridiculous. As if she cared what this man thought about her father.

Thorn studied the file again. 'Some interesting charges on Lester's credit card. He's planning a trip back to Costa Rica based on these plane tickets. And someone who's out there already is racking up clothing bills.'

Jane pulled up at the kerb in front of Pat's flat. 'I would be too if I'd won the lottery.'

'Can't imagine I'd need my current wardrobe,' Thorn said. 'I'd probably burn my suits before getting on the plane.' He threw the file on the dashboard.

Thorn craned his neck up at the block of flats in front of him before opening the car door. 'I've decided not all the houses are nice houses on your beat. Please tell me there's a lift, or Pat lives on the ground floor.'

'No, and yes, sir.' Jane grabbed the file and headed to the main entrance. 'One out of two isn't bad.'

The knock at Pat's door went unanswered. Three times. 'Strange,' Jane muttered. 'She's always in.'

'Except Wednesdays, when she's at the market,' Thorn said. 'I read the file.'

Jane couldn't decide yet if he was annoying or entertaining.

Thorn tilted his head towards a window. 'I'm guessing the twitching curtain means the neighbour's willing to provide us with information.'

Jane followed Thorn's head tilt and indeed saw a shadow in the window. One minute later, the pair was on Becky Dagny's sofa.

'I told Pat I wasn't going to lie to a copper for her,' Becky stated for the record. It was obvious to Jane she'd said no such thing. '"No way am I getting wrapped up in your shenanigans," I told her straight out. Not when they water bowl people in our country these days.'

Becky had held up under torture long enough to get Commander Thorn's name. She headed into the kitchen to make tea.

'Bring a large bowl of water along with my tea, please,' Thorn shouted into the kitchen. Becky's startled head shot around the corner, her eyes wide.

Jane stared, open-mouthed, at Thorn. 'She thinks you're going to waterboard her!'

'No, she doesn't. She thinks I'm going to water bowl her.' Thorn raised his finger to shush Jane as Becky came back into the room.

Once the tea was served and a large Tupperware container of water placed on a doily on the coffee table, Becky sat down to squeal.

'Costa Rica. She's gone to Costa Rica. That's in Africa,' Becky stated assertively.

Jane gave Thorn a minuscule shake of her head.

'And how did you come by this knowledge, Mrs Dagny?' Thorn eyed the water in the container. 'Did Mrs Rickman mention it to you directly?'

'Yes. No. Not directly.' Becky also eyed the water. 'I was sweeping outside the window and saw a ticket on her table, you see. That's why Pat didn't need to tell me, because I already knew. She would've told me, if I hadn't known already.'

'I'm sure she would, Mrs Dagny,' Jane said. 'Would she also have shared how she afforded the ticket, if you didn't already know? She didn't strike me as having the means to head off to exotic locations on a whim.'

'It was Lester's name on the credit card next to the ticket.' Becky sought answers from the ceiling. 'Must admit, that's a strange how'd you do given Lester and Pat aren't what you'd call bosom buddies. Excuse my language.' Becky avoided Commander Thorn's eyes and pulled her cardigan over her ample chest. 'Should I have called it in?'

'No, no, Mrs Dagny.' Commander Thorn narrowed his eyes. 'The drone picked up that detail.'

Jane shot him the kind of scathing look she usually reserved for rookie subordinates.

Becky's eyes leapt out on stalks. 'How long's Pat been under surveillance? And can the drone see me through these walls? I do the hoovering every day. It's the breakfast dishes aren't done before lunch. Nothing in the law against that.' Becky straightened up; the first indication of back-bone since the torture session began.

'You're right, Mrs Dagny.' Jane cut in before her smirking superior could respond. 'There's no law against that or we'd all be in prison, wouldn't we? So, when did Mrs Rickman leave for Costa Rica?'

'That's in Africa.' Thorn nodded seriously at Jane.

'I saw her get into a taxi yesterday morning.' Becky rubbed her chin, making sure she got the details right. 'Didn't ask me to watch the flat while she was gone. She probably forgot.'

'Probably.' Jane made a note in her pad. 'When you saw her ticket through the window, was there a second ticket? For Lester, maybe?'

'No, couldn't read the small print, what with those filthy windows she has. Not everyone's as good at housekeeping as me.'

'Except for the breakfast dishes,' Thorn said.

Jane cleared her throat to cover her snort. She dabbed at her nose. 'Thank you for your help, Mrs Dagny. We'll get anything else we need from Mr Hardcastle if he's still in town.' She handed over her card. 'If you'd give us a call when Mrs Rickman gets home, we'd be grateful.'

'Oh, I will.' Becky nodded violently. 'Not one to hold out on the coppers, me.'

As the trio headed for the door, Thorn turned and gave one last nod in the direction of the water bowl. 'Keep that handy, please.'

Back in the car, Jane glared at the man in the passenger seat, her hands gripping the steering wheel tight enough to turn her knuckles white. 'Keep that handy? Seriously?'

'What?' Thorn said. 'What? I'm trying to prevent the bucolic suburbs from turning into the mean streets of the city, one terrified old lady at a time. Anyway, what do you think? Pat's done a bunk to hide out with Annie?'

Jane wrestled her attention from insane interrogator to subject at hand. She turned the key in the ignition. 'None of it makes sense. I usually spot a lie a mile off, but Pat and Annie? I can't believe they're hiding much.'

'So, this running off's out of character? A holiday perhaps, rather than a ruse to escape St Albans' finest?'

'Excuse me, sir, but the best at Scotland Yard lost several Great Train Robbers in South America. Even after they put them in prison, they managed to lose them again. I'm sure I'm allowed to misplace little old Pat if you boys are allowed to specialise in losing convicted felons.' Jane scrunched up her shoulders and ducked, waiting to find out if she'd gone too far.

Thorn laughed all the way to Lester's flat.

'Can't wait to find out what you threaten Lester with.' Jane pulled the car up outside the Hardcastles' flat, a mere stone's throw the other side of the cricket pitch from Becky's. 'Remember, long after you've scarpered back to London, I've got to deal with the hysteria you've left behind. If Becky talks to the press about being waterboarded, I'm not taking the fall for you.'

'I didn't waterboard her, I water *bowled* her.' Thorn hopped out of the car and buttoned his jacket. He stopped at the main door and said over his shoulder, 'Can't get lucky twice, right? Top floor? No lift?'

'Correct, sir. How long will it take for you to catch your breath and get the water bowls set up?' Jane sprinted up two flights of stairs to stay ahead of the insults.

'Mr Hardcastle? I'm Superintendent Williams of the St Albans Special Crimes Unit and this is Commander Thorn of NCIS. We need to ask you a few questions about your wife and mother-in-law.'

'Oh, my good gawd!' Lester sagged against the wall. 'I thought that stupid Becky woman was joking when she called to say you were coming.'

'So much for the element of surprise,' Thorn whispered over Jane's shoulder.

'We have a few questions, sir. Won't take long.' Jane headed past Lester into the living room.

The flat's shabbiness spoke of making do. Someone had tried to make it a home up until about a decade ago: no updated photos, just old pillows, worn rugs and heavy, tired curtains. The empty spaces in the china cabinet exuded an air of having given up all expectations.

'For the record,' Lester said, as the trio took their places, 'I never agreed to this scarpering song and dance. I wanted to go to Benidorm. No one runs away to Benidorm, do they? You don't even need to win the lottery to go there.'

'It's all right, Mr Hardcastle,' Jane said. 'No one's questioning why you went to Costa Rica. Many people go there who haven't won the lottery. However, we need to ascertain why Annie hasn't returned with you and why you paid for Mrs Rickman, your mother-in-law, to fly out soon after you returned home.'

'Annie did return with me. She just didn't stay home with me.' Lester jutted out his chin. 'Now, what's this about Pat? I never paid for Pat to go anywhere. Why on earth would I buy her a holiday? She owes me a fortune in borrowed drinks money as it is.'

'According to your credit card records, you bought a plane ticket to Costa Rica a few days ago. We thought it was for you. Now we believe, based on Mrs Dagny's statement, you bought the ticket for Mrs Rickman. She flew out yesterday.' Thorn pulled out a copy of Lester's credit card expenditures from a file and handed it across the coffee table.

Lester studied it. 'Well I never! Dinner for the Irish lassies was expensive, wasn't it?' He drew his fingers with little resistance through minimal hair and sat back.

'That may be, Mr Hardcastle.' Thorn tapped the paper. 'But may I draw your attention down many lines to the St Albans Travel Agency charge of £600 for a round trip ticket to Liberia in Costa Rica, and another £500 for a cash withdrawal at the airport there.'

Lester followed Thorn's finger with his eyes, his mouth slightly open. He reached for his wallet and poked about inside it. 'Well I never.' Lester breathed. 'That cow stole my credit card!'

'You expect us to believe you didn't fund Mrs Rickman's escape? Why would Mrs Rickman fly out just over a week after you got back? It all seems rather suspicious, doesn't it?' Thorn stopped to draw breath. 'What about your father-in-law, Mr Hardcastle? What about Number Three? And where's the stolen money now?'

Lester sought enlightenment from the bank statement, from Jane's face, from the ceiling, and most definitely from the half-finished beer on the sideboard – at ten in the morning. 'I don't know anything about any of that.'

'You expect us to believe you, Mr Hardcastle?' Jane asked. 'You expect us to believe you knew nothing of these escape plans when you bought Mrs Rickman a ticket to join her daughter? Come on now.'

'Honest!' Lester's panic came across as genuine. 'If you must know, Annie left me. Forgot to mention where she was going. I've no idea how Pat got my credit card or why Annie would want Pat in Costa Rica. She could hardly stand her mother in the same room for five minutes. I'm only sure of one thing: I'd never heard of Number Three. Not until those reporters prattled on about it when they cornered me at the pub. That's when I confronted Pat. She didn't give me any answers, either. So, I have nothing to say except I'm innocent.'

Thorn nodded his head slowly. Jane scratched away in her notebook.

The silence lingered. Finally, Thorn stood up and headed for the door. 'Well, Mr Hardcastle, that's all for now. Don't go anywhere. We'll be seeing you again soon.' He opened the door and waved Jane through ahead of him.

Back in the car, Jane fastened her seatbelt. 'We have plenty of cause for a search warrant.'

'We'd have a lot more if you'd let me water bowl him.' Thorn folded his arms and stared straight ahead.

Four hours later, armed with a search warrant, Jane and Thorn stood on the threshold of the living room in Lester's flat while the evidence collection team in white overalls searched the place, top to bottom.

Lester sat on the sofa, head in hands, muttering, 'I'm telling the truth.'

No one in the room batted an eyelid, immune to declarations of innocence.

Commander Thorn regarded Lester. 'You have to admit, Mr Hardcastle, there's room for scepticism here. Your wife goes missing right as the papers report she may be involved in a crime, and you ship your mother-in-law out of the country. According to your credit card statements, someone's buying themselves a new wardrobe. Or should I say a new identity? Now, NCIS isn't much, but the St Albans police caught on quite fast. They think it appears …' at this Thorn checked his notebook, 'and I quote here, "fishy". Do I have that right, Superintendent Williams?'

'Very fishy indeed.' Jane nodded. 'Should I get a bowl of water, sir?'

Thorn started a little and pulled Williams aside. 'Not in front of the lads, now,' he whispered. 'They won't keep my secret methods secret. Get my meaning?'

'Oh, I do, sir. Don't want to end up in front of the war crimes tribunal, do we, now?' Jane stared straight ahead.

'I knew you'd be trouble.' Thorn stifled a grin before turning back to Lester. 'So, what do you have to say about all this, Lester? Can I call you Lester? We're going to be spending a lot of time together, so we may as well get friendly.'

Lester turned his head slowly from one officer to the other. 'Think this is a joke, do you?'

An officer rose rapidly from the table where he'd been working on Annie's laptop. 'You'd better see this, sir.' He turned the screen to face Thorn.

Jane and Thorn strode over and stood behind the officer as he scrolled through hundreds of entries in a search database.

'Well, well, well.' Thorn patted the officer on the shoulder and, placing his hands behind his back, turned towards Lester. 'Our techno-wizard here has found thousands of searches for flights and hotels all over the world, dating back a long time. Seems this little holiday you went on wasn't simply a post-lottery getaway. It was a reconnoitre planned long before the win. The question is, a recce for what? A bolt-hole as the noose closed in on you?'

'Believe me,' Lester whimpered, 'I've not been involved in any searches or recces. I can barely even switch a computer on, let alone find a plane flight on it. Annie never said nothing to me about going anywhere before the lottery win. As far as I knew, we didn't have a penny to spare for a trip to Bognor, forget foreign holidays.'

Thorn and Williams nodded at each other, Lester completely convincing as a non-techno-wizard.

'Come on now,' Thorn said. 'How long's your wife been planning her, or should I say, *your* escape? I assume you've just come back here for a few days to pick up bits and pieces? Didn't think we were onto you yet? But here we are. You'd better come clean. Where were you planning to meet up with the ladies? According to these travel searches, it could have been almost anywhere in the world. We'll find your little gang eventually. Save yourself and us a little trouble here and talk.'

Lester threw his hands up in the air and let them slap down hard on his knees. 'I'm married to a little part-time wedding cake decorator, fish and chips on a Friday night, a few drinks with the boys, nose clean, decent life. That's all. Until a few days ago, when Pat tells me a cockamamie story about Annie's father – which even Pat couldn't say for certain was true – and now you want me to believe I've been hiding millions of quid for years. You're off your rocker.'

'He has a point,' Jane whispered over Thorn's shoulder. 'About you being off your rocker. Sir.'

Thorn turned to respond but was interrupted by a knock on the door. Jane swiped fake sweat from her brow. Voices carried through the hallway and an officer appeared in the living room.

'Thought you'd want these, sir. They're from Pat Rickman's flat.'

Thorn took the file from the officer who was running the team searching Pat's home. Thorn flicked through the contents, then threw a large pile of newspaper clippings down in front of Lester.

Lester picked up each piece as though he'd been handed nuclear waste.

The yellowed photos and headlines, all of them related to the Great Train Robbery of 1963, provided the investigators with all they needed. 'Right. You do not have to say anything,' Jane recited, as she took the offered handcuffs from PC Jarvis, 'but it may harm your defence if you do not mention when questioned something which you later rely on in court. Anything you do say may be given in evidence.'

Lester's face froze, not even a blink as he stood as instructed, placed his hands behind his back as instructed and wobbled out of his door, flanked by two uniformed officers. Jane stared down from the window as Lester stepped out of the main door into the barrage of questions from the reporters in the carpark. He ducked into the police car, his shell-shocked eyes peering out of the window as the car drove off.

According to the police driver, Lester uttered only one phrase on the way to the police station: 'Bloody lottery tickets.'

At the station, Jane and Thorn sat in her office sipping coffee; Lester being processed in the holding area ready to be sent up to London. The file of musty newspaper clippings taken from Pat's flat sat on the desk between the two investigators.

'I don't get it.' Thorn stroked his chin. 'Why live the way they seem to have lived for decades if they had the money? I mean, most of us could lie low for a while, a year, five years even. But fifty years? What would be the point of stealing the money in the first place if it wasn't going to be used for generations?'

'I agree.' Jane held her cup in both hands, sipping slowly. 'Let's face it, the Hardcastles and Rickmans we've met don't strike you as masterful long-term planners, do they?'

'Someone was planning something judging by those computer searches.' Thorn slapped his mug down on the desk and rubbed his eyes. 'Someone had been planning a runner long before we got involved.'

'Perhaps they knew about the money all these years but only just got access to it. Could this "Number Three" have died recently?' The idea hung in the air, mingling with the aroma of cheap coffee.

'Possible,' Thorn replied. 'Though if Pat's telling the truth about never having laid eyes on her husband since 1969, why would he leave her or Annie the money?'

'Guilt, maybe? Men can be such bastards, though a few show a glimmer of remorse given enough time.'

'Ouch.' Thorn raised his eyebrows. 'Going to need something stronger than coffee before I hear the story behind that comment.'

'You're going to need about two weeks straight if you want all the details, though my ex is hardly worth ruining a good bottle of wine over.' Jane clamped her mouth shut and squirmed in her chair. Sharing wasn't her thing, typically. She cleared her throat. 'How much money would be left after all this time anyway? Number Three would've spent a lot of dough trying to stay out of sight.'

'Sharp investor?' Thorn steepled his fingers and tapped them together. 'We could join our two theories and at least give the lads and lassies in forensics something to get their teeth into. Let's search for a recently deceased man in his late seventies with an investment portfolio. Oh, and a will leaving it all to a long-lost daughter.'

'And if we get lucky, he'll have "Number Three" tattooed on his bicep.' Jane leapt up and caught the pencil that flew her way. Before she reached the door to give directions for the database search, WPC West knocked and entered without waiting.

'Excuse me, ma'am. We just got word on Annie Hardcastle's whereabouts. Tip from a boat charter captain that she was seen on a beach having … er … "intimate relations". Possibly a threesome with a …' PC West ran her finger around the collar of her shirt. 'You'd better read the report.'

Jane took the sheet of paper and read it twice before handing it to Thorn. 'Explains why she left Lester, then.'

'Tells me not only men can be bastards.' Thorn ducked as his pencil whistled past his ear.

179

23 - ENTER STAGE CENTRE

Pat stood in the entrance of the Paradise Resort and gaped. The Paradise Resort gaped back.

It was the sheer expanse of it all: the wide-legged, rainbow-print trousers and the knee-length tunic covered in a fish motif that literally swam before the eyes with each movement. It was the oversized floppy hat in neon green, wrapped in a floral scarf floating out behind like a semaphore flag. It was the pink-framed sunglasses and the four strings of glass beads.

'A tropical laundry pile,' muttered a woman to her companion as she passed Pat.

'Thought you were working on changing a habit,' replied the companion.

Pat dropped her gaze to her outfit, then scowled down her nose at the woman. She studied the lobby again and decided it matched the brochure she'd found on Annie's hallway table as she left with Lester's credit card. She strode over to the main desk, dragging her leopard-print suitcase behind her.

'My good man,' Pat said to the man behind the desk, recalling the phrase from an old Agatha Christie film. 'I need a key to Mrs Annie Hardcastle's room. She's my daughter.' Pat pushed her tongue up between her front teeth and her lip and smacked it noisily. She wouldn't be taking any grief from anyone in the battle to save her daughter.

'I'm sorry, Mrs—' The guest manager peered under the brim of the enormous sunhat, in a seeming quest for eyes.

'R.I.C.K.M.A.N. Did you understand that?'

'I speak five languages, madam.'

'Then you'll understand when I say you need to give me the key to Annie's room.' Pat held her hand out over the counter, the hand that had smacked the arm of the bellhop who'd tried to take her suitcase from the taxi.

'I'm sorry, Mrs Rickman We can't give out the names and room numbers of guests.'

'But I'm her mother so let's not argue about it.' Pat dabbed sweat from her brow.

'Sorry, madam. I can't disclose guest details.'

'Oh, for gawd's sake. Bloody terrorist rules.' Pat slumped against the desk, the strain of her journey evident in her sigh. Saving Annie may be harder than she'd anticipated. She wound her fingers through the multitude of glass beads swinging from her neck, clanking them against the counter. An idea: a cup of tea would soon put things to rights. She straightened up quickly and poked the guest manager in the chest. 'Give me a room then. I'll stay here until I find her. Are the sheets changed between guests? And I'll be checking the skirting boards for dust, mind.'

The manager drew back from the finger and took the proffered credit card, gingerly. 'Of course, madam. Room 242. My colleague will carry your bags and show you the amenities.'

'No need,' Pat snapped back. 'Got myself this far. Certain I can find a room by myself, but what's this credit card for? I already have one. What I need is the room key.'

'That is the room key, madam. Insert it into the slot and wait for the green light.'

'Oh ay. Suppose I'll be charged each time I stick it in.' Just because it was Lester's money, didn't mean she was going to waste it. Her new wardrobe, however, had been a necessary expense. She planned on blending in.

Pat snatched the keycard and marched off, swatting the bellhop again as he timidly reached out to take her suitcase.

She returned to the lobby four times: to get help with the keycard, then to get help to turn the lights on, then to get help to open the patio door, then to work the kettle. Pat finally settled down on the chair on her patio with her handbag on her lap and a cup of tea made from the teabags she'd brought over in her suitcase.

At dinner, the chef received a complaint. 'No reputable establishment would send out a dessert trolley without a sherry trifle on it.'

On the upside, Pat enjoyed the chocolate she found on her pillow, once it had been explained no one had broken into her room to leave it there.

The following morning, Pat sat at her breakfast table, eating what barely passed for porridge in her eyes. Boiled eggs – the chef had to do an internet search for 'bread soldier' instructions – were custom-served in a shot glass when Pat insisted on an egg cup. She frowned at two 'toffs' sitting at the table next to her. The woman said to the man, 'No, Charles, I have never made that much fuss. Ever.'

Once breakfast was finished, the enormous purple caftan with sequin trim around the neckline launched from the breakfast table and set sail for the front desk.

'My good man,' Pat said, 'I need to file a police report. My daughter, Annie Hardcastle, is missing and I've searched everywhere.' This was true, as the shrieks from many a startled staff member in various maid's closets and service hallways could verify. 'I don't want to involve Her Majesty's armed services, but I will if I have to.'

The manager sighed, cast a subversive glance over each shoulder, then leaned conspiratorially over the desk. 'Mrs Rickman, I'm not at liberty to share this, but Ms Hardcastle is not registered at this hotel. Her whereabouts are unknown to me, and trust me, I would tell you if I knew.' He oozed sincerity.

Pat rolled the voluminous sleeves of her caftan above her elbows. 'Well, here's a fine how'd you do. Now what?'

'Perhaps we can be of assistance.'

Pat turned. The toffs were smiling at her.

'We'll take it from here.' The man smiled at the manager, who offered a radiant smile back.

'Mrs Rickman, is it?' The woman took Pat's arm and led her over to one of the plush sofas. Pat tolerated this only because the straightest, whitest enamel bling she'd ever seen disoriented her. She couldn't take her eyes off the teeth.

'I'm Taylor and this is my husband, Charles. We couldn't help over-hearing you're Annie's mother. We made friends with your daughter while she was staying at this hotel. She's no longer here but perhaps we can take you to her.'

Pat dragged her gaze from teeth to eyes. 'Now then, why would you do that? We've been having a lot of trouble with people trying to be our friends since we won the lottery. Why should I trust you?'

'We're aware of the lottery win.' Charles smiled sweetly. 'But do we seem in need of money, Mrs Rickman?'

Pat raked Charles up and down with narrowed eyes before focus-ing attention back on Taylor's teeth. She squinted at the face; the high cheekbones, the dark rim around the brown irises, the furrow between the brows. She'd seen this woman with the enamel of an angel some-where before. She just couldn't place where.

Pat pondered, torn between need and suspicion. 'Nooo, you've obvi-ously got plenty of money. But we must be careful, mustn't we? We're targets of scammers and cutthroats now, you know. Mark my words, I'm being watched as we speak. Have you seen the papers? Me and Annie on every page.' Not completely accurate, but Pat figured no one here knew better.

'So, you've seen today's press about you and the Great Train Robber?' Charles blew out his cheeks. 'Bit of a surprise. Annie didn't mention it.'

Pat's eyes flew open. 'Costa Rica knows about it already? We've got to find Annie before the press does. She needs to hear it from me.' Pat swung round to grab her handbag off the sofa, making all her jewellery jangle.

'You mean Annie doesn't know any of this?' Taylor's face moved from shock to concern. Pat registered the change. It made her trust the teeth a little more.

'We'll rent a car right now and take you to her.' Taylor stood to go. 'When you've changed, meet us in front of the hotel.'

Pat smoothed down the front of her outfit. What was wrong with the caftan? Elizabeth Taylor used to wear caftans.

Taylor turned to Charles as they walked away from Annie's mother. 'Do I have something caught in my teeth?' She poked around her gums with her tongue trying to find the source of Pat's scrutiny.

'No. Do I have something purple stuck in my eye?' Charles glanced over his shoulder. Pat and her spinnaker were entering the elevator.

'Promise me she's going to change into something less purple dinosaur-like.'

Charles smirked. 'You know, if you want to better connect with someone you should emulate their dress code.'

Taylor smiled. 'Then I hope purple suits you.'

'Hey, you're the one wants Annie's business enough to get involved in all this. You play the dinosaur.'

Twenty minutes at the concierge desk saw the Newmans holding a set of car keys. Turning towards the lobby, Taylor froze, eyes wide, as the newly changed Pat tottered towards them. Taylor instantly longed for the subtlety of purple dinosaur. She pushed Charles's mouth closed with a finger.

In the car, Taylor navigated using the Google Maps app on her phone. The real estate brochure for the newly listed villa rippled in the blast of air conditioning.

Pat leaned over from the back seat to study the brochure in Taylor's hand. 'What on earth's my Annie doing living there?' She gasped at each photo. 'And how's she going to keep it all clean?'

Charles took a left at Taylor's behest. 'I'm sure there's a staff available, Mrs Rick—'

'Call me Pat, dear. Seeing as you're helping out.'

'Will do, Pa—'

'Oh, my good gawd and bless her heart!' Pat slapped Charles's arm, causing a swerve into the middle of the road. 'She needs a place big enough for me to move in with her and Lester.' Pat threw herself back in her seat and chuckled at the ceiling. 'This Casa Loony place will be perfect for us all.'

Taylor looked at the brochure for Casa Luna, then at Pat. Correction wasn't worth it. Maybe correction wasn't even appropriate.

It took thirty minutes to find Casa Luna, and that only because they missed the turn onto the secluded, unsignposted driveway three times. The car finally pulled up in front of a solid wooden gate. It gave away nothing of what lay behind.

'I have to give it to her,' Charles whispered to Taylor. 'Brilliant move to hide under everyone's noses.' He turned to Pat in the back seat. 'There's probably an intercom system somewhere. Let's check if Annie's prepared talk to us. If she's gone into hiding, she may not be too willing to open the gate.'

'My Annie hasn't turned into that daft Howard Hughes overnight.' Pat sniffed. 'Let her mother talk to her.' She started to get out of the car.

Taylor shot out of the car to apprehend Pat's progress. 'She's not expecting you, right? It may spoil the surprise if she hears from you first. Why don't you let me check if she's in?'

Charles appeared somewhat confused but kept quiet. As he and Taylor walked to the intercom box, almost hidden in the vegetation beside the gate, Taylor whispered, 'Don't want to find ourselves nothing more than a taxi service, do we? Got to get ourselves in the door too.'

She pressed the intercom button, then threw a glance over her shoulder at the waiting woman. *This plan had better work.*

185

24 - MUMMY DEAREST

Lester not breathing down her neck if she left her dishes in the sink was still akin to heaven. Apparently, his own dirty dishes added value to the flat. Annie revelled in it; the luxury of complete decision-making autonomy and the right to ignore the opinions of all animate – and inanimate –entities.

She'd refused the maid service included with the villa. 'It ruins the creative juices,' she explained to the rental agent in a wispy voice with elongated vowels. Even Jason Bourne wouldn't have thought up that ruse, she was sure.

The dishes waited, non-judgementally. She walked the beach, collected shells, watched the birds dip and dive in the morning light, and inhaled the salty aroma of her new home. She strolled back for coffee, made a grocery list and called it into the store, thankful the owner spoke some English. No wandering up and down the Tesco's aisle for her anymore – another delight. A twinge of loss for England took her by surprise. Tesco's dredged up images of custard over Christmas pudding, the memory so intense she swore she could smell it. She gave herself a mental slap. Amazon would deliver custard powder and Christmas pudding. Even in the summer. Even in Costa Rica. She made a note to check on that as she took a shower.

As she returned to the kitchen, a loud, obnoxious buzzing sounded in her left ear. She spun around. After the third buzz, she identified the source as the intercom box on the kitchen wall. An irritated tut escaped her lips, directed at the delivery people. They'd been instructed not to use the buzzer as it was a sure way to destroy a complete novel. It was also a way to ensure the delivery people didn't wait for her to pick up the cooler they left at the gate. She wanted to retain her privacy.

Placing her hand on her heart to still the pounding, Annie morphed into Dale Dante; though even to her ears the American accent came across as somewhat unnatural.

'Whaaaad?' She'd always been confused as to why Americans changed the 't' to a 'd' in the pronunciation but not the spelling. She almost added 'Go away', but at the last second changed her mind. The only person who knew she was here was Rob. Didn't want to scare him off.

'Annie, it's Taylor,' a sickeningly familiar voice said. 'We're worried about you and came over to check on you.'

Not good. Not good at all. If they could find her, others could too. 'You have the wrong house. This is Dale Dante. Author. From New York.' She screwed her eyes shut in chagrin. Jason Bourne would never have given away that much, even of his fake identify. 'Don't disturb me again.' A little power crept back into her demeanour.

A different voice now: 'Annie, stop being daft and let us in. I need to pee.'

Oh, say it ain't so! Annie stopped breathing. Her new-found freedom fled, all hope of escape evaporating into thin air at the sound of her mother's words.

'Did you hear me? Open the gate.'

Old Annie acquiesced. Pavlov demanded it. Jason Bourne sucked on his thumb and gave all the secret files to his mother.

Saying nothing, Annie pressed the button to open the gate. She stood at the front door in disbelief as the car glided down the driveway between the swaying trees; the gentle undulation of the branches an odd juxtaposition to the approaching storm.

Annie raked her brain, searching for how her mother had known she'd be in Costa Rica. All pondering ceased as the car door flew open. She'd been mistaken. This couldn't be her mother after all.

Three-inch-high wedge heels appeared out of the back seat first, followed by varicose veins, then florescent green Capri trousers topped off by a halter neck blouse displaying ample bosom and acres of pasty white, wrinkly skin. The terry cloth turban with floral appendage hid all but the grey roots. Large, hoop earrings completed the apparition. Annie gulped rapid, shallow breaths, reaching out her hand to steady herself against the door jamb.

'Said she'd be overwhelmed, didn't I?' Pat threw a victorious smile at her driver, then lurched forward to hug her daughter.

Cinched in a tight, sweaty hug, Annie gaped over the shoulder of her mother at Charles and Taylor. They had the sense to look apologetic. Annie held their eyes, raising both palms from her mother's back.

'Right ho. Enough of this huggy stuff. I need to pee.' With that, Pat tottered past Annie into the house and tripped across the tile. She turned in various directions before locating a hallway and heading off down it.

Annie stood stock-still as her old life gate-crashed her new. Was it normal to feel violated by a visit from your mother? To feel such anger that she'd found you?

The rage had to go somewhere. Annie turned towards Taylor. 'What have I ever done to you?'

'Sorry to barge—'

'How did you find me? And how the hell did my mother get—'

'We couldn't let your mother rampage around the hotel—'

'Who else knows I'm here?'

'No one, we—'

'Don't tell me Lester's here, too!'

Charles lifted his hands. 'Let us explain, Annie. Give us a minute. Please.'

Annie's pulse pounded in her ears and chest, short breaths pulling humid air into her throat. Fear, anger and resentment made a mockery of the jolly, tinkling fountain in the courtyard. 'This had better be good.' She blocked entry to the villa with folded arms.

Charles thrust his hands into his pockets. 'Let me talk, please.'

Taylor folded her arms too and jutted out a hip at the same time Annie did. This elicited a quick head turn from Charles, one to the other. Annie tried to work out why he appeared so confused, but she had bigger things to worry about. Mainly the pasty white apparition in her bathroom and how long it was going to haunt her.

Charles moistened his lips with the tip of his tongue. 'We thought you were far away from here. We didn't blame you for going into hiding at all, what with all the press reports about your family.'

Annie's mouth opened to speak. Charles raised his palm to stop her. 'We didn't come looking for you. We were too busy trying to sort out our own lives. Honestly, we never thought we'd bump into you again. Then you popped up on the beach with your … er … friend … friends.'

Annie was certain her crows feet would split if her eyes got any wider.

'We didn't let on that we recognised you. You had a right to your privacy and the paparazzi were still trying to find you, in fact, even more now.'

Again, Annie opened her mouth to speak. Again, Charles's hand gesture silenced her.

'We happened to bump into that woman, I mean, your mother, at the hotel. She was making a scene about getting the police involved in finding you. We thought we could handle it more discreetly. We were trying to help.' Charles shrugged and looked hopeful.

Annie nodded slowly. She knew – Lord knows, she knew – how much fuss her mother could make and maybe it wouldn't have taken long for the police to find her. Maybe this was the best way. Maybe.

Annie began to ask about the references to her family in the papers; her question interrupted when her mother returned from the bathroom.

'Let's not all stand on the doorstep for the neighbours to gawk at. Come in! Come in!' Pat waved her hands like she owned the place and headed for the kitchen. The others followed her.

'There's no Babycham, Mum, so don't bother looking.'

'A posh pad with no Babycham?' Pat perused the sky-high wine cooler. She tripped forward to peer at the bottles, wiping the condensation from her breath off the glass. 'How about something with an umbrella in it then? We'll make do until the good stuff gets here.'

'It's too early in the morning, Mum. No.'

Pat slammed her hands onto her hips.

'No!'

'Well, it's your house, Miss La Di Dah.' Pat scowled, then stumbled over to the pool. She didn't stay mad long, just stood tutting and 'Cor blimey'-ing while clapping her hands.

Bulges in her mother's back pocket provided ample evidence Pat had taken the little rose-shaped guest soaps from the bathroom – a surprising course of action, Annie thought, given that her mother made it quite clear she planned on staying.

'This'll be nice to wake up to, won't it, luv? Oh, yes, I'll get used to this right quick.'

Annie's fists clenched, sweat collecting in her palms. 'We need to talk.' She waved everyone over to the patio and steered herself towards a chair on the long side of the table. Changing her mind, she pulled out the lone chair at the head. The others brushed palm fronds aside to seat themselves.

Chairman and CEO of Casa Luna, Inc. called the meeting to order, carefully measuring her words. 'Obviously, we have a situation here we need to sort out. I didn't mean to worry anyone or lie to anyone. I'm sure you understand why I needed to get away. I just didn't know what else to do. I had to hide.'

'We get it,' Charles said.

'Annie,' Pat cooed. 'I'm your mother. You can trust me to keep my mouth shut.'

Annie recalled the time her mother stood at the bus stop and announced to all assembled Annie had got her first period that day. Had her mother ever managed to keep a secret in her life?

'No, Mum. I can't always trust you to keep quiet. Especially if Babycham's involved. Best never to put you in the awkward position of being trusted with my wellbeing.'

The words tumbled over her lips and down her chin to plop into her lap on top of her ashamed hands. Annie couldn't believe she'd said it.

Pat grasped her ample bosom. 'Well I never! That my own child would say such a thing. After all those years of raising you by myself, struggling with bills, giving up my life for you. Of course, *now* you're rich. *Now* you're a toff, hanging out with toffs.' Pat scowled at the couple across the table. 'S'pose I'm not good enough for you now.' Pat wiped a non-existent tear from her eye.

'Oh, please, Mum! Does everything have to be about you?' Her cheeks burned. *Why have I always allowed myself to be so … manipulated?* Annie caught Taylor's expression, one suggesting comradery, like she'd taken second place too. The reveal came as a surprise.

'I need you to think about me,' Annie continued. 'Not what I can do for you. Not what you need from me. Just about what I need. And what I need right now is time to think. The lottery money gave me no peace until I got to Casa Luna. Here, I have quiet to sort out how I want to live my life and I've come to a couple of conclusions: I need to find a permanent home that's all my own, and I don't need Lester.'

The fact she'd reached the latter conclusion about eighteen years ago, yet done nothing about it, caused significant embarrassment on her part. Better late than never entered her mind. A little smile danced across her lips. It died when she saw real pain on her mother's face.

'What do you mean, you don't need Lester? He's your husband! Of course, you need a husband.'

'What for, Mum? All Lester's ever done is hamper my life; completely set in his Victorian ways.' She stopped to catch her breath. Taylor's nodding head again surprised her. Surely, Taylor had never been held back by a man?

Pat shook all over, her face flushed. 'At least you had a husband. Me and my mum didn't.' Real tears threatened to spill from her eyes. 'I thought you'd made something of yourself, married for going on twenty years. You had everything I ever dreamed of.'

'You need to dream bigger, Mum. Much bigger.'

Pat ignored the comment. Maybe she didn't even understand it. 'Even before this new money, you and Lester were all right, weren't you? Holidays in Spain, never missing a mortgage payment? Christmas Babycham?'

'May want to ask the bank manager about the Babycham. He loaned it to us most years.' Annie took in her mother's shocked expression. *No point backing down now.* 'I had nothing, Mum. Only the pretence of enough until one Tuesday a few weeks ago. I had a sham marriage, like yours. Difference being I worked it out myself. You only found out when Dad left you for that other woman.' A glance between Charles and Taylor. 'Then you dragged us around as kids, like we were hiding from some—'

That look again. 'What? What's going on?' Annie waited. Tension ricocheted off the patio furniture and into the tropical foliage. These guests were hiding something.

'We figured you may not have seen the more recent coverage of your story in the news,' Taylor said cautiously.

'What?' Annie's shout made the whole table jump.

Pat straightened up, pushed her bosom forward and cleared her throat. 'This is why I followed you out here. The newspapers have got hold of a hare-brained story about your father.'

Annie prepared for the lie. She could spot them a Richard Burton mile away. 'Saying my dad's a film star too, are they?' She waited for a chuckle from someone in the room. The silence almost burst her eardrum.

'Mum! What?'

'It's in the papers.' Genuine concern in Charles's eyes induced fear in Annie's. 'You'd better listen to your mother.'

Annie turned from Charles to Pat, gripping the edge of the table.

'It turns out,' Pat began slowly, picking up speed to get the worst over, 'that your father may have been on the run from the law.'

Silence.

'Ooookaaaay.' Annie didn't take her eyes off her mother. 'I'm going to need more detail.'

'Your father didn't leave me for another woman. He left because the police were on his tail about a big robbery.'

'How big?' *How big could anything be if I were connected to it?*

192

'Have you ever read anything about the Great Train Robbery?'

'Of course I have.' Annie rolled her eyes. 'Biggest heist in history at the time, and happened not … far … from …' Her thoughts ground to a halt; the piercing screech of metal on metal as a train shuddered to an unscheduled stop at a fake red railway signal. 'Are you saying Dad …? No, can't be. They caught all those men. Loads of them, or so that film made out.' She'd always liked Phil Collins. She'd watched *Buster* several times.

Pat continued. 'Not quite all of them. The rumour was … is … three men were never identified and most of the money was never found. The papers have got the wind up and are reporting your dad may be one of those men and you may now have the money.'

'What? What? Just … what?' Alien births? Demon-possessed rock stars? Annie knew tabloid press. But her having millions of pounds stashed away? Before she had millions of pounds stashed away? What the heck?

'Does anyone believe, even for one minute, if I'd had two pennies to rub together, I'd have lived the way I lived for the past five decades?' Pat flinched at her daughter's angry words. Annie didn't care. 'But fill me in, here. How did we get from Dad leaving you for another woman to me being a millionaire long before I was a millionaire?'

Over the next few minutes, her mother spoke of the early years, of the good times, before the phone call, the rapid kiss on the cheek, the knock on the door. The search of the flat in St Albans.

Annie closed her eyes against imagery of a flicked curtain, sparkly raindrops, a sudden move.

Her mother spoke of the realisation of a joke marriage, of picking up the pieces with two young children. Of running from the rumours.

The cardboard boxes, first days at new schools. Lizzie.

And finally: 'So your maiden name, Rickman, may not be a real name. Luv.' The afterthought endearment did nothing to soften the blow.

Annie sank back in her chair, her eyes glazed.

Charles and Taylor left the table. Noises from the kitchen. Glasses rattled. A wine cork popped. Footsteps returned to the table.

A tiny smile, initially fringing the corners of Annie's lips, slowly spread across her whole face. Her shoulders shivered and her mouth cracked wide open to expel a belly laugh of Santa-like proportions.

'She's going into shock!' Taylor flapped her hands in Annie's face.

Charles slopped wine into four glasses, losing half of it on the table. When Annie didn't stop laughing, Charles called in the heavy artillery, grabbing a whisky bottle from the cabinet, filling a tumbler and waving it under Annie's nose. Pat snatched the whisky from his hand and glugged down a large mouthful. Annie struggled to see her mother through watery eyes. Obviously, this wasn't a Babycham moment.

Annie gasped for air and wiped away tears, pulling herself together. It took three attempts before words came out.

'You mean, Annie Rickman isn't me?' Three furrowed brows crinkled back at her. 'What a relief! I haven't been living a lie, after all. The person inside me really is someone different. I haven't been hiding anything. I've just been misidentified, filed in the wrong folder. I don't even have the words to express how good this feels!'

Annie stood, triumphant, in front of her baffled audience. 'Maybe I'm a rogue secret agent after all. Maybe I really speak Russian. Maybe I actually do have multiple passports in foreign safety deposit boxes.'

'She's gone crazy,' Taylor whispered.

'No. Crazy was when I was Annie Rickman. This is nothing!' Annie hugged herself. 'This woman in the luxury villa with the turquoise necklace could be the real Annie after all. Let me say again, what a relief.'

Pat eyed the whisky bottle. 'That's not quite the reaction I expected.'

'That's my point,' Annie said. 'I've never had the reaction anyone thought I should have, because I've never been me before. This is the reaction you'll get from now on, from the *real* Annie Hard … Annie Rick … Annie ME!' She raised her arms in victory and let out a whoop. A bird rose from the closest tree with a startled screech, liberating itself from earthly bonds as Annie felt the truth, that she could be anyone, liberate her. Why had it taken so long? Annie stared up at the blue sky, only one tiny cloud visible. It passed directly in front of the sun.

'Why didn't you tell me all this before, Mum?'

Pat met Annie's appeal, stripping off the muzzle that had kept her silent all these years. Her whisky-infused tongue fought a valiant battle to shape the words. 'I told Lizzie when she was eighteen. Told her after an argument – don't even remember what it was about – that she was the daughter of a crook and a heartless man and someone who'd thrown her away for a pile of money he'd nicked from the Queen. And that was that. My Lizzie was gone. Moved out, took up with a rough crowd. Then ... the drugs. You know how that ended.'

Everyone nodded.

'I wasn't going to risk more of the same after that, Annie.' She rubbed her eyes, as though a finger could sweep grief from a body, nothing more than wayward grit.

So, Lizzie wasn't my fault. Annie dropped her head in her hands. The inquest.

'She is ... was ... smart and funny, your honour.'

'No need to call me that. I'm only the Coroner.' The man's voice was kind.

'She tried to protect me at school,' Annie said forlornly to the man. She remembered turning to her mother sitting across the formal inquest table, asking herself if her mother knew then why things had changed; from Lizzie being the protector to needing protecting. Across a patio table, decades later, Annie discovered her mother had known all along. She felt nauseous. Pat had let Lizzie's tragic descent into addiction judge Annie. She'd let the panelled walls and the sympathetic eyes and the mournful pronouncement of 'accidental death' hound her. All. These. Years.

Annie's voice cracked as she spoke. 'Lizzie wasn't my fault, then?'

'Your dad used to say he'd pulled himself up by his bootstraps.' Pat's hands hung limply in her lap. 'Turns out they were the Queen's bootstraps and they strangled Lizzie.'

'And you and me.' Annie stifled a sob.

'My father used to say that all the time, too,' Taylor said. "About the bootstraps. Pushed my brother so hard to achieve more, Richard caved.'

Annie locked eyes with Taylor. 'What happened to him?'

'Suicide. Nothing accidental about his drug overdose.'

Annie closed her eyes and shook her head slowly. 'Our dads had something in common, then. Wanted their kids to think they weren't worth much.'

Pat poured another whisky. 'I wasn't worth much; not to Joe, not to my own dad, either. But I thought you were worth something to Lester.'

'A life of waiting for something to happen. That's what I was worth. Not just to Lester, to myself, too.'

'But you had a home. You can't give up your home.'

'You're right, Mum. You can't give up something you never had.' The words swung between the two women; a door key rocking on a lost keychain.

Pat swallowed a large mouthful of her drink. Annie recognised the decision: the inebriated state became preferable to the sober one.

Taylor sipped her own vintage of solace before saying, 'We all figured your dad was the worst of the bad news. Glad you've interpreted it in a positive light. However—'

'There's more?' *How could there be more?* 'Like I was born on Mars or something?'

'A little bit more.' Taylor paused. 'The British authorities are looking for you and … um … Lester's been arrested.

Annie turned from Taylor to Charles to her mother. Then to the whisky bottle. She grabbed the tumbler out of Pat's hand and took a large swig.

25 - THE CAMERA NEVER LIES

Charles explained it one more time. 'They won't know it's you, personally, searching the internet, Annie. It's only your email or bank accounts you can't go into without attracting attention from the authorities. Chances are good your accounts are being monitored.'

'But they see everything, as soon as you touch your computer,' Annie said. 'Have you never watched any of the Jason Bourne films?'

Charles sighed. 'I'm a Bond man, myself, though the Bourne movies are great fun. You, however, aren't part of a failed experiment that could bring down a government.'

'Could've fooled me, the way they're still looking for Dad after fifty years.'

'Point taken. Okay, let me do the search.' Charles switched places with Annie at the computer desk and started opening windows. One website after another, he showed Annie how the world viewed the Rickmans and the Hardcastles.

'Poor Lester.' Annie added spousal concern to her ever-increasing list of novel experiences. 'He's in real trouble, isn't he?' She flicked from the BBC to *The Daily Scoop*, and to newscasts from America to Australia and even Tokyo. The story was the same worldwide: Annie, her mother and Lester had been implicated in the Great Train Robbery.

'My God!' Heads spun towards Pat. 'You don't suppose they've told Her Majesty about me, do you? I've sent her a card every Jubilee for fifty years.'

'That's two cards, Mum. Twenty-five years apart. She'll get over it.' Annie felt a headache coming on. She closed her eyes and turned back to the screen. She opened her eyes one at a time, as if filtering information into smaller visual chunks would make it easier to digest.

'Jeez,' she muttered. There was Lester outside their flat in Verston, in a police car, gaping at the cameras.

'Oh, my goodness.' There he was, arriving at the station in St Albans.

'Ugh.' Lester being transferred to London, photographers holding their cameras up to the blacked-out windows of the police van. The world wanted a snapshot of the criminal mastermind who had evaded the police for fifty-four years. It didn't seem to matter Lester was only fifty-three.

Annie read a few lines from *The Daily Scoop*, then turned to her mother. 'They say Number Three groomed Lester to take over the family's ill-gotten gains. What a load of codswallop! How could Lester have been hanging out with Dad when I couldn't even pick my own father out of a line-up?'

'No pun intended.' The words were out before Charles could stop them. He studied his shoes.

Annie glared at him. 'The good news is, it can't get worse.' She turned back to her screen – and screamed. She covered her mouth, failing to prevent the hysteria from cascading between her fingers and threatening to buckle her knees. *No! No! They can't wake me up now!*

Charles turned up the volume and listened to the ITV commentator: 'The Hardcastles' lottery win is now deemed suspicious and is being investigated by the Euro Lottery Commission.'

Pat swivelled her drunken head first towards the swimming pool, then the wine cooler. She hiccupped. 'Easy come, easy go.'

Annie dry-heaved. She bent over and rested her hands on her thighs, acknowledging a sense of guilt at the contrast between her reaction to poor Lester's predicament and the possibility of losing the lottery winnings.

Fight or flee? Which one? Her choice.

She inhaled. She chose.

'Right, everyone.' The speed at which Annie stood up startled her posse. 'We have to get moving. Obviously, we must clear up this mess with the authorities. There are perfectly reasonable explanations as to why I went into hiding, why you, Mum, came out here and why we have no idea where the stolen money is. Let's march down to the local police station and lay it out. They inform the British police and we all get on with our lives. Simple.'

'I agree you need to explain everything to the authorities,' Charles said. 'But I'm not sure you want to go to the local authorities. If NCIS is leading the investigation, NCIS is who you should contact.'

'Sounds right.' Pat's head moved in circles rather than up and down.

'With all due respect, Charles,' Taylor broke in, 'we can't give advice here. Call your lawyer in England. He or she will advise you.'

Pat cackled into her whisky glass. 'You've got us mixed up with a couple of toffs. Since when have we had lawyers?'

Annie chuckled too, then stopped. 'Oh, wait, I do have a lawyer.' She slapped her forehead. 'Or rather, a solicitor. We had to get one to help us set things up after the lottery win. In fact, he was the one suggested we come to Costa Rica.'

'Not exactly a ringing endorsement of his skill, is it?' Pat huffed. 'After his advice, you've been hounded by the vulture press, forced into hiding and lost your husband.'

Annie snapped back. 'A lot of this wouldn't have happened if you hadn't hidden a criminal in our family nut tree, now would it?'

'Hard to disagree with that,' Charles said. Taylor slapped his arm.

Pat pouted, then deflected. 'This is about you, not me. Wish I could have your life. The old one or this new one.'

'Oh yeah, Mum. A good life. Of ironing, taking the bus, waiting for life to happen.' Annie sank into a chair. 'Lester's one proud man, always pretending we had enough. Then when we finally did have enough it scared the socks off him and he bolted back to the Fox and Rabbit.'

'But turned out, he was right to be scared,' Pat said. 'See where money's got you? All over the papers and Lester in the clink. Bet the Fox and Rabbit sounds pretty good to you now.'

Not being a Rickman sounded good to Annie now. Not being a Hardcastle sounded good to her, too. The Fox and Rabbit? Didn't sound good at all. Annie struggled to even picture the pub on the Verston high street. She had to refocus her mental camera lens until the pub came into view: the shabby carpet, the grubby wallpaper the smoking ban was far too late to save. She'd spent many birthdays and holidays there, its familiarity now disquieting. Her entire prior life, alien. In contrast, the beach, the monkeys, the freedom. This was home and she'd fight for it.

'Earth to Annie? Are you having a fit?' Pat waved her arms to attract her daughter's attention.

Yes, I'm having a fit, Mum.

Pat stood up. 'Despite all the fuss, there is one good thing about the money. This place. So, I have a plan: I'll stay here while you go home and spring Lester from the clink. Then you head off to Harrods to shop for clothes more suitable for our new lives.' Pat waved her hands down her body to exhibit more suitable clothing.

Annie stifled a retch. Not in response to the clothing – though possibly a bit in response to the clothing – but at the idea of leaving Casa Luna. Tears blurred her vision, misting the ocean she'd come to love as a friend. Her mother was right, for once. She had to go back to that place everyone thought was her home to take care of that person everyone thought was her husband, and to put to rest that man everyone thought was her father. But she'd be damned if she was going to sit in a police station while her mother lay by the pool at Case Luna. No, Mum was coming with her.

The buzzer sounded.

Pat grabbed her chest. 'What the hell!'

'Relax. It's the intercom from the gate.' Annie The I'm-So-Used-To-Intercoms strolled to the wall and reached out a finger to press the button.

'Are you sure you should answer that?' Taylor asked.

'The police don't know where I am, so it can't be them,' Annie responded. 'And I'm expecting a delivery of groceries. They probably forgot not to buzz so you're right, I don't need to answer it. I'll walk up and get the cooler.'

'I'll come with you,' Charles said. 'I need a stroll. Perhaps you'd show me the gardens out front? This place is for sale so we should check it out.'

'Oh, that's why you wanted to bring Mum over?' Annie folded her arms and tapped her foot.

Taylor raised her hands. 'It's okay. We don't have the listing. Nothing's going on behind your back, Annie. Trust us, for once?'

Annie needed to trust someone. 'Just this once, then.' She slipped into her sandals. 'Be right back.'

Charles and Annie wandered slowly up the driveway, stopping along the way to marvel at colourful blooms and gigantic ferns. Annie allowed herself to relax and enjoy the sociable connection. It had been a long time since she'd made new friends. Rob crossed her mind.

'It was good of you to come,' Annie said. 'I have to concede bringing Mum here was the right thing to do. Goodness knows what damage she'd have done by herself.'

'It wasn't easy, trying to decide what was best for you.' Annie was grateful for Charles's kind sentiment. 'We tried to imagine how someone like you would cope with all this.'

Annie stopped walking. 'Someone like me? What do you mean?'

'I guess the word might be "sheltered".' Charles twitched quotation marks with his fingers. 'You don't project the image of someone who's experienced a lot of … excitement.'

'Really?' Annie swallowed twice: once to suppress her irritation at Charles's comment, once to quell the irritation at the truth of his statement. 'The fact "lack of excitement" is written all over my face doesn't thrill me at all.'

'I didn't mean it as an insult.'

'I know.' Annie took a couple of deep breaths. 'It's just along with all this financial opportunity comes the luxury of more time to realise what you've been missing all your life. I'm middle aged and only beginning my life. How sad is that?'

Charles squeezed Annie's arm gently. 'Not sad at all.'

Annie smiled up at this man with the kind eyes. As she walked along the driveway she added a little pep in her step, her arms began to swing – a vision of life to come.

On reaching the gate, Annie pressed the button and the solid structure began to draw back. She caught the camera flash full in the eyeballs. The first yelled questions assaulted her eardrums, the shoving of a mass of arms and legs holding cameras and microphones kicked dust into the steamy air.

Someone tried to push through the gate, thrusting a large box in front of himself. 'Delivery for you, Ms Hardcastle. How about a few questions while I carry this to your rather lovely hideout?'

Annie could barely hear him over the cacophony of crow-like reporters, all demanding explanations: her reasons for hiding, her reasons for throwing Lester under the bus, her reasons for escaping with her mother, her reasons for not telling anyone about her father … reasons … reasons …

Charles leapt into action. Jamming his fist on the button to stop the gate opening farther, then punching it again to make it reverse direction, he grabbed the box and slammed the reporter who held it backwards where he fell into the crowd. Charles threw his arm in front of Annie's face to protect her from the incessant flashes of light.

Annie, shock replaced by seething anger, slapped at the hands reaching through the closing gate. She yelled, 'Leave me alone!' before deciding she didn't sound Jason Bourne-like at all. In his honour, she kicked out and got one reporter full in the shins.

As the gate clicked shut and cameras floated and bobbed in the air above it, held by disembodied hands, Annie and Charles turned and ran.

'You don't have eggs in here, do you?' Charles struggled to heft the box onto his shoulder as he ran.

'That's not the food cooler I was expecting,' Annie panted back.

'Then what the hell is it?' Charles slowed his pace and dragged the box back off his shoulder. He held it out in front of him as though expecting it to explode at any second.

Annie came to a screeching halt and threw her hand over her mouth. 'What?' Charles yelled. 'What is it?'

'Am … Amazon,' Annie stammered, gasping for breath.

Charles burst through the door and dumped the box on the tile floor. He ripped it open and dug through it frantically, like a stray dog in a rubbish bin. Puffing and sweating as he worked, he explained the mayhem at the gate to Pat and Taylor.

'No tracking devices, explosives, or death threats,' Charles announced, sitting back on his heels and blowing air through pursed lips.

Taylor gaped at the scattered contents of the box, her face a picture of utter disgust. She turned to Annie. 'Cake tins? You gave up your hideaway for cake tins?'

'I'm sorry,' Annie wailed. She sat on the floor among the cupcake tins, paper muffin cups, recipe books, icing tubes with every fancy nozzle attachment ever made, vanilla essence, food colourings and an apron proclaiming 'Bakers Make Life Batter'. She tried to hide the apron by sitting on it. 'Millions of people order from Amazon every day. How could anyone find me in that horde?'

'Let me explain it to you,' Taylor chided, hands on hips. 'Every day Amazon charges millions of people's credit cards, cards in their real names. Then, they put the customer's real name on the delivery label. Are you with me so far?'

Annie groaned. 'I forgot, all right? Besides, when I placed this order I didn't know I was on Interpol's most wanted list. All I wanted to do was make cupcakes.' Annie blinked forlornly at the contents of the box sprayed around the floor.

Where did Jason Bourne get all his supplies?

'Ahem.'

The voice came from the direction of the patio door. A second of stunned silence followed. Then all hell broke loose.

Pat, or rather Pat's whisky, grabbed a cupcake pan and took off as fast as her wedge heels would carry her towards the invader. 'Get outta here, ya bloody parrotnazi!'

'No! Stop!' Annie's scream was too late.

Charles leapt to his feet and stormed the 'ahem' source. His head made contact with the invader's stomach in a manner that would surely have made the Yale Rowing Team proud. Both men flew backwards, hitting the ground on the patio, the cake tin alternating between the invader's head and Charles's shoulder. From somewhere, a dog got involved. Charles's designer linen shorts proved unsuitable for battle. They ripped loudly.

It appeared Pat's duty to her daughter ended once the enemy set the dogs on her. She threw the cake tin over her shoulder and retreated – turban over one eye, a breast breaking free of the halter top as she ran.

Taylor grabbed Annie and pulled her down onto the floor behind the kitchen counter. 'I won't let them get you, Annie!'

How sweet. 'Thank you. Now, get off me, you idiot!' Annie spat the words into Taylor's face and escaped her grasp with a shove. She sprinted towards the patio, intent on separating the rollicking tangle of human and canine limbs. Instead, she tripped on the discarded cupcake pan and crashed on top of the wrestling pile. A barrage of camera clicks exploded from the direction of the beach, followed by a chorus of cheers. Annie groaned, aware the paparazzi lived for brief glimpses of their prey leaving a grocery store, so this fiasco was clickbait gold.

The hoots and hollers from the paparazzi galvanised her into action. Dragging herself, two men and a dog into the villa took mere seconds, thanks to the adrenaline rush. She flung the screens closed, then sank to the ground. Everyone else kneeled, lay, or sagged, wherever they'd fallen. There were no words; just panting and wheezing – and growling from Jackson.

Rob stood up first, brushing his chest off and placing Jackson on stay with a wave of his hand. Jackson stood beside his master in a low stance, head forward, ears back, bandaged paw slightly raised.

'May I assume this is a bad time to ask for my towel?' Rob gritted his teeth. His eyes flashed a warning that if anyone else dared to assault him, all bets were off.

Annie winced. Yoga Man was gone. This was Apoplectic Man.

Charles dragged himself to the sofa and pulled himself up slowly. He didn't seem to realise his shorts were gone and his underwear hung low enough to constitute 'out of character' – even for a disgraced financier.

'I'm sorry, Rob.' Annie sucked in air as she dragged herself from the floor, only to collapse on the sofa next to her mother. 'I am so sorry.'

'I'm owed an explanation.' Rob glared at Annie. 'Not that what you do is any of my business, but you did invite me back and you do still have my towel. A simple "Not now" would've been sufficient. In fact, don't even bother. I'll leave you the towel and get back to my boat. Enjoy the rest of your … whatever you call this.' Rob waved his hand around the gathering and moved to open the screens.

Annie leapt up with a yelp. Rob spun around, ready to deflect another assault. Annie raised both hands and stopped her advance. 'Please don't open those screens. Please. I'm begging you. You don't understand. The paparazzi are out there and you'll be hounded to death if you try to go back to your boat now. Please, stay. I'll explain everything. Please.' Annie's hands adopted a prayer position, something they hadn't done in years.

Rob perused the room. 'I guess you being hounded by paparazzi explains the motor boats speeding into the cove as I walked across the beach. Though why you're being hounded escapes me. All right, Dale, I'll bite. But this story had better be good.' He pulled out a chair and spun it around. He straddled it backwards, placing it between the sofa and the patio door. As he sat, a hand went to his mouth, another fingernail sacrificed. The knowledge she'd caused the anguish forced Annie's eyes to squeeze shut.

'Who's Dale?' Pat pulled the turban off her head and threw it on the sofa. She peered around the room.

Annie placed one hand on her forehead, one on her chest. She couldn't speak.

Pat mirrored her daughter's movements, only to discover there was nothing between her breasts and everyone's eyes. With a small shriek that set everyone's nerves on edge again, she stuffed herself back into her halter top.

Averting her eyes from breasts, Taylor let out a gasp, directed at Charles. 'Dear God, Charles! Go find something to cover up!'

Charles grabbed what was left of his underwear, then, still appearing somewhat dazed, he stood and stumbled towards the bedrooms.

Annie tried to collect her wits. 'Where to begin?'

'How about starting at the bit where that clown attacked me?' Rob nodded in the direction Charles had taken.

'Oh, I need to go back farther than that,' Annie said. 'For a start, there's my real name.'

It all tumbled out: lottery winnings, kidnappings, train robberies, Dale Dante – 'Oh, I've read one of her books.' 'No, you haven't, Mum. Shut up.' – jailbird Lester, no-name Annie, on and on. Rob interrupted at one point to ask if Annie thought he was completely stupid.

'Oh, I wish you were stupid,' Annie replied, 'but this is all true.' She knew she was describing a British 'Carry On' farce. There was nothing 'Bourne Supremacy' about it.

Annie arrived at the grand finale: Amazon and cupcake pans. She stopped, exhausted, not daring to even look at Rob. As the silence stretched on, she tilted her head and squinted at him with one eye closed, her mouth contorted in an agony of suspense. *If I were him, I'd run.*

Rob's hands unclenched from the back of the chair. 'That's one messed-up story.' Annie noted his eyes shift between her and Taylor, as though he were waiting for something more. 'Even if I only believe half of it, it's messed up.' He stared at Annie. 'You gave the impression of … less complication.'

'Um … thank you?' Resentment bubbled up inside her at being taken for boring – again. The feeling competed with relief at knowing she hadn't initially come across as the crazy woman her story would suggest. 'I'm sorry to disappoint you.'

For the first time, Rob cracked a smile. 'I'm not disappointed. I'm surprised more than anything. I usually read people pretty accurately. Though in my defence, I've not had much experience with train-robbing, lottery-winning, paparazzi-fighting, cupcake-making, fake-author spouses of jailbirds.'

Annie grimaced at the realisation being called a spouse struck her as the most offensive part. Surely that was messed up?

Charles reappeared, wearing a bathrobe way too short for him. A ripple of sniggers reduced the tension somewhat; enough for Annie to remember she was the host of this fiasco, anyway.

'May I humbly beg no one try to leave right now. It's not safe for us out there, so we may as well settle in for the afternoon. I'm not prepared for a lunch party, but I'm certainly not going back to the gate to check if the groceries have been delivered.'

Charles headed over to the wine cooler. 'I personally think something to drink is first on our list of priorities.'

Annie smiled, grateful for Charles's attempt to smooth the waters. 'Agreed, but even so, let's hope there's something to eat.'

The word 'eat' gained Jackson's full attention. He followed Annie to the kitchen, where he accepted a cracker. His personal chef placed fruit and seafood dishes on the counter. Her hands shook as she took the wine Rob offered her; more so when he closed his fingers over hers on the glass for a reassuring instant.

Charles walked over to the computer, carrying his plate of fruit. The clatter of china on tile sent Jackson running for cover. All others flocked to the computer screen.

'Orgy at the Gang's Hideout!' blared the headlines. Charles mouthed the subtitle: 'Train Robber's Daughter in Perverted Romp in Paradise!'

The photos and video footage displayed a barely dressed Charles, Pat's boobs swinging in the background – requiring more pixilation than typically warranted – Annie herself leaping on top of two men and a dog gainfully employed in stripping the participants.

Annie struggled to breathe, before a somewhat hysterical laugh broke through. After all, why wouldn't the world assume an orgy? The camera never lies.

26 – WHO SAYS CRIME DOESN'T PAY?

Jane pulled at the collar of her jacket, hating the sensation of sweat trickling down her neck. She studied the recently arrived tourists waiting for taxis at the Liberia airport. 'How do people put up with this heat?' She narrowed her eyes at Thorn, leaving no doubt she considered her current discomfort his fault. Because it was.

'Honestly. You're worse than Becky Dagny,' Thorn shot back. 'Didn't you know it's hot in Africa?'

'Oh, don't even,' Jane snapped. 'I knew exactly how hot it was going to be in Central America which is why I didn't want to come.' She dragged her bag towards a taxi and climbed in next to Thorn.

'I trust you've brought more suitable clothing with you,' Thorn said.

'Ditto.' Jane pulled her sunglasses down lower on her nose and peered over the top of them. 'Hardly going to intimidate an international crime syndicate in that Hawaii-inspired explosion in a flower shop, are you now?'

'Hey, I got this in Bermuda, one ex-wife ago.'

'The ex-wife makes perfect sense. The shirt? Not so much.' Jane gave the driver the name of their hotel in Playa Panamá. The official budget wouldn't spring for the Paradise Resort. 'And staying twenty minutes from where Annie is doesn't make sense either. Correction, where Annie *was*. She'll be long gone by the time we get there. Devious, she is, and her mother had us fooled too. Innocent Little Miss "Wednesday's Market Day". Are you listening to me?'

'No,' Thorn replied. 'It's a mental health preservation technique I learned from my ex-wife. But you may want to listen to this.' He adjusted his glasses as the taxi sped up. 'It arrived from our team cross-checking the databases. Seems there was an individual who fits the criteria for Pat's fake husband. Possibly lived in the St Albans area for a while about the right time under several aliases, including Rickman. No history before that, no history after. They're trying to find a photo now.'

'Okay, it's a start.' Jane studied the phone screen Thorn had turned towards her. He'd also leaned in a little, brushing her arm with his. A strong impulse to rest her head on his shoulder caused her to clear her throat and stiffen her back. *Jet lag. It's only jet lag.* 'Have them show the photo to Lester. I want eyes on his reaction.'

'I'll make sure I tell the boys that.' Thorn maintained a straight face. 'We're not usually into observation of that kind at NCIS, but I'll ask if they'll make an exception – seeing as the big guns in St Albans want it.'

'Sorry. Used to working with idiots. Oh, wait …'

Thorn opened his mouth to laugh. His facial features froze as he stared at his phone. He let out a curse. 'Guess we're working with the Vice Squad now. Would you take a gander at that?' Thorn cupped his hand around hers to help hold the phone steady. Jane had only a second to enjoy the sensation. The screen filled with Pat's saggy bosoms, Annie's shocked face and two men she didn't recognise, all in a heap in various stages of undress.

'Once again, sir,' Jane said, 'Thank you for insisting I be the one to support you on this mission. I'm sure my involvement in this complex and intellectually stimulating case will further my career. I owe you one.'

Thorn laughed too hard to reply.

He was still laughing when they got to the hotel. Having checked into their rooms and freshened up, the two officers walked into the patio bar to strategise. Both stopped dead in their tracks as the view of the bay appeared before them. Colourful umbrellas and hammocks dotted golden sand. Sailboats bobbed on clear blue waters. Three piña coladas on a tray floated before their eyes as the waitress briefly interrupted their line of vision.

The heat didn't seem to bother Jane anymore. 'Does NCIS have a field office out here?'

'If it does, I'm putting in for a transfer,' Thorn said. The two officers sighed simultaneously.

Jane interrupted the dream. 'Right, down to business.'

The skirt and blouse she'd changed into caught Thorn's attention. 'I see the uniform's been upgraded to … floaty. Will need to mention that in my report, in case it's important.'

'I'm trying to blend in with the floral camouflage you're wearing, sir.' Jane saluted and turned to find a table.

Sparkling waters in hand, because umbrella drinks were forbidden while on duty, Jane and Thorn pored over the reports coming in on their phones. A man had been traced through his British passport to various parts of the globe until 1970, when the trail went cold. A photo surfaced: a man, smiling into the camera from the back of a camel. 'Circa 1969. Tunisia, maybe?' was the caption on the Facebook page it came from.

Jane stared at the Facebook profile. 'You can't make this stuff up.'

Thorn blew a long, slow whistle. 'Unbelievable.' He took a steadying sip of his drink. 'Explains why the Americans jumped on this like bears on honey.'

'Just when you thought nothing else could surprise you,' Jane said, almost to herself.

'I've stopped using that phrase,' Thorn replied. 'These days I've had so many surprises by lunch time on a Monday, it's not even worth saying. Anyway, bit of a black eye for US immigration. In their defence, we assumed South America because that's where all the other suspects turned up. Number Three may have been the smartest of the bunch.'

'But no one outwits St Albans forever, sir.' Jane looked straight at Thorn. 'Shame NCIS didn't involve us after the initial interview with Pat all those years ago. We could have saved you a decade. Or five.'

'Funny, Williams. Funny.' Thorn flicked water at Jane before stand-ing to leave. 'At least Annie's still at Casa Luna. It's going to take her a while to catch her breath and get dressed, but we should leave now.' His phone pinged, signalling an incoming message. 'The FBI and Costa Rican authorities are in place. They're sending a car for us. Should be quite the reception at the gang's hideout shortly. Sorry. You'll have to change from floaty back to professional.'

'You should change, too.' Jane pointedly examined Thorn's shirt. 'Unless you're planning on acting the part of the Trojan potted palm.'

27 – CUPCAKE BANDITS

Emotion welled up inside Annie as she looked around, but she struggled to identify it. Incredulousness? Contentment? She focused on isolating the component sensations: a lack of wanting to be anywhere else, an unexpected comfort level with the people she was with, the knowledge she could afford the drinks her friends were consuming. All this wrapped in the sounds and smells of the ocean – another of her new friends. She settled for incredulous contentment. There was one fly in the ointment; the paparazzi swarming outside. She doubted they'd be there much longer, soon getting bored with her little story, and moving on to buzz around the heads of other unwitting souls.

Over the top of her slice of kiwi fruit, she caught Rob smiling at her.

'Are you okay?' Rob whispered. His air of genuine interest left Annie tingling with unadulterated incredulousness.

To hide the heat in her face, she picked up a recipe book from the Amazon box. 'I'd better bake cupcakes, seeing as these supplies may have cost me life without parole.' The comment elicited uncomfortable glances.

'Oh, come on, people! This will all be sorted out soon, and when it is, I, for one, would love a cruise on Rob's sailboat.' Annie crossed her fingers that she hadn't overstepped the mark.

'Fine with me, though Jackson may be guarding the gangplank,' Rob said. 'He's still not convinced you're a trustworthy crew. Look at him. On full alert.'

The upside-down belly of a snoring Lab took up most of the sofa. Jackson had enjoyed the tuna and appeared ready to forgive and forget. Annie walked over and rubbed a soft ear. She was rewarded with a sleepy tail wag. 'One taste of my cupcakes and he'll be putty in my hands.'

'Will I be?' Rob winked at Annie. She threw a cushion at him. Taylor and Charles shared a raised eyebrow.

'May as well fill our time productively until the paparazzi leave. Choose a recipe from the book, everyone. I'm sick of heavy wedding fruit cakes. Something light and fluffy, please.' Her new metaphor for life.

The group settled on a lemon cupcake. A slightly tipsy search for bowls, electric mixers and measuring spoons ensued with promises of ever more elaborate prizes for the winners.

'A BMW for a measuring cup!' Annie shouted.

Pat fell to her knees searching all the drawers, only to find when she stood up, Rob was waving the cup above his head.

'Don't worry.' Rob smiled. 'I can't fit a BMW on the foredeck. You have it, Pat.'

So, he's not after my money? Annie couldn't say the same about her mother. The good news: Pat was in no way capable of driving right now. Measuring out sugar appeared to be quite enough of a challenge. Jackson, leaping up from a deep sleep at the sound of falling food, helped with the spill clean-up.

'So, Rob.' Annie bustled about as she spoke. 'What's with the boat? Do you have a house somewhere? ' *Or a wife?*

'Sure, I have a house.' Rob answered. 'But I prefer the boat.' He appeared finished with his explanation.

'Really?' Taylor jumped into the conversation. 'We're weighing up real estate options in this area ourselves. Is your house in Guanacaste?'

'No,' Rob replied. 'Connecticut, actually. I also spend a fair bit of time in France. My mother was French. A baker.' He smiled at Annie. 'I'm only down here at the behest of a friend.'

A girlfriend? Annie couldn't ask. It was none of her business.

Taylor's business, however, appeared to be other people's business. 'A girlfriend, maybe?'

Charles choked on his drink, directing an apologetic grimace in Rob's direction. 'That's none of our business, Taylor! I'm sorry, Rob.'

Rob grinned. 'We're outnumbered here, Charles. I'll come clean to avoid being force fed frosting until I squeal. No girlfriend. I'm down here checking out opportunities for a friend who owns a real estate business. I'm helping him assess whether Guanacaste is a good fit for expansion of his overseas operation.'

The silence was ear-splitting. Drinks hung in suspended animation a few inches from mouths. Even Jackson's ears dropped flat to his head as the awkward vibe stopped his tail wag in mid wag.

Pat poked her head out of the Amazon box where she'd been rustling through the contents, paying no attention to anyone else. 'Silver or gold?'

'Er, neither.' Rob's eyes ping-ponged from face to frozen face, confusion all over his. 'Real estate only.'

Pat held up two small boxes. 'I said, silver or gold muffin cases. Which goes best with lemon?'

A forced chorus of 'Gold, yes gold,' and 'Definitely gold,' from Charles and Annie. Taylor remained silent.

Perfect! He's the Ashcroft bloke. Annie geared herself for Rob to storm out of the villa and her life, Taylor throwing real estate brochures at his retreating back. Taylor circled the kitchen island – face of a hungry lioness. Rob backed up a pace or two, wide eyes clueless as to how he'd become the weak impala. He lifted a questioning eyebrow at Annie. She shrugged, then dolloped batter into gold-coloured cases. The trays went into the oven and Annie set the timer for fifteen minutes, telling herself if Rob was still there when it went off it would be a miracle.

Maybe her mother's deflection tactic would help. 'Icing flavours? Suggestions, anyone?' No one answered. 'Lemon it is, then.' Annie intentionally upped the thumping and crashing as she whipped up the mixture. Anything to fill the silence

Taylor finally broke eye contact with Rob and walked away. She whispered something to Charles, then plastered on a crocodile smile. Annie

214

held in the 'Don't you dare' building up inside her, realising she had no idea what Taylor dared. Rob's eyes stopped flitting from face to face. Maybe he was thinking he'd imagined the whole safari thing?

When the timer went off, Annie removed the cupcakes from the oven and set them to cool. Chatter about the weather ensued. Running out of synonyms for 'sunny', the only plan Annie could muster involved topping up everyone's glass. She couldn't tell one bottle from another when it came to wine, but she dragged several dusty bottles of red from the top shelf of the wine rack. Charles's raised eyebrows denoted approval as he studied labels. Rob joined the grape discussion. By the time the cupcakes cooled enough to be decorated, the tense exchange had turned somewhat hazy in most minds. Annie threw silver sugar balls – remembered from everyone's childhood – at Rob's mouth. He even caught one. *Good.* The afternoon was back on track, though she vowed not to leave Taylor and Rob alone.

Annie retrieved fondant from the Amazon box and showed the group how to make tiny flowers. She filled wax paper piping cones with icing and passed them out to everyone; Taylor handling her bag like she'd been given dynamite.

Sugary lace and latticework soon covered the countertop as Annie demonstrated icing techniques. Splodges and splatters were the best the rookie decorators could do. It felt good to be the expert in the room; to have these high-flyers defer to her, ask questions, nod appreciatively at her work. Maybe she hadn't wasted all those years at the bakery. It wasn't the head baker position at a fancy hotel she'd dreamed of, but it had given her this moment.

Once the cupcakes were cool, Annie set up a production line. Taylor and Charles spread yellow icing on the tops.

Charles marvelled. 'In eighteen years of marriage, I've never seen Taylor do that.'

'And you never will again, so enjoy it.' Taylor kept one eye on Rob, which didn't help with precision.

Pat arranged the fondant flowers on a selection of the cupcakes, somewhat off centre, while Rob placed silver balls with great precision on others.

Annie piped everyone's names in impeccable cursive script on top of some of the sweet treats. She resisted the temptation to put a heart shape around Robert's name.

But he's such a good idea, New Annie said.

Lester was a good idea once, Old Annie replied.

Yeah, compared to homelessness or staying with Mum forever. New Annie folded her arms and rested her case.

Rob appeared at Annie's shoulder. He spoke into her ear. 'I haven't had this much fun in a long time.'

Annie tried to collect herself. 'You must have led an exceedingly boring life, then.'

'Actually, the opposite. Too exciting. This … and you, are refreshingly comfortable.'

'You mean boring?' Shields up.

'Hardly boring, based on what's outside the window. Anyway, why does comfortable have to be boring?' Rob's breath stirred the hair behind Annie's ear.

I am miles from bored right now.

She steadied her hands as she refilled the icing bag to put the finishing cursive touches on an unfrosted doggie cupcake. The buzzer on the intercom shattered the peace. The last 'N' in 'Jackson' took off across the countertop like a plane's vapour trail in a hurricane.

Everyone held their breath.

'Shhh! Shhhh!' Annie pulled Rob down on the floor beside her. The others followed suit and battle crawled around the kitchen island to join ranks.

'You know someone pressing the intercom at the gate can't see us, right?' Rob stood up and swatted flour off his knees. At that moment, Annie found him a little too smart.

'Oh, of course.' Annie helped her mother off the floor, signalling her to tuck her wayward boobs back into place.

The buzzer interrupted again. 'What do we do?' Taylor whispered.

But Taylor knew what to do in every situation, controlled everything, didn't she? Annie waited for this force of nature to take charge. She didn't. She looked to Annie with expectation all over her face. Wow. Give Superwoman an apron and she folds fast, Annie thought.

'Tell 'em to naff off or we'll call the police,' Pat said with boozy bravado.

'Naff off?' Charles said. 'Not familiar with the term.'

Taylor slapped at her husband's arm. 'Not time for a language lesson.'

The buzzer rasped frazzled eardrums for the third time. 'We can't call the police.' Taylor frowned. 'Aren't we trying to stay away from the authorities?'

Annie blew out her cheeks. This was her mess. She had to take the lead. 'I'm not listening to that buzzer all night. Besides, maybe it's not the paparazzi. Anyone expecting anyone?' She dragged her mouth into a limp smile. Her dry lips stuck to her teeth.

'It's your decision, Annie,' Rob said. 'This is all about you.'

Annie wiped her palms on her apron. With encouraging nods from Charles and Taylor, Annie pressed the intercom button. 'Yes?'

'Annie Hardcastle?' It was a female voice.

Taylor tapped Annie on the shoulder and whispered, 'The press is using a woman's voice to make you more comfortable. Don't fall for it.'

'Does your voice make people more comfortable?' Charles feigned innocence.

Taylor narrowed her eyes. 'Don't start, Charles.'

'Be quiet,' Annie snapped. 'Let me think.'

The voice from the wall spoke again. 'Is this Annie Hardcastle?'

Annie's face brightened. She had a plan; called in backup. 'You first,' Jason Bourne goaded.

'I'll take that as a yes,' the voice said.

'Wait a minute,' Pat said. 'I recognise that voice.'

'Oh, do be quiet, Mum.' She pressed the button. 'Okay, this is Annie. Who's this?'

'Superintendent Williams from St Albans Special Crimes Unit. We need to talk.'

217

Annie turned with glee to the watching faces. 'How stupid do they think I am? I'm not dumb enough——'

'I know that voice!' Pat tottered over to Annie and grabbed her shoulder.

Annie swatted her mother's hand away. 'You've also read one of Dale Dante's books so you're not the best judge of anything right now.' She turned back to the intercom and pressed the button. 'Listen up, you crawling, sniffling, scum of the bottom-dwelling tabloids, I have nothing to say to you and my lawyers are filing restraining orders as we speak. Go back to flicking fish poop at each other and leave me alone.'

Nothing but static from the intercom. Annie turned her back on the wall to face her guests for the high fives she expected.

All she got was a condescending snort from her mother. 'Fish poop? They know you mean business now, luv.'

A male voice boomed from the wall. 'Mrs Hardcastle, this is Commander Thorn of the National Criminal Intelligence Service. The FBI are with us too. They're armed. You have five minutes to open this gate or the Costa Rican authorities will break it down.'

Annie spun round to stare at the intercom. 'Shit!'

Fish poop was so yesterday.

28 – DEFINITELY NOT THE WALTONS

Rob spoke first, his eyes ablaze and his fists clenched. 'Who *are* you people? I'm making cupcakes like something out of *The Waltons*, only to find I'm starring in the freaking *Godfather* movie!'

Annie briefly admired the restraint in his language. Restraint didn't seem to occur to Taylor, however. A cupcake hurtled past Annie's ear and splattered all over the intercom buttons, a trail of icing dripped down the wall.

'What the hell have you got us into?' The cupcake pitcher glared at Annie, then locked eyes on Rob. 'Is Ashcroft behind this? Is he setting me up?'

Rob threw his hands in the air. 'Lady. I've no idea what you're talking about. This has nothing to do with—'

'Shut up!' Annie shocked herself. Jackson, who had been sidling towards the intercom to lick icing off the wall, scuttled back behind the kitchen counter. 'I have no idea what's going on so let me think.' *Bourne Supremacy* or a *Monty Python* skit? She'd completely lost the plot, whatever it was. The contorted faces glaring back at her confirmed this definitely wasn't an episode of *The Waltons*.

'Mrs Hardcastle!' The angry voice from the wall, though muffled by cupcake, wouldn't go away. 'Did you hear me? Five minutes to open the gate or we're coming in anyway, and things get a lot worse for you and your friends.'

'We're not exactly friends.' Charles peeked around the room and adopted a stoop. Annie bet her lottery winnings he was planning his escape.

Taylor targeted Rob. 'But we know full well who this guy is, don't we. And, frankly, finding Ashcroft's spook hasn't proved satisfying at all.'

Rob dragged his fingers through his hair. 'Who the hell's Ashcroft?' A finger made its way to his mouth, the crack of tooth on nail making Annie cringe.

Annie studied her fingers. *Maybe I should try nail biting.*

'Don't give me that "Who's Ashcroft?" crap.' Taylor didn't even bother to wipe the spittle off her mouth. 'You know damn well who he is and now I've uncovered the bastard who took my job. Get ready, mister. I'm stealing all your clients.'

'Hey, just because I made you obsolete, don't blame me. It's adapt or die in Silicon Valley.'

'I'm in Chicago, you jerk, and next time you're there, you pass on this message to Ashcroft: go to hell!'

'Taylor! Quit it,' Charles hissed from his position by the computer. 'We've got bigger problems.'

'Oh, bigger than—'

Charles strode over, grabbed Taylor's hand and tugged her over to the screen. Annie's stomach clenched as she dropped to her knees and crawled over behind Taylor.

Rob swung his open palm between the floor and the vague vicinity of the gate. 'They can't see you, for Christ's sake!'

'But I bet they can see this.' Charles pointed at the image on the screen. BBC news was switching between photos of the semi-naked melee on the patio earlier and a live feed of the massed troops outside the Casa Luna gate. Police cars lined the road. Uniformed and what looked like plain-clothed officers milled about in small groups, outnumbered by the media. The camera panned over to the gate, where a male and a female stood by the intercom with their heads together. Flashing above the news anchor, in bold red letters: 'Great Train Robbery Stand-off in Paradise.'

MORE OR LESS ANNIE

Rob, eyes opening wider and wider, read the ticker-tape feed. 'Who's the disgraced financier in all this?' His cheeks flamed red, mouth flapping open and shut like he was trying to breath through gills.

Charles moved to block the monitor. In the silent seconds that followed, alcohol evaporated, hair got smoothed down and a silly baking apron found itself slowly and deliberately folded into the size of a pocket handkerchief. No one made eye contact.

'We can safely assume they know who we are.' Charles straightened his shoulders, apparently preparing for the executioner's bullet.

'Okay. I have a question.' Rob slammed his hands on his hips, his voice raised to an un-Zen-like level. 'Two questions, in fact. One, what's the statute of limitations on a theft charge in England? Two – and this one interests me greatly – why is the FBI here? What the hell did you do to the USA, Annie?'

'That's three questions,' Pat chirped. Her alcohol didn't seem to be evaporating as quickly as everyone else's.

'Please be quiet, Mum.' Annie raised weary eyes to meet Rob's. 'Good questions, and I wish I could answer them. It's just I've never stolen anything from the Queen before so don't know—'

'You stole from the Queen?' If Rob's head had done a Linda Blair right then, Annie wouldn't have been at all surprised. 'I thought you robbed a train. Or rather your dad did. If he was your dad.'

'Cheeky monkey!' Pat spluttered, drawing herself up to her full height. 'I know exactly who her dad was.'

'You don't even know his name, Mum.'

Pat focused – as best she could with one eye partially closed – on Rob. 'For your information, it was the Queen's Royal Mail, so technically the money was stolen from Her Majesty.' Pat jiggled her bosom with her folded arms.

'Great!' Rob clasped his hands behind his head. 'I get a dungeon in the Tower of London.'

'Mrs Hardcastle!' The wall shouted again. 'Time's up. Are you coming out or are we coming in?'

221

Annie placed one hand on the wall and leaned into it, her head bowed. How much more could she take? *Woman up or shut up. Your choice, Annie.* She took three deep breaths.

'Never again.' Her voice turned to steel. 'Never again will I take the blame. My non-existent dad messed up my life, Lester made me think I deserved it and now this copper at the gate wants me to pay for it all. It stops now.'

With shaking hands, Annie pressed the sticky button beside the intercom, letting the outside world in.

29 – QUIETER THAN SILENCE

Outside the gate, Jane directed the Costa Rican policemen to clear the reporters out of the way. Cameramen poked everyone with enormous lenses, fighting for photos and videos of every move. They even took footage of the monkeys overhead.

As Thorn moved to press the intercom button for the last time, the gate creaked and slowly slid open. United States, United Kingdom and Costa Rican authorities got into their respective vehicles and cruised down the driveway, leaving enough men at the gate to keep the reporters out. The paparazzi climbed trees to shove lenses over the closing gate. Jane drew similarities between them and the monkeys, fearful she may be insulting the monkeys. She held conscientious journalists in the highest regard, but the tabloid press was the bane of her life. She recognised several of the British journalists. Neither the BBC nor The Guardian were climbing trees.

Thorn produced a low whistle at the unfolding view of the ocean.

Jane whistled back. 'That bit about crime not paying. Would you care to explain it one more time?'

'Do they have Royal Mail trains in Costa Rica?' Thorn asked. 'Let's stay here and take up where Number Three left off. No need to return home first. Can't think of anything I'd even need to get shipped over.'

'Me neither.' Agatha crossed Jane's mind. She shrugged. Mrs Turnbull next door would make a fine adoptive feline parent.

Thorn shook his head. 'Sooner or later the authorities would come knocking on our door and it would all be over. Crime doesn't pay long term.'

'Would it pay for a month? I'd take a month of this despite the prison sentence.' Jane couldn't quite believe she'd spoken out loud – and to another law enforcement agent.

She eased out of the car and approached the villa door. It opened before she could knock.

Annie Hardcastle faced the multi-national force.

First impression: she didn't strike Jane as your typical Verston girl. Skin a light tan speckled with new freckles. Auburn hair, though sprinkled with silvery highlights, shiny and vibrant. Exposed arms, toned. The obviously new skirt floated around a lithe body.

Yep, crime's paying for this one.

Jane shifted her gaze behind Annie, keen to lay eyes on the other one – the one who'd been benefitting far longer from a crime than Annie, if suspicions turned out to be true.

'You'd better come in.' Annie stood to one side of the door. 'Though do you all need to be here?'

'US and UK agents will be coming inside,' Jane explained. 'The Costa Rican authorities are here in a support capacity, as this is their jurisdiction. We appreciate the assistance they've offered.' She nodded to her official hosts before walking into the villa. Thorn and the two FBI agents followed her.

After the bright sunlight outside, the living room appeared shadowed. Her eyes slowly adjusted, allowing four figures to take shape. Clasping her hands behind her back, Jane adopted a wide stance. 'Let me introduce—'

'Oooooh, hello.' Pat staggered forward. 'Told you I knew that voice, Annie. She's the copper who didn't believe you'd been kidnapped.'

'Turns out I was right about that, Mrs Rickman. As I was saying, I'm Superintendent Jane Williams of the St Albans Special Crimes Unit—'

Pat snorted down her nose. 'Like we have "special crimes" in St Albans.'

Jane ignored the comment. 'And this is Commander Thorn of NCIS. Behind him are FBI Special Agents Thompson and Bart.'

Pat eyed the agents up and down, then hiccupped.

Annie gave Rob a pleading look. 'Could you please help Mum to sit down?'

Rob said nothing. He took Pat's arm, guiding her to the couch.

Agent Bart headed towards the bedrooms. 'We'll just check around, if that's all right.'

'No, it's not all right!' Pat bristled with apparent indignation from the couch.

'Oh, our warrant says it's all right, Mrs Rickman.' Agent Bart set off, hand resting on his gun. A few minutes later, Bart and Thompson returned from their sweep of the villa and the immediate grounds.

'Clear,' said Bart.

'Clear,' said Thompson.

'Clear,' said Pat with a salute. Rob attempted to bat her hand down.

The two agents took up position, one each end of the dining area.

Jane began. 'Perhaps you could introduce us to your friends, Mrs Hardcastle.'

Annie rolled her eyes. 'As if you don't know everyone already.'

Jane questioned where Annie had acquired her courage. If everything Jane had learned was true, Annie should be weary of police officers. Yet here she was, playing coy with multiple agencies, some carrying guns. And why the guns, by the way? Completely out of place in this setting.

'Would be nice if you'd make formal identifications, Mrs Hardcastle.' Jane waited.

Annie cleared her throat. 'My mum, Pat Rickman. Charles and Taylor Newman, who I met on the beach at the Paradise—'

A snigger from Agent Thompson.

'—Resort. And Rob … sorry, your last name is?'

Rob visibly squirmed. 'Fordson.'

'Rob Fordson,' Annie continued, 'who only happens to be here because he stands on his head behind trees.'

Another snigger from Agent Thompson.

Jane spun around again and threw her hands on her hips.

Thompson raised his hands, palms up. 'Well, come on. You've seen the footage, right?'

Jane had to admit the casual acquaintances Annie suggested didn't gel with the photos bouncing around the world. Or with the information contained in the files Thorn held in his hands.

'And lastly, this is Jackson.' Jackson sniffed a few new hands, then found a quiet corner, settling in for the long haul, icing on his bandage and nose.

'Thank you, Mrs Hardcastle.' Jane nodded towards the dining room table for twelve. 'Perhaps we could all sit down. There seems to be plenty of room.'

Rob heaved Pat off the couch, struggling to keep her upright. He steered her to the top end of the table; not because she was the head of the household, but because it was the closest seat.

'Commander Thorn will fill us in on the reason for this visit.' Jane leaned back in her chair and yielded the floor.

Thorn opened the file in front of him. 'Annie. May I call you Annie? Good. You've been connected to a criminal act committed in the United Kingdom in 1963.'

Annie tutted. 'May I point out, for the record, that's several years before I was born.'

'Yes,' Thorn continued, 'I realise you didn't commit the initial crime. However, we are investigating the possibility your father – known to you as Joe Rickman – did.'

Annie narrowed her eyes at her mother. 'Known to me as Joe Rickman. How sad is that?'

'From all the travel searches on your laptop, Annie—'

'You've been on my laptop?'

'And all the newspaper clippings in your flat, Pat—'

Pat struggled to sit upright. 'You've been in my flat?'

'—it would seem you were aware of your father and husband's involvement and may have been planning to run once your lottery win thrust you into the limelight.' Thorn checked his notes. 'We're here to find out about any funds, investments or accounts that may be traceable back to the heist known as the Great Train Robbery. Any safety deposit box keys. Any overseas accounts. Any letters containing directions or maps that could be of assistance to us as we search for the missing two million pounds.'

Annie leapt to her feet, indignation emanating from every feature. Thorn motioned her to sit down, which she did with as much dignity as she could muster. She placed a hand on her chest, appearing to steady herself as best she could before speaking. 'You know, Inspector Thorn—'

'Commander Thorn.'

'Sorry. *Commander* Thorn.' Annie sneered before continuing. 'I'm a little tired of everyone thinking I'm boring, stupid and incapable. I'm a little tired of people thinking I'm pathetic enough to live in a tiny flat in Verston, scrimp and save for necessities and give up my dreams of culinary school, when all the time I possessed a stolen fortune. I'm tired of people thinking a nameless, faceless father could dictate how I lived for decades after he stopped showing any interest in me or my sister or my mum.'

Jane noted the tremor in Annie's chin.

'Exactly how stupid do you think I am?' Annie waited a moment. 'On second thoughts, don't answer that. Because no matter how stupid, I'm apparently brilliant enough to dupe the lottery people into paying me fifty-two million quid, on top of fooling the entire police force for decades. And why did Lester and I play the lottery if we already had plenty of money? Flips me from criminal mastermind back to complete dunce again, doesn't it? So, what am I? Stupid or genius?'

Jane allowed Annie time to collect herself. 'I understand all the conflicting accusations could be confusing.'

'Confusing. Yes. That's the word.' Annie's fists wadded into tight balls.

'I want you to identify someone, Annie.' Commander Thorn pulled a photo out of the file. 'Do you recognise this person?'

Annie took the photo between thumb and forefinger, moving it in and out to focus on the yellowing image. 'No, never saw this person before. Who is he?'

Commander Thorn leaned forward. 'Take your time. Are you sure you don't recognise him?'

'I'm positive. Not from St Albans, is he?' Annie handed the photo back.

'Mrs Newman, would you take a look please?'

Taylor started at hearing her name. 'How on earth would I know who's in a photo concerning Annie? Hardly at the sharing the family album stage of our relationship.'

'Please.' Thorn rose from his seat and pushed the photo across the table.

Taylor huffed. She reached for the photo. Her eyes opened wide. 'Where did you get this?' Her astonished gaze bounced from Jane to Thorn to Charles before locking back on the photo.

'You recognise this man?' Thorn waited.

'Well, of course I do. He's my father.' Taylor threw the photo back across the table.

Pat grabbed it before it reached Thorn. She grinned. 'Let's have a gander at the bastard who messed up your life, then.' She held the photo close to her eyes and squinted. The squint and the grin remained rock steady, as though both had just been sprayed with cement and blasted with a heat lamp.

The photo fell to the floor. Pat's head lolled back and she toppled sideways off her chair in a dead faint.

Annie leaned over her mother with a glass of water, a modesty blanket placed over her ample wayward chest. The three original Casa Luna guests stood close by, having helped drag Pat to the sofa.

Finally, her eyes slowly opened. Pat gazed at all the faces peering down at her. 'Am I dead?'

'No hangovers in heaven, Mum, so you can't be dead.'

With help, Pat sat up and grasped the cup Annie handed her. She took a big gulp and winced. 'Are you trying to kill me? That's raw water!'

'Get used to it.' Annie took the cup. 'Now, do you want to explain what just happened?'

Pat blinked up at Annie. 'I don't know. What did just happen?'

Annie retrieved the photo from the table and thrust it into her mother's hands.

'Oh, I remember now. Handsome man, your father.' Pat stroked the edge of the photo and smiled down at it, then looked up.

Annie followed her mother's gaze. *Shouldn't you be looking at Taylor?*

'Right, the photo of Taylor's father,' Annie said.

'Uh oh.' The softness of Rob's voice sheltered Annie, momentarily, from the enormity of the meaning behind his simple syllables.

'Who's Taylor's father?' Pat said, no mistaking who she was addressing at now. 'This is your father, Annie. Joe Rickman. Though what the hell he's doing on a camel I've no idea. He didn't even want a cat back when I knew him. Never mentioned wanting a camel and I'm sure I'd have remembered if he—'

'Mum!' At Annie's shriek, the edgy FBI agents reached for their guns. 'Forget the bloody camel! What do you mean, Taylor's father is my father?'

Pat tried to stand. Her legs weren't up to the task, resulting in a collapse backwards. 'Stop going on about Taylor. This is the man I married and the father of you and your sister, Lizzie. He has nothing to do with Taylor.'

Williams spoke. 'Actually, Mrs Rickman, he may have everything to do with Taylor.'

Agent Thompson cut in. 'We'll take it from here. This is where the United States gets involved. The photo is of Anthony Richmann, Taylor's father. British authorities contacted the FBI after they searched international records trying to trace Joe Rickman. We tracked him through various countries, including Tunisia, where that photo was taken. Names, dates and immigration records led us to believe Joe Rickman altered his identity, becoming Anthony Richmann, when he entered the United States in 1970. Which led to this photo Mr Newman put on Facebook with the caption "Anthony Richmann". Which led us to you, Taylor. We have reason to believe you're the daughter of a suspect in the Great Train Robbery.'

What's quieter than silence? It became increasingly important to Annie she had a word for the deafening hush around her. Maybe the word would lead to clarification as her world blurred and distorted before her. She was only vaguely aware of Rob catching her, lowering her gently into an oversized armchair. Vaguely aware he pulled up an ottoman beside her and held her hand. Vaguely aware of gazing into his face. She had no idea how long she remained perfectly still.

Slowly, she turned to Taylor. Then to her mother.

Pat was staring at Taylor. 'I knew I'd seen you before,' she whispered. 'I'd seen you every time I looked at Annie. Every time I remembered Lizzie.'

'I saw it, too.' It was Charles who spoke. 'When we first met you, Annie. I saw it, too. I didn't connect the dots. How could I possibly have connected the dots?'

Agents and officers and husbands and mothers and half-sisters and Rob – whatever he was – held a collective breath. Somewhere outside a bird screeched.

Annie studied Taylor. Take the make-up and the hair dye from Taylor, add years of spa treatments and high-flying confidence to herself, and Annie tumbled into eyes that matched, cheekbones that related, hand gestures that understood and an expression of awe that could have been two souls staring into a mirror. Annie bobbed in orbit; floating around this other woman in zero gravity, trying to reach for her, spinning away at the last minute to float untethered in time and space. Until Pat hit the airlock button and everyone plunged to the floor in a heap.

'That bastard!' Pat's cheeks glowed a frightening shade of scarlet, the colour seeping down her throat into her cleavage where it pooled; a puddle of anger between two hillocks. 'Left me with two kids and no money, just so he could set up shop with some whore in America? Gave her a life of luxury? And another kid who grew up with nannies and fancy cars?'

'Taylor never had a nanny. There were a few au pairs though ...' Charles met the eyes of the FBI agents. 'May not be relevant right now.' He reached for Taylor's hand and tapped it lightly as though searching for a vein.

Taylor finally reacted. The corners of her mouth turned upwards, her hands lifted to her face. Her eyes focused on Annie. After a few deep breaths, she let out a euphoric, 'Yes!'

Annie understood, nodding her head slowly, then faster. She grinned at Taylor. 'He's not the man you thought he was, is he?' Her words were gentle.

Taylor shook her head. 'He was nothing more than a crook with a superiority complex. All that crap he gave us about pulling himself up by his bootstraps. Turns out he hadn't even used his own bootstraps. He stole someone else's!' Taylor rose to her feet, hands clasped, head high. 'Dad wasn't a great businessman after all. He cheated. I'm more of a success than he ever was.'

'And I wasn't abandoned because I was worthless,' Annie said, laughing. 'I was set free by a ... by a ... complete pillock! He was the worthless one!'

Thorn turned to Williams. 'If we expected someone to defend this Anthony-Joe bloke, we came to the wrong house.'

Annie sucked in her euphoria in hungry gulps, one of two women who weren't who they thought they were. Yes, born of damaged stock. Yes, lied to. But, here they were, celebrating. Liberated. Never had such bad news been so welcomed.

Pat stood without help, entirely sober now. She retied her halter top with firm hands. 'You wait 'til I see him. I'll knock 'is bloody block off!'

'Mrs Rickman.' Williams moved forward to stand in front of Pat, manoeuvring her into a seated position beside Annie. She grasped both their hands, about to say something, but Taylor cut in.

'You won't be seeing Dad or Joe, or whatever the hell his name was. He's dead. He died eight years ago.'

30 - TO HUG OR NOT TO HUG

What am I supposed to do? Hug her? Annie's hands shook. *Not going to happen.* But should it? Happen? Could she cope with having a sister again? It had taken decades to learn to cope with not having one. To cap it all, this sister was American! Childhoods full of summer camps and sweet sixteen parties, adulthoods full of teeth whiteners, luxury cars and therapists, if the films were to be believed. Could she embrace all that?

Agent Thompson disturbed her thoughts. 'We still have a lot of questions concerning what everyone knew about the funds that helped Anthony Richmann set up his company. If it turns out RM was financed with stolen money, we've got a whole heap of headaches here.'

'What's RM?' Pat held a cold facecloth to her forehead as she spoke.

'Relocation Management,' Thompson replied. 'An international moving company dealing in large government contracts for shipping military supplies. Though when it started, it targeted relocating families in the Chicago area.'

'RM? RM? Why does that sound familiar?' Pat rubbed her arms, then let out a hoot. 'Of course! Royal Mail! Joe always did have a sense of humour.' Pat chuckled again before remembering Taylor. 'Sorry for your loss though, dear.' She didn't sound sorry.

Over the next hour, agents filled in the details of how they had traced Joe/Anthony across the world, through Europe to Chicago. They showed photos as they spoke. RM advertisements from the early 1970s promised to undercut any other moving company quote by ten per cent; easy to do if you were laundering a fortune. A fleet of shiny, new moving trucks graced the pages of first local then national then international newspapers. Cargo ships were added, followed by planes, convoys ploughing through desert sand and frozen tundra. Corporate headquarters and private jets.

Thorn and Williams kept professional eyes on each face in the room. Annie kept her eyes on Williams and Thorn, aware they hunted for signs of deceit, attempts to cover up. They'd see nothing. The connection between stolen money and RM was news to everyone, especially Taylor. Annie felt certain of that. The humiliation and the need to disassociate with the crooked nature of the deal showed itself in winces and pained creases in Taylor's forehead.

Agent Bart questioned Taylor. 'Do you think your mother, Mrs Richmann, knew anything about your father's business dealings?'

Taylor huffed, then slumped sullenly in her chair. 'My mother knew nothing about anything. Dinner parties and keeping the pool cleaned were her duties.'

'Oh, we have soooo much in common, us Number Three wives.' Pat attempted a royal wave. 'Joe always insisted on a clean swimming pool and the best champagne at our parties, too.'

Annie recognised her mother's attempt to cover the hurt. She understood so much about her childhood now – so much about her sister. *Littlest treasure.* The pet name her father called her, once a cherished memory, now an acknowledgement she'd been the least significant of his worldly goods. But would life have been better growing up on the more glamorous end of her father's lie? Based on the little she knew about Taylor, she doubted it. Evidence would suggest Taylor grew up resenting her father's legacy every bit as much as Annie had.

Agent Bart continued. 'We haven't talked to your mother yet, Mrs Newman. Her doctor says she's fragile. We'll need your input on how to interact with her.'

Pat removed the cloth from her forehead. 'What do you mean, fragile? How *fragile* can a woman be who no doubt lives in a mansion with a swimming pool and au pairs? The only pairs I had were a couple of hungry kids and bills piling up two by two.'

'My mother is under the care of her doctors,' Taylor replied stiffly. 'You'll need to get permission to visit her nursing home, though I doubt you'll learn much. I can't believe she was in on the crime.' Taylor stared into her hands for several seconds before speaking, as though to herself; a possible revelation. 'Maybe she found out somehow? Maybe her drinking was related to the discovery of my father's dealings?'

'Wait a minute.' Pat was on her feet. 'You're telling me your mum couldn't cope with being rich? I still coped better than the woman who got everything?' She wrapped her arms around herself in a congratulatory hug. 'I'll be blowed. Well done me, then.'

'Money certainly isn't everything.' Annie nodded to herself. This place, this view, the fridge full of treats, the ordering an entire bakery-full of cupcake equipment without counting the pennies first. It wasn't everything.

Annie rubbed her eyes. Travelocity La La Land, unexploited potential, bitterness, her mother's need to be Richard Burton's daughter, Taylor's attempts to outdo her father, all of it wasted energy. Money couldn't buy back the time they'd all squandered trying to impress someone else – or be someone else. They needed to focus on who they were now.

'Taylor.' Annie began to speak but the anxiety in her throat restricted her voice to a croak. All eyes swivelled towards her. She coughed before trying again. 'Taylor, it's all right. I know how it feels to be you.'

If Annie could have imagined one utterance she would never say to Taylor, that would be the one. The Taylor on the beach, in the hotel room, at the restaurant, selling penthouses in Chicago. That Taylor remained an alien. But this Taylor, born of the photo of a man on a camel, this Taylor she knew.

'I don't even know what it's like to be me right now,' Taylor snapped back. The fight in her was over before it began. Confusion etched her features with worry lines no makeup could hide.

Annie tried again. 'What I mean is, I know how it feels to chase after a father who didn't exist. It's about the only thing we share right now. So, let's start there, shall we?' Annie from Verston took the lead, more worldly-wise, more confident, than she would ever have given herself credit for a few weeks ago.

'Okay,' Taylor whispered. 'Okay,' she said again, accepting Annie's lead, something else Annie couldn't have imagined once upon a luxury beach.

They gazed at each other – an image of 'sister' slowly taking shape.

The FBI agents had more questions for Taylor. Annie left them to it, walking over to the patio doors and peering through the small chink in the screens. Chatter from the paparazzi floated on the breeze towards her. Rob's sailboat undulated as each wave caressed the hull before throwing itself on the beach.

Money bought you a lot, Annie thought, but it required more than money to buy freedom. As for control, it was now obvious you could get that whole concept completely wrong. But there would be no more drowning herself in mouse clicks and almost complete Travelocity reservations. No more following or hiding. She inhaled deeply, absorbing her new world like ocular oxygen. She turned and headed into the kitchen, taking long, purposeful strides.

'Cupcake anyone?' Annie threw Jackson his, marked 'Jackso—', which he caught in true Labrador style.

Annie heard the exchange between Thorn and Williams.

'Bet you can't make cupcakes.'

Williams replied, 'Bet you can't catch one if I throw it at you.'

Jane and Thorn moved out of earshot. Thorn hit speed dial for NCIS on his mobile phone.

'Yeah, Bill? Yeah, release Lester Hardcastle.' Thorn listened to the voice on the other end of the line. 'Hold on. I'll ask.' He held the phone against his chest, his expression serious.

'Bill says Lester has a question. Will Annie will be home soon because they're out of milk.'

Jane smiled across the room at a version of Annie she doubted Lester would even recognise. A woman wearing tropical colours and turquoise jewellery, taking charge in a gourmet kitchen. Her face tilted upwards, her eyes reflected sunlight. Annie's smile was radiant.

'No,' Jane said. 'Tell him she won't be there.'

It never helped to lie to a beaten man.

31 – GET A LIFE!

Annie closed the door on the departing United Nations security forces. The reassuring clunk of the solid wood signalled a collective sigh and the collapsing of weary bodies into plush couch cushions. The fact they'd all had to promise not to leave the area until given clearance was of little concern. Few had the energy to move anywhere. Pat shuffled off to lie down in a bedroom, muttering something about how this never happened when she drank Babycham.

'What a complete and utter mess,' Taylor said, rubbing her temples.

'Oh, come on now.' Rob managed to move as far as the wine cooler in the kitchen. He opened a bottle of champagne. 'It's just paperwork from here on in. If you're all telling the truth, that is.'

Taylor caught the wink. 'Funny, but if you think it's all going to be just paperwork, you wait until they meet my mother. One mention of Dad's name and they'll be scraping her off the ceiling of the serene little retreat they've got her in.'

'Is it possible she knew?' Annie had to ask. 'About your dad? About us?'

'No idea,' Taylor replied. 'I'd find it hard to believe she did because Dad shared nothing with Mom. But her addiction issues preceded my brother's death. It was only after Richard died – oh, God! Richard's middle name's Morris, another RM reference for you – that Mom became more and more unmanageable.'

'How long will it take my mum to connect your brother's name to her supposed father's name?' Annie flattened out her skirt with her hands. 'Mum will probably think "Richard" was a shout-out to her.'

'Maybe it was,' Taylor replied softly. 'My middle name's Elizabeth.'

Taylor Elizabeth. Elizabeth Taylor. Annie doubled over, the name punching her in the gut as surely as any fist. Elizabeth. Lizzie. Her sister's name. Her other sister's name.

Hot tears slid down over burning cheeks to be captured in angry fists and batted away. How dare her father steal her sister away on one continent and reinvent her on foreign soil? A tentative tap on her shaking shoulders reminded her others were in the room still. The tap became a rub, became a squeeze, became a hug. Taylor leaned into Annie's body and held her. Gulping air and willing herself some semblance of control over her emotions, Annie slowly wrapped her arms around Taylor. The women rocked for a moment before Annie pulled away to look at her second chance of a sister. This shock, the latest in a long line of shocks, left her in no doubt her father had taken a part of her mother, real or imagined, and inserted it into his new family. The man who abandoned her to a life of shame and insecurity had, after all, remembered a part of her. Nothing more than a token consolation, perhaps, but it was all she had. Her throat constricted. She had to make a choice: remain angry for the rest of her life or accept a tiny morsel of atonement and move on. Moving on – though into the complete unknown – seemed simpler than continuing a life of rage.

She swatted at the last of the tears. 'I'll try to find comfort in your name. Even if Richard Burton wasn't actually part of my family fiasco.'

Taylor stretched her arms above her head and closed her eyes. 'Guess we need to find comfort where we can. Part of me feels I should apologise to you for taking your money. Though if it's any consolation, I was disinherited after Richard's death. Blaming my ... our ... father in public was an expensive move, but I don't regret a word of it. Especially now.'

Annie smiled, sadly. 'It wasn't my money. Or Dad's. Or yours. The more I think about this the more I realise you weren't the lucky one after all. We both ended up losing a sibling and blaming others for how our lives turned out. We spent years trying to outrun ourselves. Incidentally, who's going to believe outrunning our demons would lead us here?'

'Oh, I don't know.' Charles cupped his chin in his hand. 'Quite a natural segue really; from winning a lottery on one continent to losing two careers on another. From thinking I was the crook to finding out my father-in-law was. From discovering a sister to solving a fifty-year-old crime. Just another day in the tabloid press.'

Taylor didn't even try to hide her irritation. 'You know, Charles, I've seen disturbing changes in you since you lost your job. You speak in tabloidese and one of the most shocking aspects of all this is finding out you have a Facebook profile on which you could post photos of Dad.'

'Before you write me off as unsalvageable, let me explain.' Charles moved onto the couch next to Taylor and pulled her close. 'It was the eighth anniversary of your dad's death. I'd been sitting at home twiddling my thumbs, bored out of my skull. For a laugh I joined Twitter and Facebook. I found a box of photos in the closet, scanned the photo of your dad on the camel and posted it. I knew you always derided people who spent hours—'

'—posting about the lives they wished they had, only didn't because they were too busy posting.' Taylor hesitated. 'Sorry. I shouldn't judge.'

Charles stroked his wife's arm. 'You shouldn't, but you do. We all do. Anyway, I wanted to find something to make you laugh that evening. I clicked "post" about five minutes before you walked through the door with your damned cardboard box the day you quit Ashcroft. Facebook got forgotten after that.'

'Good job, too,' Taylor said. 'A reminder of my father the day I was essentially fired wouldn't have made me laugh at all.'

Charles kissed Taylor's head before continuing. 'Once in Costa Rica, I had a little more time to kill so went back on Twitter. I was horrified at what I found posted about myself all over social media. It got worse and worse. I figured I had two choices: go into hiding for the rest of my life or come out swinging. I chose swinging. I signed up on Instagram and Snapchat.'

'How on earth does that help you?' Taylor asked.

Rob obviously didn't understand either. 'Seems counter-intuitive. How would inflicting more social media outlets on yourself help in this situation?'

'Oh, it helped.' Charles waggled his eyebrows. 'Knowledge is power, and I get the last laugh. I connected with a couple of others from my old company who'd also been trashed unfairly. We explored ways to restore our reputations, to separate fact from fiction. As word spread about what we were trying to do, many others reached out to us, from all over the world. We were sitting on a tsunami of individuals who needed help. People who, through no fault of their own, fell prey to innuendo and false judgement. So, wait for it … I'm now the CEO of "Clickbait Bites Back", a non-profit organisation devoted to restoring the good characters of individuals who've been treated unfairly on social media.'

Taylor choked on a mouthful of champagne. 'A non-profit, social media company? I must admit, those are two concepts I never thought you'd be a part of.'

'Me neither,' Charles said. 'But we're developing software capable of tracking an individual's profile across all social outlets. We then identify and clarify false claims about people before they get out of hand. Bet you never thought I'd be meeting Bill Gates. He's interested in helping out.'

'A nice guy,' Rob said. All eyes turned his way. 'Oops.'

Taylor scowled. 'And your connection to Bill Gates is …?'

Rob refused to make eye contact. He checked a finger nail instead. 'I was in computers.'

'Now in real estate, apparently,' Taylor muttered into her glass. She focused back on Charles, however. 'I'm proud of you, hon. You've reinvented yourself, and in a way that will help others. Good for you.'

'Taylor!' Charles squeezed his wife's hand. 'Are you going soft on me?'

'Not at all.' Taylor nodded towards Annie. 'Annie and I will be the toughest clients you'll ever have. You've got to extricate us both from the headlines this whole mess will generate for months.'

'From high-flying financier to daytime use of Facebook.' Annie tut-tutted. 'How the mighty fall – and in your case, rise again.'

Rob rolled his eyes. 'People, I've dealt with a lot today. I'm a little too battered and bruised to stand another confession. Tell me you aren't on Facebook too, Annie?'

'Very funny.' Annie wagged her finger at Rob. 'I'll have you know all the members of the Royal Family have Facebook pages. But no, I don't have a Facebook page. I wouldn't have known what to put on it. Nothing ever happened to me.'

'That doesn't seem to stop anyone posting.' Charles nodded, sagely.

Annie figured now was as good a time as any to commit to fully embracing her failings. There was a limit to what she could blame on Lester and her parents. 'I searched thousands of travel sites, haute couture sites, gourmet food sites. I fed my needs through the computer screen. I now realise it was only giving me more reason to focus on what I didn't have and more time to blame others for it. What I should have been doing was putting my time and energy into going out and getting the life I wanted. I could have ignored Lester, worked full time and saved for culinary school. I could have been living, not observing.'

'I found observing others easier than observing myself after the collapse of my company,' Charles said. 'Pure escapism, that social media world. Not the real world at all.'

Annie waved her arm around the room. 'It couldn't be less real than me living in this house and being related to Taylor. Surely even the worst troll couldn't have conjured up our father's escapades?'

'I agree,' Taylor said. 'But it's all out there now which is a relief, somewhat surprisingly. I propose a toast: to truth and freedom.' Four champagne glasses clinked together.

Annie thought Rob was about to say something else. Whatever it was, he changed his mind. She put her glass down and folded her arms 'Before we wrap this crazy day up, we have one more piece of business to attend to.'

Taylor groaned. 'Can't it wait? I'm exhausted.'

'No. It's important.' Annie pasted on a serious expression. 'Should we give Rob his towel back or not?'

32 – CHAMPAGNE WISHES, CUPCAKE DREAMS

The first of the sun's rays rose behind the villa, spreading citron, amber and mauve hues over the lush vegetation and the sleeping monkeys. Annie tiptoed past all the bedroom doors, afraid to make coffee in case she woke anyone. With the dawn came the hope she could sit outside without the paparazzi snapping away at her. Besides, surely there was nothing more the world wanted to know. She settled into a lounger by the pool.

The moving shadow in the treeline made her jump. She prepared to leap back into the villa and slam the screens shut.

'It's okay, it's me.'

Annie sank back into the cushions as Rob and Jackson crossed the lawn. 'You scared me,' Annie whispered. 'How'd you know I was up?'

'I didn't. Jackson did.' Rob gave Jackson's head an affectionate rub. 'Once you've given Jackson a cupcake, he doesn't forget. He was driving me crazy to come visit. I also offered to lend Charles a pair of shorts.' He waved a pair of khakis, speckled with salty splashes after their journey from sailboat to shore.

Annie laughed as Jackson licked her bare legs, then her hand.

'You have got to shower more. Jackson can't be expected to take up all the slack.' Rob's eyes reflected the sun's rays that had begun their sweep across the lawn in search of the beach.

'Sorry, the shower's on a coin meter and I only won a small fortune. I'm planning on once a week showers to keep costs down.' Annie giggled, not at the joke but at the mindboggling realisation it *was* a joke.

'Jackson won't be pleased to hear his cupcakes may be rationed. Break it to him gently.' Rob bent down to rub his head against his dog's. He sank into a lounger next to Annie and stretched out his legs.

'I'd offer you coffee but I'm scared to wake anyone up. Wanted to own this morning. Selfish, I know.' Annie closed her eyes for a moment.

'I should leave,' Rob said, placing his hands on the arms of the chair.

'No. No, really.' Annie put out a hand to stop him moving, brushing his arm before drawing her fingers back. 'I don't want you to leave. Just wanted time away from Mum and my … sister.' The word rolled across Annie's tongue; a hard, cold rock as foreign as any of the strange drinks she'd tasted over the last few weeks.

'Understand.' Rob rested back in his chair.

Paradise seeped into the comfortable space between the two visitors. Gentle waves, the jovial splash of the pool waterfall, rustles of stiff palm leaves and bird chatter. Malinche trees cloaked in red blooms. Birds of Paradise, stiff and formal like floral herons, strutting their stuff beside the hammock. Annie inhaled deeply, absorbing the heady scents of the multitude of plants she had yet to identify. She stretched out her toes, reaching into the soul of this place as she had during her first night on the beach, wrapping herself in a sense of home she'd never felt before. Was this it? Her soul place?

'How do you feel right now?' Rob's words steered her back.

'Puh!' The expulsion of air was out before she could stop it. Pool water drank in the dawn rays, morphing from a black hole to an inviting reflection of the sky while Annie struggled to shape chaos into words. 'I feel I woke up on an alien planet in an alien body speaking an alien language and thinking alien thoughts that don't compute with the database I've been using all my life. And yet, I feel at home.'

'So, a bit strange then, ET?'

Her smile displayed brittle edges. 'You wouldn't understand.' Old baggage appeared out of nowhere, stacked haphazardly next to her chair. It blocked her view of the villa.

Rob's soft eyes spilled genuine concern. 'Try me.'

Annie made the decision to trust him. 'You strike me as someone who's done things. I don't know what things, but you've been involved in the world. Made decisions, taken control of something big. It shows in your face. I bet you can't even imagine sitting and watching the world go by with no idea how to join the parade, your only view of it through a fifteen-inch screen. I'm not proud I let that happen to me, by the way. There are many out there who would never have accepted my life. You must think I'm weak. I do.'

Humiliated, she turned her face away. Rob said nothing, which confirmed her worst fears about what he must think. Despite fighting back yesterday, this new Annie was still under construction. She had nothing to offer another person until she worked out what she could offer herself. She waited for Rob to get up and leave.

He didn't. Instead, he stroked her shoulder with tentative fingers until she turned back to face him. 'Annie, I get it,' Rob said. We've lived different lives. You think your life is somehow inferior to mine. That's your interpretation by the way. Here's my truth. I married young, divorced quickly. I struggled to pay the electric bill on my first office space. I slept in my office for a year and took the bus to meetings when my car wouldn't start. I gave up time after time and let others tell me what to do. The difference between us is I decided to choose my own future while you decided to accept the future other people saw for you.'

Bullseye.

'You thought about what others had, what you could have if you could only control everything and if you only had money. The truth is, I've met plenty of unhappy, rich, controlling people. None of those things has given them what they need.'

'Computers must pay well,' Annie said, 'if you've been hanging out with the rich crowd.'

'Trying to stay away from the rich crowd, actually. Present company excepted.' Rob winked, which started a chain reaction in Annie's stomach that spread to her cheeks. But what rich crowd was Rob thinking of. The ex-wife? The multiple girlfriends he'd had since?

'Money – either too much or too little – can make us forget our dreams,' Rob said, softly. 'But I'm sensing it won't make you do that. Your new opportunities have given you a freshness, an appreciation of the world, not to mention a feistiness that puts many of the people I've been around to shame. I'm pretty sure you'll never take this new life for granted. You'll never view freedom or options with anything other than awe. That's where your old life remains relevant and where our lives collide. I'm making a fresh start too. We can be the people we want to be now. An excellent plan for you and me. Us.'

Surprise spread across Rob's face. Had he not expected to hear his own words? He held Annie's gaze; his eyes questioning. Annie didn't have an answer; the silent enquiry lingering in the gently stirring breeze.

'But, most importantly,' Rob continued, 'this could all be good for Jackson. You're the first woman Jackson's taken to in … forever.'

Annie leaned down to stroke Jackson, snoring between the loungers. 'Could be because he hasn't met many women who make cupcakes lately.'

'Sadly, I believe you've hit the nail on the head.' Rob dropped his head into his hands and fake-sobbed. 'You want to hear pathetic? I'm fifty-two years old and I've only recently discovered I have a thing for lemon icing. What a loser.'

'There, there, Sir Lawrence Olivier,' Annie said, reaching out for Rob's shoulder; fingers no longer pulling back. 'Seems we've both got a lot of catching up to do.'

Rob's face snapped up. 'So, ice the damn cupcakes already, woman!'

'Ha! You control your own coffee pot *and* your own cupcakes. Ice them yourself.' It was Annie's turn to wink. Rob stood up and offered his hand to pull Annie up beside him. They crossed the lawn towards the villa together.

Charles sat at the desk, coffee and the computer in front of him. He wore the bathrobe from yesterday as no one but Rob had dared to leave Casa Luna last night.

'Morning, Rob,' Charles said. 'Did you know you're missing?'

'Missing what? My marbles? The point?' Rob threw the shorts at Charles before walking to the kitchen and pouring two mugs of coffee.

'I'm serious. You've been missing for months.' Charles beckoned him over to the screen.

Rob sauntered over to the screen, briefly pursuing the images before heading back to the kitchen. 'Oh, that. That's old news.'

'What's old news?' Annie asked, as Rob handed her a mug of coffee.

Charles fake emulated Rob's nonchalance. 'Oh, nothing. Only that everyone thought Towel Boy here fell off the edge of the earth when he sold his company to Bill Gates six months ago. That company's chang-ing the world itself, if you believe this article in the *Wall Street Journal*.' Charles spun the desk chair around and placed his hands behind his head. 'Care to comment, Dr Robert Fordson?'

'You're a doctor?' Annie raised her eyebrows. 'Good, because Mum's going to need one when she wakes up.'

'Not that kind of doctor,' Charles said. 'The MIT kind of doctor.'

'Is MIT the American version of the NHS?'

Charles shook his head. 'I doubt the National Health Service recruits many from the Massachusetts Institute of Technology. We're in the presence of greatness, Annie.' Charles bowed his head towards Rob.

'I've always said a good tech school was better than a stupid univer-sity.' Annie arranged cupcakes on a plate. 'I figured I'd get more out of cooking school than anything Oxford could give me. Don't let Charles and his fancy Yale hat get to you, Rob.'

A laugh, more a spasm of breath, escaped Rob's mouth. He appeared delighted by Annie's comment. 'I'll try not to be jealous, though I admit it stings a bit. Much better rowers at Yale.' He pulled out a chair at the kitchen counter.

Charles clamped his hands to his head. 'Honestly, you two. What's this laissez faire stuff? MIT's one of the most prestigious schools in the world and did you not hear the bit about Bill Gates?'

'We've relinquished control of everything except the coffee pot and cupcakes,' Rob said, bowing towards Annie. 'Grasshopper here doesn't give a rat's ass anymore about what the world thinks, right?'

'Right.' Annie bowed back. 'But where I come from, they say "monkey's arse".'

'Quit it, both of you.' Charles lost his patience. 'You'll care when the next bunch of cameras get stuck in your faces.'

That got Annie's attention. 'All right. Hit me with the latest from the tabloids. Which, incidentally, you obviously enjoy way too much and that could get your Yale hat revoked. Maybe you can get him into the tech school you went to, Rob.'

Another expression of pure joy lit Rob's face. Annie couldn't for the life of her work out what was going on in his head. Did he always take put downs this well?

Charles switched screens from the *Wall Street Journal* to something with more colourful photos. '"Missing GenChip Founder Seen with Lottery Winner."' Charles paused for effect, then read more. '"Technology Titan, Doctor Robert Fordson, who hasn't been seen since selling GenChip to Microsoft for a reported half a billion dollars" – that's with a 'B' Annie – "has been spotted with Annie Hardcastle in Costa Rica. The relationship between the two is unclear, though rumour has it things got hot and heavy during a beach tryst." Would you care to comment on that, Dr Fordson?' Charles held out his coffee spoon microphone.

Annie pushed Charles aside and plopped down at the computer. She scanned page after page, shocked at the photos of her and Rob smiling at each other by a pool. Even she had to admit her expression could be misconstrued as sultry and suggestive. *But that only happened this morning!*

Her entire married life, she'd stared through a laptop portal into other worlds, believing the images and stories to be representative of – or at least in the ballpark of – truth. Now, faced with her own pixilated existence, it bore not a single iota of accuracy. Of course Rob wasn't a missing millionaire. Of course they weren't a couple. Only when Charles opened other windows, from non-tabloid outlets, showing Rob on stage, Rob at white tie events, Rob with Bill Gates, did Annie believe at least half the story was true.

She twisted around in her chair to face Rob. 'Start talking, Towel Boy.'

Rob sipped his coffee, unfazed. 'That's my favourite title to date. You may call me Towel Boy Fordson from now on.'

Annie fought to control the hinge on her jaw. It kept flopping open. 'Seriously, is this true?'

''Fraid so.' Rob winced like he was confessing to extortion.

'Explains the fingernails.'

''Fraid so.' Rob curled his fingers and studied the ragged tips. 'But I'm hoping the after-effects of GenChip wear off quickly. Apparently, yoga and cupcake therapy help.'

Taylor walked into the kitchen and filled her coffee cup. 'Morning everyone. Did I miss anything?'

'Not much,' Charles said. 'A nice sunrise, Jackson making a spectacu-lar cupcake catch – oh, and the revelation Robbie here is Doctor Robert Fordson.'

'*The* Doctor Robert Fordson? The tech guru and philanthropist?' Taylor's cup sank away from her mouth. 'No way! But, wait. Why are you scouting out properties for Ashcroft? I mean, it's a prestigious com-pany and all—'

Rob threw his head back before placing his hands in a prayer posi-tion. 'I'll ask one more time. Who's Ashcroft?'

Taylor groaned, then covered her face with her hands. 'Ugh. Guess I got it all wrong. Used to be quite good at putting two and two together and coming up roses.'

Charles raised his eyebrows at his wife. 'Evidence has been to the contrary on that one for, let's see, maybe your whole life?'

Annie cast a sideways glance at Rob. 'You mean, Taylor, you've also discovered you know nothing? Control nothing? We should start a club.'

'We already have, haven't we?' Rob asked, eyes on Annie. 'But I'm here to check out the property market for an old college friend of mine. Nothing for the tabloids in that.'

'Stick around. I'm sure they'll find something unfit to print, given time,' Charles said.

Rob raised his wrist in front of his eyes with a cheeky grin. The uniform colour from elbow to fingers suggested he hadn't worn a watch in a long time. 'I can only stick around until the cupcakes run out. Then I'm gone.' Rob put his feet up on the second counter stool; comfortable, as though he belonged there.

Emotion stung Annie's nostrils and blurred her vision. Could he be part of her life now? This nail-biting, head-standing computer geek who'd apparently changed the world, yet walked away from it all to collide with Annie from Verston? *Sure! Why not?*

'Jackson, will you help me make more cupcakes?' Annie knelt to hug Jackson, who'd followed her into the kitchen and promptly lay down in the way of everything. Or rather in the way of anything that may fall off the countertop. Annie pulled out a mixing bowl and smiled at Rob.

Tech guru. Cupcake lover. Towel Boy. In search of home, like everyone else.

'Here,' he said. 'Let me help.'

'I don't typically believe in coincidences.' Rob and Annie sat at the kitchen counter waiting for the cupcakes to cool. Charles and Taylor had gone to their room to get ready to leave, Charles in Rob's shorts. 'But you and Taylor meeting under these circumstances? With these consequences? It boggles the mind.'

'Doesn't it, though?' Annie replied. 'Maybe jet skis control the world.'

Rob chuckled. 'From now on I'm changing the saying to "When jet skis fly".'

Annie laughed until tears spilled onto her cheeks. Wiping her eyes, she caught her breath before turning serious. 'And we're back to that illusive control. When I first met Charles and Taylor, I imagined they controlled everything. Yet here we all are. None of us in control of anything.'

'Good. We're on the same page then, and those cupcakes smell amazing.' Rob tried to take one from the cooling rack, but Annie smacked his hand away. 'Hey! I'm Dr Robert Fordson. I get what I want, right?'

Annie fake frowned. 'Not before it's iced you don't and maybe not even then with that attitude.'

Rob rested his chin in his hands and smiled at her. 'You have no idea how refreshing you are.'

'You mean how freakish I am?' Annie cursed her 'shields up' mentality.

'No. Refreshing.' Rob reached forward and tucked a wayward strand of her hair behind her ear. 'You don't care about what I may or may not be. I'd forgotten how nice it was to be talked to as nothing more than a guy who bites his nails and craves cupcakes. To make jokes, to relax by a pool with a beautiful woman without wondering what she wanted.'

Annie could only imagine what a beautiful woman wan—

Wait! Is he talking about me?

'You didn't know so you didn't care and you still don't care even though you know, if you get what I mean. Because MIT and tech start-ups and God knows what other crap I've been involved with still doesn't matter to you.'

'Are you calling me stupid?' For the first time, Annie dared to believe someone didn't think she was stupid.

'No. Enlightened. A cupcake guru.'

'Well, I am pretty good with an icing bag.' Annie waggled her eyebrows at Rob, who chuckled back.

'You don't care about the money,' Rob added. 'That makes you the first person I've met in a long time who doesn't.'

'A wise man once taught me money doesn't get you much.' Annie struggled to talk and recover from Rob's fingers brushing her cheek. She reined herself in, pulled her face back from Rob's. 'But turns out he's a plonker.'

'What's a plonker?'

'Well, I'll tell you.' Annie couldn't control the irritation in her voice. She just wasn't sure what she was irritated at. 'In your case, it's someone who believes if he'd knocked on my door in Verston while I was standing with the electric bill in one hand and a bank statement in the other, his money wouldn't have mattered. That's a Fordson plonker.'

'I've made you mad. I'm sorry. Would it help if I told you I gave most of the money away? After all that work, I found I didn't need it after all. My nails certainly didn't.'

Annie shook her head, furious at herself. 'No, no. I'm sorry – and good for you for giving it away, incidentally – but I'm struggling to adjust to all this.' She swept the room with her hand. 'To you. You never met Lester. If you had, you'd know compliments and interest in me weren't exactly standard fare. I'm not used to positive feedback and encouragement and … and … thinking about the future.'

'Then you need to start thinking about all that, and soon, or you'll let others steal even more of your time.' Rob stole a cupcake. 'And another thing, "plonker" doesn't even begin to fit this Lester guy. Not a strong enough word.'

Lester's name coming from Rob's lips sounded completely wrong, but in that moment, Annie knew Rob was right when he'd said her old life still held relevance in her new one. It had to be acknowledged – dealt with. No more wasted time.

Taylor thought of her grandfather as she packed to leave the Paradise Resort. Though only returning to Chicago to put the apartment on the market and tie up loose ends before relocating her business to Guanacaste, a strange sadness washed over her at leaving this kinder, gentler, country. Sand between her toes had become strangely satisfying. Having a half-sister had become strangely … she didn't have a word for it yet. A shiver of excitement ran down her spine. When the word came to her, she suspected it would be a pleasant one. Was she leaving as a kinder, gentler person? With a smile, she vowed to keep working on it.

'I promise to stop being my father's daughter and start being my grandfather's granddaughter,' she announced to Charles.

'Good,' Charles said. 'I never met your mother's father, but he's got to be an upgrade over your father.'

'True that. No more living to avenge my brother or impress my father.' Taylor said. 'Kind is the new me. Patient is the new me. I'll clean off my glasses before I start a conversation. I'll really listen.'

'Bet you'll sell more homes that way, too.'

'We'll see. At least I don't have Ashcroft as competition.' It had been a blow to hear from an old associate Ashcroft never intended to set up business in Costa Rica. She'd fallen for his pump fake to get rid of her. The knowledge stung, but Taylor was learning life was too short and changed too quickly to maintain resentfulness as her primary motivation.

During their last breakfast at the Paradise Resort, Taylor smiled at the hostess, chatted with the coffee server, then helped an elderly lady work out how to operate the hand dryer in the bathroom. *Three weeks to break a habit…*

Louis Vuitton stuffed back in the trunk, the car whisked Charles and Taylor away towards the Liberia airport. Taylor pointed to the cameras and microphones jostling for position at the airport doors. 'Okay, Mr Spin Doctor. Spin us out of this.'

Charles took a deep breath, flung open the car door and marched ahead of Taylor. 'Ladies and gentlemen,' he shouted over the voices. 'I understand you have questions about Relocation Management and Ms Newman's father. But this story is as new to us as it is to you. Please let us adjust to our new reality and find out the facts behind it all, real facts rather than innuendo. You'll receive more information, as will we, when it's released by the authorities. Thank you. That's all.'

Taylor cast her eyes down, then changed her mind. This was her father's mess, not hers. She had nothing to hide. Head held high, she strode towards the airport doors.

'Well done, Charles,' Taylor whispered.

'That should keep them quiet for a bit,' Charles whispered back.

'Is it true, your half-sister is Richard Burton's granddaughter, Ms Newman?'

'And that you're named after Elizabeth Taylor?'

'Is it true you're hiding Elizabeth's diamonds?'

'Mr Newman, did you invest retirees' stolen money in Robert Fordson's GenChip?'

Taylor glared at Charles. 'So much for "that should keep them quiet".'

Kindness took a back seat as Taylor shoved her way through the crowd.

EPILOGUE – YOU GET WHAT YOU PAY FOR

One month later:

If money was one thing, it was dizzyingly fast. It made solicitors work quicker, realtors pull strings, last-minute flights accessible. Annie clicked her heels and landed – dazed and awed – in her new home: Casa Luna.

She placed the legal-sized envelope down on the kitchen counter, having carried it in her hands almost the entire trip from England. It contained a decree nisi; such a simple piece of paper, but the power it contained overwhelmed her. In six weeks' time her marriage would be over. It gave the thick, creamy yellow paper the status of Magna Carta.

Lester had begun to protest, according to the solicitor. However, he was persuaded 'resistance was futile'. As a *Star Trek* fan, Annie imagined Lester appreciated the sentiment she'd asked the solicitor to share with her soon-to-be ex-husband, from his no-longer-assimilated ex-wife.

As she'd prepared to leave England, her mother filled her in on Lester's progress – or lack thereof. He was still in their old flat, 'weighing his options'. One option, apparently, involved recruiting a replacement shirt ironer from the Fox and Rabbit; bartender, Ashley. With the world as his oyster, Annie pictured Lester pulling the shell shut and curling up to wait for a grain of sand to make him worth something. Verston was as big a world as he could imagine. Would Ashley at least convince Lester to go to the horse races rather than watch them on the television? She found she didn't care. She knew one thing: Ashley would earn every single penny of her lottery windbag. *Oops; windfall.*

In her new kitchen, a world away from her old, and for the last time, Annie spun the golden noose around her finger. Her plan had been to walk down to the beach and throw it in the ocean. Now, she didn't want to contaminate the location. She tossed it in the air, caught it in one hand and bounced it into the rubbish bin. 'Let it sit in a landfill somewhere.'

In all this newness, she would bury herself in the task of doing her duty to herself. After all, she'd completed her duty to her mother. Pat now lived in a three-bedroom, two-bath home with two-car garage and a small garden, close to the shops with a view of the Verston cricket pitch. Annie chuckled at the thought of her mother scrutinising the comings and goings of the whole village through her front windows. God help Verston.

She hadn't informed Rob she was back in Costa Rica. They'd parted on the beach a month ago, Annie fighting back tears as she hugged Jackson first, then sinking into Rob's arms, holding on tight, refusing to turn her face upward for the kiss she desperately wanted. There had already been too much overlap. Annie needed Lester and the Fox and Rabbit and Verston bled from her system first. She needed to apply leeches to the internet searches, to the shabby wallpaper of her former home. And, most importantly, she resolved to stand on her own two feet before thinking about Rob's offer, his rather pleading offer, to meet again, anywhere in the world. Anywhere in the world used to be the sole property of her imagination and the Travelocity website.

The world was terrifying.

Rob was terrifying.

The texts between them had dwindled but wandering through the house – her home – she missed his presence.

Outside, Annie smiled at King Neptune from the patio, greeting an old friend. She welcomed herself back to the flowers with huge waxy heads incapable of surviving an English frost, the speckled islands surrounded by shimmering skirts of azure and turquoise. None of this should make sense. Yet somewhere in her soul, it all began to settle like a handful of glitter thrown into still air. She'd been searching for home since the day she'd been born into a false family on the wrong continent. Costa Rica meant a new beginning, yes, but it also held the promise of roots.

She placed the photo of Lizzie on the coffee table. She intended to live – really live – in this living room.

Flour covered the kitchen counters – and half the kitchen floor. Ten cooling trays spread across the countertops, the stove top and the breakfast table. Annie mixed various colours into batches of icing, writing down exact proportions in a notebook. On the first page of the notebook, Annie had written, 'Just because I don't need to dream anymore, doesn't mean I shouldn't.'

She had pictured her own cake business since childhood. Now, with the influx of Americans and Europeans to Guanacaste, Annie hoped she had a successful business model for supplying the local hotels and restaurants. She meant to give it her best try, anyway, currently developing an icing that replicated the flavour of the local tres leches cake. The idea of small cupcakes instead of giant slabs of fruit cake thrilled her. Wedding cakes carried too much baggage. From now on her focus would be light, easy to eat, less time-consuming, happy little treats. No strings attached.

Rubbing her shoulders, she took off her Union Jack apron – one of her only shout-outs to her heritage – and flung it over a chair. The dishes could wait. The floury floor no longer judged her and found her wanting. Or if it did, she didn't care.

Annie picked up her phone and stared at it. She'd been thinking about making this call for a while. As she got closer to setting up an actual business, she'd lost her nerve a bit. She inhaled deeply and hit the number on speed dial.

Annie had been over to the new house in Playa Flamingo several times now. The winding roads skirting the bay coated her car with dust but the views more than compensated for the mess. Driving past gorgeous homes would once have instilled a sense of missing out. Now on her drives around the area, Annie just smiled at the porches and the pools and the stunning views. She wouldn't trade her villa for anything. 'Family dinners' she and Taylor had decided to call their evening get togethers; initially in jest, then in disbelief, now in a comforting sort of acceptance. Last week, Annie presented Taylor with a photo of the two of them together by the pool at Casa Luna. Their faces now smiled out from a frame on the desk in Taylor's home office.

'Hi, Annie.' With barely a pause, Charles called, 'Taylor, it's for you.'

Taylor laughed down the phone line. 'Need another house?'

Annie chuckled back. 'Need another business opportunity? Seriously, I need your help. Or rather your reputation as a savvy businesswoman.'

'Fair's fair. I tried to use your reputation once.'

'True,' Annie replied. 'The good news is, thanks to Charles and "Clickbait Bites Back", we both have reputations good enough to share.'

'Good news indeed. The bad news is he's so swamped with work it's a sad commentary on the world we live in.' Taylor paused. 'Anyway, what's this business venture about? I'm busy with the exploding housing market here but I'm happy to help.'

'Cupcakes. I need help setting up a cupcake business. I don't know where to start and it's frankly a bit intimidating.'

'Let me get this straight,' Taylor said. 'You travelled halfway round the world, fought off the FBI, NCIS and the paparazzi, outran your husband – and, even more impressively, your mother – yet you don't feel up to opening a cupcake store. Interesting.'

Annie chuckled. 'When you put it like that.' A few short months ago, she'd never have believed herself capable of any of that. 'Okay. Let's pretend I could do it by myself. Maybe instead, let's say I'd appreciate your help. How's that?'

'Can we call it "Two Sisters Cupcakes"?'

'Nope. It's going to be "Casa Loony Cupcakes". Name's non-negotiable.'

Taylor huffed down the phone line. 'See. You don't need me.'

'Maybe not as a cupcake-making assistant. How about as a friendly support system? Somewhere to turn for advice. Be fun to find out how that feels.'

'Yes, it would.' Taylor's voice cracked a little down the phone line. 'Talk soon … sis.'

Annie hung up with a smile. Taylor would teach her to push herself forward. Annie would teach Taylor to bake – and apologise for breathing. On second thoughts, nobody needed that British skill anymore; least of all Annie.

She walked outside. New mosaic tiles depicting a sign saying, 'Casa Loony' had been added to the pool floor. It hung off King Neptune's trident. Annie couldn't help thinking it would have been a better title for the flat in Verston than here, but her mother's name for the place had stuck.

She wiggled her toes down into the succulent ground cover, working herself deep into the new soil of home. She tried to recall the sensation of socks. It made her claustrophobic. How quickly experiences lived over a lifetime faded if you wanted them to. This new technicoloured, sockless, cupcake-filled world spoke of home in a way the past fifty-odd years never had.

Her mind wandered to the question she often asked herself: was she drawn to this new place by a cosmic connection, or simply driven out of an old place by … what? Regret? The embarrassment of allowing herself to be such a weak rendition of the Annie she was supposed to be? Was Costa Rica home, or simply not so obviously *not* a home as Verston had been? Life would give her time to ponder that. Or time would give her life to ponder that. It didn't matter which.

Back in the kitchen, Annie swept the floor and started loading baking pans into the dishwasher. A shadow fell across the counter, making her jump.

'I knew you'd be here.'

Annie's tongue seized up. She felt the need to mentally practise the words before speaking. 'And how's that, Towel Boy?' Every muscle in Annie's body strained to resist leaping over the counter to hug Rob.

'It was the expression on your face by the pool the morning after you found out about your sister. Despite all the chaos and craziness, you looked … content. At home. The real you. I want you to know I'm here for the real you, and I'll be somewhere out there,' his arm swept the ocean, 'if you need me.' Rob walked around the counter and kissed Annie's cheek, placing a small collection of shells in her limp hands. He closed her fingers gently around the simple treasures.

Annie let her eyes rest on their intermingled fingers. She smiled at Rob's nails. Longer. Smoother. Ten pink signs of progress.

Jackson gazed longingly from Annie to the cooling racks. He let out a sigh before licking Annie's hand as he passed by to follow Rob back to the sailboat.

'For God's sake, take a shower, woman!' Rob's words, caught by the breeze, swirled through the foliage, drifting into the house before infusing their warmth into the walls of Casa Luna.

Annie opened her mouth to call Rob back. She abruptly snapped her mouth shut, unsure of whose voice she'd hear: Old Annie, who'd always been disappointed when she relied on others for her happiness, or New Annie who was determined to make it on her own now. She decided, just to be on the safe side, to wait a while to find out which voice was stronger. The risk was great. However, she knew something for certain: she would be the only judge of how she led her life from now on.

Rob disappeared across the beach. Annie strolled to the patio and sighed, then jumped as though stung by a jellyfish.

She shouted up at the vast blue sky, 'I get it!' She didn't need a lifetime to work it out. This sense of home wasn't because the trees or the ocean or the monkeys or cupcakes or even a sister said 'home'. It was because she was 'her' here. She could think as herself, plan what she wanted to do, to feel, to be. No more running away, she'd run towards – arms outstretched, eyes wide open.

Annie wasn't home. Home was Annie.

THE END

ACKNOWLEDGEMENTS

I'm astounded at the number of people who willingly jumped in to help guide Annie's journey. My writing community, friends and family are special indeed.

My writers group, Tuesday With Stories, for your boundless energy, support and wisdom.
Gail Anderson, Priscilla Baldwin, Cindi Dyke, Ann Morgan, Rhonda Seligman, and Debbie Troxel – beta readers extraordinaire. Friends extraordinaire.

Meredith Efken, who completed a substantive edit on an early draft of this novel and taught me much about story structure.
Wendy Janes and Pauline Wiles, for their care with this text. Any remaining errors are my own.
Anita B. Carroll, for her skill and patience with the cover design.
Erin Rhew for interior formatting.

Mike Austin, for ensuring no jet skis were hurt during the writing of this novel.
Dave Karls, for confirming no police protocols were violated.

Rebecca Harmer for reminding me of my voice.
Nicola Thornton, who always knows how to talk me off a ledge. It typically involves chocolate.

Alex and Kerry, the greatest weirdos on the planet. And Gillian, who joined our family recently. Don't say I didn't warn you.

Duke (posthumously) and Watson, my rescue pups, for asking to be let out, and in, and out at crucial times during the writing of this book. I forgot many a brilliant line – and probably a few howlers – during my treks to the door.

And finally, Scott, for the freedom to pursue my writing endeavours. Don't take it personally that you're listed beneath the dogs.

ABOUT THE AUTHOR

TRACEY GEMMELL is a British writer based in the USA. An obsessive search for home finds her ricocheting through countries like a malfunctioning satellite navigation system. Tracey has been featured on BBC Somerset Radio and received an honourable mention for her short story 'Scooby-Doo and Hobnobs' in the Jade Ring Contest, 2018.

MORE OR LESS ANNIE is her second novel.

If you enjoyed Tracey Gemmell's MORE OR LESS ANNIE, you won't want to miss out on her debut novel. Look for *Dunster's Calling* at your favourite online bookstore now.

Turn the page for a preview.

REVIEWS FOR DUNSTER'S CALLING

'It is a remarkable writer that can take you on a journey that allows you to feel something beyond the scope of your own experience and leave you changed because of it. Tracey Gemmell is that writer, and *Dunster's Calling* is that book.'

Kashmira Sheth, author of *Boys without Names*

'Perfect for Anglophiles, horse-lovers or anyone who wonders if their life has played out the way it should.'

Pauline Wiles, author of *Saving Saffron Sweeting*

'*Dunster's Calling* made me laugh and made me cry – what more can you ask of a book?'

5-star review

'As someone not living where I was born, I very much related to the emotional dilemmas in the book. I am neither a horse person, nor a lover of cream teas, but I still really enjoyed this book, especially that quintessentially English wit, which had me smiling, chuckling and laughing out loud at times. It is fast paced, involving and understated. The shifting between now and her childhood worked well. Recommended, and looking forward to the next offering from this author.'

5-star review Amazon.co.uk

'This book has left me with a longing for both cream teas and a pony. It made me nostalgic for a childhood that wasn't mine!'

5-star review Amazon.co.uk

'Thank you for a lovely story which made me laugh and cry! I could identify with so much of the narrative, not from the perspective of an émigré but as someone who grew up as a pony mad child in the fifties. Thank you for donating to the welfare of our beautiful "Dunster's" too!'

Review on author website

'Loved this book. The author insightfully articulates the path that takes us from childhood dreams to adult reality. A keen sense of humor keeps this intimate journey feeling like an adventure we want to join. Even though I've lived my life on only one continent, the book resonated deeply. Seriously. Loved. This. Book.'

5-star review Amazon.com

'I would read this book again just for pure enjoyment! Moreover, this book has piqued my interest, big time, for a visit to Exmoor one day... it's been added to my bucket list!'

5-star review Amazon.com

Dunster's Calling

A Novel

TRACEY GEMMELL

Prologue

Exmoor, England. 1960

The mare's nostrils flared with each rapid breath as she lay, fore and hind legs stretched out straight and rocking back and forth in time with her contractions. The light frost was slowly being vanquished by lemony rays as they stole into the valley below the farm. But the early spring dawn went unnoticed in the paddock except for the glint reflecting in the sweat coating the Exmoor pony's neck and flanks. The single ob-server noted the calmness of her demeanour. He remembered childbirth looking and sounding different during the birth of his own children.

She'll kill me, he thought.

"Merv! Wha' 'av you done?" He could already hear her voice as she interrogated him later, hands on hips, head on one side. But how was he supposed to know the foal would come early? No time to get the mare in the barn. No time to fetch his wife back to the farm. And besides, he didn't think she'd approve of being disturbed at her father's sickbed.

Should I call the vet? Merv knew what to do with sheep, but this was different. Each birth of an Exmoor pony was a triumph after the herds had been decimated during World War II. His wife had anticipated this foal with as much excitement as the birth of her own daughters. Deep down he knew the mare could do this without a barn or his help. She was of Exmoor: strong, hardy, from ancient stock that had survived great adversity. Like himself, really. But surviving marriage was on his mind right now.

The mare grunted, tried to sit up, then rolled flat on her side again. One rock of the legs … two rocks … three. A white bubble appeared first, then a nose, head, and neck, quickly followed by tiny shrouded hooves. The soon-to-be mother rested briefly, then finished her job, sliding her newborn onto the grass. The farmer approached, reassuring and praising the mare. At least he could tell his wife he'd done that much. He grasped the white sack that gave the foal a ghostly silhouette in the dawn light. Tearing the membrane to free the head and body, he cleared the foal's nostrils and glanced back to check the gender.

Good. He hadn't wanted to shout his mother-in-law's name across a field. The mare nickered softly, then more urgently, as she scrambled up and spun around to meet her baby boy. She licked his nose and eyes, nudged his neck and belly, breathing in the scent of her descendant, the newborn doing the same of his ancestor.

Dunster had arrived.

Chapter One

Wisconsin, USA. 2016

O h, and you need to get US citizenship." A patriotic challenge, wrapped around a xenophobic hand grenade, pin pulled … five … four …

That first shot arced across the dining room table, rattling the Wedgwood tea set and sending the dogs scurrying for their beds in the kitchen. With horror, Samantha McClintock watched the fires of global domination flicker in her husband's eyes.

"Did you hear me, Sam? The committee felt it was in the best interests of the campaign." Brody stopped eating to look at his wife. Three … two … one …

Campaign? Campaign! Sam heard the words ricochet off the inside of her skull, refusing to quietly absorb themselves into a brain that, until now, had been fully capable of comprehending most of her husband's utterances. The campaign was supposed to involve her husband knocking on about three hundred doors. He'd be clutching a flyer sporting every icon from the free clipart program even remotely related to elections, or America. She'd assumed, with some fear, gastronomically challenged as she was, she would have to bake a few cookies. She'd been told there would be a couple of appearances at the local beer festivals and a doughnut-heavy meet and greet. Knowing Brody's proclivity for healthy eating, Sam was amazed he'd even agreed to have doughnuts on the agenda, though it should have been her first clue that political ambition trumped prior values. "There'll be no polling over how your dresses are playing with the voters, no deleting questionable e-mails, and no paying for the silence of long-lost college roommates," Brody had jokingly said. But nowhere in the discussion had there ever been mention of a change in citizenship status.

"You haven't said anything. Citizenship?" Brody stared into Sam's face like he'd never seen her before. Sam came to her senses and realised this conversation was really happening.

"Umm ... what's to say?" she responded, trying to keep the incredulousness out of her voice. "We talk about me getting citizenship about once a decade. I say no, and we move on with our lives. You know my reasons. You always said it was up to me. I don't see what's changed."

"Everything's changed!" Brody's organic noodles infused with low-sodium soy sauce clung to ashen chunks of tofu. They fell from his chopsticks with a splat as he waved his arm to encompass the entire known universe. "I have a chance to influence the direction of our town! To introduce new concepts and present myself in a much bigger arena than the local banking world. This could lead from town to county to state politics!"

As if in response to this grandiose speech, a cheer broke out from the den. Some baseball game. Sam heard the crack of a willow cricket bat knocking a ball for six. *Where'd that come from?*

"Tell you what then," Sam said, still trying to shake the sounds of cricket from her head. "I'll wait to get citizenship until you run for president."

"They'll say you only did it to get to the White House."

"I was joking!" Sam spluttered, adding as the horrifying prospect sunk in, "Are you seriously thinking about the presidency?" *How could I have missed this one?*

"Well, no, but hypothetically … anyway, the point is, the exploratory committee felt that you being a British citizen could lead to uncomfortable questions about why America still isn't good enough for you."

"What? Who said anything about America not being good enough?" Sam started to hear that screech in her voice that made her turn off any talk show with multiple female hosts. "Would I have married an American, spent twenty-six years here, raised my children here, and tolerated the accent and appalling grammar—well, strike that last one because I don't tolerate it—if America wasn't good enough? This has nothing to do with good enough and everything to do with me just wanting to remain British. Not a 'dual' anything. Just British. If your committee doesn't understand patriotism, loyalty, and acceptance, you might be on the wrong committee." Sam folded her arms and waited for another rousing cheer from the den. Nothing. Just a Jeep commercial.

"But, honey," Brody pleaded, "it's such a small thing. Just fill in a few forms, hold up your right hand, say a few words—you can even cross your fingers behind you back, if you like—and you're done. You'll feel no different, and nothing will change the big picture for you. But you not being a citizen may change *my* big picture. I want to be a greater part of things. Can you help me? Please?"

Sam chose to ignore the comment about crossing her fingers during a solemn oath, though if she'd been looking for a representative of her values, Brody at that moment wouldn't have fit the bill. And she knew that statement didn't fit Brody's ex-military moral code either. Well, usually. Second time her newly minted politician husband had compromised his values. *I hadn't realised all this compromising started so early in the process.*

"So tell me," Sam asked. "How does 'The Committee' feel about your name, Mr. I'm-So-Proud-of-My-Scottish-Heritage McClintock? Should I be calling you Buck or Buddy or John Wayne from now on?"

"You're being ridiculous," Brody said as he pushed his unfinished plate away and threw his napkin on the table. "Everyone has a surname from Europe around here."

"Soooo, a European name is okay but an actual European wife is not? I'm confused." Sam felt at this point the battle was won. Apparently not.

"Look." Brody countered. "It's a small town, and I'm already an outsider. We've only been here ten years, and my competition, whoever that is, will have been here for at least three generations. The committee felt I was enough of a new concept. A non-citizen wife may be the tipping point." Brody pouted like a toddler at enforced naptime.

"Well, speaking of new concepts, why don't we start with differences and tolerance?" Sam shot back. "Not that this town needs introducing to them, or so I thought until a few seconds ago, because I've never been anything but graciously welcomed here." Sam's raised eyebrows dared Brody to disagree.

"Of course you're welcome here," Brody said, carefully replacing his water glass on the table. "No one is suggesting you aren't welcome. The committee just wanted to ensure that there were no obstacles in the way. You know, for the voters."

"Oh, the voters." Sam leaned back, folded her arms, and nodded her head slowly. "You mean, my best friend Gail? Macy at the grocery store? Anne and John at the coffee shop? People we've known for the decade we've lived here who couldn't care less whether or not I have citizenship? Do you really think Dennis at the gas station is going to make a fuss about my heritage? This is all stupid." Sam tried to imagine Dennis, who doubled as the town's snowplough driver, starting an anti-British smear campaign. The man was the biggest Manchester United fan ever born the US side of the pond.

"Maybe they do care," Brody said softly. "More than one person on the committee brought it up.

Sam started, her jaw dropping open. She unfolded her arms and slumped in her chair.

"People have said as much?" *Et tu, Macy*? "People doubt my engagement in this community because I'm British? Wish I'd known *that* before I spent all those years with the PTO, volunteered at every fundraiser, and cleaned miles of American trash off the side of the town roads. Because chances are slim it's the Brits dumping garbage out of their car windows on the way to Heathrow—via Wisconsin!" Sam paused to draw breath before delivering her pièce de résistance. "Call me barmy, but a non-meat, non-dairy leader in the middle of Dairyland, USA, gives much bigger cause for suspicion than I do!" Brody's decision to lower his cholesterol a couple of years ago had rendered most of Sam's meat and two veg meal plans obsolete.

"There's no need to take names and cry traitor. This is standard practice in politics: try to head off any unpleasantness before the opposition can sink their teeth into any skele—" The panic on Brody's face was almost comical as he grasped the enormity of his error.

"So now I'm foreign, unpleasant, and a skeleton in your political closet?! What the hell, Brody!" Sam tried to bring her voice down an octave. She stared at the floor for a moment, allowing Brody to stammer a retraction. Ignoring his back-pedalling, Sam lifted her eyes to meet her husband's, then rose slowly to her feet, displaying what Brody had learned to call her "Dam Busters" look.

"You always loved the fact I was from somewhere else," she began slowly and deliberately. "Remember you only spoke to me on the ferry in New York Harbor because you heard my accent. You used to say in the old days—like yesterday—that my British accent actually opened doors for you, an icebreaker at banking conventions. You loved telling your friends about English beer and castles and tweed jackets. And, with the exception of that one party where you told the joke about the British Isles being a slow-moving US aircraft carrier, you fit right in in England. And you made me believe I fit right in here. But now, overnight, you're saying my heritage is a liability for you? That it's okay for me to *sound* British but not to *be* British? That you get to stand out only if I agree to blend in? Well, concept this, *Buck*!"

The gesture that followed wouldn't have looked good at any election rally.

Chapter Two

The night had started on the couch, despite entreaties to "Please explain why such a simple task is so hard" and Brody's final plea: "At least think about it."

"It's like we've never met!" Sam had fired back after spitting toothpaste into the sink with the velocity of bullets. "Like you've forgotten you agreed to work towards getting a job in England. Like you had no idea I'd never wanted US citizenship!" The old Brody had understood. Old Brody had promised to take her home.

The couch wasn't a new sleeping arrangement for Sam. Many a night of fantasizing about murdering with a pickaxe Mr. Snoring-Hard-Enough-to-Cause-Vibrating-Ripples-in-His-Bedside-Water ended with Sam choosing the couch over life without parole. But most days she didn't contemplate killing him. Brody was typically the most sensitive of men: kind, grateful, and caring. This current hiccup demonstrated a one-sidedness Sam wouldn't have believed possible in her husband of twenty-six years. But he had touched a nerve or, based on her current sleeping arrangement, hacked right through one.

"What kind of self-respecting international crisis happens over a take-out dinner on a Thursday night? Seriously?" Sam spat at the ceiling. She lay on the lumpy cushions, trying to wrap her head around Dictator Brody's statement about it being a simple task to switch citizenship. "Let's see *you* switch from supporting the San Francisco 49ers to the Green Bay Packers just because I want to run the PTO," she muttered.

Tossing and turning on that midwestern sofa, miles and decades and memories from home, it took until 1:00 a.m. for Sam to remember that there were not one but two empty bedrooms upstairs that she could have used. And that was when the tears fell.

"We regret to inform you, Sam McClintock, you are no longer who you thought you were. Not a mother in the day-to-day sense. And not an accepted member of the community. Anymore."

***

"So this is a midlife crisis," Sam muttered hours later, still awake. "Nah, can't be. That's ten years from now."

She'd always thought a midlife crisis would be more exciting some-how—all personal stylist consultations, start-up gelato businesses, wide-brimmed hats on exotic beaches. And who wasn't in crisis? Everyone Sam knew had woken up at the age of forty or fifty (or thirty-five in the case of one particularly irritating, overachieving co-worker) and asked that reflection in the mirror, "Who the heck is that?" Not for nothing was it the clichéd opening of every baby-boomer film.

Could first town administrator be Brody's equivalent to gelato and hair dye? Sam pulled the blanket tighter around her shoulders and pondered. Possibly, she had to admit. But from the day they'd meet all those years ago, if you put the word *first* in front of anything, Brody wanted it. So it shouldn't have been a complete surprise to Sam that when an exploratory committee asked Brody if he'd be interested in the first town administrator position, the bull just had to charge the red flag. The minor local position suddenly took on the importance of an ambassadorship to the United Nations.

Sam turned over, curling into a foetal position to protect her feet from the chilly air. Her last conscious thought was that if Brody had been offered the chance of a run at *second* town administrator, there would have been no crisis tonight. She'd have continued repainting the picket fence every year until she reached midlife, ten years from now, the seeds of discontent slumbering on, waiting for a less embarrassingly mundane reason to sprout.

After a terse breakfast and even terser peck on the cheek from her work-bound husband, Sam sat at the kitchen counter trying to focus on the crossword puzzle. Her first patient of the day had cancelled so she was free to dawdle a bit. She'd scanned the front page; another immigration headline. The crossword puzzle seemed less threatening.

Three down: Cornish word for homesickness with a sense of loss.

Usually, for Sam, the word *Cornish* evoked pleasant thoughts of ice cream and clotted cream, preferably one on top of the other. But today, the word dredged up more, a dawning sense that something was askew. Sam googled "homesickness with a sense of loss." The search resulted in forays into websites for college counselling related to homesickness, which led to remedies, which led to families, which led to a brief encounter with an old Jerry Springer website (*blimey!*), then onto ancestors, which led to archaeology, which led to Druids, which led to the Cornish word *hireth*, with the Welsh version, *hiraeth*. Sam gazed, stunned at the meaning: homesickness for a home you cannot go back to, maybe a home that never was. She shivered. A six-letter word on top of a fight with her husband induced a sense that her expat existence was in jeopardy. Walls she didn't even remember erecting began to tumble. Scars across her heart tore open. Breathing hard, she found herself doing what she often did for comfort. She composed a letter in her head:

Dear Dunster,

I need your help …

CONTACT TRACEY GEMMELL

email: tracey@traceygemmell.com
Website: www.traceygemmell.com
Twitter: https://twitter.com/TraceyGemmell17
Instagram: https://www.instagram.com/traceygemmellauthor/
Facebook: https://www.facebook.com/author.traceygemmell/

Printed in Great Britain
by Amazon

76734085R00166